# Rhapsody of Blood

## Volume Four—Realities

# Books by Roz Kaveney

## Author

### Fiction

Rhapsody of Blood: Volume One—Rituals
Rhapsody of Blood: Volume Two—Reflections
Rhapsody of Blood: Volume Three—Resurrections

### Poetry

Dialectic of the Flesh

What if What's Imagined Were All True

### Non-Fiction

From Alien to The Matrix: Reading Science Fiction Film

Teen Dreams:
Reading Teen Film and Television from "Heathers" to "Veronica Mars"

Superheroes!:
Capes and Crusaders in Comics and Films

### (with Jennifer Stoy)

Battlestar Galactica: Investigating Flesh, Spirit, and Steel

Nip/Tuck: Television That Gets Under Your Skin

## Editor

Tales From the Forbidden Planet
More Tales from the Forbidden Planet

Reading the Vampire Slayer:
The Complete, Unofficial Companion to "Buffy" and "Angel"

### with Mary Gentle

Villains!

### with Neil Gaiman, Mary Gentle & Alex Stewart

The Weerde Book One
The Weerde Book Two: Book of the Ancients

# Rhapsody of Blood

## Volume Four—Realities

### A Novel of the Fantastic

## Roz Kaveney

*Plus One Press*
*San Francisco*

This is a work of fiction. All of the characters, organizations and events portrayed in this novel are either the products of the author's imagination or are used fictitiously.

Plus One Press

RHAPSODY OF BLOOD, VOLUME FOUR—REALITIES. Copyright © 2018 by Roz Kaveney. All rights reserved. Printed in the United States of America and the United Kingdom. For information, address Plus One Press, 2885 Golden Gate Avenue, San Francisco, California, 94118.

www.plusonepress.com

Book Design by Plus One Press

Cover artwork by Graham Higgins, copyright © 2018 by Plus One Press

Publisher's Cataloging-in-Publication Data available on request

ISBN-13: 978-0-9977453-1-3
ISBN-10: 0-9977453-1-2

2018951102

First Edition: August, 2018

10 9 8 7 6 5 4 3 2 1

*To the memory of my mother*
*Joan Mary Kaveney*

# Acknowledgements

My thanks are due to Leslie Arnold,.Simon Field and Tim Concannon for beta listening, to Jacqueline Smay and Deborah and Nick Grabien for editing and publishing me and to Paule for 30 years.

# Realities

"The World Is Everything That Is The Case"
— *L. Wittgenstein*

"You Make Me Feel Mighty Real"
— *C. King*

# The Sound of His Horn

This is how my story nearly ended. There, among the rocks at the end of the world, rocks which still bear the marks of that fight in broken stone and cliffs that crumble and fall into the sea, rocks that were barren many many years and now speckled with grass and shrub and heather and little more—and the place where I fought and nearly died is gone under the beating waves these many years, crumbled and shivered from that fight and their fury, as they nearly ended me.

Teeth held me by the back of my neck and though they could not pierce me, as yet, still they could hold me and dash me against the rocks as soldiers kill infants in a massacre and do it over and over again until even I grew dizzy and thought that I would faint or die.

And around us rocks fell from above and crumbled beneath us from the force of our blows.

A horn jabbed at me as I lay stunned so that I had to roll and roll near cliff edge and rock fall with salt spray in my eyes and broken stone under my skin.

Hooves unshod but vicious and feet with great splayed claws trod at me so that I could only move and dodge and try to regain my feet and try to find a standing point from which I could strike with spear or sword or the small knives in my hair, at flesh which melted and reformed as I struck at it and which could seemingly take no hurt from me.

And their force was the force of her last hatred and of the love which was even more part of where that hate came from.

It might have been my end, I think, if anything can be.

That was not my end, but it was almost the end of this story, and this is how that story began.

***

After I said angry farewells to Hekkat, who loved me, and to my former apprentices, who did not, I hunted alone for a season and for many seasons more.

The flooding of the great lake north of the two rivers drove people from their homes all around the new dark salt sea, and desperate people will take desperate remedies of a kind which kept me busy; some I found before they had done anything unforgivable, and others worked the Rituals and the Rituals worked results which were their own punishment, and I had little to do save a mercy stroke to what they had become, and others still quickened into godhood of a sort. And those I punished as well as killed for I was not in the best of moods.

And yet this is the story of how I came to give mercy to The Hunter whom I would always before have considered unworthy of it, and of how I had my reasons.

I wandered the shores of the new sea East for a time and then North and then West and South, hunting and killing as I went, and in due course I came to the new mouth of an old fast river that one day people would call the Danube but which then was just called the River as so many other rivers were.

2

It had had a delta, with lagoons and marshes, and one day would again, but for now they were lost under the sea. Angry gulls fought and tore over the dead trout and perch which had been caught by the salt and drove the waterfowl upstream to find new homes or starve.

Crowding the cliffs which were its sides were the last outliers of the oaks and elms of the great forest that lay to the North and stretched away into the lands I did not yet know, all the way to seas whose existence I had only heard as rumour, seas greater than the one I knew and thought so vast. Seas to the shores of which I would come in due course.

And that is a part of the story of my hunt for the Hunter and of our fight.

I heard the snarl of his horn and the baying of his hounds long before I set eyes on him and I did not know what it was that I was hearing. It was a noise in the distance like nothing I had heard before and I thought it just a thing of the forest.

The old great forest was different to anything I had known to the South and the East—dead wood piled on dead wood, the smouldering of old wildfire, new saplings in the char, the smell of centuries of fallen leaves gone to mulch and mud and endless slow fierce growth. The dung of great cattle and the tracks of innumerable deer and the singing of chaffinch and thrush, and the silencing weight of the years and the constant piercing note of life through that darkness and the patches of light where a tree had fallen in a storm and created a gap that would last a score of years and then go back to dimness.

Men and women lived in that great shadow—they burned charcoal, but carefully lest their fire become an inferno, and they cooked their food, for they had brought fire with them from the South; they ate the mushrooms that grew in the mulch, and brewed the ones with red and white spots to tip their arrows; they took small game in snares made of gut or killed them with pebbles taken from the streams where they dabbled fingers to take trout and perch

3

by silent delicate tricks; they picked berries from the briarbushes and crushed them as sauce for their meat; they climbed great trees for small sour fruit and the wild honey of bees.

And, as in the land of the two rivers and the great lake, men wandered the trails back and forth, and wandered out of the forest south into lands where they could sell their great packs of charcoal to smiths and tinkerers who used it in the forging of small bronze needles and arrow heads and rasps that went back north and into the forest where men gradually became less clever beasts skilled at survival and more creatures of will and wit. And malice.

And in due course, but not quite yet, they harnessed the smaller cousins of the great aurochs, and they built sleds and then carts, and took ever greater loads of charcoal to the South where it was needed, and felled more and more of the forest to make it, and to graze their cattle, and then their sheep and the goats that they brought North in trade.

Men and women died in that great shadow and their flesh and bones went into the soil and the piles of leaves. Bears fought them for the honey and tore out their throats; wolves lurked where they could take a young child but had learned to fear sharp stones and the charred hard points of tree branches and the wit of men that might prowl and lurk and take the lives of wolves that grew too bold. And sometimes the great cattle came running between the trees, panicked by flame or wolf or sudden mushroom madness and every creature that was in their path, be it man or wolf or bear, was smashed into the mulch by the rushing onslaught of the bulls.

It was in those woods that pups of the wolves were taken by hunters, or came creeping to the warmth of the banked charcoal fires, and that first friendship started.

A little later he turned that friendship into something else, for good and for ill.

He fought the killing beasts of the forest, and perhaps Great Beasts as well, for he became a god as much because the peoples of the forest came to love and worship him, as they did to fear him. He was a god to them, or almost a god. She brought sour fruit and mushrooms and fishguts among them and salved their hurts and stitched their wounds, and delivered their children, and they loved her and they trusted her but they did not worship her, and she was not a goddess.

He hunted all the creatures of the forest with hounds that were still wolves that he had reared from lost pups or cowed into his service as his might grew and among the creatures of the forest he hunted small game, and deer, and wolves, and boars, and bears, and cattle, including the great cattle that men came to call the aurochs.

One such, the oldest and fiercest bull, tried to gore him with its great horns—perhaps it did and he took a wound from which he nearly died, and she saved him from festering death with a poultice of small berries and fishgut and mushroom and honey, for she understood all these things and their properties, and he grew strong again and killed the great bull and broke off its horns as a trophy to keep after they had grown fat and strong on its meat and its fat and its heart and liver and lights.

Or perhaps he took it first time but brought her its horns for a pretty.

I do not know, for he was a god of few words, rarely still long enough to talk of such things, and when we talked in later years he did not talk of her and I did not make him, for his grief was a thing that has lasted almost as long as time.

I think it was she who first thought of hollowing the horns out with a rasp and piercing the tip with a small bronze needle and waxing it with beeswax until it glowed. I know, almost to my cost, that she was the clever one, the wicked one.

I think it was to her that the Enemy first whispered that they would be stronger if they hunted the wisest and fiercest beasts of the forest, which is to say their fellow men and women, and their children. She and her love learned in ways that were hard, only less hard than what they did to those whom they killed, that the Enemy lies, and that the years more of time and love that he promised them would also be years of change and ache and pain, until they ended.

And when they were done with men and women, when he had taken their flesh and their hearts and their livers, he hung what was left on briars and thorn brakes to rattle in the wind.

She was witty and malicious where he was fierce and bold and she made small cakes of the honey of bees and enticed small children with those cakes to where she could take their blood, slashing their throats after hanging them upside down on briars and thorn brakes. She added their blood to her mash of small sour fruits and fishguts and wild honey. There was power in her brews, but also power in her blood, her flesh and her bones, power that I learned to my cost and to hers.

They had killed for many years before I came upon them, for they were already old, older than I was, and he had taken more benefit from those deaths because he had remained youthful in appearance and strong, where she had retained vigour and strength enough, but not the appearance of youth, nor any ability to take on a glamour of youth for more than a few hours at a time, and that at the cost of young blood.

Some stories are true memories.

She never built a house of sweetmeats that you might live in, and she never built an oven for the children she killed for when she ate them, she ate them raw.

But these things I knew later.

I wandered in the forest and wondered why I no longer found the trails of wicked men and worse gods. I was young and had not yet learned that if there are few such it is because the worst of men and women brook few rivals.

In the distance I heard his horn and his hounds and I did not know what it was that I was hearing, until one day I came where they had been a season earlier and found the dismembered bodies of men and women and children hung on thorn trees or scattered and knotted among briars.

There is a scent to the Rituals that lingers and pricks within the brain like a burn to the hand or a harsh note in music or a foul taste of decay on the tongue. I knew that scent and knew that I had work to do, and that quite soon I would find a man turned god for my killing. Perhaps not that day or the next; I knew how vast the forest was and did not know yet how much of it he had taken as his range, but I did know that he had been here and that sooner or later our paths would cross.

I had the scent, and I run fast and I do not tire. And I listened for screams because the sounds of men and women and children in desperation are one of the ways we know where the wicked are to be found.

And in due course I heard such screams. And with them the sound of his horn and the baying of his hounds. Sounds which, as I have mentioned, I had heard before without knowing them for what they were and which I now knew to be my quarry.

More important than the fact that screams would lead me to him, was that they would lead me to his victims and that I might be able to save those whom I seek to protect—the sight of all those corpses had affronted me. I cannot save everyone, but I am angry with myself when this fact is borne in upon me.

I ran towards the screams, by the fastest route I could find, in and out of the light and shade of trees and in and out of shadow and the Mundane, for the forest was huge and dark in both.

And I came to where a man and a woman stood at bay against a great oak with great dogs that still had much of the wolf about them snapping at them to hold them in place and to make them know that their fleeing was over and their death near, but not yet. They had skin that was dark with soot and fume and they smelled of the charcoal which was their trade even more than of the sweat of fear and panic and urine where they had soiled themselves in flight.

I walked among the hounds and struck at them with the butt of my spear so that they barked and yelped in anger that anyone more or less human should treat them with scorn rather than terror, and then whined for their master. I shooed the couple away and, when

7

one of the hounds tried to seize her by the ankle, smashed its jaw for it to show that I meant business and so that it would whimper some more and bring its master down upon me, for I wished to meet and have done with him.

I was young then, and thought every kill an easy kill.

Then I heard the sound of his horn close to and wondered that I had ever thought it a simple natural thing, and at that sound his hounds yipped in joy and menace that their master was coming to avenge their hurts, and the earth shook under the weight of his coming and I heard the noise of the tree branches he pushed his way through as they cracked and fell to the ground, not just beech either but great oaks that he tore up and tossed aside in his hurry. And as he came, when he set the horn aside and ceased to blow it, he bellowed in incoherent rage.

He was fully ten foot high, and the span of horns on his head was some five foot and he stank of the Rituals as if they were dung and he had rolled in them to be sure of stinking.

I turned the shaft of my spear in one hand and drew one of my swords in the other and I took my stance. At first he did not even notice me but walked to the hound I had injured and reached down, patted it and with a firm grasp of his hand reset its jaw where I had dislocated it, then stroked it with power that shimmered and healed. For he loved his hounds as if they were his children.

Then he turned and looked down on me in a rage surprisingly cold and calm.

I had hurt one of his hounds.

"Who are you? That you dare?"

I glowered up at him. "I am Mara, the Huntress, and I punish evil men that would become gods by working the rituals. And from the look and smell of you, your punishment is well overdue."

He laughed, and it was not a happy laugh. "Little girl, little girl," he said. "There is only one Hunter here, and only one who gets to punish."

I thrust with my spear so that it pierced his thigh and then pulled it back. His leg gushed blood like a spring when you move the stone that blocks it. "That remains to be seen," I replied.

He touched his own thigh, and again it shimmered and healed. "Indeed so."

In his passage, he had split an oak in two, as if he were a walking thunderbolt, and he reached down and tore the lesser part of it from its roots, and struck at me with it. The ground shook at the blow, but I had danced away from it with whole moments to spare, and dodged also the lighter stroke with which he tried to sweep it sideways and knock my feet from under me. I had guessed that his movements were not as slow as he tried to deceive me into thinking. We were as yet sounding each other out.

I noticed though that he had not learned the knack of watching his opponent's eyes; I guessed that this meant he had rarely fought other men or gods. He was not accustomed to enemies that fought and were perhaps as strong as he was.

He hooded his eyes a little with a sudden frown and waved his dogs back, that I not hurt more of them as much as to ensure he did not have them under his feet or need to take thought for them, and could concentrate on me.

I knew that I too must not underestimate my opponent—I had fought men and gods and beasts that were clever and were as strong, or stronger, than I was, and I guessed almost at once that, balancing one thing against another, we were evenly matched, that he might even defeat me and kill me and hang my flesh on his thorns like a butcher-bird.

It was a fight of blow after blow—my blows landed and his did not, but he healed where I struck and I knew that I might eventually tire of dodging and ducking, though that time would be hours away and I would flee to fight another day should it come to that.

I am proud, but I am not stupidly proud.

He was slow and I was fast and yet it was a dance of equals, for the moment.

9

Yet we were not to try conclusions to the limit on that day, for suddenly his dogs were yelping in fear and it was not on the account of the small mice and rabbits and hares of the forest, nor the tiny savage pigs and their greater cousins, nor deer nor elk nor cattle, though all of them came charging among us. It was not even the wild wolves and bears and lynxes, nor the screaming trumpeting creatures covered in coarse hair that I had never seen before and which tried to gore him with their great tusks when he failed to get out of their way.

It was the flames and the choking smoke from which everything in the forest was running and which was leaping from broken branch to broken branch in the wake he had left. It was not, of course, a coincidence or a sudden mishap—the charcoal burners were trying to take revenge on him and his dogs and were displaying a certain level of ingratitude to me for saving them. I have found this reasonably common.

Flame does not inconvenience me in any serious way, but they were not to know that. From his size and his horns, it was clear that the Rituals had affected him enough that he was not going to be burned either; but he cared about his hounds and so led them out of danger, picking up and carrying any that fell behind.

Some he took and laid across his shoulders and some took a grip with their teeth in the long hair of his head and others found themselves a clawhold in the thick hairy skin of his back. Some clung to others. It was as if he could wear his pack like a cloak of wolves, I thought idly as the flames rose up about me.

"We will meet again, Huntress," he shouted back and the irony in his voice was louder than the flames.

Indeed we would, I thought to myself, but saw no point in boasting about what was self-evident, nor in hindering him at this time. His hounds were mere beasts, however much he used them to work evil, and I would not see them burn.

Nor did I wish to see the fire grow out of control—I doubted that the charcoal burners had thought of more than revenge but I could not be sure of that. Fire can serve as a focus for the Rituals just as poison or the knife. It is always best to be sure of these things and so I sheathed my spear and dashed some little way ahead of the flames and began to fell trees and pile deadwood in the hope of creating a fire-break and a backburn. The wind that carried the flames died down a little and there was some chance I would succeed, and as I created a line across the path of the flame, I found I had a partner in the work.

He looked at me in surprise that my own face mirrored.

"This changes nothing," I said to the Horned God as I shared the load of a great oak with him.

"Why should it?" he shrugged. "But the Land is more than us or our quarrels."

It was tiring and dirty work and his sweat stank of the Rituals, but I grew up in forests and I hate to see their destruction. There would be time for his punishment...

After a day and a night and another day, during which we had moved the line of what we were trying to save a time and again until we came to the bank of the River, where we made a third line, that held, the flames died and we stood looking out over a band of char that stretched for miles, with the game, great and small, quivering behind us and taking sips from the river. Many had not succeeded in escaping and the air smelled of smoke and of burned flesh.

"Thirsty work, Huntress," and he gestured at the river. "A truce while we drink our fill?"

"Granted." For there are rules in these things even with the enemy, decencies to uphold to which not all who work the Rituals are lost.

Though I am not a fool, and I kept my eye on his hands to check that he did not pick up a branch of a rock to bash out my brains. Just as he watched my hands and was sure that I did not reach for the weapons in the quiver at my back or the small knives in my hair.

He sat and cooled his feet in the water and so I did likewise—he reached down and took a great handful of water and wiped the ash and smoke from his face. He cupped his hands again, and filled them with water and one after another his hounds drank from his hands which he filled over and over, and only when the last dog had drunk did he take a series of draughts himself.

He lay back and his hounds clustered around him, taking no thought for the easy prey that stood apprehensive nearby drinking as well, or for the few beasts that might have been threats to them.

I had no such concerns and drank from my own cupped hands until my thirst was done.

"What is your quarrel with me, Huntress?" This time there was no sarcasm in the title he gave me.

"You work the Rituals of Blood, as I have seen, and smelled on you. I am tasked with punishing such, to protect the weak against those who would be strong."

"Tasked by whom? If I might ask?"

"By a young god who was friend and briefly lover to me and to my two sister-lovers. Along with whom he died most terribly at the hands of those who, like you, work the Rituals."

"Ah." He sighed and then said nothing more for a while. "And the power of those Rituals comes to you without their guilt, at second hand. You protect and you serve, but you also take revenge, for those whom you loved and love yet, across the long years. Well, alas, we all do what we must." He paused a little more, then spoke in the voice of one who has considered much. "I have my hounds to care for. One burned his feet badly and needs more salve, and one is about to pup and I am concerned for her. I will give you the fight you crave and I will not hold back, for I do not choose to die. But, for my hounds' sake, I ask a pause before we see which of us is the strongest. It is a vast forest, but we will meet again."

I nodded at him, for courtesy in such matters is one of the decencies I choose to observe. "How came you to the Rituals?"

He sighed again. "Love and time. We all do what we must."

He stood and he bowed to me and he turned and dashed across the hot ashes and into shadow and the shadow of the trees and was gone from my sight. For now.

I did not tell him that the Rituals stank on his skin so strongly that I would be able to track him however great his start, because there was an advantage to that from which I would not forbear. I am courteous, but I am not stupid.

Nor was he, for there was an advantage he had which he had not mentioned to me and which I had not thought of, until, as I sat by the River for a night more, she came to me.

There was mist over the river and the shadow of the unburned trees on the other side, so that the night was dark and yet soft, and her voice came to me like the mist on the river, only sweet-smelling.

Yet a flower scent or the scent of new grass would not have overwhelmed ash and char the way this did and so I was not fooled and breathed it in a little more deeply. His smell was on her, for one thing, and the scent of his Rituals but also the scent of something else, sweet and yet tainted, honey and blood and a version of the Rituals I had not met before.

"Daughter" she breathed. "Would you be a good daughter and leave your mother in peace?"

The word she used for daughter was not one I would have known—it was blood child and birth child and clan child, all and more and alien, for I and my sisters were reared by several mothers and they were blood mother and clan mother and birth mother, but there were only certain times of day or season when which particular right they claimed was something that any cared about.

I was in a land where kinship was different—I had met other ways of kin before, but not ones where it was so taken for granted in a word, and a tone of voice, that kinship was one thing and unchanging. I was in a foreign land.

"Mother." I used her language back at her so that she might think me deceived.

"If you would leave us in peace," she whispered, "I have honey cakes for you." And the words themselves dripped honey at me into my ears, and I was deaf to them because she could not know that the last promise my sister-lovers made to me before their deaths was just such and down the ages the only honey cakes I have eaten are those Sof makes for me in the ages when she is alive again, and that had not, in that age, happened yet nor did I know that it would.

"I will not eat your cakes," I whispered back, but not yet harshly. "And I fear for those who do," because I had noticed the small children among the corpses hung among briars and on thorn breaks and I knew, in the way I understand these things, why her version of the Rituals smelled sweet and why that honey savour in her voice smelled of fresh young blood.

Children love sweet things and children lost in the woods are all too ready to think that the next voice they hear might be their mother. And I am, in my appearance, young enough that she might take me for one just of an age still to be deceived.

But birth mother and blood mother and all my other kin were swept away from me by murder or by that gentler murder which we call time. She deceived many but she could not deceive me, for I knew all that I had lost.

"You need not try to trick me, Huntress, for I am the deceiver here and you, alas, the undeceived." She laughed, and her laugh was sweet there in the dark. "You gave truce to my beloved," she whispered. "Will you give it also to me? For I have other honey. Feel, here."

And she was at my side and had taken my hand and I felt her wetness.

"I will not," I said. "For you have the taint of the Rituals and of blood on your lips as well as the taste of honey and salt. And I am sworn to others, dead though they be these many years at the hands and wicked small knives of those who work as you do."

Yet her scent was sweet and not only with honey and death.

She pulled away, but only a little, and my fingers were still wet with her.

"Liar," she whispered and I knew that she spoke truth. "For I smell her on you yet, one you love, who is witch as I am witch, and murderer as I am murderer, and who loved you and whom you love,

14

and she is on your fingers as I am on your fingers. And she is in your heart."

And I swore to myself that that last saying at least was not true. And I hoped that I spoke the truth.

"You could go across the river, or around and beyond this new sea that was once a lake, and never bother us more. The world is big enough for you and I and him I love and you whom I could love."

Her whisper was further off and then it was near and then I reached up and took her knife from my throat not gently, pulled it from her hand and threw it into the river where it glinted in the water and was gone.

"Truce, you say," I shouted at her, not angry but yet half-regretful that it had so soon come to this as I had known it would. "What you call truce, I call treachery and it is over."

She laughed and it was like the mist on the water and the glint of starlight and moonlight on the blade as it sank. "I smell the games you two played. And bladeplay and bloodplay were in your head if not carried through. I know you, Huntress, because I know what you smell of. And you lie to yourself, you lie so very much."

I did not know what she meant.

She went on. "You scorn us, me and my beloved, and you do not know our story and you do not know our love. We live by the blood and lives of others, cut with my knife or torn by his hounds. Yet why do you still live, Huntress?"

"Because I am the protector of the weak against the strong."

Her laugh was sarcastic. "Tell yourself that down the years and hope that it will not grow hollow. As for me and my beloved, we wish to have time together even if we cannot be together."

And suddenly the sweetness was gone from her and was replaced by a carrion reek.

"Do not look on me," she gasped.

He was the Hunter God and so went horned and massive; she was the Witch of the North where things go by seasons and are lush for a time and then decay and wither for a time and so it was with her.

She could seduce and she could be lush and gorgeous, but I had rejected her, and so the other half of the bad bargain they had made came upon her. Until she found a new child to kill or lover to take and mar.

I am sure that she took and marred many a young man in the wood. And thus it was for this and many reasons that her husband was the Horned God.

Not everyone who is changed by the Rituals in ways that they would not wish becomes a Flat Ogre; the Rituals, like other workings, can be wittier and more malicious than that.

So she fled from me, in disappointment, envy and anger and I did not find her again for a long time, nor did I find him, nor hear his horn and his hounds, and though I thought to trail them by the stink of their Rituals, they and their hounds were hunt-canny and knew to cross and re-cross the river, and take no lives save those they needed to live.

So I cast wider and wider, in all directions and into shadow and I learned much of the forest and the lands that bordered it. I stood at its Eastern edge and looked at hills that turned into more hills and across great plains and wild grass and wheeling birds and herds of wild horses, and the wind came fierce and cold from the East and the North and there was no scent of them on it and so I did not go there.

I traced the river North and then West and then North again a little and then I cast into the forest again and after a while I came to another great river and followed it North to a great sea where the forest ended and around the coast following the line of the forest to another smaller sea.

I met the people of those Northlands and I met the men and women who were not yet quite their gods, brawlers and war leaders and healers and midwives, and the gatherers of honey and the growers who were taking the small sour fruit of the forest and over the generations and the ever longer years turning them into something larger and sweeter, and the ones that brewed salt and sour juices and turned and boiled and turned and soaked pot herbs in great wooden vats so that there would be something green to eat in the long cold winters of the North.

I scented godhood and the beginning of godhood among those useful folk but I scented nothing of the Rituals, the Rituals of those I sought and others I might find in the line of my work, and I left those lands and walked back into the heart of the forest, crossing it and criss-crossing it many times before I caught his scent, but never hers.

I had his scent, and I realized after a while, he had mine.

He was the Hunter and I the Huntress, but he had learned his skills before I was born, when he was still a mortal man, before he acquired his pack. He knew the trails of the forest, for hundreds of miles in all directions, had watched trees grow and fall and knew where the rocks were loose in high places, where narrow valleys might be flooded in minutes, where high trails might turn and crumble under foot. He was sounding out my strength while keeping his distance from my spear and sword and I was learning—not to fear, but at least to respect his skill and his art.

Once only I saw him and that was as a face looking down at me in a pit into which I had fallen.

"Leave us alone, Huntress, and leave these woods. I will always know them better than you."

I laughed. "When I have killed you, Hunter, I will have an eternity to learn them as well as you do now. And be assured that I am implacable and I will kill you, however many times you outwit me."

"Let us see the truth of that," he rumbled, and he jested, for suddenly I was in darkness for he had placed a great oak, roots and all into the pit on top of me so that it pinned me where I lay.

He knew, or at least guessed, that I would take little hurt from this, any more than I had from his other snares and traps, but he inconvenienced me for a time while I dug my way out from under the oak and in and out of shadow—where he had placed snares in the ground that tangled me further as I dug like a worm, like a mole.

17

When I came out into the air, covered in dirt and with fragments of fish-gut snares still tangled around my arms and legs, I heard his laughter in the distance. He thought to shame me into abandoning my pursuit.

I had told him the truth, that I am implacable, and I thought that if he would not face me close at hand, I would take this hunt more seriously. He was strong and so I would weaken him.

I went back to where I had first met him and cast about me for the dugouts where the charcoal burners lived. I kept my weapons in my quiver and in my hair and I walked with arms outstretched so that they could see I meant no harm, planned no vengeance for the forest fire. For I had two things I needed, and one of them was information.

The man and the woman whom I had saved rose up out of the dead leaves—not to ambush me but to show me that they were wood-canny and that I was not, that they and their families and friends might be all about me and I would not see them. As indeed was true—but I did not tell them, then or later, that I could smell them and taste the soot on their skins a mile away.

"I am the Huntress," I announced myself as they stood silent. "I am the protector of the weak against the strong. I seek the Horned God, the Hunter, and his wife, the Witch of the North, for they have lived too long by killing and betrayal."

"He was our god once, who killed the killing beasts of the Forest," the man said. "And he turned on us long ago, in my great grandsire's time, and hunted us and killed us as if we were beasts and he grew strong and strange."

"She was our helper," his companion added, "who healed hurts and helped women in childbirth, and she grew old and he did not. And suddenly she was young again, part of the time, and part of the time a lich. She takes our children, and she takes our young men."

This was not the time and the place for rebuke—but I thought then, know now, that the people of the forest had sinned against the Hunter and the Witch. She had helped them and they had not paid her in the worship that would have kept her young. As always, we make snares for ourselves, and there is one who seeks our undoing, who helps us tangle ourselves.

I have known love and lost it and I felt for the Hunter ever young and newly a god and his love, the Witch who had been a Healer. All they wanted was to help and be in love forever, but that is not given. We all do, not what we must, but what we think we must, and they had become monsters out of all that was good about them. They expected reward for right action and that expectation had made monsters of them.

But they were workers in blood and terror whom I must slay, and pity them afterwards.

I listened to the tales the charcoal burners told me and to their family and their friends and I asked them for four things. The skin of a rabbit, or some other small game, that I might make a sling; some mud and straw that I might make small balls and dry them into sling shots; some splinters of wood that I might set within those sling shots before they dried; and a pot of the salve they made from stewing the mushrooms with red and white spots.

I might not kill him thus, but I might perhaps weaken him, or at least annoy him.

The gifts given me by the Young God, either in the cave, or when he chose to die at my hands, shielded me from most wounds and all toxins. The Rituals are less kind even to those they favour. I do not know why this is, except that perhaps the world is, in some respects, just.

First though, I needed to find him, and not be found by him. I know, for enough of my friends and enemies have told me this, that my besetting weakness is arrogance, but when I have fallen into a pit through folly, I can learn to dig myself out of it.

The Horned God was my equal in most things and my superior in some and I needed to narrow those gaps by coming where I could learn. He was older and wiser and more wood-canny, so I must learn what I could from those who could teach me. In return, I taught them things that I knew and which they did not—songs of my homeland and the shape of the world beyond their forest and stories of gods and monsters; how to turn a pot on a wheel before baking it. They knew much of setting limbs but did not know that when the heart seizes in the chest, there is a blue and purple flower that may help, if stewed in a potion. They knew of parsley to sweeten the breath, but not of willow-bark.

I take no credit for passing on things that had been told to me by the mothers of my clan, that my sisters Sof and Lillit knew far better than I.

I could travel in shadow, and they could not—and in times of hunger, when snow fell, I brought them fruit from lands in shadow mere steps away from me, fruit and strange rainbow fish and the small voles that chitter in the grey beeches of those lands and which are delicious cooked on hot stones and crunched whole beneath the tongue, their fur like the skin of small peaches. I did not travel far, however, for part of my hope was that he and his wife would think that I had gone away or given up, that they would think it safe to return and prey on the people with whom I guested and whom I hoped to defend against any trouble I brought down on them by being apparently gone.

And when I was ready, and stealthy enough, I took the first step to weakening him.

I found and followed his pack and one at a time, I stole his dogs.

I did not hurt them, for they were innocent brute beasts and I try to be just, and because his connection to them might mean that he knew their pain, but I took them into shadow and left them there, where they were unlikely to be found. He was the Hunter and was less without his hounds.

I found him sleeping one night and for the mischief of it, smeared dung on the mouthpiece of his horn, that thereafter he would sleep with one eye open. And I took some of the shots studded with splinters and sauced with the red and white mushrooms and I put them into his clothing where they might scratch him in his sleep and cause him to wake feverish.

20

With his lessened pack, he came looking for easy prey to the diggings of the charcoal burners, and they all had slingshots and they peppered him so that he ran away in confusion and delirium.

The children and the young men only went into the woods in pairs and trio, and let themselves seem dazed and confused and lost. When a voice came to them in the dimness, and called them "Son" or "Daughter" or "Beloved", they waited until they could tell the direction of her call and they let fly at her.

It was not just the pellets and the poison that stung them; it was the lack of respect and fear. Part of godhood is worship and part is fear—and I took much of the fear away from them and they began to dwindle a little.

There was nothing magnificent or epic about the war that I waged against them. It was a slow diminution—the charcoal burners sent out emissaries to other groups elsewhere in the forest and passed on my suggestions. It was mean and petty work—and sometimes they caught those messengers and killed them horribly and sometimes he was with her and they took children together and hung them on briars. I cannot save them all and sometimes I put my allies in the way of danger—but they were in danger even had I not been there and I cannot save them all.

One day I saw his trail, and he was limping in his path and the scarring of trees meant that the span of his horns was less. On the other hand, his tracks were followed by those of his hounds again—he had gone deep into shadow to retrieve them lest they wander there forever.

That must have tired him.

And I thought that the time had come to weaken him further by taking him into despair. I sought her out in one of the small huts where she made her honey cakes and to which she would take young men to love and to mar. I thought to kill the weaker of the pair, for it would be worse to leave her to mourn him than him to mourn her. I thought to have compassion for another woman.

My besetting weakness is arrogance and again it nearly undid me.

I came to her hut and she was sat cross-legged in front of the banked ashes of a fire and she had her lich form, but her eyes were as bright in the tight-drawn kidleather skin that lay lightly over the bones of her skull as if she had been a young and lovely girl and the smile on her withered lips was gleeful and lush.

"There you are, as I expected you, Huntress, Mara as those who love you call you, I am told. You have undone me, I think, and I cannot change to my other shape as I would wish, to greet visitors, even you Huntress."

She coughed and the lushness of her smile was red until she reached up and wiped it away with her fingers. With her other hand she reached into the ashes and winced as her fingers burned a little. She brought out a bundle of charred leaves and she unwrapped them and held up what she had been baking. Small clay models of a beast with hooves and one long horn, and another with claws and a great mane of hair.

She wiped the blood from her bloody hand onto them and then she spoke again. "I will die and he will live on, because you will die, Huntress, of my dying curse. And these are the last and only children of my love, rage and fury, Huntress, rage and fury. But they are not my only gift." She snorted with laughter. "Since you have come to our forest, I have had a great fear upon me that my time with my love is over. And now I know that to be true, and I return to you the fear you brought to me. You have been fearless for so long, little girl, and have brought fear to so many…"

And she drew another small knife from her clothing—or perhaps she had retrieved it from the river somehow for it looked like the one I had taken and thrown away—and she slit her own throat and she cupped her hands for her own blood and she threw it at me and then cupped her hands again and threw it on the clay beasts and then, somehow, she waved her hand and the banked fire burst forth in wildfire and she threw herself into it and she burned in it and she screamed.

"My curse, Huntress, my curse. You will die and he will live and my vengeance on the folk of the forest."

She withered to ash and there was a great smoke and as I breached it in I felt madness and fear rise up about me and I heard a roaring and a whinnying and I ran.

For the first time since the cave and the flame and the spear, I felt fear. I felt terror. I felt my bowels open and my bladder let go and I soiled myself and I could not breathe for the fear that rose in my chest and the tears of shame and humiliation that gushed from my eyes and the roaring and the whinnying in my ears and in my brain.

I ran into shadow and I ran through the trees and rocks that I found there and I dashed into each river that I found and did not pause to wash myself clean though clean I became again and soiled again until there was no more in my bowels and my bladder with which to soil myself and I ran through one more river and was clean for good and all.

The whinnying and the roaring were still in my ears and every so often I felt the leather at my back almost tear as a lazily swung claw or a thrusted horn grazed it. I could not know whether I was outpacing them or whether they were toying with me—my fear told me that either they had caught me or they had not caught me yet and either was a terror of itself. And I could not think for fear or turn and fight for fear and the whinnying and the roaring filled my mind and I knew that this was what it was to die and yet it continued and there was the fear that it would have no end.

I came to a high cliff over a great river and I wanted my fear to end and I plunged from the cliff into the fast-flowing river and I could not would not drown and I let the river carry me away and I let the whinnying and the roaring fall behind me though I knew that they would follow and my mind cleared somewhat from the fall and the current and I gradually found peace and was myself again, somewhat.

I reached into my store of power that I do not normally squander on such petty matters as my own welfare, my own sanity, because it is not for that, it is for sometime when I need it, when the world needs it, desperately and I will not squander it lest in that moment of need it come up short. But nonetheless there was, there is, a need for me as the bearer and accumulator of that power, the power of the innocent which was stolen from them and cannot be returned and can only be stored and sometimes used.

I let the river wash from me much of that fear, much of that horror, as it bore me further and further from the ashes of the Witch of the North—but not all of it, for I needed some of that fear so that the beasts she had brought into the world would follow me and remember my scent.

I knew even then that they were the wild magic that comes when the power of the Rituals is let free upon the world by the death of those who work it at other hands than mine, or sometimes when I cannot contain it. They would follow me and they would perhaps destroy me and the rage and the fury would go on forever, fires fed by their own essence and by all they might destroy.

And they might destroy all, in time.

I thought of the seas, the great seas I had not yet seen more than the first shores of, and the greater seas that I had been told lay beyond them. These creatures were born of flame and hatred and perhaps there was a sea beyond those I knew that would quench them.

I knew the Lord of Salt and I had seen the Middle Sea summoned by the Bird and perhaps even the greatest seas of all would be wise as well as great and see the threat that these beings would pose to the world. For all that seas tear at the land, for it is the nature of seas to wash away and tear down, yet land is born again out of sea, and being limited by land is part of the sea's nature too.

I swam to the shore and I waited for a while until the whinnying and the roaring became audible again, and beyond them the horn and the hounds of my other enemy, whose wife was dead and who would wish to see her curse destroy me, I guessed. They had my scent and he and his hounds had tracked me before, so they would follow me where I went and perhaps I would trap them or they would trap me.

24

He was the Hunter and I the Huntress and he had his hounds and he had the beasts, sole children of his dead wife. We would see what we would see, because we all do what we must.

I raced on, through hot days and cold nights, the trees and briars catching at my clothes as I ran, the ground sometimes hard and sometimes stony and sometimes soft with mulch and mud beneath my feet. The fear was not gone so much as changed—it was a back-note which I had taught myself to ignore but which was there if ever my will faltered for a second, the pain that you do not notice except on the brink of sleep, the chafing of a shoe that you lose in the dance.

I had remembered who I was. And all it took was a long plunge into cold water.

I came to the river's end, where it broke up into rivulets and brooks that contended with the tide, where the land constantly broke and dissolved and formed again where the river forced itself for a while into the sea and the sea tried constantly to push it back. There had been a bridge here once—not a bridge built by the hand of man, and most of it still stood and much of what had fallen was still there—foreshore becomes salt-marsh becomes sand-bank becomes treacherous footing where you might still see a confused crow that had just gone too far and found itself picking at the eyes of a half-rotten fish as water and grasping sand built up about it. It was an economy of fast exchange where the price of meals was being trapped and becoming the next meal in the next trap.

This was no place to take a stand and I raced on.

Sand-bank became salt-marsh and salt-marsh became fen where patches of solid land were there to be seen among the hawthorn bushes and straggly beeches and willows. I heard the honking of geese as they pottered around the soft wet ground, their heads down, and I took a quick turn into shadow where, on solider ground, a pair of great elk tussled for supremacy, their antlers interlocked.

I hoped that the creatures that raced behind me would not pause to take easy kills but I could not be sure and so I jinked and twisted my course, in and out of shadow and the Mundane, so that to keep their attention on my traces they would need to pay attention. Or so I hoped, without knowing what I would do if I saw people in this so far largely empty land. Shoo them out of the way of harm, I supposed, but had enough of the terror she had inflicted of me still running in my mind that I was guiltily unsure.

In the Mundane world, rolling hills and thicker and thicker forest; in shadow, fields where great beasts with armour on their thighs and long lumpy muzzles grazed and produced prodigious amounts of dung—I had seen the like before North and East of my home, creatures that sometimes wandered out of shadow into the desert of the Mundane and met with misfortune. I had guested with wanderers in that desert and can report that great slabs of those creatures' flesh thrown into the ashes of fire and left for hours are good eating.

I never hunger and I never tire, and yet in that chase I found myself growing weak, and seeing those beasts reminded me that memories do not feed hunger. And as I paused a moment to lean on their pillar legs, I heard the creatures behind me stumble into shadow again, roaring and whinnying, and when I slipped back into the real and leaned on a tree instead I heard the baying, the howling of the Horned God's pack and the whooping of his horn.

I came to rivers and some I forded and others I avoided by shifting from one world to its neighbour, leaving them behind me when I emerged. I did not hope to evade what chased me—they were beings of wild magic, remorseless and inevitable followers, and I could not hope they would have been designed in such a way that they were even capable of losing my scent. All I could do was hope and try to shake off fear and try to find a place to stand, a promontory from which I could beg help from the sea.

I crossed one river and, as I did so, narrowly missed a white wall of water that gushed up it from the estuary beyond—I called out amid the din of the waters but I heard no answer. I had no hope that, should I call on the great waters for assistance, they would answer—but I had the headache of great fear only partially overcome and I could not think of what else to do.

I never plan ahead and so I have no especial gift for it. Yet the vast ocean that I sensed lay at the end of my path seemed at least a possibility. I had no other ally in mind.

For mile after mile woodland and rough ground and occasional patches of clear green grass. There were people in this land, I could tell from axe marks in the trees and laid stone pathways in the woods, yet I never saw one. Perhaps the fear that was now a bearable thing for me travelled as a miasma around me and the beasts and birds and men of this land hid from me—I did not know then and I do not know now. I walked the same lands later and they were full enough.

As I raced I came to the land I had expected, as if I had seen it in dreams. Broken cliffs where the spray crashed almost to the top and great waves scores of man-height below me that tore against the rocks as if hungry to take back land that had once, so long ago, risen from it in fire.

In the end, as I had known I would, I came to the end of things and I turned and I slashed my hand with one of the small wicked knives in my hair, because of course I can wound myself if I choose, though I rarely choose to. I scattered large drops of blood into the foam below me, and looked out at the sea. Ocean I had been told it was called, and I thought as we thought that it went on forever. Or at least until it came to the Lands of Silk and Spice, for even then I had heard from the Lord of Salt, who loves to boast of his kin, that one of them had told him so.

If so, either he lied, to seem more important and closer kin than he was, or they deceived him—for even the gods of the sea are a family with petty rivalries and meannesses. The Lord of Salt is after all a being whom even his close family may find it hard to like.

"Oceanus, greatest of all seas," I cried in my need. "I am the Huntress, protector of the weak against the strong. But I fight two who are stronger than I and I fear that I may fall and fail. I was there when the Bird called upon your smaller weaker brother the Middle Sea. Aid me now, for even one as small as I may one day be able to do you a service."

There was no reply save the clashing of the waves and the cry of gulls, and then what felt at first like a great burning wind was upon me and I found myself overpowered and thought that, perhaps, this was the end of my story.

Except, clearly, it was not.

I heard the sound of the Horned God's great horn and suddenly his hounds were there, harrying the Lion with nips at his lashing tail and darting in among the Unicorn's hooves, yet carefully, because they knew like any wise beast that they were outmatched and could do no more than annoy.

They bought me precious seconds in which I rose to my feet and reclaimed my spear from where it had fallen from my quiver or been knocked from it by a well-placed hoof.

For the first time, in the concentration of fighting and my sense that the crisis of that fight was upon me, I saw the beasts of rage and fury more clearly.

You must not think of the elegant beasts of art and heraldry— these were the real thing, vast and terrible and rough hewn, with patches of armour on their backs and thighs and rage and fury in their eyes and hearts. They were not Great Beasts, not the idea of Lion or Horned Stallion as manifested by the world—they were a witch's dying anger at me and the world and all save the lover she was trying to save made into a sort of flesh. They were made of magic and of that wild magic which can live on when the one who has worked the Rituals that summoned it has gone where they trouble the world no more. Worked more precisely than most dying gods and godlings can manage in their extremity, but for all that also like a child's daubings or something stitched together in haste and then come to ramshackle life.

The Hunter blew his horn once more, so close at hand that it

28

deafened me and I thought to cast my spear for he was my enemy and one who had worked the Rituals—but I had more pressing concerns, and clashed my spear against that spiral deadly horn as it darted at my eyes. I carried through with the stroke so that that white terrible head was overthrown against the soil and I kicked the Unicorn hard in its forehead just below the horn, guessing that that would be a place that really hurt. Its head knocked against the rocks from my kick and again the rocks flaked and shattered and fell into the sea.

The Lion rose up out of the crowd of hounds that worried at him, and their teeth had found purchase where my sword and spear had not. I paced towards him—the Lion was flamboyantly pendulously male—and kicked him where he stood rampant. That the beast felt, and I felt the last of the fear drop from me.

The Hunter was here now, and he smiled down at me as he took both beasts by their manes and banged their heads together and threw them to the ground at his feet.

"If you will bear with me, Huntress, I have these to dispose of."

He picked them up again and banged them together brutally over and over, like a cat that toys with a rat, or if a housewife beats two rugs together and dust flies off them, because as he hit them together they became less and less. As he did this, he wept and his tears were blood and his sobs sounded like the breaking of rocks, the tearing up of trees.

"They are my love's magic and so I can break them," he explained. "I loved her and mourn her but some things should not be done."

"They were her dying curse on me."

"But not on me because nothing she made would ever have harmed me."

"They were made out of love for you and rage that I might harm you."

"That they were, and a pretty piece of malice too. I love—I loved her, but some things are just wrong. They were her rage and her fury and if left—well, they might have killed you, but then they would have harmed the Land. Their rage and fury was not just a curse on you. My love understood me very well, but not that there are some things I care about apart from my love for her." He took what was left of the beasts and ripped them apart, then raised one hand with them in scraps on it and blew them away like thistledown. "They will be back, of course. She has brought a great evil into the world, but you will be able to control them, next time, when I am gone."

He knelt before me. His hounds whimpered around him and not in pain.

"I bow to your justice, Huntress, for with her gone, there is no point left for me and I wish to die, because my love is dead for whom I killed and ate many. And there was no point, for we should have died and not killed, for she is dead in spite of all that we did."

He wept and I, who had also lost love to death, wept with him. He had come to save me, and then to die at my hands and I could not, I would not, do it. I wept with him and then I sheathed all my weapons and started to walk away.

"Huntress," he cried out.

I turned back and I reached out my hand to him. "Hunter." I took his hand and raised him up, and I looked up at him and straight into his eyes. "Hunt and kill no more men and I will delay your sentence. You were a godling or a god before you worked the Rituals, one of those whom men make into gods because they save lives—go back to that and I will delay your death. Your life is a burden to you, without her, and so I give it to you until you ask me to take it from you."

I like to think that I was severe to him, but not cruel, but I cannot be sure. I had spared Hekkat for that we had fought together and because I could have loved her and perhaps I did; I spared him because he had sinned for love and his love was dead.

Without the Rituals, he would dwindle unless he was of service and men and women forgave him for that service and forgot that he was a monster. Also, though he talked of saving the land from the beasts of rage and fury, he had come to my aid against them when he might have waited until I had been killed or taken some great hurt.

That was not the end of the story of those days, though. For as we stood on the cliffs at the end of the world, a great wave rose up against the land and then hung suspended over us.

In a voice that was the clashing and smashing and beating against the shore that remained suspended, it spoke and I heard. "Little Huntress, little Hunter. You are beings of justice and mercy and the seas know not such things. Yet we all do what we must. We did not help you this day, nor did you need us to. One day, though, one day—do not call on us again for we will know when to come. When the ring of flesh shall burst, and the sleepers shall awake, and all will be undone."

Then the great wave was gone that would have smashed us both and the cliffs on which we stood, and he flung his arms around me in terror and friendship and whispered in my ear.

"When he came, the one who taught us how we could live in love and not die and misled us, he warned us even so that we could not live in love forever and those were the words he spoke."

I shook my head. "Do not think of it, for it will drive you mad."

I kissed him once in fellowship and left him there with his dogs and fled back the way I had come, sick at heart.

I did not know then, how often down the years, I would see him again and how many times the Lion and the Unicorn would find their way back into the world.

Some stories have no end.

# *Waking*

Sof screamed some more.

A perfect C sharp, she should go on the stage, whispered the part of Emma that was still Berthe.

"Why is that lady screaming?" whispered what was left of the little girls.

Sof was a ghost in Emma's head, a memory of some life she did not remember, a ghost with a face that was and was not hers. Several faces, from several lives.

Sof ran through all the halls and corridors of Emma's memory palace, screaming wide-jawed, trailing a white robe behind her that was somehow part of her flesh, part of her memory. Yet at the same time Sof noticed every picture, every hanging. The mind behind those masks, those faces, those lives—it might be mad but it was also alert and enquiring.

And then she was suddenly back, staring into Emma's eyes, as if into a mirror, and still screaming.

Emma suspected that slapping her to shut her up probably was not going to work. She tried it anyway, and for once it really did hurt her as much as it hurt the person she was slapping. Which was predictable.

Sof broke off screaming a moment. Emma's hand-print was dark on her brown skin. "Lives," she explained, almost pedantically. "Lots of them."

Then she started to scream again, but her heart was no longer in it and after a while she petered out.

"So —" she was obviously intrigued enough to forget being batshit insane, "— let's have a look at who I am these days. And why you presume to wake me."

The sensation of fingers riffling her memories was not one Emma particularly liked, she decided instantly, and she thought, aggressively, of a piano lid being slammed down sharply and painfully.

That, Emma thought with satisfaction, isn't one of mine. It wasn't from some film she had seen, because it actually hurt.

Thanks, Berthe.

She fixed Sof with a glare. "I suggest that we take this gently. Apart from anything else, I've got the casework on thousands of the formerly damned locked away inside here with us. I think those count as confidential."

Sof pulled the face of one taking a long breath even though she didn't need it to start screaming again.

"I know that face," Emma smirked. "I've practiced it in the mirror."

Sof laughed. Better than screaming.

"Not to pull rank," Emma pulled rank. "I'm a goddess, so I think I can guarantee to win."

Sof looked at her with sceptical consideration. "Worse things happened to me than have ever happened to you."

"Thousands of damned souls, remember. Every last breaking on the wheel, every last red hot pincer." Oh god, Emma thought, she is me. We're competing.

Sof fixed her with her own steely glare. And opened her mind as if she were laying out a weaponized deck of cards, and…

It was, after all, Emma's palace and she chose, in that instant, both to experience the memories Sof aggressively shared with her and to see them as a creature, a small wiry spiky creature that climbed out of Sof like dark pus spurting from a boil, like a tooth rotted past blackness pulling itself from a jaw.

Emma reached out, and grappled with it, suddenly so much bigger than Sof that she towered up to the ceiling, which moved to make room for her. Her hands bled and tore where the spikes and hooks that covered it stung her; the memory of immortal flensed flesh lapped in corrosive liquid until every fragment of her was dead and gone…

She twisted the creature's arms behind its back and the torn skin of her hands healed itself as she shrunk back to its size and frog-marched the vicious little thing down and down a spiral stair and past cells where other demons lurked and howled at her—the storm-troopers kicking Berthe where she lay on the floor and breaking those speaking musician's hands with clubs, one of the little girls coughing lung blood on to her first communion dress, John blowing away as white powder, the ogre crunching through Caroline's neck…I did not know I had this place, but it makes sense that I would, a cellar of suppression House of Usher deep, the Iron Box with Many Locks.

She was strong now. Goddess-strong. And she knew all about how it is to be cast into a dungeon of hopelessness. All she took away was the facts and she gave those to Sof to replace the creature, the agony of remembering. Facts that could not hurt either of them.

She did the same to herself with Berthe's memories, and the little girls' memories, and her own.

"We won't be needing those anymore, dear." Her voice was prim and sharp. "We are both better off without them."

Sof blinked, as if she were suddenly in bright sunlight.

That was the right thing to do, Emma thought, but presumably without all that pain—and that really was bad, I had no idea—one of us is going to absorb the other, right about now. Hope it isn't me, wasn't me –

Sof was still there, and so was Emma.

They both thought hard. Emma knew she was thinking hard and could see those thoughts echoed in the face opposite.

"Oh, it's because I'm—you're just a bit too different," they both said at the same time.

"You've been everyone; you slept with Socrates; you're Mara's lost love. You're…" Emma could hear the breathy fan-girl in her own voice, and also heard it echoed when Sof spoke.

"You fight gods and sea monsters and…Platonic Solids from Another Dimension?"

Emma realized that, since Sof had been Hypatia of Alexandria, this last must be kind of a big deal for her.

"But," Sof went on, in tones even more awe-struck than Emma's, "you're a hero. Like Mara. Only cleverer. I was never that." She sounded almost envious, but reconciled.

"You survived something I couldn't imagine surviving."

"It broke me. I am not sure I will ever be whole. Except, you are me, unbroken, mended, better."

"I don't think we will ever agree." Emma knew she would never be able to console this woman, her other self.

"How could we?" Sof smiled. "Because we will never be of one mind."

They were united in sudden laughter. The hug that followed was nervous, was sisterly, and, once they both knew it was not going to blend them, warm and extended. But not sexual, not in the least, Emma thought with relief—there are limits to my lust, apparently.

They broke off at a rap on the pane of one of the windows that both were and were not the actual eyes in Emma's face. Emma moved to the latch and let Josette in.

I suppose that once you construct the interior of your head as a single vast metaphoric building, a lot of quite odd consequences ensue, she thought. After all, she's had, and not used, a telepathic back door ever since she helped me with the card I'd given John. And she did knock, politely, now she's using it.

Josette was wearing slightly faded jeans and a t-shirt with a sacred heart design. "I just wanted to check –" and then Josette caught sight of Sof, and she of her.

Nothing was said, for achingly long moments.

Well, that's a moment of silence you could not improve by setting it to music, thought a side of Emma that was still somehow Berthe. But I would love to try.

"Well," Sof finally broke the silence. "That explains a lot."

Josette shrugged and then blushed.

"I thought I was an abomination…And everyone expected so much of me, and. Well, you were kind to me and taught me stuff and you were so clearly in love with the Huntress and…"

There is nothing quite so embarrassing, Emma thought to herself, as being stuck in a room, eavesdropping while two people explain their back story to each other. Especially when one is someone you are sort of attracted to, who is clearly besotted with your previous avatar. There's seeing people naked, to which you grow used, and there is seeing their hearts and minds and souls naked, to which, even after millennia of judging the formerly damned, she would never get used.

So she hugged them both consolingly. Josette's hair smelled as nice as it had on previous occasions; Emma wondered how that could be, inside her head, and reflected that her memory would just project how Josette smelled.

Then she realized that Sof smelled of incense and opium and shuddered a little to think why that would be.

Josette suddenly remembered to look baffled. "What are you doing inside Emma's head?"

"Mind-wiped reincarnation thingy." Emma thought she had

better be the first with an explanation. "Terrible trauma. Morgan tried to fix it—bit of a bodge, but I've sorted it. There are some things you can only really do for yourself. You can go under the hood, sort of thing, if you've got the dashboard of your mind in front of you. We'll go into the details later once she's back in her own flesh."

Sof shook her head, almost apologetically. "I'd rather stay in here, if that's OK with everyone."

Emma was not sure about this, really she wasn't, but, well, it would be bad manners to say no. After all, the inside of a head that both was and was not her own had to be some sort of comfort zone to Sof, who had been through a lot, poor lamb, even if Emma had just sorted it for her.

Sof went on in a voice that was just a bit too arrogant to be described as pleading. "You may have hidden my past agony from me, which probably means I am sane and functional. I don't think, though, that I want to be out in the flesh where bad things could happen to me again; it's much safer being a goddess' passenger. At least for the moment. And you know so many things—it's like being in another library just riffling through your mind."

We might as well be comfortable while we try to sort this out, Emma thought, and in the same thought created some couches so that they could all sit down and discuss things. A big over-stuffed purple sofa for herself, and a chaise longue on which the other two sat down, or rather reclined, snuggling in a vaguely non-sexual sort of way.

Which is nice, she thought, though now Caroline is back, I am trying not to think of Josette that way.

"But what about Mara?"

Josette was clearly being very noble about the one true love of the person she loved more than anything. It made her look slightly constipated.

Maybe, Emma grumbled, to herself, all she's ever seen in me is a vague family resemblance...

Sof's expression was enigmatic shading into cynical. "Last but one time I saw Mara, she had to dissolve me in That Which Devours. It was the right thing and the loving thing to do in the circumstances. Last time I saw her, she asked this woman who is totally in love with her to erase my memories and personality. That was also the right and loving thing—but possibly time and chance are trying to tell us something about our enduring love…"

She giggled.

I thought I had a dark sense of humour, Emma thought to herself. Oh well, with her and some sort of vestige of Berthe, and Josette making house calls, I'll never be lonely.

And then the French windows of her mind opened again, and Caroline appeared.

It was weird, because a mental projection of a living Caroline was a lot more different from her ghost than one would think. She probably hadn't really changed out of the sensible military outfit she had been wearing a few minutes earlier, but inside Emma's head, she was wearing something slinky and black, with a big hat. Likely a quotation from Erte or Beardsley, Emma reflected, but I am not going to ask.

"Apparently now I'm back in the flesh, I can do this. Hope I'm not intruding. Who's your friend?"

Sof was suddenly standing there, in the middle of Emma's memory palace, with her mouth wide open in amazement. Then, very deliberately, she walked over to Caroline, slapped her very hard and threw her arms around her and started sobbing.

All three of the others were totally confused.

Eventually, Sof spoke, her voice at once relieved and astonished. "Where have you been, all these years?"

None of the others was any less baffled.

Caroline put an embarrassed arm around the sobbing avatar. "We've never met. I'm Emma's girlfriend and what are you doing inside her head?"

Now it was Sof who looked baffled. "But you're Lillit. My sister-lover, who died horribly at my side on a trail in the land between the rivers before history began. On the day we met the Young God. The day we died for the first of so many times. You must remember." Sof was almost in tears, almost shouting with hurt.

Emma tried to explain. This was all very unexpectedly awkward. "This is Caroline, my lover except that she was killed and became a ghost before we got a chance to do anything. Until now. But still not yet. She was abducted by Lucifer and I came to Hell to find her."

Then she turned back to Caroline and pecked her on the cheek, and how nice to be able to just do that, without making a fuss about it or anything. Even if it was a mental construct.

"Sof here is the Huntress' long-lost sister, and apparently I am her current incarnation, only we're different because she had her memory wiped and only got it back when I woke her up. And there's a lot of back-story—some of which is hanging around with Josette here and some of which is so awful I won't tell you about it yet."

The more often she said it, it started to sink in how messily mythological her life had become.

Caroline looked blank for a moment, sat down on the sofa next to Emma, put her arm around her, then spoke tentatively. "Really not. I mean, I suppose what with reincarnation seeming to be a thing...And if Emma didn't know she had other people's memories tucked away, then..."

"If she is," Josette sounded authoritative, "she doesn't know she is. I've been inside her head a lot and I would know."

Emma thought she had better speak up and try and get everyone to make sense of all this. "Actually, you've been in my head at least once and you never noticed that the love of your life was tucked away in there. Your endless visits to Caro's subconscious mind really wouldn't make a difference. After all, if Lillit has been hiding from everyone for seven thousand years, she'd be quite good at it by now."

Caroline butted in, "Also, amnesia, right. It seems to be a thing." She obviously liked the idea of not really being the youngest person in the room.

"Well…" Emma looked from Caroline to Sof and then to Josette. Something had come to her, something that was, belatedly, embarrassingly obvious. "I know another candidate for being Lillit. One I got to know very well indeed. You did too."

Josette nodded, "Now you mention it."

Sof and Caroline looked blank until Sof riffled Emma's memories again and went, "Ohhh!" as light dawned.

Emma thought she had better put Caroline out of her misery. "My armour, when it was being an independent being, had a face that looked like you in the same way that Sof here sort of looks like me."

Caroline pulled a face. "Is that what I look like to you?"

"Give or take being made of gold or something like it. And, as I said, sort of Assyrian. Like her."

Sof clearly objected to this. "The Assyrians were a long time after our time, and smelled of hair oil."

Emma ignored her. Sof might be her other earlier self, but Caroline was her newly restored lover, so Sof could lump being offended. "It sounded a bit like you too—honestly sweetie, it had your snark, more or less. Only it's clearly some sort of alchemical being –"

"We don't call it alchemy. It's the Work." Sof was surprisingly tight-lipped about it. "I'm not responsible for the misunderstood mess people made of it in the Dark Ages."

"Whatever. And it, she, could do something a bit like what angels do, receding into perspective. Only into time rather than into space."

Caroline jumped in. "If she does things with time, that explains how she could be in the same place as me. If I'm her. Sort of."

Sof clearly knew how to do this whole bouncing of ideas off each other thing—of course she does, she's me.

"Back at the beginning, just before we were killed, she asked to set aside the workings of time and chance. I'd never thought about what that would mean."

Emma realized that if she and Caroline were versions of these women, their choices affected them as well.

"These choices?"

Sof pulled an 'are you sitting comfortably then I'll begin' sort of face, but then seemed to think better of spinning the story out.

"There was a young god; we were nice to him; he insisted on giving us boons, the way gods do. Whether you like it or not."

"Oh great." Emma felt that sinking in her stomach she usually associated with being in fast cars, or planes—someone else totally in control of the next minutes of hours of your life. "What did you choose, then? For yourself, and presumably for me and Berthe and the rest of us."

Pretty much simultaneously, Sof intoned, "Understanding the workings of time and chance," which Emma thought a little pretentious, and Caroline snarked, "Being an utter smart aleck all the bloody time, and now there's two of you, oh imagine my joy."

Josette had been standing ever so quietly—inside Emma's head, she didn't have to breathe—and looking interested. "So what did Mara choose? Because clearly this is one of those things that come in three; that's just the way the universe is."

Sof looked at her with the slight disappointment of a teacher whose beloved star pupil has been uncharacteristically slow on the uptake. "To protect the weak against the strong, of course. Why would you think she chose anything else?"

"And so she's always needed." Emma was excited in the way she always was when the universe seemed to be making more sense than it had a moment before. "And so she cannot ever die or rest."

"And she cannot save us all," Caroline added ruefully. "And yet she is the Hunter, not the Protector. Why?"

Sof smiled. "Because, when you've lived more than one lifetime's worth, you know that is sadly how things are."

She really has the patience of a good teacher, Emma thought, which I do not have, and that is one of the ways in which I am not her. We share a soul, or my soul is a copy of hers, but I made different choices along the way—I might have been her, but am not. And I do what I can to protect and no, like Mara, one of the few bits of wisdom I know with certainty is that I cannot save them all.

But we do what we can. And it looks as if I have saved Sof.

For the moment, at least.

Caroline snuggled up against Emma even more tightly—Emma could smell her hair which was like spring and a breeze. From the slight petulant thrust of Caroline's lower lip, Emma could tell she wanted to get the subject back to her. But, for a moment, she was silent and kissed that lip rather than merely observe it. A welcome change after all these years, she thought.

They took a moment, and then Caroline pulled back, her eyes wet with tears and joy. "She was the playful one. The tease."

In all the years they'd known and loved each other, Emma had hardly ever seen Caroline think so hard about what she was like.

"And now she teases the central forces of the universe and plays games with our lives," Emma shivered. "I hope she knows what she is doing."

Sof nodded. "If she did what I think she did, she is as ruthlessly compassionate as Mara. She danced her way through time and stole things in one century and put them where they were needed in another. And helped me die when I needed to, but could not help me escape into death a moment earlier than seven centuries of agony. Because she needed to die herself, and be reborn from my death as the Fifth Thing. She was always the cleverest of us, and she solved what I could not. She accomplished the Work."

There was a cold pride in her voice that made Emma and Caroline shudder—Emma in particular because she knew just what Lillit had let happen to her sister.

"These older women –" Caroline talked as if one of them were not there, right there, in the room with them, "– they're kind of cold, heartless and amoral, aren't they? I thought you were a bit chill and ruthless sometimes, sweetie, but you're an innocent beside them."

Emma decided she had better not break it to her beloved that actually, these days, she had many centuries of subjective time locked away in attics of her mind. She supposed that the fact she had spent them being professionally compassionate had helped her preserve her sunny disposition—that and locking it all away. Repression—the cure for wrinkles in the mind.

Josette coughed, and then she convulsed a bit. Sof put a hand on her shoulder and then hugged her in mild panic as Josette hacked and hacked like a cat getting rid of a hairball.

And suddenly Alexander was in the room, looking truculent.

"It's all very well you women having cosy little chats in here. Judas and Asareth and I have been doing all the clean up. And we need a council of war and…"

He noticed the fourth woman in the room.

"Oh, hallo Sof, old thing. Didn't see you. Where did you spring from?"

Sof was visibly less pleased to see him than he was to see her. "I was here all the time," she grudgingly admitted, "in a magic sleep. Hekkat."

He hooded his eyes and nodded. "I've had dealings with the lady."

Which seemed plausible, because all of these elder beings knew each other.

Emma really did not feel like being hospitable, but she made him a sort of military folding chair thing because it seemed like what she ought to do. He ignored the chair, clearly preferring to stand, his legs apart and his hands at his side, not quite at attention, but with the firm definiteness that she supposed military geniuses regard as part of the job. In other company, he would have dominated the room.

"So, anyway," Alexander went on, "while you've been lollygagging around in here, we've buried all the bits of dead demon. Asareth says they'll be good for the crops next growing season, which I suppose she would know all about being a fertility goddess."

43

This seemed to Emma a fairly cold-blooded attitude to a lot of dead sentient beings, but then, neither he nor she had had anything to do with their deaths.

"But we really have to decide what we do next. And we can't get all of the others in here, nice as it is."

He clearly wasn't about to apologize for barging into the inside of Emma's head through some back door he had into Josette's. And what on earth was that all about, Emma wondered?

"Well, I don't plan on going anywhere." Emma recognized the stroppy tone and firm set of the jaw with which Sof said that. She had seen it in mirrors. "I'm sure that if I have anything useful to contribute, I can tell Emma and she will tell the rest of you."

Just what I need, Emma thought to herself, a big sister back seat driver. Only she couldn't think quietly in here any more, she realized because Sof obviously heard her, even if the others didn't. Or maybe they were just being tactful.

Alexander sat down in the chair Emma had provided him with and looked at Sof with an expression he probably thought was soulful. Oh god, Emma thought, he's going to try to be helpful. "You know, Sof dearest, having been cooped up in someone else's skull for several years myself, I honestly can't recommend it in the long term. And that was just two of us."

Josette winced at the memory.

"But I'm not an interloper trying to take over Emma's body in order to conquer the world again."

Clearly Sof had a point, and Alexander shrugged, "Fair enough," with an apologetic little twist of the mouth. He really is quite charming when he wants to be, Emma noticed; I suppose you can't rule half the world and always be a ranting egomaniac. You have at least to pretend to be noticing other people's feelings.

Then she started worrying whether people thought that about her.

"But," he went on, "I've had this utterly splendid idea and I would love you to be part of it. You'd be really useful."

44

Emma realized that her head was hurting; it was just too crowded in here. And then Tsassiporah's voice was cawing in her ears.

"Oh there you are, mistress."

It was the smell of feathers in her mind that did it.

She sneezed and twitched her brain and suddenly she was back in the world and so was everyone else, including Sof, though she was just a shade.

Everything was tidier than when she'd last seen it. You would hardly have known that there had been a battlefield and a monster-slaying and annihilation weapons being fired, and demon bits strewn, in all directions.

There were tents, in neat rows, with banners, and vines up and down their flagpoles, with small sweet-scented flowers and fruit. A little further away, the Wild Damned were doing drill, as if they were in a display rather than preparing for another battle, and a lot of the ordinary former damned were standing round applauding them.

Judas and the Recording Angel were hovering nearby, meticulously smoothing out the pocks in the castle walls. They were using trowels and some sort of putty or mortar, while shouting down to minions who were erecting some sort of scaffolding. Asareth was lounging on a chaise longue, sipping something—though she was clearly owed a rest from all the horticulture that had obviously gone on in Emma's absence.

Sof, though, looked entirely discombobulated and was having a mild fit of the vapours at being out in the open.

"I'm most awfully sorry," Emma flustered at her "It was just so crowded in there, and then its feathers got up my nose, and I didn't mean to throw you out as well and –"

Out of the corner of her eye, she saw Josette and Alexander nod at each other, and Caroline nod as well a second later. Putting someone back into flesh apparently went much faster if there were several of you doing it.

Once Sof had shoulders to shudder with great honking sobs of outrage, Josette walked over and put her arms around them, consolingly but with a certain steeliness that Emma knew well.

"We just can't afford not to have you in play. We can't have you wandering around inside Emma's head when she has her own work to do."

"And I really don't want you kibitzing," Caroline butted in snarkily, "when Emma and I get our very belated first night together. I don't want any of you anywhere near us—and that means you, boss, and it means Asareth over there and it especially means you, sister Sof or who ever you are to me really. Privacy—you can appreciate that."

Then she looked at the bird. "And especially not you."

Tsassiporah looked crestfallen—only a bird that actually has a crest can look that droopy, Emma thought.

"I don't have a sex myself," they cawed. "I don't see why humans would expect me to be interested."

Emma could not deny that she agreed with Caroline about this, though she would never have been tough-minded enough to say so herself, or to put Sof back in the flesh against her will. I think I am a terrible person, Emma thought, but I'm not remotely as ruthless as all that. But then she reflected that Josette and Alexander and Caroline really didn't know just what Sof had been through and it was better that way. Not that Josette or Caroline's pasts were exactly free of trauma, but nothing quite that bad.

Asareth seemed blithely uninterested in what was being discussed, but she gave a cheery wave.

Judas shouted down to them, "Oh hello, Sof," and then returned to what he was doing. He was clearly enjoying himself, being the son of Joseph instead of the Son of God.

Emma found it reassuring that they had things they were more interested in than this rather private conversation. It must be nice having a hobby that you can always go back to—though in Asareth's case, maybe doing gardening was her main job as a fertility goddess, and being worryingly sexual all the time, whatever she was doing, was the hobby.

Raziel, though, was hovering as if he wanted to say something, which probably meant he was keeping notes; it was, after all, his job. We probably need a minutes secretary and he is the best in the business, after all, Emma thought.

She turned her attention back to Alexander. "It's all these guns and bombs. Bad enough having spiritual conflicts fought with Mundane weapons, let alone when they're powered by some sort of annihilation magic," he said. "I pay attention to these things—it's important to keep up—and none of it looks like the stuff you get in the Mundane. It's not just Mundane arms factories being retooled to do magical stuff—it's magic all the way through. And things like the bombs the Dukes of Hell used on the Heavenly Host, or that nasty little pistol of Simon's—well, they smell of—not the Work exactly, but something a bit like it."

He'd clearly got Sof's attention.

Josette had it even more. "The Enemy is doing something—it's like there's this other version of the Work that's malignant."

Sof nodded, deep in thought. "Anything like that—we could call it the Work's Dark Twin—well, it would have the same structure as the Work, probably. Which means that you'd have to do some of it in shadow and some of it in the Mundane, so we need to look for it in both…"

"We need you Sof." Josette wasn't only sweetening the pill of what she'd just helped do with flattery, though that was part of what was going on. She really did believe they needed Sof, in the flesh.

"I saw it in Iraq," Emma said. "They were taking fragments of dead gods, and bringing them back half-alive and turning them into weapons that wandered around the landscape cancelling existence, and eating people. Eating them down to their essence. And when I was Berthe, in 1912, well, she saw them using a black powder that was a product of horrible deaths and provoked more, to generate more of it." A further memory came to her. "Mara knew about it.

She came across it with Berthe. Why didn't she do something about the powder?"

"Not the sort of thing the Huntress ever pays attention to," Josette shrugged. "When you get to know her, well, over the aeons, she's become sort of focussed. She doesn't believe in planning things. And two years later, well, it was the so-called war to end war and everyone had other things on their minds."

Sof laughed, bitterly and bitchily. "She likes to say it's about not abusing the power she gets by killing the killers, but that's self-deception. She was just as bad when she was a small child, never saving a honeycomb for later and never biding her time with a slight. And she was terrible about doing her share of the housework, back when we ran a wayside house. No, you're right, we do need to know about these weapons."

"And," Josette pointed out, "you are one of the great mathematicians and two of the greatest devisers and practitioners of the Work. It's what you do. I've acquired the odd bit of skill with it down the years, but you taught me everything I know, and I have never excelled you."

This was, Emma noted, clearly the way to get Sof to do what you want; since she was in many ways the same person, she noted that she should probably be aware when people tried to use it to persuade her.

Alexander clearly was not feeling the love. "Mara.... Mother and I did listen when she gave us her standard lecture, and we didn't ever do anything she'd disapprove of ever again—well not hardly. She kept hanging around the edge of battles and orgies, with her eyes narrowed as if she suspected us of something underhand. I wish I knew where Mother ended up after her murder; it would be ever so handy to have her here."

Sof and Josette looked at him stony-faced. "We don't think we'd have liked her." Josette's tone was sharper than usual. "She may not have been doing the Rituals but she had an unpleasant taste for watching you killing things. Most people don't find it your most attractive quality."

Alexander smiled ingratiatingly. "I promised I'd mostly give it up. I meant it, but I do miss it—good at it, you see. Still, probably not what we need right now. So anyway, I have this plan—Sof, this is what I need you for."

He really was someone you'd pay attention to even if you didn't know who he was.

"I've got all these troops, you see, and a lot of the formerly damned are content to sit around scratching the dirt and growing things with Asareth for the rest of eternity, which is a perfectly respectable thing to be doing. And building things with Judas—I should imagine he'll keep them busy."

"Or doing my filing." Emma thought she'd break in because she owed it to the people who'd helped her. "Or Judas and Raziel's filing now I've broken the back of the work and can take a little personal time as a sabbatical."

Alexander was not especially irritated at the interruption. "Just so. Anyway, my people, we spent a long time drilling up in the back hills of Hell, because you can never do enough drilling when there's eternity to play with. Then you brought things down without our getting round to it, so I have this army and nothing to do with it now we've dealt with Simon—and you even did most of that. I thought we'd march off into shadow—a lot of charting to do and maybe we'll find their factory, and maybe we'll have to do the odd bit of fighting. But it's an adventure; I need one of those." He looked wistful. "I never got to the land of Silk, and what it's become in the Mundane world doesn't interest me enough to bother with, but the far reaches of shadow, well that's an expedition...And I really need you along, Sof, because you'll be able to explain what we find to me. Better than m'tutor, actually, even if he weren't busy being in Heaven and too grand to talk to the likes of us any more, I'm told."

The theologians were still hanging around. I should have sent them off days ago, before the battle, Emma thought. Glad they're OK; presumably the Scots one kept them safe. From what I remember, he's capable.

The very fat theologian had perked up his ears at Alexander's words and waddled over. He looked very pleased. "Sorry to interrupt," he lied. "But did you just say that Aristotle is in Heaven? I always assumed he was one of the Virtuous Pagans, but they don't seem to be here. No sign of a place for them either. Not to criticize His plan, of course, but Hell is not what was thought it was going to be like, wasn't even before you lot took it over."

Raziel looked down at him benevolently and explained. "The Prophet insisted on bringing The Master of Those Who Know –" he clearly thought the title inexpressibly funny, so much so that his usual sniff turned into a snort, "– to Heaven as a personal adviser. Poet, you see, and needed someone to explain philosophy to him once his successors took up with it."

Alexander smirked. "Everything I've ever heard about this father of yours, Josette, Aristotle would fit right in to his Heaven. Love the man, he taught me everything I know, but he really is the most terrible toady. Sucked up to my father dreadfully, and Philip wasn't a man who took to flattery easily."

Judas had finished with his point-work, or whatever it was he was doing, and walked over to the theologians. "I never thought of the virtuous pagans thing in the early days, you see and none of you did until much later. After we settled accounts with the Olympians, Lucifer just shut down the Elysian Fields and flung almost everyone there into torment. Obviously I made an exception for Plato; Philo would never have forgiven me if I'd let harm come to him. But Socrates refused to be freed. He said it was a matter of justice. Of course, he was right and we were totally in the wrong, I see that now."

Alexander was clearly not impressed by this belated repentance. "Good job he was one of the first souls I liberated, back when I started the Wild Damned. What were you thinking letting Lucifer have him—he was lying on his back under a harrow trying to convince the demon torturing him that it needed to see things from his victims' point of view. The demon wasn't being persuaded, so I gave it a practical demonstration." He smirked and made a lewd gesture with several fingers. "Socrates didn't approve of my methods—said it was typical behaviour for a Macedonian hooligan, but I counted to fifty and didn't hurt him, asked him to teach me. Or at least ask me questions. He said he had better things to do; he wanted to go find the soul of this rope-dancer he'd known."

"Lovely man," Sof said nostalgically.

Josette shook her head at her brother. "What were you thinking?" Judas looked shamefaced.

The fat theologian stuck up his hand. "A lot of it was our fault...Can we go now? We promise not to do it again."

"I promise no such thing," the Scotsman grumbled. "The rest of you may think something's changed, but I am not fooled. This is still Hell, and it's even worse than it was before."

"What do you mean?" said the fat theologian.

The Scotsman looked at him in scorn. "Well, obviously. There's a load of women suddenly in charge. That's clearly Satanic. Whores the lot of them. And all these damned flowers—that's obviously a subtle ploy of the adversary. Sinister I call them—and their colours—all purple and red and pink. It's all an encouragement to lechery and fornication."

His face grew ever more craggy and disapproving as Emma watched him—he's actually controlling it really well, she thought.

Asareth suddenly towered over the lot of them. It's very disconcerting being around her when she does that, Emma thought; I mean, I suppose I could do that now I am a goddess, not just inside my own head, but out here—but why would one want to?

"You lot, you were free to go days ago—and you just hung around being useless. And now you start being insulting. Well, dammit, I'm one of the Queens of what used to be Hell, and you will mind your manners in my realm." There was mischief in her eyes rather than anger or hurt pride. She kissed each of the theologians in turn and suddenly the old men weren't old any more. "Just think," she laughed, "of all the things you think of as sins that you can do, with a second chance. You're free to go."

51

They looked around in confusion and felt clumsily at chins that were no longer bearded or even stubbly, at pates that were no longer tonsured. They scrubbed up nicely, for the most part—especially the dark-skinned quiet one, who looked thoughtful and suddenly felt inside his robes and smirked.

Asareth glanced down at him and, intrigued, shrunk down so that she was looking up at him, put her hand on his inside his robe, then pulled his lips down to hers. "Make me chaste, but not yet, I think you said…Maybe I'll keep you."

He laughed—his laugh was as lecherous as hers—and suddenly he was enthusiastically joining in the kiss, his free hand behind her neck and pulling her head back.

Asareth gave a shudder of pleasure and suddenly neither of them were clothed and their limbs wrapped round each other and they were off the ground and he was in her and oh gosh! Emma thought, they really are going to do it here in front of everybody and Caroline stroked the back of her neck and Alexander stared amused and hungry and Sof seemed to be taking notes.

Josette and Judas both looked as if they felt they should say something but did not know what.

Several of the theologians looked away, shocked and blushing. The young fat one looked on intrigued—it was as if he had never actually realized that people really did these things and might enjoy them. A couple of the others—Emma realized she did not know who half of them were—at least not in her conscious mind—just stared hungrily.

"Don't let her tempt you, laddie." The Scotsman sounded genuinely protective. "Somehow we're damned, and purgatory is a papist invention, but you really shouldn't act like a heathen. Even if we're damned there's no excuse for whore-mongering." He reached out a muscular arm as if he were going actually to try to pull them apart.

And perhaps it was Asareth's peculiar power as a goddess of fertility but the moment of pause lasted for what seemed like hours until they were finished with a shudder and a sigh and suddenly clothed again. and just kissing.

The North African broke from the kiss a moment. His dark eyes had the glare of someone who was pulling rank, as well he might in the circumstances. "I know a lot more about being a heathen than any of you. Especially you, you young puppy—and frankly it was a lot more fun than anything I've done since. Listen, the lot of you, don't you see—we're supposed to be intelligent—clearly nothing we thought was true was. Which makes our lives meaningless or worse."

The Scotsman made as if he were going to defy him and the African glowered at him until the Scotsman stepped back like a wild dog who has met the leader of a pack of wolves.

The African stared at each of the others in turn—the ones who had turned away turned back at the pressure of his glare and then lowered their eyes. The fat young one was the only one who could meet his eyes, and even he just shrugged and lowered his head in submission.

The African returned to kissing Asareth and the others stood there in silence, as if they were waiting for orders that they knew would come in turn.

Eventually Asareth broke the clinch. "You need to talk to them, dear," she said. "You moulded most of them so they are your responsibility. And we have plenty of time. Later." Decades of lechery were implicit in that 'later'.

Emma and Caroline looked at each other and Caroline tapped her feet impatiently. Emma pulled her 'I know but intellectual curiosity?' face and Caroline pouted and shrugged resignedly.

The African turned round and looked at the others in contempt, some of it at himself. "I mean, original sin…What was I thinking? How did that even make any sense? How did you all swallow such nonsense? At least making love to a heathen goddess is worthwhile. I wasted my life. It was all nonsense. You wasted your lives too…"

Then he looked round at Emma. "Mother's not around, is she?"

Raziel reassured him, "The Blessed Monica sings among the Matrons of the Church in the seventh rank of Heaven."

Augustine looked relieved and turned back into the kiss for a moment. Then another thought struck him. "Where's your man, wosisname, Calvin?" he asked the Scotsman.

Knox shrugged.

Raziel explained. "Him we let into Heaven, but he didn't like the company. Too many Popes. So he left. Somewhere in shadow, I'd think."

Augustine kissed Asareth some more. They really were very ornamental together, Emma thought—and went on watching rather than getting on with business. After a while, Asareth grew a little more, tucked Augustine under her arm and made as if to leave.

All the time this had been going on, Judas had been getting more and more embarrassed and Josette had been getting more and more of a fit of the giggles. "Why didn't I think of that?" she managed to say finally. "I could have sabotaged centuries of theology and the damage it causes just by wandering around seducing you all."

A couple of the theologians were experimenting with their bodies—it had obviously occurred to these actually quite intelligent men that they could do that. The Scotsman suddenly grew six inches, and acquired intertwined knots of muscles on top of his already muscular arms.

The no longer noticeably fat, but still quite chubby, theologian looked serious. He looked where Augustine had gone and talked as if he were answering him, even though he was talking to himself. "Because we needed to learn the hard way. I had a vision once, and thought it meant I could put reasoning aside, but I never did, not really. We needed to be humbled. Pride of intellect, pride of spirit, pride of virtue. And Paul said love, and his Master said Love and we did not hear them."

He wept, until Josette patted him on the back and led him aside.

"You know, Thomas, I'm going to be investigating a lot of people, back in the Mundane. I need to reactivate my networks, I could do with an intelligent young man to organize an office for me…"

The theologian looked slightly confused. "You would be…"

Emma thought she had better take charge. "That would be on a need to know basis."

Sof whispered to Alexander, who walked over to the Scotsman and slapped him on his broad shoulders. "John," his voice was full of command. "You were a man of action in your youth. We need bright young men on our journey into shadow. And my friends here don't need you around causing trouble."

Josette's voice whispered in Emma's mind—from the look on Caroline's face she was talking to her as well. "That'll be interesting—Alexander always did like them butch and was always good at the slow chase…And neither of them can kill the other."

The other theologians milled around with sour expressions on their faces like children who haven't been picked for a side. Emma thought about it for a second and glanced at Caroline, who shook her head in agreement.

"Where would we put them?" Caroline said. "The flat's going to be cramped enough with both of us in the flesh."

"I am sure I could fix that quite easily." Emma looked smug. "Because, goddess."

"Planning permission." Caroline pulled her best 'you're not thinking this through' expression. "Load-bearing walls." Then her eyes went soft and wistful. "Can we go back there, soon, please? Or now? And alone." She drew out the last syllable into a whimper. "I spent three decades watching you eat salt beef platzels and onion bagels with cream cheese and salmon and now I can finally eat them again. And I want to…"

Emma snapped her fingers and suddenly there was a small table heaped with bagels with a variety of fillings. Caroline started stuffing her face, and most of the others wandered over and took one.

After a few mouthfuls, though, Caroline looked disappointed.

"These are lovely, but they're not the same. I want to eat bagels in the flat, after saying hello to the nice goblin lady."

Emma clapped her hands and most of the people still present turned to pay her attention.

"I want to leave," she explained. "Caro and I have decades of ungratified desire to make up for, but business first."

She started counting things off on her fingers. "Well. First someone needs to sort out the gods of Canaan and Olympus—we haven't heard from them since we left them building a citadel we don't now need. And then there's all the inhabitants of Dis—they didn't all end up part of Simon's body and I'm sure a lot of them were just too cowardly or bored or possibly good-natured—though they are demons—to get involved. Someone has to go and talk to them. And one of you two is going to have to explain how things work now to your father."

Judas and Josette looked stony-faced at this last, and then smiled simultaneously.

"We'll get Mother to explain," they said in unison, as they had obviously done many times in their past. "She'll know what to say. Or not to."

Asareth, who was suddenly back from where she had gone, put Augustine down, made a 'stay' gesture with the index finger of her right hand, and took a big bite out of a piece of cheesecake, which she then put down again half-eaten. Then she walked over and put one hand on Emma's shoulder and another on Caroline's.

Tsasipporah came and perched on Emma's outstretched hand.

"I'll take care of all that—I've got lots of people to help," Asareth explained. "The whole point of being a goddess is that you really don't have to do everything. Always worshippers and acolytes and demi-gods to delegate to. You really don't have to be the Judge of the Damned the whole time, you know." She smirked at a private piece of amusement. "As to the gods of Canaan and Olympus...I talked to them about how they stayed out of the recent unpleasantness and they were sorry...And they talked to me about their plans. About which I will say one word to you—deniability."

Emma sighed, knowing that her co-regent was right, and the sigh became a sudden shudder and a sense of just letting go. And very consciously leaving the bird behind.

She waved as she and Caroline left but she wasn't sure anyone saw this.

The flat was a lot tidier than when she had last seen it, and there were potted plants and vases of flowers all over shelves she didn't remember having put up. Next to the silver statue—which was still there, odd because Emma had thought it was some sort of manifestation of Josette—there were two perfect little bonsai trees.

"We told you you'd feel ever so better when you stopped being human." Eithne turned round from where she was doing something delicate to a browning frond.

Aspara flustered round and pecked a kiss on Emma's hand. "Your divinity."

"So who am I?" Caroline said. "Chopped liver?"

A sudden delighted thought came over her face. "Do they do that downstairs? You never eat it, but I remember liking it..."

"Oh, look," Eithne cooed. "She's not a ghost any more."

"Hell flesh, so much more tasteful."

"Almost as good as trees."

"Do they have trees in Hell?"

"Wouldn't they catch fire?"

"They'd be special trees, silly."

Emma realized that the sweet girls could go on all night and she and Caroline had an agenda that consisted of bagels and then bed, perhaps not in that order. Delaying gratification is one thing, but prioritizing between them can be a bitch. She didn't want to be aggressive but...

"What exactly are you two doing here?"

"Miss Wild," they chorused. "We do her plants, you know, and she is ever so scary."

57

"She wanted to put someone in to take care."

Aspara pointed to the bonsai. "She got Tom to put bits of our trees here."

"But you'll hardly know we're here..."

Caroline started tapping her right foot, meaningfully.

"Anyway," Eithne could see a certain urgency creeping in. She was almost terse. "The Huntress."

"She's going to be in London."

"Miss Wild says she's coming to kill someone."

"Miss Wild said she wanted you to know."

"And now we know." Emma was pleasant but firm. "And we want some quiet time."

Suddenly, the two dryads were gone, or at least apparently gone. Their little trees were glowing slightly, making the statue glint when Emma reached out with her mind and dimmed the lights.

There was an embarrassed moment—they'd waited so long, had so often despaired, had found so many stratagems and workarounds. Caroline sat down on the bed and started undoing the fifteen buttons down the front of her dress. Emma sat down beside her—she could have removed her own t-shirt and leggings and fleece hoodie with a thought, but that did not seem to be the right thing for now. After all, given that Caroline could apparently still work some sort of clothes magic she could presumably just dissolve the dress or not be worried about tearing it off and scattering buttons in all directions.

Emma unzipped the front of the hoodie and shucked off her t-shirt. Caroline was by now on the thirteenth button and Emma thought that a good time to reach over and peck her on the cheek. Caroline stopped even trying with the last two buttons and turned, let the dress fall off her shoulders and arched her neck so that Emma had to move her kiss to Caroline's lips.

It felt like water in the desert, like flame in the cold, like milk in the throat, like a soft firm pillow under an aching head. Like a spark and a slow delicious explosion. It was coming home at last to a place they had never been.

And a sense that it was not just them, but the world around them that had changed a little forever.

After a while, Caroline turned her head on the pillow.

"That glow, is it you being all goddessy?"

"Don't think so. Something else. Not apotheosis but a bit like it."

"I wouldn't know," Caroline grumbled. "Civilian here. Person who gets killed and kidnapped in order to build the heroine's character."

"It's not quite like that, is it? I mean, you escaped from Lucifer and trekked across Hell to join the Wild Damned. That's pretty heroic."

Emma hugged her close to show how impressed she was, but Caroline pulled away, shaking her head as if she felt she didn't deserve it.

"Well, that's the thing. I gather I did all that. I remember coming into the flat, and he was there and going bwahaha. The very next thing I knew, I was shaking hands with Bloody Alexander the Great in some green valley surrounded by triangular mountains and the sky was exploding with dead angels."

Her eyes flickered a moment. Her voice was suddenly slightly different yet well-known to Emma.

"That would be because I took over for a bit. I needed her safe and I couldn't afford slipups."

It was the voice of Emma's armour.

And suddenly Caroline was back behind her own eyes, and looking aghast.

The voice continued, only now it was coming from the mouth of the statuette, and however had they failed to see that it wasn't cold stiff metal, but just staying very still? "I just wanted to get the backrush of you two being together. It tastes delicious."

The two women sat up and Emma stuck out a hand imperiously, while suspecting that there was nothing she could possibly do that would affect outcomes. She put her other arm around Caroline so that she could at least pretend to be protecting her.

Emma found the idea of being watched bad enough—she had

specifically tried to arrange it so that no one would—and Caroline was freaking out more than Emma had ever seen her do. She looked slightly sick, as if she were suddenly on a boat and she did not know where it was going.

Emma stared at the statuette and stony-faced as she could manage for something which, oh ick, she had lived inside for a while and which knew her skin better than a lover.

It stared back at her with metal eyes that were none the less cold for the fact that they were glowing.

It went on. "Don't stop making love just because I'm here. It's something you need to do it a lot. Magic, you see, like in Berthe's opera. Do it a lot, and store it, because you need it, the world will need it."

The statuette, which was absolutely the armour, and always had been, Emma realized, stepped down from the table and stood up, and grew as she did so to the size she had been when Emma was inside it, and slightly more. She hummed a few bars from Berthe's opera.

"Thus it was, thus it is," she sang.

"Lillit?" Emma and Caroline both said wonderingly.

The armour laughed, "Oh yes, and so very much more...When you were Berthe, you understood so much that you seem to have forgotten—ask her, listen to the music, listen to the words. And make love a lot; a lot depends on it."

"What are you doing here?" Emma could hardly not ask.

"Being cryptic and annoying." Caroline was clearly quite vexed with this other self, far more so, Emma thought smugly, than I've been with mine.

The armour laughed; it was annoyingly like tiny bells. "Just so, my sisters." She bent down and kissed Emma, first, and then Caroline. When she kissed her other self some of the silver of her skin flowed with the kiss, glimmered briefly in Caroline's lips and eyes and hair and then was gone.

"I can't protect you from everything. But that should help with most ordinary danger." She tapped her left wrist where a watch would be. "Time, always time. And I must be away. I have an appointment in Alexandria. To collect some things. And you need to be downstairs, buying yourselves the bagels you neglected to eat last night." Her tone was suddenly almost nannyish. "You need to keep your strength up. And the Huntress will be downstairs ordering cucumber and cream cheese in ten minutes' time. It's time you met her, both of you."

And then she was gone. Into time.

# Horrible Murders

I went directly, through shadow, from Crowley's dingy funeral to the outskirts of London, but thereafter I took my time. I walked, mostly not through shadow; I even, against my usual habits, rode on the red omnibuses and on the Underground, and at last I came to the centre of what was still a great city.

I had already noticed what I saw more of the longer I looked— threadbare clothes and sorrowful faces, a scent of cheap tobacco and despair and clothes too rarely washed, buildings chipped and scarred and left for rubble. And the green and white of bindweed and the bright red flowers that grew amid the grey wastes of broken brick.

Yet the people had—as often as not—grim smiles on their faces, especially those, and they were many, who walked with crutches or had lost an eye or bore the marks of terrible burning. There were so many ghosts walking among the living as if they did not care to abandon their comrades yet, and were prepared to make Heaven or Hell wait for them. They too had the same grim smiles, even those, living and dead, who had no faces.

I have seen cities that were sacked and cities that had known defeat; what I saw around me was neither of those things, but a city that had known victory but paid the butcher's bill in full.

I had seen one Great War and had not expected that there would be another so soon. Clearly the thunder that had vexed my long sleep had been no mere clash of clouds.

I wondered how much had changed that I had not yet seen, and yet, I trod the same alleys and pushed at the same door in an almost anonymous wall in the courtyard of a building that still stood though much around it was rubble and dereliction.

Polly was not especially glad to see me, but she poured me a cup of hot coffee all the same. The tobacco smoked by the people in the street might be stale, but Miss Wild was not being deprived.

"'Ere she comes without a by your leave. Once everything is done and over and we don't need her to finish any job. Save the Russians, which being hideous atheist Bolsheviks, her specialty is probably not called for."

"I was detained."

"The late Mr. Crowley?" she snorted sardonically. "Time was when it took someone serious to inconvenience you."

"Not Crowley alone," I said in my defence. "He was part of some conspiracy. Hassan had supplied him with some special concoction, for one."

"Well, if you will go taking people's toys away from them, you must expect some little inconvenience from their attempts at vengeance. We did look for you, and we saw photographs of you with Crowley. But when we puts him to the question, he claimed to have mislaid you. And now 'e's dead, so presumably that's why you're back."

"Just so. I didn't want to leave myself in a situation where someone might try to use me while I slept. So I betook myself to the heart of the mountain where I could sleep undisturbed among its flames."

Polly snorted. "Very restful, I'm sure. Also very mythological. But we really could have done with you in the last little scrap, and it's only recently that I knows for certain that the beastly Hun was not up to the sort of games you deal with. Though you would certainly have done him some useful damage finding out to the contrary."

"Another war with Germany?" I had made this only my second port of call—the damage done to her city had implied warfare and whichever German Reich it had been by now seemed the most likely candidate. "Crowley mentioned that he had colleagues there. I had been wondering if I had them to thank for my period of inaction."

"As to that, I couldn't say," Polly replied, "there being little necessity to round up all the men of the Thule society, they not having for the most part been around once the serious killing started."

"Killed in their turn?" I ventured.

"No, pensioned off or given cushy jobs abroad by jumped-up clerks what were prepared to lower themselves to actual office politics. They wouldn't flatter, not the real mages, because being Germans and mages, they thought they were better than their masters, which was unfortunate for them, because they mostly were."

This was not the first time I had witnessed the most talented and wicked of men come to nothing because of envy.

"The late Herr Himmler, what I had the pleasure of seeing hanged—he was the one most interested in all that, wanted to believe in the Holy Grail, the magic of the German forest, Secret Masters in Tibet who were secretly blond and blue-eyed and the world being a bubble inside a vast block of ice. So people that told him to pick one damn idea and forget the other as nonsense were out, whichever one they believed in, and the ones who'd say Yes Mein Herr, No Mein Herr were in. And to our great good fortune, the file with your damn Rituals in it got lost behind a radiator or something."

I breathed a sigh of relief.

She looked at me sadly. "Oh, they still killed uncounted thousands of people in the most 'orrible of ways. They really wanted to do that, and they really did it. They just didn't do it for any reason that made sense. Even magic sense."

She shuddered. "You talked to me once about Mexico. That was nothing. Genghis, 'e was nothing. But I had to lose good people making sure, while you were all tucked up comfortable-like in some fucking volcano. I wanted to stop it, anyway—on general principles and just in case—but bloody Churchill said it weren't our business. We had better things to bomb, 'e said, that would shorten the war by killing Germans. And their sins would be on their heads. 'E talked about it –" she did an imitation "– 'the abyss of a new Dark Age made more sinister, and perhaps more protracted, by the lights of perverted science,' but really 'e fucking loved the idea. Made 'im a dragon slayer or something. I was so glad he lost the election—too keen on other people dying, that one. Always has been, since he was a kid orficer going wherever he could get into trouble and kill people."

In two hundred years, I hadn't seen Polly so angry with a mere politician.

"Remind me. Which party is he now?"

"Vile old Tory again. Same as 'e ever was, really."

"But you won the war."

"The Americans won the war. The Russians won the war. We— well that remains to be seen, don't it? Empire's shot to pieces, is the good thing. Never liked that for all I served it. Conquest is a game played by ruffians without the guts to be honest thieves is what I say… But then, all the rules got changed now. How does anyone win when there's weapons that could kill all of us in seconds?"

She explained to me about the new bombs, and about bombers that could fly half-way round the world to drop them.

I had met Einstein once, when he was dapper and wore hair-oil and spats and fancied himself quite the ladies' man round the dance-halls of Bern. He never quite made a pass, but told me all sorts of things about the nature of the universe that I did not quite understand. I had known Newton and this young man was nicer, and more importantly, not interested in magic.

I had not thought of him as a man who would someday tell us how to undo the world.

"Bombers ain't the worst of it. The Germans hit London with rockets. Imagine a rocket with an Atomic Bomb stuck on the top of it. That'd piss on anyone's chips for good and all. What price stopping the Rituals when all anyone has to do is press some fucking button? And we're either ashes or having our hair drop out from poison. Anyone who does that to half the world, well, do they even need to get the words right?"

"The Rituals are a matter of wicked will. The same as ever. I shall be there, I and my spear and my swords. And my will is to punish the strong and wicked."

"But 'ow are you going to know who is working the Rituals and who is merely killing half the world on general principles?"

I looked at her and I was not sure which of us was being naïve.

"Polly Wild, you walk among the powerful of the world as their peer. Let it be known to them that anyone who uses such weapons will die at my hand, were they the last man or woman on Earth. If we cannot tell them of the Rituals, lest it put ideas into their heads, just inform them that there is one whom it is best not to offend. That should suffice."

I have always known Polly for a persuasive woman, and clearly she convinced the powerful of the world because those weapons have never been used to kill again. Yet.

I defend the weak against the strong, and I cannot save them all, but sometimes I have my uses.

"No matter how virtuous a ruler, or how benevolent their rule— even if they think it is in self defence…"

Polly nodded. She knew me well enough to know that I was serious. She walked across to the drinks cabinet, poured herself a large whisky and downed it in a gulp. I am aware that I have that effect sometimes, even on my dear friends.

Having decreed how things would be, I thought I had better move on. "What other news is there that I should know of?"

Polly's face grew wistful. "Sweet young Herbert died last summer. He saw so much of what was to come. He did not die a happy man." She looked sad, and I shared her sorrow. "I know you play for the other team, Huntress, but you should have tried him, at least once. He was thoughtful and delicious and his breath was like honey on your mouth."

I reflected how little she knew me—I had delighted in the body of the young god on that day when my life changed forever. If he had had no male successor in my bed, and only one female and that for a moment, it was less inclination than my deep mourning for the sister I had never seen again and the sister I had so often lost to death and chance.

We live on, and bright young people full of hope become old and full of age's sadness and sometime its despair.

It is the way of the world.

Young Herbert, dead—so many are, but his death, even in the course of nature, saddened me...

I thought back to that autumn of blood and madness when I met him.

...Not all who know that I am the Huntress care to enquire too deeply what it is that I hunt. Learned men and daring men, they suspect that knowing too much about me might bring them to my attention, and they are not entirely wrong. Though I would never maim or kill for mere curiosity; that is one of the many things I dislike about gods.

That summer, in Africa, the heat was such that the labourers on the new canal would faint and die like wheat snapped off by a fierce wind. It is always thus; the wise men and the rich men and the powerful men decide to connect the Nile to the Red Sea, or the Red Sea to the Mediterranean, and many of the poor die, and there is much profit for a century or five, and then the mud creeps back and soon it is as if no passageway had ever been. I have lived so long that I see the works of man rise and fall and rise again and go to utter oblivion. Sesostris and Darius and Necho and Ptolemy and Omar, and now this man Lesseps.

Many things lie buried in the mud where once ships made passage, and some of those things I have killed and placed there. Whenever there is digging, I cast an eye over it; it is never to be assumed that what is dead cannot pass from death to mere sleep. Because that is an assumption that is folly, and puts the weak in danger.

So I stood alongside the labourers and wielded a pick with the strongest of them and felt through the thick dark silt that gives the land its name. They were shocked to see a woman working among them, and one whose flesh was not decorously covered; any who spoke, I looked at. And they spoke no more.

I found things, things that I had put there for safe-keeping and others that I had not, but nothing that was alive or undead. Deep in the silt into which I passed without breath, I found a cage, and what I had placed therein had died eventually, and would trouble the world no more. There were pottery shards, and lost signet rings in the mud, and a marble faun with a sneer on his face. And a flask of glass overlaid with lapis that I recognized by the voice that moaned from within it.

There are stories of such things, of course. The Thousand Nights and One Night, and the Sea of Stories, are full of them. Last living dregs of forgotten gods, or the sort of low spirit that Nameless and Star recruited as their enforcers, or the souls of living jewels, trapped in glass or fine pottery by charms and trickery so that the world might be free of them, or at least so that they might learn better manners.

This flask had once held a fine vintage that I had poured on the ground both to make room for the surly spirit it now contained and so that he might lick it as it fell and from the dust and become drunk as such do on the idea and scent of wine as much as the substance.

"Is that you, Huntress?" he cried out to me. "Are you here already to release me? After so few days?"

"No, spirit," I replied. "I am not here to free you and it has been almost a millennium."

I had imprisoned him, and several like him, for serving the mad Caliph Omar on whose face it was not lawful to look. They wandered the streets of Cairo on torrid nights, whipping up dust-storms to flay drinkers and fornicators, and the Caliph claimed to be doing the work of God, but it was the Rituals he served and himself.

"What would you do, if I freed you?" I asked.

"I would try to destroy you, and then I would go about the godly work my master set me."

Like most hypocrites and deceivers, Omar had set a spell on the djinn who served him that they could not lie, or even prevaricate.

"Then it is best I leave you to lie until the sands wear the glass away."

"That is true, Huntress. Bury me deep so no random foot can smash the glass, for I will have my revenge. When I am free."

I buried the flask, and the djinn, deep and deeper in the mud where even Lesseps' men would not disturb it.

It was grimy work and afterwards I allowed myself to bathe in a remote pool I know of, where none go. It was a shrine once, to nymphs that had come from Greece in the train of that Solon who gave laws to Athens and to many creatures besides. The Pharaoh and learned men of that time were intrigued by tales of the many creatures, not divine and not human either, who lived among the Greeks, and asked Isis for permission to live in her realm.

Isis met the nymphs and they flustered at her, for she was more approachable, less quick to anger than the goddesses that they knew. She was charmed, and gave them this place—they were long gone from it, into shadow or into final death, I know not. But the charm of seclusion still held, and the splash of clear water from a spring onto clean brown pebbles and the scent of the few frail white and yellow flowers that grew there.

There were fish there in the pool, small silvery darting fish that were not afraid. I thanked the pool and took three, and dried them on a stone in the hot sun with a little of the salt I had in my wallet, and ate them, slowly and reverently. Isis is long gone from the lands she once cherished but her gift to the nymphs remains to please wayfarers, and I thanked her in her absence, making a note that I should mention it when next I saw her in that part of shadow which is called the Land of Reeds.

I had nothing especial to do, and so I set out, knowing that wherever I go, I find iniquity sooner or later.

That is the nature of the world.

Some miles away, there was a track, almost a road, that ran down into the South. An army from the black kingdoms of the South had marched along it centuries before, answering a summons in the name of old alliances, when Nectanebo the Accursed fought his last war with the Persians. They came to grief, not in battle but in the treachery of the Pharaoh they had sought to help; and I walled up the creature that Nectanebo had become through their deaths, in his obsidian tower of sorcery. Where for all I care he groans still, crawling on the ground like a broken spider, after limbs that unjointed themselves when his magic went astray.

If I had killed him, his fate would have been easier. Either dark Anubis would have weighed his rotten soul and tossed his heart to the beast that devours those who prove unworthy, or—alas and more likely—he would have learned enough from his extensive library of Books of the Dead to sweet-talk his way out of punishment for his many crimes and gone on to make trouble in the Land of Reeds.

Isis, who has set up a system of Judgment that enables repentance and rehabilitation—which does her credit—is not naïve and has been known to ask favours from me, who does not always forgive. In Nectanebo's case, I chose to circumvent the inevitable and condemn him to pain before he could work even more harm.

One day perhaps I will behave unjustly in a matter of this kind— but that was not that day.

But now, on this day, on that track I had known down the millennia, I heard the gentle whinnying of one horse to another, for horses talk among themselves, although they are but beasts, for the most part. I was curious to see who was travelling there, with horses smart enough not to be deceived away by the pool's spells, which normally kept men a league away—though I was not strong enough to cope with an army, obviously.

My curiosity serves me well and my interest was in this case further piqued by the sunburned hands and neck of a Frank, as they call the peoples of Europe in those parts, though not a Frenchman like the engineers of the canal, for he sang to himself gently in German one of the songs of those other nymphs who chanted men to their deaths in the wilder parts of the Rhine, until I persuaded them otherwise.

One of his two horses was a high-stepping Arabian, as well groomed as if it were on parade or part of an exhibition dressage contest. It amazed me that he brought so fine and costly a beast into such debatable lands—I guessed that he was the sort of European who believed himself deep in his soul to be untouchable by lesser breeds.

The other horse was a mere pack-drudge but it had livelier eyes.

The man wore gracelessly the fine cottons of wealthy men who adopt the dress, but not the style, of the peoples of the Levant—a man in middle age with an unbecoming moustache that he wore unwaxed and a beard sufficiently trimmed to be a problem in places where something fuller is considered godly.

I stepped into the middle of the track—without taking any of my weapons from their place.

"Well met"—for even if often not true, it is a pleasing opening gambit—"What brings you here?"

"Fair maiden, what brings you here? A woman by yourself in the desert. Even if you are well-armed to the point of madness." He spoke kindly but with an air of superiority.

"They call me the Huntress. And I walk where I choose, and none can stay me. And not because of my prowess in arms alone."

"Huntress." His tone was polite but questioning and querulous. He clearly did not know who I was: knew that I was a danger but did not know enough to be sure that he was not my quarry. "I am a seeker after knowledge, and after old things that I can study, while I sell them at a profit. Hans Langenschmidt at your service." And he made a gesture of respect—like his clothing, copied from the people among whom he worked—and dismounted.

Horses sometimes like me, and sometimes not. It has nothing to do with whether or not I smell of the blood of my work. The pack horse was skittish and restless and he walked over and stilled it with a whispered word. Men who have that particular skill have in general no bent for other magics, save sometimes those of the forge; I have learned to trust them. Nonetheless...

"These are lonely roads for a man by himself, who travels with wealth and with fine horses. There are soldiers, and bandits, and those somewhere in between, who would take both from you and your life beside."

As I spoke, he took a draught from a water-bottle at his side then offered me some. I took none, because though I thought it unlikely I would need to harm this man, I did not know it for certain, so would not give him host-right.

I learned that rule before time and chance took me and made me what I am.

"And so they might." There was humour in his voice, but also relief that I was not one such. "Twice as I travelled through the realms of the Emperor Johannes, and those of his rebel subject King Menelek and the lands conquered by that dead man they wrongly called the Messenger, I had to buy my life and my liberty, but I was able to pay in the coin of knowledge, which is more use than gold or horses." And he brandished a tablet, baked clay but with a charm upon it that spoke to anyone who held it, and to those around them.

It said in an insinuating whisper, "I am the knowledge men kill for or spend kingdoms." I speak all tongues—as is convenient when I walk through so many lands—and it was in all tongues that it spoke to me. I knew from that fact alone that it was a powerful magic; the voice, though, was one I knew, for I had heard it last begging for mercy as I walled its owner into his own tower of sorcery.

I walked over.

I had to use little of my power to compel or persuade, and Langenschmidt thought hardly a second before offering the tablet to me. It was foul to the touch, and I recognized the bindings as if they were a bad man's handwriting. There was much else written on the tablet, in Akkadian, and Egyptian and the languages of the South, a simple further message, and one I knew well.

I had idly wondered with what Nectanebo had tempted his allies North, and now I knew. I felt less sympathy for those long-dead kings he had betrayed to their deaths, and even more for the men that they had led into the darkness with them all unaware. It was a short form of the Rituals, which said much that I will not say at the present time.

"Knowledge?" I was uncertain how much this man actually knew.

He laughed sardonically and with the peculiar arrogance of Europeans who believe that science and law are the only things worth knowing in the world and who think, even when they hold it in their hand and talk to it along the road, that magic is a lie. "It is some rigmarole, promising long life and power to those who kill to gain them, which cannot be true since there are no murderous gods walking among us. It would be of little interest, save that it is a first hint of the forgotten script of Meroe, I think—nowhere near as useful as the tablet Champillon used, but something."

"And you bought your life with its message."

"Of course. There is war brewing, and I was arrested by both the Ethiopians and their ambitious neighbours. But they did not kill me out of hand, either of them, and I was taken first before the man Golden Mouth, who serves King Menelek as courtier and flatterer, and I whispered a translation of the charm to him and he looked thoughtful, and wrote it down. Then he took the paper and twisted it into his beard as a pretty, and ordered that I be given food and drink and sent on my way."

"And the others?"

"I had fear of the Mahdi's men, for they are pious and abhor sorcery for the most part. But as fortune would have it, they brought me before the one they call Osman, though he is no Turk, and he is one of the Scarred Folk, who demanded accommodations when they took the Way of Submission. They are pious after their fashion—they pray and they abstain from pork and they cut their daughters—but they still have a fondness for sorcery. And I whispered the charm to him too, and he let me go, though with less generosity in the matter of food."

I held in my temper, for this man seemed likely to have cost me much work and peril, but I would know all, and I could see that there was no malice in him.

"If they aspire to use the charm, why did they not keep you until they had seen whether it worked? And indeed, used you as the first victim of its rituals?"

He chuckled into his moustache. "I told them both that it had to sit in their minds unused until the next full moon. And that it would be useless if they harmed or detained the person who gave it to them. I am not foolish, you know, and for all their courtier's wiles and skill at arms, they are not learned men."

"Foolish." I spoke in my most quiet voice, the one which goes with a patch of red on my cheek, just above my scar. "Or not foolish, perhaps, but nonetheless a fool. Did it not occur to you that the charm might be real…What is it, think you, that I hunt, little fool?"

He looked clearly worried now and not merely fearful for himself. "I confess, I once read of an immortal huntress in a book of tales, that I took as merely a version of Artemis. Are you claiming to be that immortal huntress? The book said little of what she hunted—I had assumed it was the usual—wild beasts for their flesh and their fur and their ivory."

I shrugged. "That would be because I warned the storyteller not to say things that might put bad ideas into people's wicked hearts. I hunt those who use that very charm, and the godlings or worse things that they become as a result. You trade in magic, little man, for all that you do not believe in it. And magic has consequences, and prices that you are not prepared to pay."

His face grew pallid and he began to quiver as if in fever. I do not set out to terrify, but neither do I always avoid it. "Who, what, are you?" He crossed himself as he spoke.

"I am the defender of the weak whose lives they would take against the strong who do such things. I defend them, and I punish—and I cannot save them all. Especially with men like you who think they know, who think they understand…But go from my sight—it was not your fault. As a friend of mine once or twice said, go and sin no more."

He glanced at the tablet I still held, as if remembering what he had paid for it and wondering whether to ask for reimbursement.

I caught the grimace and laughed at him. "It has bought your life twice over, Herr Langenschmidt, and so was priceless whatever you paid for it. And regard it now as the fee you have paid me, for the work you have cost me, and for what I will say next."

"And what is that?" He touched, thoughtfully, the sabre scar on his cheek.

"I give you fair warning. Do your best to forget this tablet and its contents. I think we would both rather not meet again; you might put me quite out of temper should you tell others of it, or worse, try to put its words into practice."

"I promise –"

"Do not promise; just bear consequences in mind. These things so often go wrong, and, believe me, there are less pleasant ways to die that at my hands—and many whom I kill die weeping."

75

It is best to make these things clear.

I stood perfectly still and silent as he backed away and swung himself back into the saddle, then waved him adieu as he rode off, periodically looking back to check whether I followed.

After a while, I ceased to watch him and thought what to do with the tablet. It was a foul little thing, but it might be useful one day and its sheer age gave it some protection from me.

The water of the pool had charms of innocence and purity on it strong enough to resist any taint. Nectanebo was a mighty sorcerer, but Isis is a powerful goddess even now she is largely gone from a world, from an Egypt, that no longer wants her. I waded into the centre of the pool, whispered—not a prayer but a request for a favour—then bent and pushed the tablet deep into the heart of the rock. It would wait there, secure for an age.

As I travelled South I heard further talk of war. The intermittent war of Johannes and King Menelek—and their alliance against the forces of the dead Mahdi, who had sought to take advantage of that kinstrife only to find, as many armies have down the centuries, that the people of Ethiopia and of Nubia and Meroe before it, have survived so long because they resist invaders with even more vigour than they fight each other.

War is not my concern. It sometimes happens, though, in time of war, particularly those wars which are fought over the right way to worship my former apprentice, that men of faith talk themselves into the early stages of the Rituals. They do this in order—they tell themselves—to make themselves more effective champions of their God, or in this case, the divinely appointed viceroys of God whom they serve. Because corruption will always find a way into the proud hearts of men, they rapidly confuse the idea of being His champion with being His equal or rival. And then mere monstrosity takes over.

I went to both camps, and talked softly to the man called Golden Mouth, both for his eloquence and for the small fortune he wore there as replacements for teeth lost from the kick of a mule, and to Osman of the Scarred Folk, but soft words were of no avail.

"I would never use dark magic," Golden Mouth assured me. "Magic is for weak women and for savages like the Scarred Folk. I bought the charm from the Frank Langenschmidt so that, should the forces of the Prophet be so wicked as to employ it, we would have a defence. I let it be known that I possess the charm, to discourage Osman from using it."

Osman was more hostile. He made as if to strike me until I seized his hand and forced him to the ground, and batted away the spears of his bodyguards as if they were straws. I made him order them to bring me mint tea and flat bread so that I could exercise guest right.

In a while, he calmed down and agreed to speak to me. "All is lawful in struggle," he argued like a lawyer, "but some things are not needful. We are the warriors of the Messenger and the men of Sawa will fall before us, as the followers of Johannes will fall to our forces in the North. I shall hang on to the charm nonetheless because those with an imperfect understanding of God, whom they call Three who is One, might try to cheat us, and God, of our victory."

Then I tried speaking harshly and uttering threats, but both young warriors thought themselves safe from a lightly armed girl among hordes of armed men, and were mocking and arrogant.

I am the Huntress, and I serve the weak against the strong, and I like to think I retain a certain humility in the face of such mockery. With very few exceptions, those who practice the rituals have to die, and these were not yet such. But I was patient no longer.

I spoke to Ras Gobana, the wise servant of King Menelek, and to the Mahdist Khalil Al-Khusani, about their ambitious subalterns. I used the word "blasphemer" much and pointed out that young men who would not shrink from rivaling God, would certainly move against his more senior servants.

They knew, to some degree, who I was, for they were wise and scholarly men. They sought oracles from me that I could not provide them with, for that is not what I do, but I answered their questions with good sense, which is the best oracle of all.

"Will the British come again?" Khalil asked me. "I saw the dog

Gordon fall with the spear of the righteous through his kaffir heart and I saw his head on that spear and his body thrown aside. Will his masters come and take their vengeance?"

I looked at him with the sad certainty that he knew the answer and knew in his heart that that vengeance would be his death.

"I care not," he boasted and lied. "They are not what they were. Weak. They cannot even kill that righteous man who slays the whores of London." He was perhaps at this point carried away by his mood into excessive candour, or perhaps he chose to be insulting. "They are weak because they are ruled by a woman. Perhaps that godly man will tire of killing whores and put her from her throne, where no woman has any business being."

I knew nothing of the man of whom he spoke, yet, and was silent. Which he took, because it suited him, for agreement. Whereas I was merely choosing to prioritize. I had men to kill for attempting the Rituals and he was nothing to me—he would find his fate in due course.

"We are the army of God," he went on, "and in his name we will prevail."

I crossed to the other camp again.

"If the British come again," Ras Gobana grinned, "as they came against Theodore, we will be ready for them. Johannes has bought many guns—some from their enemies the Russians and some from their unfriends the French. And many that have been stolen from them. For the moment, we will parlay with the Italians, but we are ready for them when they make their move. And Johannes has given some to us, his disloyal subjects. We are angry with each other, but as brothers are angry. The Mahdists are not our brothers."

The British had punished Theodore, and the Italians were threatening both Johannes and his rival Menelek. The Ethiopians had learned a lesson from their conflicts and other dealings with the Imperial Powers, but not that lesson which the Europeans would have wished to teach them. They were the last strong unbroken power in Black Africa. The fact that they could afford to fight among themselves was proof of that, in its own way.

"And the current fight?"

Ras Gobana laughed long and hard, and swilled harsh red wine from a jeweled cup. "The followers of the Prophet think that God is on their side whereas he is of course on ours. And has shown us his blessing by providing us with three Hotchkiss repeating cannon and ten cases of Austrian needle guns. It is all my master the Emperor Johannes would spare me."

Since his master Menelek and Johannes had been fighting intermittently for years, it was a little surprising that Johannes bothered to spare any, but Johannes was a wise king and so was Menelek and they knew that their little war was not all that important, a pastime, whereas their war with the Mahdists was a serious business.

But as to the matter in hand, both commanders were wise enough men that they did not wish to have me take a side in their battle, and agreed to dispense with the services of those I sought, to send them on errands to places where I might pursue my business with those young men away from the fog of battle.

Where chance might confuse outcomes.

I followed Golden Mouth to the town of Nejo where Ras Gobana had sent him to requisition what little flour was still to be had in the market place and then to extort more from the merchants who were hiding it in the hope of later profit. Someone had told him that there was a woman seeking him, and he guessed who was on his trail—thus it was that by the time I tracked him down, he had summoned those merchants, and their families, to a feast. Sometimes, for I am a prisoner of time and chance, as are we all, I bring about that which I seek to prevent.

I was late to the feast by a matter of ten minutes during which he had his men shoot and club down the merchants and their families. His men thought that they were doing the King's work, for they knew that the merchants were guilty of starving the poor, right up to the point where he bade them shoot each other. And some obeyed and others disobeyed, but it was all one for he had started a little storm of killing and betrayal.

From which he profited little, for two of his men, dying, had seen him start to quicken and to change. He achieved a degree of godhood, but with a bullet lodged in his skull and a cutlass pinning him to the inlaid wooden floor.

It was at this point that I arrived. Too late, for I cannot save all, but there were dying children to be cared for and dead men and women to be taken where their bodies might be honoured. I gave orders to those soldiers who were not dead and what was needful was done.

Then I turned my attention to Golden Mouth—for I would not see suffering extended longer than it had to be even in a man who had done such things. It was a mercy to strike from its shoulders a head that had begun to reorganize itself to hold its skull together and was moulding and mashing what lay inside it so that the thing he had become screamed constantly. His intestines had taken on a life of their own and had come questing from the rent around the cutlass like a nest of vipers in the spring.

The severed head did not die at once—that was the worst thing—and though it was no longer connected to a throat or to lungs, it had enough of godhood about it that it went on screaming for fully an hour, and his spine kept crawling out of what was left of his neck trying to find it, and lashed at the guts that crawled all around his body, spreading filth wherever they went. I kicked the smashed and screaming head well away—I would not have him digest himself, for there are some ends that no one deserves. He screamed and he stank and he died forever, his soul gone to wisps that dissipated like smoke.

As he died, his last whimpering sobs were drowned by a noise that was like thunder in a clear sky. Once he was gone, I followed the noise of guns, and the screaming of horses and men.

Khalil had expected an easy victory, for he had all the arrogance of a cavalry commander in a land where horses were few and thus prized. He had come thundering down a pass from the high hills into the green valley where roads met and Nejo stood. A few miles from the town was the hill of Gote Dili, little more than a rise above the road, and there Ras Gobana and his allies had taken their stand.

On the other side of the road was a meadow where the people of Nejo let scrawny cattle, that had been brought there by drovers, graze to ready them for the market and the slaughterhouse. And it was there that Khalil drew up his left wing and his right wing and his centre, driving the cattle away to fend for themselves.

They outnumbered the warriors who stood on the little rise though not by much and Khalil thought that the pitch was not too steep for a charge, since they had the meadow to ride out of gathering speed as they crossed the road. The charge was never completed, for the meadow and the road and the bottom of the hill were Ras Gobana's killing ground. He had buried barrels of powder in the road and in the meadow and small boys darted out of the shallow ditch between them after lighting fuses of a medium length that meant some of them got clear, though others died.

At the ends of the rise, and at its centre, Ras had placed his three artillery pieces and between them his riflemen and those troops he had armed with needle guns. The barrels blew and as what was left of Khalil's army milled around trying to keep its footing in ground suddenly falling to craters and the bodies of their friends, the guns opened up with shells and the riflemen and the men with needle guns took their time, and made every shot a killing shot.

I have a distaste—as you will see—for that slaughter of beasts which kings call sport and especially for that death ritual where hobbled deer or netted quail are just butchered where they struggle. Such deer, such quail, had more chance than the Mahdist armies in the South, who neither conquered nor went home. So few went home, indeed, that their stories were not believed and a greater army met a similar fate outside their capital of Omdurman.

But that was no concern of mine, any more than was Menelek's

81

great victory of Adowa eight years later, where the same skills were deployed.

Khalil had offended me, but I am not petty, and he escaped the battle, with a few men and horses, and lived, for a time. I had no business with him personally as yet.

One of his men fell behind because his horse had caught a fragment of shrapnel in its hoof and was limping. I caught up with him and pulled him from his horse, ungently.

"Where did Khalil send the man of the Scarred Folk, called Osman? That I suggested he send away? Quickly, for I will help your horse and otherwise you will be left for the men of Shawa who have their own ways with stragglers." And I stroked the horse into calm and prised the hot metal from its hoof as I spoke for I would not see it suffer. I am not a healer, but the power I have in me is a cure-all when I choose to use it in that way.

"Him? He got the easy job—and missed the glory of being shot to pieces. He was sent off to hurry reinforcements to the front. You will find them on the road from the West."

I helped him back on to his horse, and slapped it on the behind— they headed off after Khalil and I followed and then overtook both him and the main group he was trying to catch up with, and continued.

As misfortune would have it, Osman was some way off, having found the reinforcements he had been sent to bring up to the front already nearly there, bringing with them the great gourds in which they carried flour. And which, when they had eaten, served them as trumpets, drums and the shells of great lutes.

The Berta, the Scarred Folk, are swordsmen and spearmen and slingers of deadly accuracy; they are also great exorcists and traffickers with the spirits that bring rain, magicians of a small kind but not a petty one.

Thus it was that when I came up with him at a small oasis in a waste of small stones, Osman had hidden himself among dancers and drummers, their faces covered in dust and sweat, who were scarifying each other's faces so that enough blood was being shed to confuse the issue.

I strode into the middle of the camp, and called on his name—may he be forgotten!—and he did not step forward. And his men mocked at me, for they did not know of their own danger, either at my hand or at his.

And then spurring their horses, so that white salt of sweat was snow on the horses' black flanks, there came up what was left of Khalil's cavalry, and he among them in the worst of tempers. He swore at the men of the Berta as crypto-idolaters and drunkards, for they were sipping as they danced the weak beer made from sorghum which they used in their rain-making. They had converted to the Way of Submission some generations earlier—but their submission did not include giving up on the rituals they thought essential in the dry lands or the beer to quench their thirst.

The Mahdists had persuaded them to fight and die for them, but not to those sacrifices.

Then Khalil saw me, and leaped down from his horse, tossing its reins to one of the Berta who rushed to catch them, and started to yell abuse at me, nerving himself to do, poor silly man, actual violence, as if he could. "I let you into my camp, Huntress, and I sent my lieutenant Osman away on the eve of battle at your request. What have I done to you that you betrayed me?"

I looked blankly at him.

"The guns," he screamed. "They had European guns, the kaffir bastards. And you did not tell me."

I laughed in his face. "I am the Huntress, little man. And the petty wars of men, who wins and who loses, are no concern of mine."

But he had taken my mind from what I should have been observing, for the Berta who had taken the reins of his half-blown horse had swung himself up into the saddle and rode at a gallop through the camp, his knees guiding the horse as he swung a great long two-handed sword smashing and slashing any of his tribal brethren that he could.

It was Osman, and he was muttering the words Langenschmidt had taught him. He had not yet killed nearly enough to change, but then, I realized, he had a better plan. The horse was near dead, but it took him where he wanted to go, just far enough from the oasis that when he slashed its throat, the blood fell on small stones, a hundred thousand of them.

And he waved his hands and all of those stones took flight, and plunged, like hail, like arrowstorm into the half-naked bodies of the men and the women and the children of the Berta. He directed a particular stream of sharp pebbles in my direction; stones that were putting out eyes and tearing off fingers of the people who stood near me merely tickled, even refreshed, like hail. Such are the charms on me.

But I had to watch for whole seconds, as I reckoned my aim and calculated a clear path through the storm of pebbles, as he maimed and killed his fellows. Killing of kin, killing of those who trust you implicitly, is always a strong version of the Rituals. I have lived so long and there is always a way for the workers of the Rituals to surprise me with wicked ingenuity. I underestimate them.

And they underestimate me.

He thought he was out of range of my spearcast and he was wrong. My lance stilled the Rituals in his throat. I ran to where he lay, not yet certainly dead; my Japanese sword settled the matter. I brought his head back, and flung it in a camp fire.

Then I turned to Khalil; I did not rebuke him for distracting me from my work at what had been—it transpired—a crucial moment. I looked at him sternly though—he had taken no hurt from the storm of pebbles because I had turned to him and thus by chance protected him.

"And that is why"—I continued what I had been saying to him two minutes earlier—"I take no interest in the wars of men. I have other concerns—and right now, it is my concern and yours to ensure that as few of these people die as is possible."

Osman was dead and gone beyond recall—the camp fire which

was charring the dead flesh from his severed head was making stinkingly sure of that—but the Rituals raise magic, even when its planned beneficiary is not there to be changed, and that magic, left wild and without a master or mistress, is not something to be taken lightly.

It attaches itself to any of the bystanders whom it chooses—and Khalil was not a man whose moral compass I would trust in those circumstances.

An old woman of the Berta, who had had the sense to throw herself to the ground and received little hurt, clapped her hands. As one in authority.

Many of those women who had been tending the cook-fires at the edge of the camp, or carving flesh and pith from the great gourds, had taken less hurt than most and began to move among their neighbours, tearing strips of cloth from their robes to bind a torn hand, or pulling brands from the fire to cauterise a wound.

A tribe that goes to war has a set task for everyone, and those women, from the calmness with which they laid one task aside, and turned to another, were the best people to care for their own.

She joined us, making perfunctory obeisance to Khalil. "And what was that? And who are you?" She turned to Khalil. "I know who you are, my lord. Of course. But who is this foreign woman? And why did my nephew Osman suddenly act like a madman or a sorcerer?"

"I am sorry for your loss, but –"

"I never liked the boy. He disrespected his elders and had a nasty temper. Still…"

"He learned the secret of godhood and was prepared to try it. It is my task to kill such."

She nodded, and turned to a child who had stood near me, and now lay bleeding on the ground. He showed no sign of life, but I knelt beside her and breathed into his mouth, as I have done many times before.

She looked at me with new respect. "Healing magic?"

85

"I have a little," I acknowledged. "My skills are otherwise. But I can heal the smaller injuries of men and horses with my power, and I have known healers, among them him you followers of the Way of Submission call Issa, and they taught me, as I teach you now. See, thus."

And I showed her, and the lord Khalil, and presently the boy choked and roused and with them I went through the devastated camp. He concentrated first on the hurts of the men who had arrived with him as was only proper; she and I had more people to tend to—she because they were her family and people, I because those most hurt and most like to die needed saving with the small healing magics that are all that I possess.

I cannot save everyone, but on this occasion I was able to save far more than I had hoped.

She came and stood by me, some of the time, using what small magics she had—and poulticing wounds with herbs that did not grow in those barren scrublands, but in the lush pastures that surrounded them in shadow. I nodded to her in respect, and vague surmise.

She laughed at me. A little. "No, Huntress. I am not she whom you seek. Grown older than you have ever known her."

"How do you know?"

"She who taught me the little I know is one known to you, who loves you. And who said that, should I ever meet you and assist you, to remind you of her love. She heals, but cannot heal herself of her own grievous hurt, her lost eye."

It had been almost a century since I had seen Hekkat who was now Morgan. I was glad to know that she was making herself useful.

"And you will stay, until all are cured." She was speaking to both me and Khalil, and not asking a question. I felt the mild tug of a failed compulsion—but then, a compulsion that orders you to do what you would have done anyway cannot be said entirely to have failed. I think she compelled Khalil, but again, he was going nowhere without saving those of his men who could be saved, and depended on the Scarred Folk, for the moment for the food and drink of which I had no need.

She deferred to Khalil, as women sometimes must, but there was irony in her eyes that he chose not to observe or comment upon. Nor did I moralize; I think though that he took our point, for he spoke with respect when we parted.

I did not see either of them ever again—she led her people back where they belonged to the west and the south and Khalil was forgiven, after a fashion, by his leaders, and died bravely fighting the British a few years later, as he had known he would, torn to pieces in an instant by the bullets of that revolving gun men called the Devil's Paintbrush.

Some wild bad magic remained in that oasis for all my care, once we were gone. Small lizards that, when I returned years later, looked at me with curious thinking malicious eyes; a stunted tree that grew fruit that I picked and left to rot, for that it would have given men bad dreams and women worse.

Some time later, when in the city of Munchen, I found Herr Langenschmidt's place of business, stole a bottle of schnapps to give an informant and left him a note, an account of what his purchase of his life had cost others. I like to inform people of these things—it deters them from repeat offences.

But, after two and a half weeks, I had terminated my business, and it occurred to me to go South a little and East a little from the wastes beyond Nejo to Sidiamo, where the coffee beans are small and grey before roasting, and have a slight tang of lemon amid their sharpness. I thought that I should take Miss Wild a present—she has been my hostess so many times.

I was brought up to good manners, though that is not something people speak of when they talk of me.

So, a few paces and I was gone from the Western border of Menelek's realm of Shewa to the Southernmost province of the rival, Johannes, whom he would shortly supplant.

I had asked Ras Gobana for a letter to the merchant roasters as a favour, and I slung a small sack of the beans across my shoulder. In my other hand, I held a small pan in which they had brewed me a thick soup of the stuff, as they drink it. It was still at a rolling boil as I stepped out of shadow and into Miss Wild's parlour, where, I discovered, she was taking tea with an elderly woman whom I had never met, but whose face I had seen on coins in every Mundane realm I had visited in the previous forty years.

I put the steaming pot down on one of the many tables, and dipped my head in respect. "Your Majesty." Politeness costs nothing.

She peered at me with the unforced haughtiness of those born to rule. "Who is this under-dressed young person, Miss Wild?" She was wearing far too many clothes herself to conceivably be comfortable.

"One as is come timely to address your concerns, your Majesty."

I further took my cue from the fact that the respect in Polly's voice was not merely formal and turned the dipping of my head into a curtsey, if not one so low as quite to satisfy Victoria, who asked further. "That is as may be, Miss Wild, but I think you need explain further."

As Polly spoke, she went to a cabinet and produced three small cups into which she poured the coffee while it was still hot enough to drink. "Your Majesty, if I am not mistaken, this coffee was brewed five minutes ago in the Abyssinian Highlands for our particular pleasure."

I placed the sack beside the table. "Enough fine coffee to see you for several months, Polly."

For the next few moments, the three of us sipped the hot brew. Victoria pulled a face at first but then was caught up in the rich aroma and the sudden rush of concentration that followed her sipping. She looked at me with a sharper intelligence than I had expected from her. "Is that really how the people of Abyssinia drink their coffee? Like a thick soup?"

"Them and much of the East, your Majesty. And here too in the coffee houses where it was first drunk by men like Addison and Swift."

"Swift was a foul-minded rascal, I am told, a lazy cleric and an Irishman who made trouble. I have seen too many such. Addison was a godly man."

"He had an annoying cough, 'adn't he?" Polly remembered. She had met him as a young girl, before immortality and responsibility took her.

The Queen stared at both of us, suddenly aware that of the three of us, she was vastly the youngest, for all that I seemed to be a girl of some sixteen summers and Polly hardly older. "Enough chatter and mystification." She was good at imposing her impatience on those around her. "I take it that this young person"—there was bitter irony in her tone—"is another immortal of some kind."

"That she is, your Majesty. And one whose task it is to punish the unrighteous. Men as would kill to make themselves as Gods."

"The first of all sins, and the second," the Queen noted. "Is that what is going on in my city? The six dead women were of the unfortunate class, but their sins were as nothing to that."

"Six," I shrugged. "Too few for a man to take godhood from their deaths."

"Six in three months, if we count the one who was killed this last night," the Queen insisted. "Surely that is many. Too many, at any rate." I could see her upset at what she might have taken for my callousness.

"Too many, to be sure," I conceded, "but not, as a rule, enough to be even the beginning of the Rituals. But he may not know that."

I was impressed by the deep sorrow with which she spoke. I am not, as a rule, impressed with rulers, least of all those who inherit a throne, but at least she took her subjects—even what she called "women of the unfortunate class"—seriously.

"Miss Wild has still not told me your name. I wish to ask you something and I do not like to make requests of people whose identity I do not know."

"She's called Mara, your Majesty. They call her the 'Untress.'"

The Queen looked at me long and hard. And then a thought

came to her, that made her smile, with the eyes of a young girl, for a moment. "Albert spoke of you once, I think."

"We met. Some years ago. My condolences on his death."

She nodded—clearly she expected such things to be said even though they would never allay her grief. "Mara," she began, and used my name as if it were an honorific. "I know that you are a Power. Not an Angel of Vengeance, even, but something greater. I speak with respect, as a Queen to one who serves the Lord in a loftier position than mine, and I would ask you a favour. Find this man and prevent him."

I smiled at the thought that she, whose armies terrorized most of the world, could not bring herself to say "kill," but she was, in the end, an old and tired and sad woman who did not deserve my mockery.

"It shall be done, your Majesty. Polly, may I have your assistance in this matter?"

She smiled. "As ever, 'Untress. And since the request comes from my Queen, not even on terms of favour for favour."

Talk of dead women had minded me to intervene on their behalf, without the Queen's asking me. Her request, and the quiet respectful tone in which she asked it, would make my task easier.

I do not take sides in human affairs, as a general rule, but sometimes taking no side is taking a side still, with less chance of doing so effectively. I would do as the Queen Empress asked, because I would not be on the same side as Khalil al-Khusani, whose contempt for this woman had irked me; it was unlikely that he would ever know what he had done, and that thought itself amused me.

After some further pleasantries, and some talk of politicians in whom I had no interest, the Queen took her leave of Polly, who rang a bell. The Queen rose from her chair with the aid of a stick which I had not noticed, and Polly helped her from the room. At the door to the outside, a large man was waiting, an Indian wearing a turban. The Queen addressed him in Hindustani as he bowed to her.

She turned back into the room.

"Huntress," her tone was almost light. "I know you consider yourself above such things, but I have met Inspector Abberline and he is a man easily shocked. I have the reputation of a prude—but he is the thing itself. Wear more clothes, or at least put on the glamour of so doing—it will make life easier with him. He is a man of little imagination."

I cast a glamour over myself that men and women too might see me dressed in the height of fashion, nor know the knives in my hair, nor the weapons at my back for what they were.

She clapped her hands and her eyes were once again those of the excitable young woman she must have been. "Brava," she cried aloud as if at the opera, "brava!"

After she had gone, Polly sighed.

"The best of them who have reigned while I served my nation and my Lord; she is wise enough to know that I consider being obliged to her as very much the third thing. And she grows old, and her son is not a wise man, and his son is a mean-spirited fool. And her other grandson, the Emperor of Germany, is a fool of a different kind, who will, I think, bring much to ruin. He loves her, in his way, but he hates her country and that her attention to its concerns takes up love he thinks should be his. It will end badly, for him and for all of us, I think."

She sighed again, even more deeply.

"I set her on her throne, did you know that? She was the heir apparent, but there were those who would have put her from it, or used her as a puppet—the King of Hanover himself, and Sir James Conroy, as was her mother's leman and thought himself a magus." She looked at her watch. "But my day wears on, and I have Russian anarchists to talk sternly to. I will give you a note for Abberline. Come back if he is difficult, and I will bring down the Commissioner on him like a hammer of wrath—and try not to break him, as he is an honest copper."

I spent that evening and the night that followed walking the streets of London, getting myself re-acquainted with it, taking in its stinking smokey air and listening to rumour as whores talked to chestnut sellers, and stockbrokers' clerks to the women who served their evening lambchops or the men who drew their pints of porter. It was a city that grew quiet, eventually—but if it could ever be said to sleep, its sleep was fitful.

At around four in the morning, there was a light drizzle, and I took shelter, not because I needed to, but because those who did not have the penny to sleep in a penny gaff might know something, if I gave them the penny they needed.

Whitechapel alternated over-crowded lodging houses and small workshops; it was hard to say which smelled worse, though at least there were sewers now and, if people or animals died in the street, men whose job it was to take them away whether or not there was profit to be gained in doing so. I had seen many cleaner cities but also many that were worse—this one sixty years earlier had been less crowded, but smelled far worse.

The shock was to come suddenly upon slums when less than a mile away all was wealth and austere grandeur—the City of London was, in this age and for years to come, the beating heart of the world's commerce and this was the rubbish piled untidily near its doorstep.

Even at dawn the police station in Leman Street was a grey depressing building, a six-story box with large windows that stared down into the street below as if daring criminals to come near. Its reception area smelled of carbolic soap, furniture polish and overboiled cabbage; which was a significant improvement on the streets through which I had walked to get there.

"Inspector Abberline, Miss?" The young policeman at the front desk seemed hardly old enough to shave but was trying to grow a small moustache but without much success. He glanced at the note I showed him—the authority to investigate that Polly had given me. He had, I realized, been trying to flirt with me up to that point, something I only noticed when he stopped. "Miss Wild." He looked impressed. "I've heard of her. Lives forever and rules behind the throne. You work for her?"

"That's an exaggeration," I told him. "And she doesn't like her loyalty to the throne questioned. But yes, she is a person of importance, and I am her friend and not her servant, or the Crown's. I have some knowledge of killings and she and the Queen have asked me to bring a pair of fresh eyes to bear on your problem."

He looked at me with concern. "How can a little thing like you know of horrors like ours? I've heard of the Bulgarian massacres, of course, and you look like you might be from that part of the world. But still…"

"I am older than I look," I explained. Then let the tiresome illusion of respectable dress drop a moment.

He assessed me knowingly, surprisingly unperturbed by my sudden change of aspect. "Oh, you're one of them. Peculiars. As it happens, the Inspector is off up in Spitalfields, where most of your particular sort live, taking some statements."

"My sort? Peculiars?" I let him see just a little of who I was without the glamour I had cast. "There are no people like me, and the few that might be considered to come close are nowhere near London in this age that I am aware of. "

It was possible, I supposed, that Hekkat had taken up residence here again, though I would have expected Polly to mention it if she had.

"You know, ma'am. Special people…But no, not like you. Just ordinary special people. Wassernames, druids and such. That can't come all the way on to hallowed ground, which is why he is interviewing them from the steps of Christ Church."

I knew the place; I had seen it built and the other churches that went up as charms against another fire.

"Personally," he went on. "I like you people. You give the place a bit of tone. You've always lived here, and you get on with people quietly and without a fuss. I like your lot, and I like the Jewboys— don't mind the Irish. And the Chinkies are over in Limehouse, so I don't need to bother about them."

I do not bother to correct young men about such matters—life usually does that for me. Instead, I thought about Christ Church.

There were ugly rumours about the man Hawksmoor, Wren's colleague who had built it, but he was just a Vitruvian who liked to pretend he was more.

"It's the ladies, you see." He had swigged from a flask of the genever of which he was clearly far too fond. "Explain it's all about sacred shapes and due proportion and I might as well whistle for cunny for all the good it does me. Let'm think it's about the Dark Arts, and I have to beat them off with a pair of dividers."

He and his churches have always had a vaguely bad reputation, mind you, not just because of his idle necromantic chat. It really wasn't his fault. Go digging through old plague pits—and London is full of those, going back long before 1665—and sooner or later you will find yourself answering to the angry ghouls who live, eat and sleep there. Especially, if like Nicholas Hawksmoor, you think that a blunderbuss is the best way to handle the hungry undead.

Luckily for Hawksmoor, I was around, and smoothed all the hurt feelings, or at least mostly so. Later I made a courtesy call on their nest during the Gordon Riots, to remind them of ancient pacts and made sure they were minding their own affairs, and I arranged that they not protest when Bazalgette built his sewers. I had not seen them since; sometimes the creatures of the night disappear into it, or into shadow. Humanity are unquiet neighbours and there are many who cannot take their mess and din and have to get very vexed to go near them. Even creatures who dine on centuries-old putrescence.

So now I left the young policeman and his moustache and genever and passed through shadow quickly, to where Christ Church's white tower and curt portico now overlooked the new red brick market building. I made a note to check lest its construction had disturbed more things best left buried with the long dead.

Abberline was holding court from the steps—which would not have made him safer from those he was talking to, but superstition is a great help to the nervous—and I realized the moment I stepped out of shadow that the young man had not meant Druids at all.

"Oh look dear," Eithne cooed. "It's her ladyship the Huntress."

"You'll want to talk to her, Inspector," Aspara chorused with her. "This is so much more her thing than ours."

"We don't know about blood and death."

"We grow things. Green things."

"The Huntress kills people. But only very bad people."

"Like this man you humans call Jack."

"It's what she does."

Abberline turned towards me, raising a hand to keep the two trolls he had been talking to exactly where they were in the conversation.

"You kill people? Not on my patch you don't."

The dryads had rustled away the moment attention moved from them. I saw their slightly green shapes disappearing North towards Bethnal Green. There was a flower market up there on a Saturday, I remembered, where people bought shrubbery. That would be their element.

I thought I had better explain. "By the time I kill them, they have ceased to be people. They have become something far more powerful and far worse than you want to know."

He chuckled sardonically. "This is the East End, Miss. I doubt there is anything I have not seen, that you have."

I had promised Polly that I would not break him, but I put forth just a whisper of my power. I had promised to help, but I was in a hurry to get on with this favour.

"Inspector,"—my tone implied, though did not state, that the word was synonymous with 'fool'—"I have moved among the Powers of the Sea and Sky and put them down from their high and deep places when it seemed needful. I am here to help you with your little murderer, with this Jack, as a kindness to an old friend." And I passed him Polly's letter.

"You work for her? I saw her file once—almost two hundred years old, it said, though I can hardly believe. Attractive young thing, and well-spoken, the one time I met her, for all they say she used to be the Queen of all Beggars, Whores and Thieves."

This was Polly's city, but I thought I had better make myself quite clear. "Polly is my particular friend, but she is a mere child beside me. I saw Rome rise and fall, and it took less time than this conversation seems likely to. Can we get on? Neither the trolls nor the goblin woman standing next to them smells of blood or dark magic, so you may trust them, take down any information they have and then get on and show me the place of the most recent killing. If you would be so kind. Gentlemen? My dear?"

Minor beings defer to me.

The trolls mumbled that they knew nothing, but that there were chitterings and squeakings in the night.

"Them's just rats, on their way to my larder." The goblin woman tossed her bonneted head in contempt, her purple eyes glinting, and licked her lips.

"No, not rats," they mumbled some more. "Like, but not."

She looked superior— they were after all just trolls and she was a goblin. "That's as may be. But I think I saw him. Two nights ago when the last girl was killed. And his leather apron...It was all polished and it shone in the rain. And stank of old death."

Abberline looked as excited as his melancholy phlegmatic face would let him. "And? What did he look like?"

She shrugged, "What did he look like? He was a human. You all look and smell the same. He was a male, ordinary height. No beard on his face; mebbe a line of it above his lip, but that could have been a stain. He looked at me—a lot of you can't see me unless I want you too, but he saw me, and smiled and licked blood and rainwater from his knife. So I tipped my bonnet to him, for politeness, and went about my business. Which was pigeons that night, because they were all piled up in shelter, and drowsy and easily taken."

"Where was this?" Both the Inspector and I came in at once, and caught each other's eye in shared excitement.

96

"On Brick Lane. Near where it crosses the Bethnal Green Road. Odd, now I think of it. I saw him, and he saw me. But there were other people around, and they didn't seem to notice him."

Whether or not he was engaged in the Rituals, or just killing for the love of it, this man had some small skills, it seemed, whether they came from his murders or just made them easier.

"Magic." Since I was the expert, it behoved me to say it.

"I wouldn't know," the goblin woman said. "My people have our own ways. We don't meddle with such stuff. We leave that to humans and elves and the like." She spat, and it sizzled where she caught the church steps.

"Mind your manners, girl," the inspector said harshly, and then softened his tone. "Thanks for your help. If you think of anything, you know where I can be found."

She turned to go, and the trolls started to follow her, but I detained them with a glance.

"You are here, and the dryads, but what of your neighbours?" They looked at me blankly, as did Abberline. "I used to know some ghouls who haunted this churchyard and the pits beneath it, very decent ghouls, as these things go—respectful when talked to firmly."

The goblin woman thought hard. "They used to come to market," she eventually admitted. "They'd bring pretties they'd found in graves—rings and lace and the like—my old da used to buy them cheap and soak out the smell...Haven't seen them in months. Da thinks they'd taken everything there was to take and moved on to some other graveyard..."

The trolls nodded.

Abberline looked intrigued. "Never heard of such around here. Just goes to show, you think you know your manor, and it turns out there were corpse eaters here all along. Keeping themselves to themselves and not causing trouble, suppose that's a good thing..." But he did not sound convinced.

Clearly none of these people knew anything.

"Ghouls never ever leave," I explained. "Once they've found a place they like, it takes forever to get them out of it. They just go deeper, because there are always more bones for them to gnaw. And then they come up to the surface, because there's always more fresh meat...This is a city, an old city—you're never more than five foot from a rat and you're never more than twenty foot from a ghoul. Usually straight down."

Abberline looked unwell—rather than let them see, he waved the trolls and goblin away. Then he turned to me.

"Men call me the Huntress," I told him. "And now we know the likely trail to follow. If he was bloody, he had killed, so let us walk the streets between the place where his victim was ended and the place where our friend saw him. Tell me what you know."

The bad thing about dealing with the official police, in any century, is that it is not a trade which encourages imagination, or coping easily with the unusual, so that I have to do more of the actual work in cases that concern me than I like. The good thing is, a solidly competent police officer will at least keep on top of the more Mundane sort of detail.

Abberline pulled out his notebook, less as something that he needed to refer to than as a talisman of memory, and he talked to me, and I listened, as we walked from the Church and the market back into the heart of destitution.

"It rained that night—like the goblin lass said—buckets of dirty sooty London rain. You'd think even the penny knee-tremblers would stay in shelter on such a night and not look for clients—and Mary Ann was better quality than that. She could afford a room— most of the time she let less fortunate women of the unfortunate class sleep on her floor or in her chair. She had a good heart, they tell me...And she was still a pretty young thing in spite of rough men and strong drink."

He pointed to a public house that we passed.

"She went in there to sit and drink—since her man left, she was getting sozzled regular like. And then she went to that cookshop for fried fish and potatoes so as to sober up a bit. Then she stood in the street and gossiped with her neighbours—some of them were respectable women, but they still talked to Mary Ann because she always had good crack—as Irish like her call it—and sometimes she'd break into song. She had a pretty voice—I heard her once or twice singing Irish ballads to get men to buy her drink when she was broke."

He hummed some air or other under his breath.

"She was seen taking a man back to her room, a couple of times, but they were seen to leave. And she was still singing, much later—and she called out to a man she knew to lend her six pence 'coz the rent was due and she needed another drink."

It was the last and worst night of her life, but only at the end.

By now, we'd walked into the squalid alley Dorset Street, and were standing outside her ground-floor room, in the shabby little yard people called Miller's Court after some earlier landlord. Abberline's tone grew more like a story-teller, less like an officer giving evidence in court. "About four, her upstairs neighbour was woken by a cry, but she thought it was her cat's new kitten mewing for food, and went back to sleep; later, she remembered the cry as murder, as people will.

"It was only in the middle of the morning that the landlord's man went round for the rent she had been so anxious to earn, and, when he saw the door was locked, looked in through a window whose curtain was drawn a little aside. And he saw horror."

I went into the room, and it smelled of blood, shit and despair, and of a whisper of power. Too many policemen had traipsed through it for there to be much more than that impression. He had taken power from the killing, to be sure, and from the way he had cut her, and sliced her, and laid the parts of her in patterns around her dying body.

But mostly, he had taken power by taking her heart away with him. Her good heart, as Abberline had remarked—just as he had slashed her voice away, and ruined her pretty face and destroyed what she sold, but also what she gave and took real pleasure with.

99

But it was her heart's blood that he licked from his knife for the goblin woman to see.

"Has he taken it to eat?" Abberline asked me, once we were outside the death room and in the courtyard again. "Is that the sort of thing you know about?"

"Perhaps, but not for the sake of the meal." I thought a little more. "Did anyone think to draw a map of where the pieces of her were found? If he were looking for omens, I could tell much from where he placed them. Some cults lay stock in patterns and pictures made of guts and flesh. Others, well, they look at the bits for warts and ulcers and the like and tell the future from it."

Abberline had seen her actual desecrated body, but it was at my words that he retched. "I thought people only did that sort of things with chickens and such."

"Anything we do to birds and beasts, someone has done to another human. Count on it. I have seen slaughter-houses where men were carved for the table, pyramids where they patiently waited in line, without fear, to be flayed and gutted. Taking a man or woman apart to small living pieces so as to know the disposition of the enemy's cavalry, the stores still in his granaries—that's a small thing by the side of that."

Somehow this did not smell like the celebration of a god or the seeking of an answer—I say smell, but not in the literal way of how it stank in my nostrils. Dark magics have a feeling for me that is like what we know from other senses, and yet not.

"The knife work. Was it a butcher's knife or a surgeon's scalpel? Did his blade notch her bones or perhaps break on them?"

"A lot of it was frenzied hacking. Our surgeon, though, said that how he spread the adhesions in her right lung was very pretty work. My guess is that the frenzy is a fake—he wants us to think him madder than he is. He was alone for hours to work on her—I think he had lots of knives, a scalpel yes, but one of those little filleting knives chefs turn red meat into roses with. That's what he did her breasts with…"

I was glad he did not spare me details, less pleased that he was testing me a little—but it is thousands of years since I went pale at horrors, even ones I have reluctantly inflicted on the guilty.

Beside the door to her room, out of the way so that the busy feet of police would not trample them, there was a sad little pile of posies.

Abberline caught my glance. "The other girls loved her, because she was kind, and shared the little she had. And, like I say, even her respectable neighbours liked her. And they leave flowers…"

I bent and picked up one of the posies. They were red and purple flowers, and I knew even before I sniffed their heady scent that they came from no market around here.

"Not them alone, Inspector."

Dryads would not deal in dead plants, nor is it a human custom that trolls or goblins have picked up in centuries of living among us. Of course there are exceptions, but…

"If you'll wait here a second, Inspector? Our friend has more skills than I imagined."

And I stepped sideways into shadow, expecting to find clear fields.

And the clear fields were there, beyond a veil of mist and nightmare that took me whole minutes to push through, as if it was a thick curtain, with all the while something howling. Something that did not make me fear, but gave me concern. I have faced down the Wild Hunt a time or two, and fought Great Beasts of one kind or another; this howling gave me concern—it thrilled in my bones as few other things have ever done. There was a wrongness to it as of something that was turned from its proper purpose.

And there was the veil—it was like a shadow beyond shadow and that too was something I had not seen before, that had a wrongness. There is a patch in London, where that monarch known as Merry, but all of whose jests were grim, created a bridgehead for nothingness by selling his country to French Louis, but that is merely blank. The veil, the fog—it was as if London were dreaming and dreaming its own deaths, its many deaths—I saw cities in flames one after another flickering through each other like the light and dark of flames—the town Boudicca burned, and the London that burned in 1666, and a London that seemed quite like the one around me, but different, that burned; there were Londons that were empty, with white bones in the street and a London that was a heap of moulder and Londons that were sunk as deep as Ys. But the heaps of moulder most of all.

It felt as if someone had torn things, and then a breeze came up, and the veil, the fog was gone, all save a stench above the sweetness of the meadow.

Sometimes, when bright sunlight shines on wet streets, or on London's many gardens, there is a crisp clear breeze that seems to bring pleasure out of nowhere; that breeze comes from parts of shadow, just as sometimes a sense of unease and foulness blows in from other parts. It has always surprised me that more people do not guess that there are other lands as close to them as breathing and find the many simple pathways there...

But the man I was already thinking of as Jack was, it seemed, unfortunately one of those few. I would not have guessed had he not, like so many evil men, been incapable of leaving well enough alone. He had killed Mary Jane, and tortured and disfigured her, but that was not enough—he had to come back and mock the simple piety of ordinary people, thinking himself so clever, so gifted with impunity...

And did not know that one would come for him who would recognize the flowers as ones that grew in shadow.

He was vain, and because he was vain, he made my task easier. And perhaps he had a right to be vain, because if there was something deeply bad and wrong here, that I had never seen in all my years, it was unlikely to be a coincidence—and he had some part in it.

But for the moment, I had found what I was looking for.

The most evil of men are usually the most prideful.

There it was, in the middle of a meadow of the red and purple flowers, completely out of place and a few handy steps from the scene of his killing. He had set up a work bench to which he could retire with what he had taken—a work bench so like the one my love had had in Alexandria all those years before, and yet not, and not only because she traded in life, and not in death.

There were the crucibles and retorts I recognized, and the small bowl in which there burned a fragment of eternal flame. Those I recognized, but also the small wicked brass knives I had seen in Simon Magus' work place, and a cylinder-within-cylinder contraption wound by hand and also full of wicked sharp knives, but even smaller ones, a little like the machines butchers use to make sausages, yet clearly for no culinary purpose.

There was an open leather box hard worn and stained with blood and gunpowder; inside were more knives, these ones made of steel.

There was a pentagram—the most perfect that I had ever seen, and no wonder because sitting right next to it were a set of compasses with red chalk attached to them, and set-squares and protractors. Most people make the quite unnecessary mistake of thinking that they have to be drawn by hand and few are as accomplished as my beloved—which is why so many fatal mistakes get made. Inside the pentagram, nailed to the bench with golden nails, was a small demon, which wailed and mewed because it had been painstakingly dissected yet still lived.

Outside the pentagram was a small rack of glass tubes in each of which sat, preserved in spirit, the organs that had been taken from the demon—all save its heart, which still sat on the scales of a small set of balances as if Jack had been distracted from one task to a more important one.

Which was strange, in a way, because the way that the work table was organized was tidy and methodical in a way I had not in general seen in magicians or practitioners of the Work. There is a methodical nature that goes with those skills, but it is more like the growth of a flower than the working through of an equation.

I had only seen one work bench even slightly like this—and it had been that of Isaac Newton, in the day when he experimented with the Work and tried to reconcile it with his mathematics. Perhaps Robespierre had had something like this, he and Saint-Just, but so much of their science had been mere engineering or superstitions like the ideas of Mesmer. Not that these things did not work, because evil will is like water: it finds its own level...

Another set of glass tubes had some kind of vegetable matter in them. It looked dead and inert.

Another seemed to be full of dirt—I sniffed it and it smelled of graveyards. Another had a powder in it that looked at first sight like the tiny beads magma sometimes solidifies in, except that some of them had cracked open, and were hollow inside. Or rather had been cracked—there was residue in one of them that looked a little like the vegetable matter. I am used to magicians thinking the filth of death and decay has power, but usually they are disappointed. This one, perhaps, not so much.

There was an hourglass whose sand had almost run its course, but was moving significantly slower than it ought to have been—time magic of some kind, I thought, and resolved to investigate it further later on. Most people who acquire a modicum of power can alter the rate at which time passes—few tie it up in a device, though doing that had become more common as timepieces became more reliable, I had noticed. There is a limit to the harm you can work with a sundial, but modern chronometers, like the one developed by the man Harrington? I had seen real damage to the world worked with those, so I did not pay much attention to the hourglass.

A mistake, as it proved.

This man, I could see, was trying to blend magic and the new natural science and it was clearly working for him; it had occurred to me over the previous hundred years that one day I might face something as deadly and vile as the Rituals or as Simon's craftings but inexorable in its logic and rigour. Some would say I had been remiss, because sufficient unto the day has always been my motto, and rightly so; I had cast my eyes over the work of Newton and his successors and some of it had made my head hurt in a way that Euclid and Galen never had.

The time had come, I feared, to do something to make up for my deficiencies.

I walked back into the Mundane and carried the work-bench with me. It was quite heavy and needed both my hands to keep it level.

Abberline was still standing, his mouth agape, at my disappearance. "You just walked into thin air," he remarked, redundantly. Then he looked at the bench I was carrying with me, and looked queasy almost to the point of retching for a second, before collecting himself.

I thought it best not to mention his delicate stomach and so answered his actual question. "Yes. I did. It is a thing I can do—and so it appears can our Jack. He maintains this dissecting bench a few feet away, but not feet that you can walk unaided—he can do a lot more than walk unseen, it seems…Inspector, could you set your men to walking the routes between here and where he was seen, those that mortal men can walk? I will come and find you at Leman Street to see if there is anything I need to see—I will, so far as is possible, walk those trails elsewhere that occupy the same space. But first, I need to find a second pair of eyes to do it with me. Our man is a worker of science as well as of magic—and I am not capable."

I raced through shadow back to Polly's chambers, carrying the work bench with me.

Polly looked askance at this. "I don't know, 'Untress. Bringing second-'and furniture into another woman's apartment without a by your leave. Stinks too—and livestock—there's an empty room down that corridor, through that door; do what you 'ave to but put it out of sight."

I did as she asked; the demon was screaming silently but I had no obvious way to end its existence or its pain, and I might need to try to talk to it later. Right now, I had other issues to resolve.

She looked at me with amused tolerance as I started to explain my quandary, and interrupted me before I had fumbled too far. "So, it's of more interest to you than you thought. I guessed it might be. I don't think our Jackie is any kind of common criminal or simple pervert—what I've read doesn't have that feel. All that stuff about the Jews and about eating part of a kidney—that struck me as a clever sane man pretending to be a stupid lunatic." She sighed. "I loved a man of violence when I was a young girl, and it left me with a sense of what men of violence are like, even once I grew out of loving such. Wish I hadn't been so ready to break with French Frankie—I was a child back then and did not know when I was well off. He was better in bed than Mackie, apart from anything else, but I wasn't ready to appreciate that."

She shook herself slightly to focus her mind, like a dog ridding itself of moisture. and tightened her mouth a little in the annoyance that came along with that focus. "So what is it about this one that's different?"

She'd seen me deal with Newton, had settled her own accounts with him. She'd helped me and Georgiana fight Robespierre and Saint-Just, and listened with glee to the tale of how I finished them.

"Newton was a great man of science who was also a mediocre magician. Simon Magus was a magician who, luckily, only had Greek and Babylonian knowledge to work with. Robespierre was a wicked man who understood very little but was for a while lucky with what he knew and could do. This man—well, he works with shadow, which none of the others even knew about—and he applies science to magical beings—cutting up demons and weighing their insides. I think he might be a lot more dangerous..."

She looked sceptical. "If he's that good, what's he doing cutting up whores in Whitechapel?"

"That's what I don't know. And that is what worries me—I don't think the location or their trade is why he's doing it. I think it's just convenient—you may think he's drawing attention to himself but imagine how much more attention he would be drawing if he were cutting up duchesses in Mayfair…But he needs to be in London, so he has to earn a living, otherwise he'd be cutting people up somewhere where no one would notice him doing it at all. I need to understand him better and so I need someone a bit like him— obviously someone who isn't him, of course."

Polly walked over to her filing cabinets and started riffling. I'd guessed she would keep notice of a lot of potentially dangerous people.

"I need a man of science, but a young one, not set in his ways, capable of accepting that magic is real and not some elderly savant who would be useless in a fight. I at least need a man capable of firing a pistol. Someone who understands the discipline of a workroom, but has the soul of a poet."

I recalled young Jack Keats. He'd understood me as well as anyone. I'd met him in Rome and he helped me, in his last weeks, with a cardinal who was selling off manuscripts that belonged in the Vatican archives, where no one would read them.

"Sometimes, back when I studied surgery –" he broke off to cough and then to wipe the blood from his mouth with a handkerchief already stained to brown "– I smelled the rot in the flesh and bone, and saw the beauty of the cutting, healing steel…You are that steel, Huntress, except, unlike my teachers, you stay clean.

"I should have had her while I could," he moaned to me between bouts of coughing. "I should have stuck to medicine—imagine how much more use to the world a cure for this damned disease would have been than any poem I might write…"

He was wrong, I think—I don't bother with books much, but I read some of his odes and tales… But then, he thought his name would be writ on water. And we know he was wrong about that, as well.

"Ah ha." Polly had pulled out the file she had been rummaging after, and then a couple more, which she laid out on a table, and pointed to as she talked. "I have just the man. Young. Bit chippy, bit of a Red—could do with some sense knocked into him. Hangs out with the Socialists out in Hammersmith a bit—now, they're an artyfarty crowd, but Morris, who runs them, is friends with old Marx's daughter…Nice girl, bad taste in men…"

She sighed with sisterly sympathy. "So any way, young Herbert— well, mother in service, father was a cricket player until he did his leg in—Herbert fancied himself as more than a servant or a draper and worked his way through pupil-teaching and got hisself a place to study. Huxley hisself helped him out…Shiny new degree and not sure what he is going to do next—his file says he reckons he wants to write, and not just books on science…"

She offered me the files to read, but I waved them away—she had told me what I needed to know. She shrugged and put them back where they belonged.

"So where do I find him?"

She smiled. Clearly something was amusing her.

"Well, I knows you're much too grand to pay attention to the days of the week. But it's late now and tomorrow it'll be Sunday. When Morris has his Socialist tea parties. Because he's a godless old revolutionary, with a messy beard. And young Herbert will be there because there's a lot of pretty girls in arty clothing for a young man to yearn after. He's probably a virgin."

She rang a little bell. "Speaking of which. Some of us needs to eat and those as don't can watch, or take their share. And some of us needs to sleep—and I know you do it, even when you don't need to. So, bread and cheese now. And kippers and devilled kidneys and bacon and eggs in the morning. And my couch in between."

I don't need hospitality, but I will take it from old friends. I grew up in a world where I met few save my sisters and our people in the hills. Yet acting hospitably to strangers was our role in life, to our cost; though I never had the taste for it that Sof and Lillit acquired, I am not unfriendly when it is warranted.

Nonetheless I was not certain that I wanted to be at a tea party when I should be chasing an evil man, who might kill more women while I was eating sugar-coated buns or cucumber sandwiches—but

I needed the young man Polly had mentioned, and from what she said, I was most certain to find him quickly here.

Yet my mood lifted as I walked beside the river; it was a cold autumn day with a hint of rain, but as I approached the house and its garden, for a few hundred yards around it, it became that autumn poets speak of, where leaves are brown and not yet fallen into mulch, and where the sun is warm and the skies clear.

Some men have the magic of imposing their desires on the world immediately around them, not because of evil practices but because of the force of will and sheer amiability; I have met this from time to time and it is one of the things that gives me hope in the world. It is not that thing that Jehovah's various followers call holiness, though it often coincides with them.

But, I repeat, as I turned a bend in the road and saw the large red-brick house and its garden, which was somehow more spacious than there was room for, the air grew warmer and a feeling of kindness crept over me. There are few magics that can seduce me, but this was more like weather...

All became clearer once I lifted the latch and walked into the house. In the large living room there stood a broad bearded man with sad wise eyes, his arm slung around the uncorseted but lean waist of a tall, dark-eyed woman with hair the colour of night, who looked at him with amusement as he laughed uproariously.

This was clearly Morris, the host.

Around them were clustered a number of hearers—a wispy man with a wispy beard, a tall angular young man with red hair and an unbecoming tweed suit, a striking dark haired woman whom I took to be Marx's daughter from a vague family resemblance. They all smelled to me of intelligence, even genius, but they all deferred to Morris. The warmth that I felt in the air radiated off him without burning those near—and yet there was something thin about him, as if he were consuming his own flesh to create that energy. He lived for several years more after that day, and I confess I was somewhat surprised—clearly there was just more of him to consume than is normal in mortals.

He caught sight of me as I entered and I felt his gaze; this was a man whom no glamour could deceive. He turned to the woman I took to be his wife, and to the smaller wispy-bearded man.

"We are visited—look Jane, look Ned. A power is among us."

"Surely not, dear. A chance resemblance." Her voice had a slight burr to it.

He shook his head, and so did the other man. "Just as poor Gabriel painted her."

I did not know what he was talking about. "I have never stood around to be painted. Certainly not by anyone you would know." Then I recollected something, and conceded, "The Florentine sketched me, when we met in France…"

Morris looked unimpressed at my mention of Da Vinci, and then explained. "Gabriel never claimed to have met you. A woman with an eye-patch commissioned the painting, and then he saw someone who looked just like you in a dream. He painted the picture he'd been asked for, and one of the woman with one eye as well. Some of his best work…"

The man with the beard nodded.

"He finished them," Morris went on, "and then they were gone— and when we asked him about them, he did not know what we were talking about."

The smaller wispy man explained further. "The drugs made Gabriel vague towards the end, but his forgetfulness about those paintings had a different feel to it."

Morris continued, "A couple of the studies stayed in his studio for years—those are the ones you saw, dear. He thought they were studies for a Diana—but I knew they were quite another Huntress."

I try to move unseen among those I protect, but…

"Old books of tales." He waved a hand. "An old woman in Iceland who knew Eddas no one ever wrote down…I am surprised to see you here—shouldn't you be in Whitechapel?"

Did everyone in this city expect me to catch their damned killer for them?

"I shall return there shortly, but I need to borrow one of your guests."

He and his wife looked intrigued.

The tall tweedy redhead had paid attention when Whitechapel was mentioned.

"At least these killings draw attention to the terrible conditions in that part of town..." he started.

"Show some respect, Shaw," Marx's daughter glowered at him. "These are dead women you're talking about..."

"Wouldn't your father have..."

"No." Her voice was curt and anger underlaid it. "He would have done everything in his power to help catch the depraved aristocrat who does such things."

I cut in.

"There's a young man I am told can help me. A young scientist..."

Morris nodded to his wife, who smiled back at him.

"Jane," he nodded, and then turned back to the other woman.

"How does the dialectic work with this?" he asked in the tone of one genuinely seeking instruction. "What can be the opposite of some pervert killing women, and how can good come of it? Shaw's version seems so cold and yet..."

Morris's wife took me by the arm.

"I think I know who you mean. Nice lad, doesn't really belong here. But then, which of us does?"

She led me out of the living room and down some steps and out into the garden, where the leaves on the trees were lushly brown, around blossoms that belonged in spring. The balmy air was heavy with the scent of roses and lilies.

A couple of people were playing recorders as young women, and one or two rather older ones, were doing some kind of round dance. It was obviously meant to be something from the late Middle Ages, but the rhythm was all wrong and their muslin dresses, gathered at the waist, far too clean. These were women who had never known famine or discomfort of plague—perfectly useless, like the art they practiced.

Still, for a second it took me back to those long warm evenings before the Death came.

I fight so that sometimes people can be that happy and useless.

Jane Morris pointed beyond the dancers to the wall at the end of the garden, where a plump young man with already thinning hair, slightly goggled eyes and a moustache was sitting with a plate of food. The expression in his eyes mixed lust and disapproval in a way I did not wholly take to…

"That's Herbert; bring him back when you're done with him."

A large man with long hair caught us looking past the dancers, and smirked a little.

"Ah yes, Wells. Came for the socialism and stayed for the sandwiches."

He was talking almost to himself rather than to us, as if he were trying the feel of his words on the tongue.

I pushed past him and walked around the dancers, taking care not to get in their way. It was only when I got close to him that the young man Wells realized that I was about to talk to him.

He put his plate down on the wooden garden bench he was sitting on, and stared around as if there were someone else I could possibly be trying to talk to. I got the impression that he wasn't used to anyone at these occasions ever talking to him.

I sat down next to him. He smelled, ever so slightly, of strong harsh soap, as if he used the same stuff to clean his body, his face, his hair and his shirt. Which seemed likely.

"I'm told," I was trying to be ingratiating because I know that some men find me challenging and off-putting, "I'm told that you are a very clever young man indeed, and that I should involve you in some work I am doing. I need someone who understands science and who has an open mind."

At first he looked flustered and flattered that a pretty woman was talking to him at all, but then he started paying attention. His eyes focussed on me a little more—I got the impression that he had suddenly stopped seeing whatever the general glamour I had cast was showing him, and started seeing me as I am. Someone who belonged at this tea party rather less even than he did.

I had his attention.

"I need to talk to you about science. And murder. And magic."

He started to bluster. His voice was squeaky as an unoiled wheel. "There is no such thing as…"

I put my finger on his lips. "You know better than that. You just saw me as I am. You have always known, or hoped. And what you hoped is true. As true as your science."

Then I took his hand, as if I were leading him across to where the dancers gyred in their round dance, and we both stood. He reached down and stuffed the last two sandwiches from his plate into a pocket in his suit jacket, smearing butter lightly on his fingers, which he licked reflexively as I walked him round the edge of the bench and through the wall, into shadow.

"There was no door in that wall," he said in wonderment. "And where is the river?"

Because in shadow, the Thames flowed two miles south of there.

And then he turned around, and there was no wall behind us, the way we had come, just a pathway and a small bust of a faun.

"I needed to show you. So that you would listen."

"Where are we?" Now he was all business.

"In shadow, which is adjacent to the fields you know, but goes further on, and deeper in."

He nodded, and looked thoughtful.

We had places to be so I set out at a sharp pace along the path—I knew where I was going and as long as he kept up we would get to our destination faster in shadow than in the Mundane. I didn't have to tell him, I noticed; he strode out at high speed—clearly not as unfit as his slight pudginess might have indicated. He kept up even though he periodically stopped to stare at the various flowers and trees he did not recognize.

"As I said," I took him by the arm to encourage him not to linger out of curiosity, "beyond the fields you know. Did you expect an English meadow here? These are that meadow's shadows, and they still carry on well into the shadow of a city which has forgotten the green that used to be. But do keep up, for shadow is wild and has its own beasts. Tigers are small cats here, but foxes—no one would hunt the foxes of shadow but rather pray they not find your scent..."

After a while, he asked who I was.

"I am Mara, whom men call the Huntress."

"And you hunt –?"

"Wicked men and the gods they might become."

He thought a little more and weighed his next words. "You're here for—the one they call the Ripper? He could become a god?"

"I don't think that's what he's after, exactly. It's as if he knows bits of the Rituals of Blood but not all of them." I could not help adding, "You seem to be taking this all very calmly. I mean, I said you had always hoped it was true, but really I was guessing..."

He pulled a serious and slightly smug face. "Well, you see—you can shift your clothing between heartbeats, and you brought me here. I believe my eyes—as a scientist I have to. So, either magic is true or some science massively advanced of anything we know—which would nearly amount to the same thing...So I'll go with the simpler hypothesis—which seems to be magic." He considered further. "So there is magic in the shedding of blood. That's bad enough. What else is true? Astrology? Please say astrology isn't true."

"Not as far as I know—not the Persian version, or the Greek version, or the Chinese version, or the modern mishmash. Shame really, I'd find it terribly useful if someone could predict where I would find malefactors and how I would kill them. But cleverer men than I or you thought it real..."

"So malefactors? These would be gods."

"Not all gods. Just the ones who work the Rituals of Blood. They're my job, my vocation, my compulsion."

He looked wise for a second, as he tended to when he realized he actually knew what someone was talking about. "What that man Yeats who was at the party would call a geasa."

I don't remember seeing Yeats there, but I hadn't met him yet so I wouldn't have noticed.

After a bit, he asked, "Alchemy?"

"Not recently."

He looked at me hard, to see if I were joking.

"Not since Alexandria fell to the Christians and then the followers of the Prophet. They never understood it—and it's not really called alchemy at all. Anyone who calls it that has read the wrong books and misunderstands it altogether—it is the Work. And it has very little to do with gold."

His face lit up with that particular brightness which usually foreshadows a misconception. "But that's why you're immortal, right. You drank the elixir of life."

I shuddered at the thought, and spoke to him seriously. He was just the sort of enthusiastic young man who might make bad choices with which he would have to live a long time. Or not.

"If you ever come across it, do not drink it. Most people who do, do not live a very long time—they rarely live long enough to regret it. My friend Miss Wild –"

"The mistress of spies, her that tells the queen what to do –"

"That's not true, but they do take tea together. And counsel."

His ears perked up. Oh good, a scientist who recognized Mr. Pope when he heard him misquoted.

"-She drank it and is perfectly well, which means the odds are against anyone else I know for the rest of time. That's not what it's for. No, young man, my immortality is mostly a matter of the gods I kill. What they stole, dying is bequeathed to me; I am the protector of the weak against the strong, but I cannot save them all. And…"

I hate it when mortal men look at me with compassion because it means that I have said too much.

"How long?" he said.

"Since before Atlantis sank. Before Troy, before Persia, before the Three Kings and Five Emperors of the Xia. Not before Egypt or the Indus or Jericho."

He picked up a faster stride and started to whistle. It was a bit tuneless, but better than conversation—after a while I recognized it.

– Go thought, on gilded wings –

"I was there, too," I told him. "My old comrade Jah took offense and cursed the king with madness—he was tetchy in those days."

He looked at me, slightly shocked, and then smiled.

After a while, we came to a patch of white flowers I knew, and I took Wells by the arm and stepped sharply rightwards and through one of those twists in shadow that are there if you know how to spot them. I knew we were about to emerge six inches above the floor but Wells would have stumbled if I had not held him tight.

"And there you are, 'Untress. With your young friend that I kindly suggested to you."

Miss Wild had set a small table, with the coffee pan I had brought back from Ethiopia simmering on a trivet over a flame that hovered above the table. She has no particular gift for magic, but some cantrips almost anyone can pick up with a few years to master them.

Other things she has always known—how to fascinate a young man sexually with a hand on the wrist and a lowering of the voice and looking intently into his eyes when he says something moderately intelligent.

She asked Wells about Huxley, and Darwin's theories, with just that air of being seriously interested in what he explained that I had seen some years earlier, when she talked to Darwin himself.

At first Wells was caught in her nets, and blushed a little. If I had had a hand on his wrist, I would have felt his pulse race perhaps. Then I saw that smile of being undeceived that I had noticed earlier when I had spoken of Jehovah as an old friend whom I did not especially respect.

Wells was not, then, the player of those games he later became, but I realized as he reacted to Polly with the same air of innocent

116

attention that she had turned on him that he recognized what she was doing and was making moves from his side of the board.

"Gosh, Miss Wild –"

"Call me Polly," she breathed.

"I don't know why you would think I had anything of especial interest to explain. I'm just a student—a new-minted graduate—and from what I've heard, you spoke to Newton hisself."

She laughed.

"That I did, and he had cause to regret it. 'Orrible old man that did for my sweet criminal old da…and others I cared for as well. But yes, a learned man when not trying to be a bad one."

Wells looked genuinely fascinated, and patted her hand with genuine concern when she mentioned her losses. I do not always understand such things; those two had a bond, almost on sight, that I had not seen in Polly's life since her doomed French captain, or my friend Voltaire.

But they were both serious people and there was work to do.

Wells finished his coffee with a slurp, patted Polly's hand again and stood up, turning to me.

"You have things for me to examine?"

I led him through to the room where I had put the work bench. He walked around it, very slowly, as if memorizing every item that was on it, and its position in relation to everything else. A couple of times, he stood by it as if about to work there, and reached out, to see what he could reach from that point, and what he could not.

"You found his work bench and you stole it and brought it here. Won't that alert him to the fact that someone with—erm, Powers is on his trail?"

I shrugged. "I should hope so. Scared evil men generally make more mistakes. And if he is worried about me, he may not get around to killing any more women for a while."

Wells nodded. "Fair enough." And continued to circle the bench.

The hourglass had almost finished its work and he reached over, turned it, and disappeared, save for a slight trace that whizzed around the table, continuing his examination at high speed. I have seen men grow old and white and turn to dust from such accidents, and I needed him, so I reached over with a small hammer I had picked up from the work bench and smashed the glass. Wells gradually re-appeared and seemed unaware that anything untoward had occurred—he was a young man with remarkable powers of focus.

After a while, he reached into his jacket pocket and pulled out one of the two sandwiches; he ate it as he paced, without looking at it. Probably for the best, since it had some sort of gray fluff on it from his pocket. When he had finished one, he took out the other, and ate that, still without speaking or ceasing to pace.

Then he reached down, and shut the leather box, revealing a brass plate on it, which read 'WEISS for the Army Hospital Department 1854'. Then he took out each of the steel knives and scalpels in turn, examined it, and put it back in its proper place. He did the same for the bone saw that clipped into the other half of the box.

He sniffed the tubes of plant matter, the volcano dust, the graveyard dirt and the dissected organs of the demon, which looked up at him piteously.

He turned to me. "Can't we put the poor little thing out of its misery?"

I shrugged. "Hard to do, and it wouldn't thank you for the mercy. It will all grow back eventually—in fact, those organs will try to grow their own demons, there in their tubes. Demons are solid, after their fashion, but not alive in quite the sense that we are. Made of different stuff…"

He nodded, fascinated. Then he pulled his attention back to the matter in hand.

"Miss Wild, I take it that somewhere tucked away you have a myriad of clerks and files on just about everyone and everything. I'm here, after all, which means you knew of me, and knew where to send the Huntress."

"They'll be here, bright and early, Monday morning, the which is tomorrow. I don't see as there is much point in ruining their Sunday evenings. If it were wartime, perhaps…"

Wells looked at us both. "I don't suppose you've read Arthur Doyle's novel that came out last Christmas…Or Edgar Poe…I'm sure you know the idea—you're both detectives, of a sort. It's not just science as a set of facts you need; it's the process. You were right to bring me here."

He pulled out a notebook from one jacket pocket—the fresh butter stains were only the newest of many—and a pencil from the other, and started to write.

"Your man is probably about five inches taller than me, unless he has freakishly long arms. I'd find it annoying to work at this bench because I couldn't reach everything, no matter where I stood. He's been an army surgeon, and here's the odd thing—his box is the model they issued for the Crimean war but some of the scalpels are much older, Wellington's time. And the bone saw is an American model—I'd guess this man has lived a very long time. Can someone who isn't a god, yet, just live a long time, taking a death at a time? Because it occurs to me that a battlefield would be a good place to do that? No one would notice."

It had never occurred to me that there were disadvantages to the fact that Hekkat and her bird no longer haunted battlefields looking for worship and eyeballs. In their day, someone working a version of the Rituals, and only gradually discovering what he was doing…A surgeon, letting amputees bleed out, or debriding a burns patient with a dirty knife…My thought changed direction—I realized that they would probably never have noticed and neither had I.

I was at Balaclava, a couple of days after the famous charge—and yes, just stupidity. But I had to check.

And shouting at the senile Raglan, the proud Cardigan, the insane Lucan and the merely reckless and angry Nolan for several hours each—I had had to walk among all those corpses of men and horses looking for signs of magic and I was very angry by the end.

"Not any more," I thought aloud. "And if he has been at it a century or so, he'd have started after the last point when..."

Polly chimed in, "So, if he started letting people die for the hell of it, and noticed it made him feel healthier, he became one of them when he was already in the wars, not someone who went to the wars to pursue another career. So –"

Wells smirked. "He'll be on the army lists. Course, he might have faked his death and changed his name. Over and over."

Polly looked sceptical.

"'E'd have to forge his papers, every single time. Much simpler to keep one set of papers and fiddle with the dates—keep the same name and be his own grandson. I've never needed to do that, but I thought about it when Castlereagh—god rot him—asked awkward questions and wouldn't believe the answers."

"If he was in the war for the Crimea, there's someone we can ask."

We'd never got along, of course, but she'd do what the Queen wanted however much she thought me a demon and a nuisance.

"Oh, of course," Polly made a note. "She's been sick for years, but she isn't bed-ridden so much any more. Will tomorrow do? I'll send a note round to South Street."

Wells looked impressed.

"Of course we know the Nightingale woman," I explained brusquely. "Something young men like you never realize is—women have endless conversations when men are not around. Sometimes we even like each other."

"Though that don't apply in this instance," Polly added. "She once told me that I was a woman of loose morals however useful to the State, something even the Queen would never actually say, even if she thought it."

"I doubt she knows anything useful. If he was there, I did not smell the reek of blood on him. But then, I was not looking for him. I was looking for soldiers, not sorcerers. She does not strike me as more observant than I am." Then I added, "But he has no great aversion to killing women. So send one of your stronger messengers with the note. Do not delay until the morning and tell him to wait there until I come."

She started to scribble a letter.

Wells looked down at the demon. "Also, he is interested in cutting things up. So maybe he has a license for vivisection. Or maybe he is one of the unlicensed ones the Anti-Vivisection League has a dossier on against the day. Something else for your clerks, Miss Wild."

Wells picked up one of the tubes of vegetable matter, one of the tubes of dust and one of the tubes of dirt. "I wonder what these are? I'll take the plant stuff to people at the Museum—they might know what the dust is too. The dirt?"

"The dirt's from graveyards, mostly," I told him.

"Any idea which one? If we had Doyle's annoying detective, he'd have written a monograph on it, but as it is…"

I decided that I would expand his education. "I know who to ask—there are experts in these matters and I'd been meaning to call on them and ask if they had seen anything. Abberline has talked to those beings he could find, but there are some creatures out there that a prudent policeman lets come to him, or not. I, on the other hand, am the Huntress and I have no need to be prudent."

He looked wary. "Am I supposed to come with you?"

I smiled, and he looked even warier. "Ghouls are much misjudged creatures and rarely pose a threat to the living; we don't taste right to them alive and killing us means waiting around for days before we ripen. You'll be quite safe as long as they don't feel frightened. Guns and blades, for example—well they don't care for those and see them as threats you'd better be prepared to back up. A stout stick would be more the sort of thing—don't want them to see you as a pushover."

He looked at the quiver on my back, the knives in my hair.

"I'm the Huntress. Ghouls and I had that conversation back in the graveyards of Persepolis and I taught them to be polite."

121

"I hates ghouls," Polly muttered, looking up from the letter. "Always have, always will. Beastly foreign things, not like a good old British lich. And there aren't any liches any more are there? And why? Ghouls ate them all. And your good old fashioned decent British cannibal, your Sweeneys and your Sawneys. My dad used to say…"

She trailed off for a bit. Typically inconsistent of Polly, to moan about ghouls, who actually arrived in Britain with the Romans, rather than trolls, who used to eat far more living people and got left behind by Harold Hadrada.

"Down in their beastly stinky dark tunnels…" she went on grumbling.

"I'm not asking you to come with us; you've clerks to organize and messages to send."

She stopped moaning almost at once. Wells, on the other hand, looked concerned.

"I'm not very good in confined spaces…"

Polly laughed at him, but in that way men and women who are flirting with each other do, as if they were both in on some far bigger joke than had been told. "You'll be too busy shitting your pants when you see your first ghoul to ever be scared of tight spaces or the dark ever again."

I noticed that she winked as she said "tight spaces" and that he smiled toothily. I am not completely blind, I know an assignation when I see one.

Wells was clearly still worried, however, even if he had something to live for. "I'm not good in the dark, my eyes…I'm assuming that ghouls don't like oil lamps."

I reassured him. "I can glow. It's one of the things I do. Ghouls may not like that—but they accept it rather than complain to someone who doesn't have to listen to them whining. They have to put up with light sometimes anyway. When they do business."

Wells looked at once confused and intrigued—it was one of his standard expressions when I was talking, I realized.

I explained. "Teeth. They don't like the taste of human teeth—too much sugar, they say. And ever since Waterloo, they found there was something they could actually sell. Your basic ghoul has simple tastes, but they like a good story; so they do business with dentists, and the dentists pay them off with books. You can always fend off even an angry ghoul with a magazine—bop them on the nose with it to get their attention and then pass it to them."

"Why Waterloo?"

"Some young ghouls came to the surface for a lark and got blind drunk," Polly explained. "Took the shilling, didn't they?"

Wells giggled. "The scum of the earth, enlisted for drink…By god they frighten me… Did Wellington even know?"

"Know?" Polly snorted. "He sent them in, under the ground. Came up among the Imperial Guard's horses and terrified the poor brutes. And afterwards, he let them have the battlefield. And they brought back teeth, teeth in barrels. Young healthy teeth, as you saw in Lady This and Lord That's mouth for years. Couple of those young ghouls bought themselves mansions with the cash, but they never lived there for long—missed the tunnels after a bit."

Wells was laughing and amazed and shocked all at the same time, so I took his arm while he was distracted and we plunged through Polly's floor and cellarage into the ways under London.

Well, obviously there were the new sewers with all that pretty tile work, and there were in places the underground railways with all their stink and smoke and steam, that would go away within a couple of years as they put in electric rails, and all the tunnels that had always been there. Places where old cellars had been extended for no honest purpose and the secret tunnels that bankers and other criminals had built. And the old places gone strange—the Londinium that Boudicca burned and the one that followed it with all its temples and shrines to gods that those above had forgotten but those below remembered, if not to celebrate, to placate.

And all of these tunnels in the Mundane had their extensions into shadow, where great worms had gnawed away like mites in cheese and where the rats' clever cousins lived lives in the glowing dark that I never chose to find out more about. Once and only once I went into their places, because it occurred to me that rats and mice have their gods—and why not their cousins?—and I was hailed by their king.

Mundane rat-kings are just a mess of tangled tails—their shadow is something else. And no business of ours. And more particularly none of mine, for they knew of the Rituals and appreciated my concern but said it was unnecessary that I worry about them, for they were not humans and did not do such things, and if they needed me, they would send for me.

Their tone was haughty, and yet not something I could resent, for I know my betters on the rare occasion that I meet them.

So I raced with Wells caught up in my grasp to the great death pits under Spitalfields, and the chambers below those pits where I had last talked to the ghouls that dwelt there, in Hawksmoor's time and once after when London rioted against Popery and I needed to warn them of the flaming floods when the distilleries burned and lead roofs dripped hot death into the underworld. It is always a good idea to put dangerous beings in your debt.

Only this was a debt I would never be able to call in. The nest where I had last talked to them, a century or so before, was abandoned, and no-one home; dead rats lay on its floor, tattered flesh with white bone showing through, not eaten by other rats, but by the small black beetles that do their work if they are not there…

But there were stairs from the old nest, down to a new one, some hundred feet further down, through brick earth and sand and chalk and into the thick blue-grey London clay. They had taken trouble— this was no mere hole but lined with brick and supported by beams. Ghouls with money to spend will live as snug and safe as humans.

They had even put in two cast-iron spiral staircases, one at each end of the nest. We came down the one nearest to hand—that led down from store-rooms, full of barrels and ossuaries.

Those chambers, usually so loud with the howlings that are the music of ghouls, and the gnawing of bones between strong jaws, and the grinding and chipping of bones into useful tools and powders, and the mewling of ghoul cubs in the crèche chamber where they were kept from being underfoot, and the clatter of empty skulls as young ghouls played at football with them. And there was silence.

The chambers had always smelled of putrefaction, but now they smelled of dust and death.

The dead ghouls lay in rows. At first sight they seemed whole, for neither rats nor blackbeetles will dare to eat of the flesh of ghouls; but someone had been among them, straightening their limbs but not out of piety. Some of the bodies were slit open, and crudely stitched together; others had eyes or fingers missing. He had been taking samples here, as he had among the whores aboveground.

When a ghoul dies, as even they sometimes do, their already pale skin grows whiter and whiter, and gradually develops a crust that turns to thick horny plates. None of that here; instead their skins were a dark purple at the lips that faded down to cherry along their necks and pink at their extremities. Their tongues lolled from their mouths, swollen and puce, and their eyes, normally white even at the pupil, save for a dot at the centre, were bright red with swollen and burst veins. No ghoul is lovely to look upon, but these faces were distorted as if to madness by some great agony.

Their great white teeth bore marks where they had ground them against each other in their last paroxysms. Otherwise, there was no immediate sign of what had killed them.

I looked at Wells anxiously, for death curses this effective can linger, but he showed no sign of anything malign affecting him.

Instead, he sniffed as if savouring the unwholesome air, and then shook his head. "It's been too long—months at least if the rats upstairs are anything to go by."

"What would we have smelled had we come sooner after their deaths?"

"Bitter almonds, I should think."

I looked at him questioningly—this was, after all, why I had involved him. I detected a slight smell, of decay perhaps, but nothing like almonds.

"He used cyanide gas to kill them. It's not especially quick, but they are at the bottom here, so it will have concentrated—pooled and only slowly drifted up to kill the rats. I don't know how he introduced it into the chamber."

"And you know this how?"

"A fellow-student used it to kill himself. Failed his examinations. When we found him, his head in a fume chamber, his body and face were twisted like that. Except he was not a ghoul, obviously." He then looked at me sadly. "These creatures were your friends? I am sorry for your loss."

I hadn't actually liked these, or any other ghouls, very much, but I appreciated his attempt at concern. Then I noticed that all of the dead ghouls were adults or adolescents—he had obviously left the cubs in their crèche, I thought. But then it occurred to me that I should check, because thoroughness has always been one of my virtues.

I explained to Wells, and we proceeded through the dead chamber to its other staircase—the crèche lay off to the right at the top, with a stout door to prevent the ghoul cubs escaping. They are, for a while, vicious little things whose scratches can maim or poison even an adult ghoul…

I opened the door, which was unlocked, and found the crèche empty save for a couple of cubs with their over-large heads shattered open by high calibre bullets. They were near the door, half-out of the deep cribs in which they were mostly confined. Killed no doubt, as a warning to their peers. Ghoul cubs are not very intelligent, but they have enough cunning to know when they are beaten and when an example has been set. Not that I have ever had to do anything like that. I wondered where they were, and what he had done with them—more samples for his experiments I thought.

I was wrong, though. And found out how much within moments.

I heard again the howling I had heard before—it was almost

articulate, with hoarse barks and phthisic whinings mingled among it, that seemed almost on the verge of being speech, as if the creatures making the noise had caught the general idea of speech without actually learning to use it.

Wells looked at me enquiringly.

"Nothing I've met before. But it sounds like something of which we should be wary; we are in a dark place at the bottom of the world with no way out except past whatever creatures are making that din, save through shadow—but they may have the trick of that as well, and we should not assume they cannot pursue and attack us there."

I saw him take a firm grip on his stick, with both hands and his wrists slightly outstretched in parallel. It was no fighting style that I had seen among stick fighters, and yet he seemed to know what he was doing and to have done it many times before.

We started back the way we had come, and suddenly we were among them. They snarled and they snapped and they clashed great metal teeth that had distorted their jaws and which struck sparks in the darkness. And they gouged the stone of the floor where they pranced, nerving themselves for an attack.

There were choke collars around their necks, whose studs pressed inwards so that they were in constant pain—my guess was that he sometimes leashed them, but that the tunnels down to their parents' tomb was their place to run free.

The worst of it was, they were not mere beasts, though there was little light in their eyes.

They were children, or rather cubs. He had whipped them—their backs bore the marks of it—and he had taken their teeth and given them monstrous ones and he had stitched claws to their hands. I say hands and not paws in memory of the intelligent beings they would have grown into. Because they would never be whole in mind—he had taken language away from young children by killing their parents and slitting their tongues and putting those fangs into their mouths, and, I saw, cutting into their throats.

And what he had done to them was the work of years or at least many months—I thought about what else he might have done with the extra time the hourglass gave him.

I said as much to Wells, because we clearly had a few moments left before they attacked and I wanted to distract him so that he would not lose his nerve. "Did you not notice how you speeded up when you touched his hour glass?"

He shook his head.

"For a few moments, you passed almost unseen."

"But I was examining the work-table for hours...Oh. Dear me..."

And the creatures continued to pace, and slaver, and scratch at the floor, and to stare at us with a cunning that had little intelligence to it—I noticed that several of those nearest to us, perhaps all of them, had old scars in the side of their heads, as if he had passed a knife or a hot auger through their temples and into their brains.

They should not have been dumb brutes, but he had made them such. There were only twelve of them and there had been thirty cribs in the crèche—allowing for the two he had shot, that meant that some sixteen had died on the tables where he cut them, or at the block where he whipped them.

Newton had made manticores of adult prisoners; this Jack had turned children—ghoul cubs but still children—into his hunting dogs.

I cannot decide which was more vile.

But now they were done with snarling and prancing and their eyes glinted—but with malice, not intelligence—as they readied themselves for the attack.

I drew my spear, but for the moment held it near the blade; I would not take these lives if I could, though I could not see how they were other than worthless, but the only thing left to these children that had been robbed.

Wells looked at me. "But they're..."

"Children," I said, "though they will tear you apart and eat you for all that."

As he nodded, one of the braver cubs, that had guessed he was the weaker of us, lunged at him. I had been interested to see how this pudgy young man would handle himself in a fight, and how this strange fighting style of his would work out.

I was impressed—he stepped forward and brought his stick up sharply so that it smashed into the creature's jaw—driving it back whimpering and then followed through with a sideways swing into the muzzle of the child who prowled next to it. I swung my spear butt-first and drove back the eight that had come for me.

We would have to hurt them, over and over, but it was better than having to kill them. Though, as we struck time and time again, and they did not break, but continued to come at us, it seemed that it would come to that. Some of them slunk back, but only to sidle round the ones at the front, and come at us from the sides, and potentially from the back.

I was worried that Wells would tire or that he would not be able to see an attack coming. He was my responsibility and I would not let him die, because I had brought him here. So I struck harder and faster at those cubs which were still between us and our path out of here, not caring how badly I hurt them as long as I drove them out of our way. Because hurt is better than dead.

A space cleared and I shouted, "Run," though Wells had seen what I was doing and needed no instruction. He had a clean pair of heels, that young man, and ran confidently into the darkness ahead of me as I turned and struck at the cubs behind me and then followed him.

What impressed me about him was that he did not hesitate—I was behind him and he could not see very far ahead by the light from me and yet he ran confidently, but without letting go of his stick or showing any sign of losing his nerve, into the darkness, the way we had come, nor did he lose his footing when the tunnel started to climb up and up.

The creatures behind us regrouped and paced—I looked over my shoulder and they were following us, but warily, and now staying out of easy reach of my spear. Some prudence, then, if no intelligence.

Each time I looked, I counted—lest some of them peel off and come at me or Wells from some side tunnel.

I mentioned, did I not, that even so minor an adept as Polly could make and maintain a small flame on which to boil her coffee. I knew that spell before Troy fell. There are beasts so brute-stupid that they have no fear, but I had seen burn scars among the whip-marks on the ghoul-hounds backs and what had worked for this Jack in their training would work for me.

When the tunnel narrowed and they started to form a single file as they chased us, it grew harder to keep track of how many still followed. So I sent a great gout of flame behind me into their faces to deter them from following us at all. And they yelped and whined and howled—and broke and ceased to follow us. At least for the moment.

Wells continued to run and I paced after him—I could have overtaken him easily, but what would have been the point? It is of course harder to keep pace with someone slower, but it is often the lot of those of us who serve.

After a while, as the yelping died away in the distance, he drew to a halt and looked back at me.

"Where now?"

We were at a fork in the tunnels, and here is a thing—I have lived for thousands of years and have strength equal to those who call themselves god and I have fought great beasts and travelled in every land. Yet faced with a fork in the road, I know no more than the next woman whether I should take the right, or the left. It is not a power I have. Nor do I know any who have had it.

Both tunnels led upwards and clean air blew gently down from them. And so we took the right hand tunnel as most of us do, most of the time. There was no point in running for the moment and so I walked briskly and Wells matched my stride.

There was something by which I was intrigued.

"I watched you as we fought. I have trained stick-fighters a little, and watched others, my betters in that skill, train others—and yet the style you use is not one I have ever seen before. Effective, to be sure, but new to me—and I have watched men and women fight in many lands and times."

He laughed. "That would be because I am not trained in fighting—I bluffed when I said I could cope because I did not think I would ever be in danger. And it turns out that I lied to myself—I had a skill but I did not think of it as fighting."

I was even more intrigued.

"My father taught me, but what he taught me was the game of cricket. Which, until he wrecked his leg, was what he played for a living, alongside gentlemen amateurs. I have no particular gift for it, but it turns out that a strong pair of shoulders put behind a firm controlled swing has more uses than I ever knew. It is strange what abject terror teaches us."

I thought of rebuking him for putting himself at risk, but it seemed pointless—he had been foolhardy and then he had been truly brave. Now he knew something about himself that he had not known before and would be helped by that knowledge.

And suddenly we stood behind a door, the upper part of which was latticework. Its hinges were crude stuff—ghoul work if I guessed right. I pulled it open and beyond lay a larger higher broader tunnel, with loose soil as its floor. I had got a little turned around in our flight and for a moment I did not know where we were.

Wells caught my slight confusion. "This would, I think, be the excavation for the new section of the Underground. We are somewhere under Whitechapel."

And so we were.

But before we left the tunnel, one last thing happened. Wells stumbled against a pile of soil that lay at the side of the digging—earth that had been displaced where the sides of the tunnel needed shoring up with wood before being finished with strong iron and brickwork. He sniffed, and then reached down and dabbled his fingers in the dirt a little, then raised his index finger up, slightly smudged with a grey dirt, particles that were not London clay.

"This or somewhere like it is where he comes. This is the dust that was in one of the tubes you showed me—dust that comes from old deep places. I was going to look at it through a microscope, but doing so has become considerably more urgent..." He was eager and excited at the thought of finding out something new. Then he yawned, and I realized he was close to falling asleep from exhaustion where he stood.

Most men have stupid pride at such times and those I have to knock unconscious before I sling them across my shoulders and carry them to where they need to be. Wells struck me as better than that, so I reached out and took his stick from him before he could drop it unnoticing, and put it in the quiver at my back.

"You need to sleep, and look at the dust tomorrow. It will keep until the morning. As will Miss Wild."

He smiled wistfully and I reached across and rumpled his thinning hair. I had known so many younger men who were more fully the person they would be than he was in his twenties. I was not used to feeling, well, maternal.

And then he tottered slightly and before he could protest, or fall to the ground, I swept him up, slung him across my shoulder and raced into the City of London and out again to the nameless clumb of buildings, somewhere near the Inns and the Temple, where Polly sits and keeps the state she serves secure.

Polly was waiting.

When she was only a century or so old, I used to see her sleep, but increasingly she seemed not to. I must warn her of this, I thought, it is not a luxury that we should leave to mortals. Nor is it good to think of ourselves as above it—that way lies the folly of godhood.

I put Wells down on one of her couches.

"'Ave you worn out that nice young man? I had plans for him."

I gave her a serious look to remind her that we were all about business, and then relented. "He will be fine in the morning—he's had a busy night." I took his stick from my quiver and noticed, in the gaslight of Polly's rooms, that its lower part was thick with dried blood. "We had an adventure. He surprised me. He'll do, your young man, he'll most certainly do…"

She did not enquire further—Polly knew that I would tell her all later.

"Did your messenger go over to South Street? I am coming to think that this Jack is more formidable even than we thought, and I had rather wake Miss Nightingale than take any further chances with her…"

Polly confirmed that she had sent a messenger moments after I had left, in the fastest carriage at her disposal. "I sent one of my best-mannered, prissiest clerks so as not to offend or perturb her Ladyship—and a couple of likely lads hanging off the back of the carriage to do any violence as might need doing."

Nonetheless, since Jack could slip in and out of shadow, the likeliest of lads, the most perspicacious of clerks might not see him coming…Any more than had a nest of comparatively civilized, but nonetheless potentially ravening, ghouls.

I raced across from Polly's offices, past the boundary of the two cities and into Mayfair, almost to the park. For most of my route the streets were empty, save for the area around Piccadilly and Haymarket, where whores male and female were still plying their trade and the few police could hardly be bothered to move them on. There were more whores than usual in the brightly lit streets of the West End—where as yet Jack had not struck.

As I neared South Street, I heard first one and then another police whistle, and running feet followed by oaths. I quickened my pace—there would be no finding a fleeing man in a warren of streets or the shadow that surrounded them, and I needed to know what had happened. I had sent Polly's men into danger—had perhaps failed to protect Miss Nightingale sufficiently from any knowledge she might have—and needed to make whatever redress was possible.

Outside her house, two bodies lay, their throats slit—a thin man who was presumably Polly's messenger, and a stockier one who was one of her bullies. A police surgeon was stitching a gash in the cheek of another, whose bloody hand missing a finger showed how he had avoided the fate of his companions.

Nonetheless, though he was whimpering with pain, he looked up at me and knew who I was.

"Miss Mara," he reported, "sorry we failed you. But he came out of nowhere, hacking and slashing. We didn't stand a chance. Miss Nightingale…" And then he lapsed into unconsciousness.

I knew that the Nightingale woman had been bed-ridden for years and I held out little hope for her.

Most of the blood was on the stairs, where Polly's men had been ambushed—nearby, servants, most of them in nightclothes, clustered around, looking as if they were in shock.

At her bedroom door, a maid stood crying—she was unhurt, but a tray and some shards of porcelain lay broken at her feet.

"'E just pushed past me. She'll take it out of me wages, I know she will. It was her favourite teacup—Wedgwood it was. With 'Am I not a man and brother' on it and everything."

There was much to be disliked about Miss Nightingale, but she had taken the right position on the War on Slavery. Unlike many of her class.

From her room, I heard her sharp husky voice. "Don't fuss, man. He never touched me."

At least something good had happened.

I walked into her fussily decorated room, which smelled of gunpowder, blood and burned chintz. A pudgy man in a dressing-gown, whom I took for an upper servant of some kind, was holding Miss Nightingale's left wrist and checking her pulse against a pocket watch.

Next to her on the bed lay a shot-gun, recently fired. I turned and saw that, on the wall to the right of the door, the purple and green wall-paper was peppered with shot and bloodstains. By the wainscoting, there lay the upper half of a human ear.

Miss Nightingale laughed.

"He thought to catch me sound asleep. I never sleep sound. One of the few gifts that God gives us to go with pain...I remember you—the Wild woman said you would be calling and that you were working for the Queen in this matter." She clearly disapproved. "It does her Majesty credit," she went on. "She cares for all her subjects, even women of the unfortunate class, or Miss Wild, who is little better. Still, I should be grateful that she sent her men to warn me that I might be in danger. Even if it was not a warning I needed."

She patted her shotgun.

"Ever since the killings started, I have kept this under my pillows. It starts with women of the streets, but men like that know no limits. I have heard of such things. No woman is safe from blood-lust or –" she lowered her voice, "– the other kind." She stuck out that arrogant chin. "A man who hates women, will sooner or later turn from the girls of the streets to women who are famous. Even he would not start with the queen. Apart from her, I am the most famous Englishwoman alive, so I knew he would come for me." She looked a little abashed, then. "I had not realised that he might have other reasons."

"Miss Nightingale, had you seen him before?" I needed to be sure that she realized that he had come to kill her for her knowledge not her sex.

She looked at me pityingly. "Of course—but not seen, so much as smelled. We knew less then than we do now, but he was disgusting even for a surgeon. A leather apron that could have stood against a wall, it was so stiff with blood and other things. But Raglan insisted he was a good surgeon—or I would not have had such a man in my hospital. He seems not to have aged a day since then, and smells no sweeter."

Then she burst out. "Do I have to call you Huntress? Such a pretentious, heathen title—But yes, I recognized the man who came here with his knife, and his apron. And his stink. I met him in Balaclava. Where I met you." She narrowed her eyes and there was quiet resentment in her voice. Our conversations back then had not been amicable—she minded someone she had never met or heard of interrogating sick men in her hospital and I had not perhaps been sufficiently respectful.

Then she laughed. "Still, you put fear into the hearts of those stupid butchers, and I should thank you for that. I think you scared Raglan into an earlier grave—would you had done so years earlier—and Lucan still talks of you in dread. But yes, I recognized him, as I think you thought I might. He was a surgeon, and a butcher, even then, I suppose—but he was full of excuses for every death under his knife and we were over-stretched and men were dying every day. I should have noticed; I should at least have insisted he wash his hands, and get rid of that apron."

So she should, and so should I. I at least have smelled killers out for thousands of years.

"And I should have wondered about his name. But I suppose some people are just called John Smith."

"He is well-practiced in deceit, I should think. His killings have extended his life, we think, so he has had years to learn."

And a name so boring was one he would never have to change.

Her face softened—she had not expected me to console her for what she was obviously feeling guilt and shame over. For a moment I could see the young woman she had once been, and how she had learned to do without friendship and how that saddened her a little. Then it hardened again, and she smiled. It was not a pleasant smile.

"At least this time, I hurt him. That pays a little for all those poor men. See that he pays the rest."

I picked up the piece of ear. "This," I said, with a smile that matched hers, "should ensure that he pays in full."

The worst thing was having to tell Polly that we had sent two of her men to their deaths.

She sighed.

"They knew the risks. Good men as had worked for me for years. On borrowed time, really, both of them. Still..." She dabbed her eye with a handkerchief in a way that was strategic, and yet sincere.

"Worst part of this job 'as always been the funerals. Bad enough when they've retired and cop it from old age, but…Least only one of these was married."

I looked around for Wells, but he wasn't there. I forbore to ask whether he had stayed and been entertained.

Polly caught my glance. "Herbert left, early. With only a hurried kiss as a promissory note for his lodging. Said he had to go and look at things through microscopes and the like. He left a lot of instructions for my clerks. So what will you be doing this morning?"

"I need to contact an old friend. That will involve me in errands."

"Miss mysterious as always. Why can't you be a normal person, if you don't want to tell me? Just say you're going to see a man about a dog?" Which was uncannily perceptive, even for Miss Wild.

The snug of the public house down by the river was full of tobacco smoke and the smell of spilled porter.

In pubs like this one there is always such a man if you ask the publican, and buy him a glass of spirits. In this pub, the man he pointed me to was half-drunk, even at nine in the morning, and there were shreds of bacon and pipe tobacco in his white beard, but when I asked him, he talked like a man who knew his business.

"Well, my lovely, a pretty girl like you could do worse than a brace of ferrets. They stink a bit, but they're wery affectionate like. And they can take a rat, quick as you like, that would wear any cat's fur for a hat. But I dunno, some of the rats we see down this way—well, a bit much even for ferrets. If you really want to go after rats, and be absolutely sure, what you needs is a good rough little terrier. The which, as it happens, I have for sale at a very reasonable rate. Lovely little chap even if 'is ear is a bit chewed orff."

The terrier he produced from under his ragged coat was a nondescript colour and looked at me suspiciously. Still, I wouldn't need him for very long and once I was done, Polly would find him a good home. Or perhaps Wells would want a dog.

I paid the man the sovereign he asked—yes, I carry money when I need to, actual money, not a glamour—then seized the terrier by the scruff of its neck and took a step down through shadow into Bazalgette's great sewer. In great cities, rats are always easily found, and if this terrier was as good as I had been told...

In thirty seconds, it had found a flurry of sewer rats, some of which made the mistake of squeaking disrespectfully in what, in the last seconds of their lives, they vainly imagined was a threatening manner. It dispatched ten rats in thirty seconds with a snarl and a twist of its head, then padded over and laid each of them in turn at my feet.

I assumed that this would do.

As it did.

There was a positively Wagnerian horn-call somewhere behind my left ear. The old brute does love to make an entrance.

"So, Huntress," Cernunnos boomed, "what are you about?"

I turned—he knew he could not intimidate me but he was going nonetheless to try because some gods will always play the game at which they will always fail. As if I was going to be affected by mere titanic bulk, or by antlers that stretched the entire width of the great sewer, and past Mundane into shadow, or that half-face, half-muzzle he had taken to affecting even though he could, if he chose, look like the man he once was.

His shoulders were broader than ever and the weight of his upper body would have made him stoop even in a place where there was more room—the blue ink across his chest shone bright even in the gloom.

How much of this was glamour these days, now he was weaker than he had once been, I did not know nor care.

These days, in this city, men called him Herne.

"Hunting, clearly, as you demand from those who seek audience with you."

"Uncommonly polite, though. From one who holds me under suspended sentence of death."

I had not merely suspended that sentence but cancelled it, as far as I was concerned; he had made himself useful enough.

But there is no point in telling reformed malefactors that they have been forgiven—it is best to keep them on their toes.

"I have need of your services." There is an etiquette between judge and reprieved convict, just as there is in summoning those to appear whom I could choose to compel, but instead request. I passed him the fragment of Jack's ear. "We need the rest of him. You are the best tracker I know, and your dogs are as good."

My terrier whined and Cernunnos looked at the rats at my feet, then patted its head. "Hush, little one. If your mistress permits, you have earned a place in my pack."

Which was handy, because it saved me finding the beast some other home.

"May I ask," he continued, "whose ear this is?"

"It is my property now, a token of the imminent execution of the man known as Jack. A killer of women and of patients in his care, but whom I suspect of intending far worse things. I don't want to take the chance of missing him."

Cernunnos started reckoning on his fingers. "My pack are dispersed—there is a fine beagle in Cumberland and a mastiff misbehaving on Dartmoor. I worry about that one, but his appetite may come in handy. Give me a couple of hours to fetch the best of them and we will cast about and find his trail."

I fretted a little, but this was no ordinary huntsman and his dogs would be the best there were.

"In the courtyard of Miss Wild's offices, then."

That would let me find any information that Wells had gathered with his seeing glass and that Polly's clerks might have found.

The clerks had found several John Smiths, in a variety of armies, some at least of whom were probably our man. They were now looking for addresses associated with each and making lists of people who might have served with him and were still alive—all this was useful work and would in time have caught him, and might yet if the ear failed to be as useful as I thought it would be. Yet I sensed that the pace of things had picked up and we needed to be hasty if we were to prevent whatever it was he intended.

I fretted as I waited for the Hunter God—time was passing and there was no sign of Wells. Still, at least he was safe in his laboratory where he belonged; he might yet be needed to explain things to me, but his methods were slow. Too slow, I thought.

And then there came the horn call from the courtyard outside Miss Wild's offices.

"Do you want to join us?" I asked Miss Wild.

"I'm a town girl, me. Never liked the sort of people who hunt—pack of red-faced drunken bitches, and their husbands are worse—and I don't know as I would care to spend time with their god. Just find the Ripper and bring him back more or less alive—I has a queen who wants to have particular sharp words with him, for she don't appreciate his activities."

She stretched in her arm-chair as if she was ready to curl up and sleep for a while.

"Besides, you told me long ago that I should not any longer exert myself in the sort of adventure where a person might do herself a permanent mischief. It's sad I send other people out to die and don't go myself, but them's the necessities of my condition, and ever since Paris I've paid attention to them. And when there's a man that cuts up pretty whores...well, I got Gibbon to tell me what he guessed that night in Lausanne. And I thinks I know why you gave me the advice you did, and good advice it was. And I am sorry."

She is one of my dearest friends and at that moment I hated her for her compassion.

Then she hissed, "So go and catch that man. For her, for those dead women and for all of us. You don't have to be gentle with him."

And that moment of anger was past.

Outside Herne was holding the small torn fragment of flesh to each of his dogs in turn—the little terrier which looked at me abashed for a moment as if concerned that it had changed loyalty so fast; the big black mastiff and a beagle with almost comically long ears; three lurchers that were mostly greyhound but had many and various other parents; some dogs that looked frail and others on whom cords of muscle stuck out so vehemently I was not sure how they could move. They all barked or bayed and jumped up and down excitedly.

I had run with the Wild Hunt once, before it was stolen from Odin by darker forces—and even then it was bleak company and its hounds and horses were vicious and unkindly. Herne's pack was not without menace—but I felt comfortable with it.

I hunt alone, but if I felt the need of dogs in my hunt—these would be the sort of dogs I would choose. Odin was always obsessed with a matched set that looked good—and it did him no good in the end for he had bred brain out of them and they had just enough of it left to dislike him for what he had done to them down the generations. Wicked will does most of the harm in the world, but resentment is the door left open for it.

Cernunnos knelt to each of his dogs in turn and whispered in each one's right ear while stroking just above its left ear. Even the great dangerous-looking mastiff got its share of attention, though he took especial time with the little terrier. Obviously it had charms that I could not see.

Wells walked into the courtyard, brash and brisk as if he knew something I did not. And suddenly all the dogs were clustering round him sniffing, as if he were the tastiest treat they have ever smelled. He reached down, and he too stroked each of them just above the left ear—clearly this was a piece of wisdom known to many, if not to me.

Wells smiled at Cernunnos in wonderment. "Herne," he breathed.

"That is one of my names," Cernunnos acknowledged. "And you are?"

"Herbert George Wells, a student of man and the universe." Then he turned to me. "He's growing something. Spores of something old—spores encased in beads of magma, as if they spend aeons somewhere deep, yet somehow he found a way to wake them –so I thought I'd find out whether it was some magic from the deaths, or something in their blood, or just the rain-water and soot he must have got all over the heart he stole."

141

He shuddered. "So I tried blood and that didn't work. But then I went up to the roof and got water from a rain-barrel, London rain, with a little bit of soot and a little bit of sulphur, and I tried that. And suddenly the spores burst and this white flabby stuff started to spread, it burst the glass slide and then it started to eat its way through the wood of my worktable. And not just the spores I had treated—it was as if the others were bursting too without anything touching them. They started to grow in the test-tube. And the dried vegetable matter—well, that came back to life too."

This wasn't like anything I had ever seen. But then, if birds had had a lord, and the creatures of the sea, why shouldn't mould or mushrooms?

He looked at me as if I were slightly dense, which I suppose I had been. "The thing is, with both you and him, well, you think of everything the same way. Why would something that has no blood, need blood to be reborn? But the atmosphere of ancient earth— well, that was full of volcano dust, and soot and sulphur. The magic of killing may have helped him—but it rained the night he killed Mary Anne, and on no other night that he killed."

Somehow it made it worse that the women had died because Jack was as set in his thinking as I was.

"And while it was growing, it was as if it were talking in my head. Pictures. Pictures of other dead Londons…"

That was familiar, and worrying. I hate it when something or someone trespasses inside my mind, and it is worse when I don't notice.

"So what did you do?"

I had noticed a touch of triumph in his voice, so I assumed he had dealt with it. "I used the first thing that came to hand. The cleaners in that workroom sometimes have need of strong stuff— carbolic and the like– so I poured it over everything and the strange white flesh burst into flame and sizzled like a fried mushroom… There was little left by the time I was done, and no damn whispering in my mind. Do you think Miss Wild's office will pay for a ruined work bench?"

"Enough." Cernunnos voice was suddenly more like a bark than a word. "My dogs are ready, and so am I. So follow or stay, it is one to me."

Those gods that are all about a single thing—sometimes forget to be anything other than that thing once it is in play.

But he was doing me a favour and so I let him chivvy us, and now he and his dogs were up and away, in and out of shadow and racing down London streets with no concern for anything that lay in their path. The mastiff bayed and the beagle snuffled and the little terrier yipped.

I could follow easily, although the dogs were moving not at their natural speed but at some faster pace that Cernunnos gave them from his store.

Wells, though, would never have kept up of his own abilities, so I grabbed him by one arm and carried him, though I think he thought his feet were still touching the cobblestones. I wanted him with us at journey's end because I feared otherwise we would never understand what Jack was about. I did not need to understand him to execute him, this was true, but I am no mere butcher.

Another thought struck me as we raced, sufficiently in shadow that we passed through drays and omnibuses in the street, took short cuts and right turns through crowded shops without disturbing a shelf or disarranging a customer's coat.

"How old might this thing be?"

Wells pondered. It took him the seconds during which we crossed the viaduct and were thoroughly into the City. "At the start of all things, there must have been a beach, a desolate beach of stone and sand. And tendrils of sea-weed washed onto that shore and took root, and something with flippers flopped after it, half-choking on the open air. And something will have been there to meet them, and perhaps devour them...That old."

He thought some more –"And some of the spores were coated in magma. Imagine, the time it took for them to sink that deep in the earth, or to be swallowed up in ages of chaos and thrown up again. Imagine the violence those spores have survived. And still to be

143

capable of growing, with blood magic to help or not. Aeons old, Huntress, aeons. What that fungus could tell us if it can speak, or if those dreams are its thoughts forced into our brains. Imagine."

Even when you are as old as I am, the new vistas of the past opened up by science over the previous few decades will make me as dizzy as anyone.

"That's strangely vivid."

"I know." Wells looked at me in concern. "That may have been another thing it put into my head."

Cernunnos blew his horn—we were somewhere near the Bank by now—and it was strange to see passers-by look up as if they had half-heard him, half-been called to follow him, and then returned to the sleep of their daily lives.

We plunged beneath the street and passed through the vaults and tunnels of the Bank itself, and into sewers and even deeper tunnels, fully in shadow now and passing like smoke. Herne cast his own light as did I, but I noticed a phosphorescence on the black hide of the mastiff and noted that it was some kind of paint or powder that someone had placed there. I wondered momentarily what purpose it served, then noticed the convenience of having an outlier that shone almost as much as Huntsman and Huntress, and moved on. I am a woman with many tales to tell, but there are always stories that I do not know.

In the distance we heard a baying that Wells and I knew well. I reached for my lance with my free hand.

The pack of mutilated ghoul cubs was suddenly upon us—and within seconds some of them were bleeding and fleeing and whimpering as the mastiff at the head of the pack seized them by the scruff of the neck and tossed them like rats he could not be bothered to kill, or some bitch's puppies he was not minded to be gentle too. They tugged at the beagle's ears, but the terrier snapped at them. Other dogs were fiercer—it was not that the hounds were stronger, it was that they were older and the cubs, however vicious, were still children, and unused to pain.

The blood of Cernunnos was up and he let his horn fall, for he had no longer hands to hold it with nor lips to blow it with.

I had seen him like this before, when we fought side by side all those years before. Back then, though, though monstrous, he still kept to a human shape of sorts. Now, at such times, he ceased to be the hunter and became the hunt—the paws of a great hunting cat and the baying lungs of an enormous hound and the beak of a hawk and the mad eyes of a stallion frothing with rage, exhaustion and lust. And those great antlers covered in torn and bleeding stag velvet, his and some others'.

I took my ground before him, and struck him once on the beak and once across his horns to remind him what we were about. "These are children, Herne, to whom a terrible wrong has been done. See, they fly from you into the tunnels—they will not hinder us again. We have other prey, he who did this to them."

The cubs fled. I do not know what became of them later. Nothing good, I would imagine.

Cernunnos shook that beaked head, and before he was done shaking it, he had returned to man's shape or something like it. His dogs clustered round their master enthusiastically and he blew the fierce double notes of one encouraging his hounds to hurry after a quarry he senses is nearby. The mastiff in particular bounded forward and Cernunnos blew the double notes again and again as the dogs raced round bends and corners so that it was all I could do to catch up. The mastiff ran so far ahead that its glowing hide was almost lost to us—I wondered again what prey it was used for that ran through the night. Cernunnos at his old practices?—he would not dare…

Then, from up ahead, there came the cry of a man in terror, and snarling and barking. Cernunnos blew the kill, though I doubted that Jack would be more than moderately injured by the time we got there.

The hounds had caught him and pulled him down near the staircases down to the vault where the dead ghouls had lain. The mastiff was worrying the stub of the ear that had been shot off—it worried me that the brute was so clearly invested in causing him pain rather than devouring that part of him or just holding him still for us. It was too human a trait for a dog to be encouraged to have. The brute was uncanny enough already.

They kept their jaws well away from the leather apron that hung stiffly around him—even hunting dogs, whose own mouths are none too clean, know better than to dabble in foulness.

Cernunnos reached out to pull the mastiff away but he did not hurry and I did not tell him to. Wells averted his gaze, but he made no move to pre-empt us.

Once the mastiff had released him, Jack stood up and dusted some of the grime from his hands. Not that that made much difference—Florence Nightingale had been right. He stank of a century's worth of blood and malignant power. I've smelled worse things—Samarkand aflame, the dung of an undead dragon—but Jack smelled worse than Herod when the worms got him.

I had seen him before. A face so utterly unmemorable had its own distinction—it was a glamour of a sort, and yet, now he was at bay, with no need for pretence, it was of a sudden more distinctive. It had the harsh lines of years of cruelty and pride and the twisted smirk of someone who thought himself superior and entitled. It also had blemishes—broken veins in the cheeks—that a man who was vain, rather than proud, might have taken the trouble to mend.

For a man so deft with razors, he was inadequately shaven and there was an unpleasant oily sheen to the patches of stubble along the side of his chin.

And that stink.

Wells put a dirty handkerchief to his mouth and nose and even so went slightly green. Still, given that he had led a sheltered life, he was coping remarkably well. That young man had steel under the pudginess.

Jack reached into a pocket in his apron and produced a small clay white pipe—it was oddly pristine for something that had knocked around for so long in adjacency to such filth.

He put it in his mouth and then pulled out a lucifer.

146

His hands were deft and his movements practiced—for a man at bay he was worryingly calm.

He struck the match back-handed on the wall behind him and lit the pipe. It was some foul mix of hemp, tobacco and opium that burned slow and steady.

Now they were not holding Jack down, the dogs retreated from his stink and started to play around Cernunnos' feet. He stroked their heads and tousled their ears as if no conversation were taking place. It was hard to keep his attention on anything save the hunt.

"So," the sneer seemed to be directed more at me than at anyone else. "You would be the legendary Huntress. I saw you from a distance at Balaclava, but I did not know then who you are and what you attempt to do."

"Most of the time, and eventually, I succeed. This would be one of those occasions. Consider that the only reason why you are not already choking with my lance through your throat is that I am mildly interested in what your ultimate goals were."

I was mildly interested. After all, most who work the Rituals are told about them—he, though, seemed to have worked something of them out from first principles and it would be interesting to know what his end-game was going to be.

I reached for my lance. Contrary to what some people suppose, most villains are somewhat reticent at the end, and need a little encouragement. I let them think that they are buying the time in which they can think of a way of escaping me. Of course, this means that on occasion some have, for a while. I am inexorable, but not always omnipotent.

I walked towards him and looked past him into shadow. He had set a fire, and on it, balanced on some sort of giant trivet, was a cauldron of something hot, sticky and smelling of magic.

"How very enterprising of you." I was genuinely impressed. "I haven't smelled Greek Fire since the fall of Trebizond."

The terrier had wandered away from the main group of Cernunnos' hounds, sniffing the foul air as if it were looking for something. It started down the staircase to the ghoul's vault and suddenly it yelped.

From below a strip of fibre had sprung out like a noose and snared its forepaw; I reached down with my Japanese blade and slashed the fibre free. The terrier dashed back to its master's side, whimpering. Its paw wept slightly from a mark that was like a burn.

I started to sheathe my sword, but Wells reached up with a small blade of his own and scraped a sample of the fibre free. He started to look at the lump of it with a magnifying glass from his pocket.

Wells' fungus, the intrusions on my mind and his...I thought, though, that I knew. Jack had understood something about the Rituals—a way of not having to commit a hecatomb of people. He had murdered to bring back into the world something that might be nearly a god, but that was helpless—and if he culminated his plans by killing that...

"I think I see. You've done rather well from first principles."

Jack snickered, then took another draw on his pipe before speaking. "I got the idea from you. Someone put a copy of that chapbook about you on my bed. I don't like that someone found my place. But it is always useful to be warned of women. And their ill-gotten power."

Every so often I am reminded that there is another very powerful player in all these games. Who likes to have catspaws.

"Wandering around massacres...And killing gods, they tell me. Kill one person, take something from their death. Kill hundreds, or something, someone big enough—well, it stands to reason. And this thing has power—it killed thousands in the Middle Ages. Though it says it didn't mean to, and it died too. Again."

The plague pits of Spitalfields—the cattle murrain and famines of King Henry's reign that people confuse with the Death and the Plague.

He looked at us smugly. "And now I've given it life. And you have to let me kill it, because otherwise it will grow and spread and eat everything that there is."

A voice sounded inside my head. I hate it when something does that, though I had in fairness to accept that it was hard to see how else an intelligent fungus could communicate. "The rest of life can have the sea, but the land is mine. It was taken from me by stupid brutes and green things that could grow faster than me, and they ate me, a piece at a time." The anger in that voice was cold and vast.

"You may not have noticed," Wells seemed not at all abashed by the thing, but he'd already destroyed a fragment of it and perhaps that made him feel entitled to cheek it, "but we are on an island."

"Little man," the voice deigned to notice him. "You do not even know that the earth moves under you. It is an island? Very well then, it will not always have been one, nor will it always remain one. I can wait. And spread my spores. Into the air you breathe, into your brains. I am not ripe yet, but when I am…When I am fully awake."

So the visions I had seen of other dead Londons were its dreams, or rather its daydreams. And the miasma…

"I find," Jack smirked, "that this smoking mixture of mine keeps the damned beast out of my head. Mostly. It was a while before it realized what I was about, and now I keep well away from its strangling bits. I brought it back to life, with the help of those useless drabs. Yet it isn't even a bit grateful."

"You stupid butcher," Wells snarled; I noted that the squeakiness of his voice almost entirely went away when he was angry. "You'd have got the same results from ordinary rain water. You just wanted to kill some women. And gave yourself a reason to indulge yourself. Butcher and coward."

I didn't feel any need to interrupt him.

I glanced down into the ghoul's vault—there was no longer any sign of their bodies, just an amorphous grey mass of what I had seen in the test-tubes. It pulsed as if it were bread-dough rising before the oven. Both Jack and the fungus seemed bizarrely happy with each other's agendas.

"So, I am supposed to let you kill it and become a god."

Jack laughed. "As I understand it, you can't kill it yourself. You have your rules."

The fungus was a thinking creature, acting according to its kind. As yet, it had done naught that would justify its death. I kill beasts and I kill wicked men and other wicked creatures.

Somewhere in the back of my mind, the fungus laughed at my dilemma.

Wells put his magnifying glass away. "Actually, Huntress, you really don't have a problem. You may as well kill the Ripper straight away for the magic he tried to work with those dead women, and all he has done in the past. Because you don't need to kill the poor creature; it's dying."

"No I am not." That voice spoke in my mind, but suddenly it lacked the certainty it had had earlier.

Wells shook his head. "Poor thing, did you think that living walking thinking creatures with guns and fire were the only enemies life has thrown up to keep you in your proper place? In the past, in the childhood of the planet? A myriad tiny creatures are eating your cells even as we speak—I looked at the tendril with which you attacked that dog and it is half rotted already."

He turned to Jack. "Coward and butcher and fool. You studied medicine once before you took to murder and magic. You would have done better to pay attention and kept on learning your trade. You have killed the creature already and not as you intended. Huntress, you understand such things—the magic act has to be the one that was intended, does it not?"

Magic is all about will—you cannot cast it by accident. I grinned; I had done so well to bring this young man into my work.

Encouraged, he went on. "It's the apron. He's been cutting off legs and arms for decades, and every speck of filth, every bit of gangrene and misery—it's all splashed onto him and stuck and stunk there. And his knives, they're filthy. He cut out her heart thinking that somehow it would feed the thing he was trying to bring back, and he contaminated his own experiment. Like some stupid first year failing his exams."

"I passed top of my class," Jack blustered. "Dr Knox himself commended me."

Wells' voice was full of scorn—I relished it. "Butcher and coward and fool. You probably think the germ theory of disease is new-fangled nonsense. I don't expect the Huntress to keep up to date but at least she knows that there are things she doesn't know."

In the back of my mind, I felt fear and weeping. It was an old creature, lost out of its proper place and hoping to seize its world back. Now it knew that this was not to be, just slow withering and decay. Again. As in 1258 and other times, countless other times. And now it knew why…And that it would happen over and over again.

I readied myself for the kill—Jack had done enough to deserve death many times over and I did not intend to make his end especially quick.

But then Cernunnos seized him by the shoulders, threw him out of his way and strode over to the cauldron, seizing its handles in spite of the heat of the iron, and carried it towards the mouth of the vault. Then he paused and looked at me. Suddenly the chamber we were in was full of the fungus' miasma and the smoke and fumes of its fear of imminent death.

"What are you doing?" I said to Cernunnos.

"Putting a poor sick creature out of its misery as quickly as possible. I am the God of the Hunt and that is part of what I do."

It is part of what I do, also, when the Rituals go wrong and a wicked man becomes a Flat Ogre or the like. I reflected that it was unlikely that there was magic to be gained from the death of this creature, largely Mundane as it was—but it was best not to put temptation in the way of a god of less than sterling character.

I kicked the cauldron over and a gout of liquid flame shot from it down into the vault.

The creature's death smelled, as Wells had said, like the frying of good mushrooms in melted butter. It could make no sound of its own, but it screamed in my mind and in Wells'. The dogs set up a howling and a whining that was painful in itself because it meant that they were in pain and there was nothing I could do for them—Cernunnos had the face of someone who is under necessity. He stroked the mastiff under its jaw, and pulled at the beagle's ears with his other hand; I do not like dogs but I picked up the whining terrier and scratched at the top of its head, hoping it would bring it some comfort. Cernunnos reached out to all his other dogs in turn.

Wells was on his knees, mumbling—which surprised me because I had not thought of him as a godly man—but who can tell what happens in a crisis to faith or its twin faithlessness?

Then I realised he was trying to talk to the creature, and comfort it. He was a kind man.

I looked around as the smoke and miasma started to thin. There was no sign of Jack. Cernunnos caught my gaze. "I am the God of the Hunt. I am not your personal jailer, Huntress"—his voice disputed my right to the title—"when your attention wanders a moment and the catch gets out of the trap. I caught him for you and the task I promised you is done. For the rest of it, you are on your own."

I shrugged, because I know of old what it is to deal with gods and their monomanias. There is no arguing with them, merely occasional negotiation and the granting or withdrawing of favours. Cernunnos and I would do business again, one way or another, and I would remember this, on that occasion.

As for Jack, I knew his face and his name. Very shortly, so would Polly and the other agencies of the state she served, or embodied. If he killed again, they would find him, or I would—and without killing he would age and in due course die.

In due course, as I told Crowley, I caught him, though it cost the lives of four more women. I cannot save them all. But he troubles the world no more.

Cernunnos blew the call which is known as 'Gone away'. The

terrier jumped down from my arms and joined his other dogs as they clustered around his legs and disappeared as he did—some of them to their other masters, and some to his kennels, wherever they are.

I heard the last whisper of the dying fungus in my mind. It creaked "Thank you" but it was not talking to me. Then, in an even quieter voice, "I shall see you again, Huntress…" It did not sound especially like a threat, but who can say?

And then Wells and I were alone. And the flames below us guttered and died. He stood up and shook himself lightly, brushed dust and spores and the residue of smoke from his jacket and trousers, then looked at me quizzically.

"Jack escaped, which is annoying." I shrugged. "I shall find him sooner or later. But the thing he planned did not happen and from what you said, could not happen. Also, I am not sure that a creature without blood would ever have brought him quite what he expected. I just wish I had noticed him earlier. Women and men died horribly because I did not. I am the protector of the weak against the strong, but I cannot save them all."

"You could, perhaps," his tone was almost that of one who wanted to console me, "if you let people help you more. You asked for my help, and we did not entirely fail."

I shook my head. "People have helped me from time to time. And often it has ended badly for them. I am the Huntress and I hunt alone. Because, in the long term, I must."

He looked at me with a compassion I could not find it in me to resent. "One day you will have help of a sort. Whether you welcome it or not." There was certainty in his voice. "I've often thought what's needed is to recruit young people. A corps of them. To work for a better world under socialism. Not like those sweet girls in muslin that Morris keeps around him—they're part of the problem. Pretty and useless. You will not always be alone."

I shook my head. I had had apprentices once and they meant well.

As we walked through the tunnels and then the streets of

London, it was a fine late afternoon. I led him back to Miss Wild's apartments, where he wished to go and be with her, but first I instructed him a little in the ways of the world as I have known them. Because I wished—not to break, but to inform his idealism—I told him of the perfectly organized city, as I have seen it, the Bird's Atlantis, and what came of it, and of my first companions, and what became of them.

He grew more and more excited. "That's the secret, isn't it? You find people, and you tell them your stories, and they join you in your mission for a while, and they tell stories of their own. Thank you, Huntress. For all you have given me –"

I looked at him incredulously. "I have given you nothing, except danger and puzzles and disappointment at the end. I will leave you now and see if I can catch the trail of this Jack again, though I suspect he is long gone and it will take me years. I wish I could pay you for your help."

He laughed. "A man who walks and kills unseen. Vile creatures underground that catch and tear. The accelerator. Minds with vast knowledge and no compassion that plan the utter destruction of all that is not them. Experiments that fail because the experimenter is unworthy. Paths that most never see. Oh Huntress, you have paid me in full…"

We went our ways and I never saw him again.

He called after me. "And last, Atlantis, Huntress. Great birds that fought and tore"…

# Three Sisters

## London 2003

One of the best things about being a goddess, it turned out, was that human food tasted as good as it used to when you were a child.

"I could go on eating these all day." Emma had just eaten a smoked salmon and cream cheese platzel followed by a straightforward bagel with salt beef and french mustard. "And I would only stop being hungry if I wanted to."

"Well, great. I imagine that with hell-flesh, I still have to watch my weight. Hardly be hellish otherwise."

Caroline dabbed a smear of cream cheese off her chin and started looking in a hand mirror to check that her lipstick was still in place. She was utterly gorgeous, Emma thought, but I do get that now she can't fix her slap with a single thought, she is feeling a little insecure, poor love.

"Will that be all?" The goblin woman was clearly not about to be impressed—she'd known Emma for years and always been vaguely surly except when saving her from elves—and apparently being a goddess didn't get you any special favours in her book.

It wasn't as if there were tables or anything—as always, you ate at a shelf round the front end of the shop, that was just enough to hold your tea, if you were drinking tea—and the place was hardly full. The queue didn't even stretch back to the kitchen.

The goblin woman was making a territorial point, which was fair enough, Emma supposed.

"I gather this is the dead girlfriend. There's people as dislike the stink of hell-flesh, but me, I can take it or leave it alone. Just so you know. Anyone complains, they're out."

"That's nice," Caroline twinkled at the goblin woman, who narrowed her eyes slightly in the universal sign of not being especially impressed.

Emma smiled sweetly. It's important not to go around expecting to be worshipped all the time, or even getting basic respect. Good service you should get anyway...

The goblin woman wiped the rest of the shelf with a bit of absorbent towel that instantly went dark brown from the memory of spilt teas. "So, saw that the dryads moved in. Not complaining. They buy cheesecake sometimes, and giggle a lot. They haven't change much in two centuries." Then, with genuine curiosity, "Isn't it all a bit crowded?"

"They brought their own bonsai trees," Emma explained. "Half the time we hardly know they're there."

The goblin woman was still wiping the shelf. It was almost clean. She clearly wanted to ask something, probably about how Emma was suddenly a goddess and what she was now goddess of, probably.

Emma decided there had been too many questions and too many dark hints that tolerance was being exercised in the face of provocation, and she had something she needed to ask.

"I gather the Huntress is going to look in. If she has a standard order, you might want to get it ready."

156

"Bagel with cream cheese and two thin slices of cucumber. As anyone who knows her would know."

"I only met her the once. We're not intimate. But you might want to get her order ready nonetheless."

The goblin woman looked sceptical.

"It's all right," Caroline explained. "There's this time-travelling alchemical suit of armour version of me which told us she'll be here shortly and said that's what she has."

This didn't help, especially when the next person to enter the shop was a small dapper man with a goatee and annoyingly tight shorts. He had left a very expensive looking bicycle up against the window—he did not seem to have locked it, but Emma noticed that he had placed some sort of minor cantrip which seemed likely to deter all but the most gifted and obstinate thief.

In previous years, Emma would have felt the need to extend some degree of professional courtesy, but in her new circumstances that would probably seem patronizing, all 'Look how far I've come compared to you'; so she contented herself with a subtle nod, which he seemed not to notice at all.

He was looking in horror at the big steaming piece of salt beef that was just being put on the wooden cutting board at the far end of the counter. "What's that?" His voice was that of one who knows perfectly well what he is looking at but wants to make a rhetorical point.

"It's a nice hot fatty piece of salt beef. Like every other time you ask." The goblin woman was clearly already bored with talking to him. "It'll go nice down with a platzel and some mustard. If you want some. Which you don't."

He shook his head in a disgust that was clearly genuine, as well as theatrical.

"You'll be wanting your usual, then." The goblin woman pulled six bagels down from the rack and bagged them.

The man paid.

"Anything else?" She clearly knew that there wouldn't be.

157

"They're the only thing you sell that an ethical person could eat." He stalked out of the shop, rather ostentatiously averting his gaze from the beef and from the half-eaten smoked salmon and cream cheese bagel that Caroline was clutching.

Disapproval was his art, the way that woman in the Plath poem had suicide as hers.

The goblin woman sighed. "Oh well, that's him bin and gone for the day."

"He does that every day?" Emma asked.

"Him or one of the others. At least there was only one of them today. Sometimes they all come in and they all glower at what everyone else is eating. They have an office on Bethnal Green Road. Sometimes they go into the Bangla cafes round here, sit down, order the veggie dishes and then complain that they've got dairy in them. And walk out. Without paying. At least they pay me."

She sounded weirdly diffident. Emma could not imagine a world anywhere in which anyone would dare to try and cheat her, but people's self-image is not always what you think it is.

Caroline looked intrigued. "You say they have an office. What do they actually do? Apart from prat around being the righteous scourges of the local catering trade."

The goblin woman shrugged. "Who knows what humans do? People used to wander in talking about start-ups and dot coms and then that stopped a couple of years ago, mostly. And now it's all NGOs, whatever they are."

Caroline smirked. "Good people who like telling less good people what they ought to be doing or not doing. Which a lot of the time is a very good thing. Emma does it all the time."

Emma shuddered. "Please tell me if I ever start patronizing people, though, dearest. I mean, being Head of the Dread Tribunal of the Region Formerly Known as Hell must not be good for my tendency to self-righteousness—you would tell me, wouldn't you?"

The goblin woman pricked up her slightly pointed ears. "So that's what's going on…No one tells us about these things."

Caroline rushed to explain. "You know how when you're a bit self-centred, everyone tells you that it's not all about you. Well, of course that's sort of true…But well, half the angels in heaven destroyed, Lucifer and his Dukes overthrown, the Gods and Titans released from the Pit, Hell under new management—actually that was about me. Lucifer abducted me to piss Emma off, and, as he learned, pissing my girlfriend off is never a good idea. And then we discover we're avatars of the Huntress' sisters."

Then all three of them realized that they were not alone—the small leather-clad woman Emma had met the night of Caroline's death had silently entered, not through the door. Her face was unreadable.

The goblin acknowledged her with a nod and passed her the cucumber and cream-cheese bagel she'd made during Caroline's rant, which the woman ate slowly in silence.

No one felt like saying anything.

"We met," Emma said, eventually.

The small dark woman nodded; she didn't reply because her mouth was full.

Nothing was said for a while. She seemed to spend an awfully long time chewing each morsel.

At last, Caroline couldn't shut up any longer. "We haven't met. I got eaten before you got there. Hi."

The woman remained stony-faced for a moment, then laughed, and suddenly looked amazingly young. "So you two have messed things up for Star. That's the best news I've heard in a very long time."

Emma asked, "I thought all of you elder beings were sort of friends?"

"It's been a long time since Star and I were friends. He's needed a kicking for at least two thousand years. I've been too soft on him, and so have Nameless and the Son. Not that they don't need kickings of their own." She pulled a face when she mentioned Judas.

Emma rushed in. "I think you'll find Judas has started to get over himself, finally. He seems to have packed in his old job for one thing; he's been building things for me, and Asareth. In Hell. We must find something else to call it now."

The small dark woman looked at Emma very closely, and sniffed. "I remember you now. You didn't use to be a goddess. And your hair wasn't that annoying shade of scarlet." Her voice was disapproving.

"It sort of happened." Emma thought she ought to explain. "I didn't plan it or anything. You must know how it is."

"I wouldn't know," the woman answered. "I've never been a goddess."

Emma, Caroline and the goblin woman looked at her as stony-faced as she had been earlier.

Then Caroline giggled. "If you say not..."

"And there's a lot of things I need to tell you." Emma realized that it would be unforgivable not to update Mara about her sisters. "Sof is back in the flesh and has gone off to help Alexander explore shadow and look for Dark Alchemy; Lillit is some sort of time-travelling alchemical being made of living metal."

Mara looked stunned for a moment, and then had the look of someone to whom a long unsolved mystery had suddenly made sense. "You mean, the Quintessence. That was Lillit?"

There were going to be things it was even harder to tell her, Emma realized.

The goblin woman had already turned back to help serve some other customers who had turned up and patiently queued while the other serving woman took up the slack. From time to time, she glanced across disapprovingly but her customers didn't seem to be paying much attention to the conversation.

"Sof says that part of what happened was some vast amoral scheme of Lillit's. She needed to be the Quintessence...Part of her—part of her apparently became Caroline here, though Caroline never knew that until now. Just as I only recently discovered that I am Sof, sort of—well, the version without all her memories."

Mara snorted. "They're my sister-lovers. I think I'd know if you were them."

160

Emma shrugged. "Well, apparently not, because anyway I found Sof asleep in the back of my mind and she ended up getting put back in the flesh and gallivanting off with the Conqueror. That's just how it seems to be."

Mara sniffed disapprovingly, unconvinced, and then her face screwed up and she almost sneezed. "I'd have noticed before if you two hadn't been babbling at me."

She really was the most impatient woman, Emma thought.

"Who's been here? I know that smell."

"Obviously lots of people," the goblin woman said. "I have a lot of customers. I'd have a lot more if you bloody goddesses didn't keep hanging round after you've finished your meals having complicated domestic arguments."

"I'm not a goddess." Mara was still sniffing.

"Neither am I." Caroline was not going to be left out.

"Well, sweetie, that seems to be something that remains to be seen."

Mara went on sniffing, and then, with an air of reluctance, reached into the wallet that dangled from her belt and produced a small hunting-horn, which she blew.

Suddenly the street outside was full of dogs, or looked that way—a couple of beagles bounded into the shop and started eyeing the salt beef and a small terrier licked Mara's hand.

"Here," the goblin woman snapped, "take them outside and take the ones outside somewhere else. Health and Safety –"

Mara looked abashed. "Sorry." This was obviously a word she was not used to saying. "I only just inherited them. I'm not used to them." She looked at the beagles and they snuck outside. Then with a slightly embarrassed air she looked down at the terrier, which was snuffling round the floor excitedly as if it had found a scent it knew. "Lead us, boy. Show us the way."

The terrier bounded outside and the other dogs formed up behind it—there were fewer than Emma had at first thought. Then she looked again—there were about ten actual dogs but far more ghosts of dogs; she'd seen the Wild Hunt and this was different, healthier, but somehow a bit like…

Mara walked outside and started to follow the terrier as it sniffed its way down the street. "You two coming, or what?" she called behind her.

***

Yes, well, my dogs. As they now were.

They were my inheritance, that I had not expected. My responsibility after giving their master Cernunnos the mercy stroke.

Sometimes, if they ask it, I come to old gods as a mercy, when they have outlived their time and the blood of worship grows thin, and they feel the cold when their season changes to winter. Not often, because I do not wish to acquire the habit of taking the power that comes with their deaths.

I will take a gift freely given; I will exchange a boon for a favour; I will let them pay me the headsman's fee.

It was not thus with Cernunnos, precisely. It was the execution of a sentence long deferred.

He had kept his word to me. For what that was worth. He had no longer practiced the Rituals but I had had constantly to check that. But all through the great forests that were later to be France and Burgundy the Lost, High Germany and the lands of the Slavs, he was worshipped and his worshippers bound their captives, his prey, in great wicker baskets in his image. Sometimes they burned those captives in his honour and sometimes they released them for him to hunt and catch and give living to be devoured by his pack. Alive, without a mercy stroke first. It is hard to say which was the more terrible end.

He had nothing to do with those killings, but he benefited from them, at least somewhat. The Rituals raise magic, which has to go somewhere, and worship is worship. The wild magic forced itself on him, and also on some of his priests who became imitations of their god, for a while.

He and I sometimes had to hunt those priests together. I because

162

it is my job, he out of a mixture of wounded pride and determination to keep the implications of his oaths to me.

There were trails then that wound in an endless labyrinth from sea to sea, from the Rhone to the Danube, paths that were knotted like the briars among the trees and the grass underneath them. The counterparts of those woods in shadow were vaster and more thick. I had learned my trade in forests of pine and cedar; his lands were full of oaks and elms and thick briars.

Between us we tracked down those priests turned murderous demi-gods and punished them. We were not friends but there was a sort of comradeship between us down the years. He had helped me once in my desperate need, without thought of bargaining, and had not asked to be spared. I had taken his love from him, and condemned him to live in grief that pained him still.

Two great beasts had pursued me from the dark heart of the forest that ran from the Black Sea to the Northern Shore as far as the land to the island that was not yet Britain, and the lands that surrounded it then, but are now sunk beneath the waves; the Lion and the Unicorn haunt the memory of that land still, though few now living there are descended from those who survived their passage through it. I say, great beasts, but these are not like the Snake I slew once in the hills above Mycenae with the two boys that were friends then, but became the satyr Marsyas and the god Apollo, and whose tale ended badly or the Leviathan that swims in the seas of Shadow. Nor were they like the Bird, that wise evil being.

These were—and are, for they are constantly reborn—creatures of fury and utter devastation that only somewhat resemble the beasts from which they take their names. They were also part of the dying curse of his wife on me for my pursuit of them both, along with fear and madness that came close to destroying me. And he had killed, for the moment, his love's creatures.

The Lion and the Unicorn leave nothing in their wake, and little was left in those lands that now lie beneath the sea, Dogger and Lyonesse. I could not, I think, have stopped them at all, or in time.

Much that came into the world in those lands would not have come in the landscape of dust, ashes and overturned stone that they would have left.

He slew them to save me and for the love of the land, even though they were part of the woman he loved, for whom he had become a monster.

Most hunters lie when they claim to love their prey, but Cernunnos was prepared to die—at their teeth and claws and horn, or at my hands afterwards if we survived—to save not only the beasts of park and clearing that he chased and devoured when it was not his season for manflesh, but the small beasts and fowl that scurry for safety into bracken and small burrows as the hunt thunders past and the land itself.

And after he had torn and shaken to dust a tawny corpse and an off-white one—I shook his new-blooded hand and took his promise not to kill men again and said that if he kept his promise, I would suspend his sentence until he asked me for the mercy stroke. He swore that he would hunt no more men and women or children, and content himself with the little lives of stags and hares and foxes and the like.

He was useful to me, and charming enough in his way.

It is possible, of course, that he hoped to lie with me, for he was a Master of that Hunt too, but if so, he was capable of greater subtlety and patience than I think the case. Though I do not think so—for her death lay between us.

I did not forgive him, either. But I knew that time would punish him and that he would need my knife at his throat by the end.

In time, the Romans came to the lands where he was most loved, and they had a distaste for human sacrifice, save for those they did themselves and lyingly called the old justice of Rome against parricides, traitors and enemies, or thought of as mere games to placate the mob. And he betook himself from their grasp to Britannia which they conquered late, and where men sometimes hunted their own kings in time of famine or murrain, and he took his share but no part in the hunt. He was welcome there, to the Lord that oversees it, for that he and I had helped the land, before it had a name or a Lord.

Slowly, without the meat that had made him a god, he dwindled there—still a god but a weak and minor one. He was not the man hunted for poaching in the reign of Fat Harry Tudor, though he came to that man where he hung on his oak and took his phantom as his henchman, for they were twin souls. By the time that phantom faded, or went elsewhere, many confused the two. And when worshippers confuse the name of their god, that god's name will in due course change. If he or she is unlucky, their nature will change slowly too...

He grew gently old. And his time had come.

Cernunnos who men mostly called Herne now had no more sincere worshippers—only rich men at their nasty pastime offering thin worship—and now the land's great Parliament had voted to end the hunt for good, and he felt himself fading. The Lords and the Commons were bickering about when it would be good and final law, that the Queen would sign at her desk in that ritual of ink and wax that is as powerful as blood.

It was his winter and he felt it in his bones and he chose not to wait, and called me to him to end him with a quick thrust, the mercy stroke he had given men and beasts. That we had jointly given to minor gods and to the fungus that Jack raised.

There is a square, a small green park, at the centre of which is a bad statue of that treacherous unMerry monarch of whom I spoke earlier, the stonework of which is as rotten as his memory ought to be. Even in the coldest of weather, people sit on the park's many benches or on its straw-like bruised grass—lovers often as not. Old men, or men who look old, take some of the benches; some of them to drink cheap wine or strong ale there because they have nowhere else to go, others to bask in what little winter sun there is, because at the end of days you take what solace you can get.

Cernunnos sat among them, the oldest and frailest of them,

165

sipping strong cider from a can as if one of them. They did not notice his great span of antlers or were too polite to mention them. Old men and in particular old drunk men have often learned tolerance from the bottom of the glass of their time.

The Lord of Cliffs and Shores was there, for, as I have said, he and Cernunnos had had their own dealings, and Herne the god had long been English for all that he attained his godhood elsewhere. The Lord brought Polly his servant with him, for she had a fondness for things that had guarded the land before she was born.

She walked over to me and hugged me, something she had only rarely done, and I let her, because I guessed that she had something she wished to whisper in my ear.

"When you've seen to the poor old dear, don't leave. I have things to impart, the which are to your advantage I am told, though you may not think so."

I nodded my thanks, then walked to where Cernunnos sat.

He looked up at my approach—his hearing and sense of smell were still as in his prime, but his eyes were white with blindness. No wonder he wished to die, for his keen sight had always been one of his proudest boasts.

"I can see my quarry twenty miles away and the wrong side of a hill," he would say.

Now he peered with those dead eyes—he may have been able to see light and shade still and perhaps it was just that I stood between him and the winter sun.

"Huntress?" His voice, that had been almost as much a horn-call as his great hunting horn itself, was uncertain and quavery and that broke my heart.

"Hunter."

"My hunt is over." His voice was clearer now, and more decisive. "I will not serve rich evil men for whom the hunt is a whimsical pastime that takes place in fields and forests for which they have no care. Fields and forests that they are sacrificing to the heat of their greed and the smoke of their refusal to see where that greed leads.

There will be no hunts when the world is dead, Huntress, neither my hunt, nor yours. I choose not to see the end."

There are many advantages to choosing not to plan or to foresee, and worry about the future has always, for me, been one of them. Nonetheless, I have seen visions of ends, and have talked to learned men; I know that the end will come. Sooner or later.

"If there is an end, I will persevere. I have a task to perform which will be needful"—I touched the hilt of my sword of that name—"until that end. Whatever fire comes, or smoke fills the air, I shall endure."

Further, of course, though I did not wish to trouble the old god, I have always thought that the end, when it came, would somehow come through the adversary, the lord of smoke and mirrors, that creature who had tricked and evaded me for so many centuries.

I did not know then, what I know now.

I hoped—I hope still—if not to save the world, at least to avenge it dead.

That was for another day and I had business here. I cast a glamour over all present save Polly and the Lord. And I drew my long sword.

"You are sure, then, Lord of the Hunt."

"I am sure, Huntress. The mercy stroke, if you pl –"

The sword was through his neck even as he spoke and I caught his head by the antlers as it fell. I would not let it fall to the ground. Even when they are not as close to being my friends as he had sometimes been, I owe the dead respect. Once I have killed them.

Once he was dead, the Lord his friend took what was left of him away, and left me alone with Polly. She was weeping a little. Something very old had died this day. I wished I could weep with her, but I shed my last tears long ago. I hope.

Polly wiped her eye, put her handkerchief back in her pocket and pulled out a small box. "He said I should give you this once you and he had finished your business." She passed me the box, which slid open the moment I touched it—it was a sort of reverse puzzle box where one panel slides inside another, one after the other, until there is no box left at all, save in some realm beyond shadow, and what was inside is in your hand as if it had always been there. It was a small perfect copy of Cernunnos' great horn; I knew without asking what its purpose was.

Polly smiled sardonically. "He said as how his pack needs a new master, or a new mistress—and it might find many worse than you and none better. You are, after all, the Huntress and it has always offended him that you have no pack—I said to him that you have something better, which is your friends living and dead, but he looked through me as if I had not spoken."

"He knew how little I like dogs; I am the Huntress and I –"

"I said as much to him. He stopped looking through me with those blind eyes, and laughed aloud. 'Not any more she doesn't. She is too precious to the world to be left to hunt alone...' Talking of which, I said I had a second thing to tell you..."

Polly pulled out an old-fashioned gentleman's watch—Victorian work so that I could be sure that she had not filched it in her days as queen of thieves, but who can say whether or not she keeps her hand in—and ostentatiously looked at it.

"Round about now, I think, you should go and get yourself a bagel. At the usual place. Go through shadow and you'll get there just about in time. There are people you need to meet. Get along with you and we will see each other later."

I took the urgency in her voice seriously—Polly jokes much of the time, and there was ironic whimsy in her voice as well, but I knew there was something up that she wished to show me, and not tell...

So I raced across London, faster than thought. And there in the bagel shop, with the goblin woman I had known for so many years, there were two women, who seemed familiar, but I could not place.

At first glance, they were ordinary enough—one had bright scarlet hair but I had learned to be used to that, except that this woman's was not dye but grew in that unnatural shade, I realized. Then I caught something further that I had missed from the breadcrumbs and mustard smear on her chin, that she dabbed when she saw me looking at her—she was a goddess, not merely in the sense that she was intoxicatingly beautiful to me in that moment, but in the sense that she was literally divine. Yet lacked the arrogance that usually goes with it—her companion had that and, no, was not Mundane either. She had the slight stink of hell-flesh on her, though mingled with something almost headily sweet.

Who were these women, and why had Polly sent me to talk to them?

I was sufficiently struck by them that at first I hardly registered the conversation they were having as I arrived, but then I listened more attentively, and got news I had never expected to hear.

Knowing that Sof had returned to the flesh and had not rushed to my side I felt like a blow; knowing that Lillit had somehow manipulated Sof's long agony to her profit was sickening. However necessary it had been.

I needed to talk to both of them, but for the moment I had work to do.

The one with scarlet hair looked up, and she smiled. She did seem familiar. They both did. There was a confident charm to the redhead—it reminded me of Berthe in 1912. But there was something else in the air. A different, earthy smell that I knew well.

*\*\*\**

Emma looked at Caroline, shrugged and followed Mara down the street.

Behind her, she heard Caroline saying, "Six large slices in a bag" and the rustle of money. A few seconds later, Caroline was trotting to catch up to her, clutching a very greasy brown-paper bag.

"I know they're super-special supernatural dogs of some kind, even the cute little one, but I bet they'll be all the happier if they get treats at some point. Since I'm the one without special super powers these days, I'd better start being the practical one who thinks of things like that. Makes a change…"

Suddenly she had a pair of Velmaish spectacles on.

169

"I don't think the pudding basin hair cut would suit me. Or the sweater—there are limits to what I'll wear for a joke, even if I can make it go away seconds later. Anyway, Scooby snacks!"

Emma wondered for a second how Caroline had picked up Josette's skill in quick changes to replace what she had had as a ghost, then reflected that, between a telepathic link to Josette and the strong hints that Lillit sometimes fed her avatar stuff, she really did not need to know.

The terrier started running hard and the dog-pack followed—Mara picked up their pace and, effortlessly, Emma and Caroline followed suit.

"Who exactly are we chasing?" Emma asked.

"I don't know," Mara answered. "Someone that smells of a fungus I met once. A while ago. It said it would be back, but I hoped it was gone for good. Someone that smells of it is probably bringing it back and if they're anything like the last one who tried...."

Emma thought of the obnoxious cyclist, and Caroline did too.

Caroline explained, "He's probably on a bicycle. Can the dogs follow him in traffic?"

But then the terrier stopped dead and ran back to them, yapping, and the other dogs started whining and shrank back too.

"Something's up. Back." Mara gestured and Emma stood in front of Caroline, who was the most vulnerable here, assuming that dogs that appear from nowhere when a horn is blown can probably take care of themselves.

Just ahead of them, on the other side of the street, with a decorous bang and surprisingly little flying glass, there was a gout of flame and smoke from a small office building made of red brick with obnoxious white plastic siding. Then it collapsed into a small pile of rubble leaving a space in the street into which the two adjacent buildings leaned slightly without at first starting to fall down.

Emma looked at her companions. "Caro, evacuate. Mara, rubble. I'll hold the buildings up."

She didn't know how she was going to do that, and then she did.

It wasn't that she grew to titanic size—it was that her strength and her reach were those of a giant without her growing. She stood on the pavement and she desired that the two buildings that might have collapsed did not, and they did not.

Up to now, she had not really quite got what it was to be a god. She had become one out of duty and she had already been a warrior of sorts—and all she had known since was war and duty, and coping with them. Oh, and building stuff, but the people around her were doing that. Creation as the result of peer pressure.

Now, she felt the need to do something, to save whoever was in those buildings, and she did it. Oh, and told Caro, and did I just give Mara an order, and did she just take it?

Caroline seemed to be able to move fast—she already had one building cleared but Emma kept on holding it up because—well, Mara could survive having bits of it fall on her but there might still be someone in the ruins. And she really was very good at moving big hunks of masonry with one hand while reaching under it, and sniffing all the time—oh that will be this thing she is looking for as much as humanitarianism.

Mara pulled out a body—the head was so badly smashed that there was no way it was a survivor. All Emma could be certain of was that it wasn't the man in cycle shorts unless he had not only had time to change into a snappy charcoal suit, now in rags, but put on a hundred pounds, two inches in height and at least thirty years. The corpse was a mess—his face was almost untouched except for a trickle of oddly dark blood from his nose, but his back was torn away so you could see bits of spine and shoulder-blade.

Emma thought hard, but she didn't seem to have the knack of bringing him back to life. She must ask Josette about that next time. Obviously I have my limits, she thought, which is a good thing but a nuisance in this particular instance when you need to ask the dead questions.

She looked around but his ghost had buggered off somewhere.

Caroline shouted "Clear" from where she stood, surrounded by the people she had evacuated and being chatted up by two cute boys and a very chic woman with dark glasses, in her mid thirties or perhaps a little more.

Mara stepped away from the rubble, shaking her head.

Holding the buildings up wasn't taking a painful amount of energy, but it also wasn't something that Emma wanted to be doing all day, so very gently she let go of the walls she had been holding up by force of will, and very gently they peeled away from the sides of their buildings. The noise they made was a delicate crump.

The rest of the buildings stayed up, for the moment—Emma wondered for a little whether she had been a drama queen, but then one floor in the left hand building crashed down on the one underneath it, and all the desks and chairs and book cases from the office that had suddenly become more open plan than before slid gently out and dropped onto the rubble Mara had stopped searching.

The woman with dark glasses walked over to her. Behind her, Caroline was mouthing something Emma did not quite make out, until the woman planted a kiss on her lips, took off the glasses and looked her straight in the eye. A few years older and she had had some very quiet work done, but she was still gorgeous and she was still Elodie.

"Damn you, Emma," she said, half-joking, half-serious. "You turn up after years and save my life, again. Or was it just that taking office space just down the road from that scuzzy little flat of yours automatically puts a girl in danger? You're looking well, and super powers? And when did Caro come back from the dead? And who's the dark girl in leather? Another girlfriend? Didn't know you still liked them young?" Her voice had a slightly resentful catch in it now.

"She's seven thousand years old, Elodie. And she really isn't my girlfriend, not in this incarnation anyway."

"That's probably true but is not the most convincing excuse I've ever heard." Bitter was suiting her...

172

"So what are you doing with an office a few hundred yards from where I live?"

Elodie didn't even blush. "Girl's got to be somewhere. Office space is less expensive round here than in the West End and I moved here some while back, when it was really cheap, and got a good deal."

Emma realized that they were so out of touch that she didn't even know what Elodie did these days.

"The thing about a failed Hollywood career—and almost every woman's career in Hollywood ends up a bit of a failure—is that it still counts for something back here. And the contacts, darling...." She narrowed her eyes a little. "If I'd wanted to see you, I knew where you live. As it was, I have secretaries to send over for bagels."

This was getting uncomfortable, and Mara was looking impatient. The dogs were not looking especially comfortable either—Elodie hadn't been a vampire for decades, but dogs don't forgive these things.

Elodie turned to Caroline. "So anyway, thanks for the heads up. Insurance will cover the office. I'm assuming that it wasn't you three that blew up next door..."

"Nothing to do with us."

Oh well, Emma thought, at least Elodie isn't being snarky at Caro. I didn't know she was so pissed off at me.

Mara wandered over and put an arm on Emma's shoulders.

"They get older, most of them. Not just lovers, friends—and they resent it when they see you the same, or in your case better, after years. And this one used to be your lover? That never goes well, even if you're both immortals."

She was talking too loud, in the circumstances—Elodie obviously heard.

"And you'd be?"

"The Huntress." Mara put on a stern face.

"Oh!" Elodie was genuinely interested. "You know there's a treatment going the rounds about you. It's not very good, but girl power is in."

"Oh god," Emma moaned. "Discourage that even if you have to threaten people. Elodie here was in this awful rom-com back in '96, playing sort of Caroline. Cameron Diaz played me. It was embarrassing." She realized that even as a goddess, she could still blush with the memory.

"I almost got a nod for Best Supporting." It had been one of the few high points of Elodie's career, even if it was a terrible and insulting film, Emma realized.

Someone tapped Emma on the shoulder and spoke low in her ear. He had an unpleasant and insinuating voice. "We need to speak to you, Miss Jones."

He flashed a warrant card at her rather too fast for her to catch his name. He was accompanied by a number of policemen with inscrutable expressions, flak jackets and very large guns. His expression was unreadable but it was clear that he wasn't feeling especially benevolent towards her.

"Inspector?"

Emma had no idea of his rank, but she thought it a good guess. Better err on the side of caution and politeness. She was invulnerable these days and so was Mara, and probably the dogs, but Caro wasn't and there were all these civilians.

Thinking of the dogs, and local bylaws, she created collars and leashes for them. The leashes were variously in her hand and Mara's and Caroline's. She really should have done that earlier, but she had other things on her mind.

She really hadn't meant to tangle up the ankles of the police officers with them, but it would have been quite a good idea if she had.

"That's Superintendent...You're regarded as sufficiently important that they ferreted me out of a meeting to come and talk to you, even before that building blew up; you've been flagged rather a lot in the last few days. And here you are at the site of an explosion in the company of yet another IC6, like the man who beat up a couple of our informants down the road a few nights ago."

174

"He was just being gallant..." Emma thought it better not to mention that Jehovah had tried to poison her a few minutes later. Interesting that the racist skinheads were police contacts. Just how long had the police been watching her?

"And then there's Reverend Green. Has a row with you in a television studio reception room and then he disappears and is never seen again. Then you show up on Eurostar with yet another IC6, and someone from the Spook squad, and—it says here—a man in a crocodile suit...People waving guns around and swords—and you tell the punters it's a movie shoot, but we checked. It wasn't. It all looks very suspicious, Miss Jones—I think you ought to come with me to Paddington Green so we can talk about it."

She didn't have to do anything of the kind of course. On the whole, though, the price of having a civilian identity was that she had to at least pretend that human laws applied to her still.

Still...

"As to Reverend Green, that's all being dealt with at the very highest of levels. Perhaps you didn't get the memo? Above your clearance, perhaps?"

That clearly stung, which possibly wasn't the best idea she had ever had.

"Don't be absurd, officer," Elodie butted in. "She and her friends were clearly out walking their dogs and when the building blew up did what any concerned citizen would do. They cleared the endangered buildings and searched the rubble and—well, held up the other buildings somehow until they'd been cleared. I certainly don't know how she did that, but Miss Jones has powers or something. In real life, not in that stupid film about her..."

Several of the police lowered their guns; one of them actually put the safety on, tucked it under his arm and felt in his flak jacket for a pen and a notebook. Her career might have faded, but Elodie was still in the being asked for her autograph level of celebrity.

She caught Emma looking impressed. "I did 'I'm a celebrity, get me out of here' two years ago," she explained. "After living on puked up blood most of my adolescence, spiders and cockroaches hold few terrors."

Emma realised that something peculiar was going on. "Where were emergency services?" she asked.

"This idiot decided that you were dangerous, and with civilians on site he didn't want anyone else put at risk." Tom had arrived as silently as ever. "I outrank you. Go away. And stop harassing the people I work with. You're out of your depth, sunshine."

Tom clearly didn't have even to show his warrant card—the armed police all tucked their guns away and looked vaguely guilty.

"Yes, so you should. Miss Jones is essential to the security of the state. Oh, and congratulations on the promotion, darling. Hi Caroline, you're looking well. And you, Elodie, And who's your friend? Not –?" He suddenly looked very impressed indeed. "It's the Huntress, isn't it?" He wheeled himself up to Mara and looked up at her adoringly." Gosh. I love your work."

Emma supposed that in the world of international sort of super-powered assassins, people would be all fannish about the woman who had been doing it since the Bronze Age.

"Who's he?" Mara asked. "And how did he get here? Not through shadow, because I would have noticed."

Emma really did not want to explain Tom's back-story to the Huntress, any more than she had Elodie's.

"I don't do magic," Tom explained. "You'd think I would, given I used to be an elf, when there were elves, but apparently I'm a mutant. Or something like that." Which was succinct and to the point.

"He works with Polly. But not for her, if you see what I mean."

Mara looked knowing and unhappy. "You mean he does her dirty work and they convince each other it's all for the best. I'm not sure I like being admired by him; I kill for my own reasons and he does it because someone points him like a gun."

Tom looked a little crestfallen, but only a little. "So, have any of you actual police bothered to start identifying the stiff?" He pointed at the corpse in the suit.

176

"He doesn't look like anyone who's normally in those offices." Elodie had wandered over and was as insouciant about the presence of death as one would expect from the formerly supposedly undead. "They're all natty goatees and very short cycle shorts and perpetually disapproving expressions. When they moved in, I sent them a box of cupcakes to be sociable and one of them came and sat on my desk and lectured me about the e-numbers in the frosting." She paused, remembering. "She said they were called Planetary Voice or World Save or something like that. I don't think she meant by that the sort of thing you all do. They're environmentalists, which is nice, but I got the impression that they were the prattish kind..."

Caroline joined her. "Oh look, Emma. It's that famous logical positivist whose name I temporarily forget. Wotsit, Professor Braithwaite. He writes in the Times about how believing in magic is a really bad thing and when he says magic, he means everything from the cards to theology; he's someone else the good Superintendent is probably going to think you killed."

Emma gave her a loving glare, then looked at the dead face again. She riffled the files in the central office of her memory palace. "I remember him—when he was younger he used to hang round Browning. So, maybe not actually evil, but capable of being duped. I wonder what he was doing in someone else's office."

Tom gave her a pitying look. He is a professional after all, and is entitled, she thought. "In all probability, he was there to try and blow the place up. The simplest explanations are always the best. He probably dropped the bomb, realized it was likely to go off, and tried to run. Most of the damage is to his back, which means he was running away from it, which means he knew it was going to explode which probably means he brought it there."

Mara looked at him a little less disapprovingly—professional to professional.

"But why is he the only body?" Emma asked, Socratically, because she thought she knew but wanted to hear the expert say it.

"Presumably because they knew he was coming, knew what he intended and had all left."

Tom wandered over, looked at the rubble very hard, reached into it and pulled out a length of wire. "In fact, they left a tripwire for him so that he would blow himself up…"

The superintendent looked both impressed and baffled. "If I didn't know, I'd think you genuinely just found that there. Best bit of evidence dropping I've ever seen, not that I'd ever participate in such a thing myself you understand…"

Emma stage whispered at him. "Actually, he really did just find it—don't be sceptical about his Sight. He gets sensitive. And you really wouldn't want that."

Caro knew that they needed to keep the questions going rather than get stuck when they got one or two of the answers. "So we're talking some sort of war between environmentalists and philosophers? What's that about?"

"It's probably to do with the fact that the man whom I was following smelled of primordial intelligent fungus," Mara explained. "I know the smell and the terrier knows the smell—we were there last time someone thought it would be a good idea to bring it back."

"What would that have to do with saving the world?"

Emma could actually think of several answers and none of them were all that comfortable.

"So that's all been blown up, right?" Caroline's tone of voice conveyed that she wasn't expecting any kind of good news.

"No smell of it in the rubble. And it's not that easy to kill—I'd know. I killed it once already. Besides, we were following the cyclist, and his bagels. If he knew they weren't going to be in the building, he'd have taken their snack somewhere else. So I should probably start the dogs tracking him again."

She looked down at the terrier with poorly disguised loathing. It got that she was paying it attention and started wagging its tail happily.

Caroline reached into the bag of meat she had somehow kept safe while evacuating people, and tossed a corner of a slice of beef to the

178

dog. It leaped up and swallowed it, but did not stop gazing adoringly at Mara. Caro distributed the beef among the other dogs, who fell to it happily; a couple of the larger ones licked her hand with big greasy tongues once they were done.

Emma felt rather left out—then reflected that it was a bit greedy of her given that she had the worship of most of Hell.

Elodie pecked her on the cheek. "Must fly, sweetie. I need to take my staff round to the flat and do a whole bunch of things, including find a new office building. Toodles."

She strutted down the street and her decorative minions followed her.

With increasing vehemence each time she did it, Mara pointed in the general direction they had been heading before the building blew up, and the terrier instantly started looking like a very depressed dog indeed. Clearly the explosion had made it lose the scent, which Emma supposed, was only to be expected.

Emma was quite surprised to see the superintendent still hanging around now they'd been ignoring him for some minutes. Most of his men seemed to have gone away, except for one that had gone into a cafe and come out with a Flat White and a croissant only to find everyone had left.

The Superintendent had clearly been paying attention to their conversation. "So," he said, "let's get this right. You lot all have ESP or superpowers or something, but you have to chase around just asking questions. How does that work then?"

Tom smiled at him with the air of someone who had been pleasantly surprised by a small child's insights. "As you may have noticed, I sort of teleport. But I can't go somewhere without knowing where I am going—doesn't work like that, which is why I'm not embedded in a wall somewhere. Same with the girls here; they can do all sorts of cool stuff, but it takes legwork to know who you're going to do it to."

"All for the best," Caro added. "You may think my girlfriend is insufferable now, but imagine what she'd be like if she just knew stuff the moment she thought of wanting to know it, rather than having to find it out."

Emma decided not to say anything about who among the three of them were the insufferable ones.

"Lucky for us that these days, doing legwork mostly means sitting at home sipping coffee and checking things out on the Internet."

Mara suddenly looked—and it was an oddly touching look on her—abashed.

"I've been meaning to ask. Everyone keeps mentioning it but I am a very old person and I don't always understand these things. What is the Internet?"

***

So, it turned out that the one who thought she might be part of Lillit was far better at explaining things than the one who thought she was sort of Sof and was definitely Berthe.

After she explained for several minutes, I decided that I understood as much as I needed to of what the Internet was; it was the Museion reborn, only with a slightly better catalogue and not tied down to any one place where it could be burned.

This struck me as one of the better ideas the human race had had for a long time and I really did not need to understand exactly how it worked, because neither they not their friend Tom seemed as sure as they pretended to be.

Their flat was full of shelves and tables, all of them piled high with things—yet somehow there was a small neat space just as broad as his chair into which he had slotted very neatly when he arrived with a slight displacement of air.

I told them, "It's all right. I think I get it now. You can stop. It's not like I can imagine ever trying to use it myself. I see it's probably important. But once I nearly killed a theatre full of people by not understanding pneumatic messenger tubes and for a while everyone had them and then they mostly went away."

Tom looked blank as did the Lillit woman—Caroline.

The Sof one—Emma—looked haughtily at them.

"You can tell which of us actually goes shopping. They have them in some supermarkets still to get the money around. Sometime you must tell me about the theatre—times when you nearly got everybody killed, but didn't are the best and oh, I remember now. Gosh, first night of the Sacre…"

The other two looked blankly at her. Again.

"Oh, I was Berthe too—actually I still am. More or less. We amalgamated—which I couldn't with Sof because we are quite different, mostly."

"I already knew that. Her, I recognized in you almost at once. Even with different hair and no tuxedo."

I could swallow that this woman was Berthe, because yes, she had the same air of competence and I wished I'd not been asleep when Berthe got killed and she died young.

"I, she, wrote an opera. It had you in it, sort of. Lots of stuff about the Enemy, Berin, Browning…"

Caroline looked slightly bored. "Any moment now, Emma's going to tell you how she met him and hit him wham in the balls and got away with it. Actually, he taught her for years after he got me killed and she never noticed a thing at the time. Nor did I—hours of bloody tutorials and we never guessed until we looked at Berthe's list."

I was moderately impressed. After all, I'd only encountered him once or twice myself in seven thousand years and that had mostly taken the form of his explaining to me how he had just outwitted me.

"When I saved you from that ogre? Which had presumably just eaten you?"—I turned to each of them in turn—   "He was there? In the room?"

The fact that he had not even bothered to mock me upset me quite a lot.

I save many, but I cannot save them all, and the source of much that is worst in the world treats me with contempt as if I were irrelevant.

Emma and Caroline walked over to me and wrapped their arms around me.

"Someone needs a hug."

I hadn't realized until this moment how tall they were and how spindly their arms and legs. They towered over me and wrapped round me and...

I felt a wet nose on the back of my left knee. I had sent the pack away before we had come up to this over-cluttered apartment, but the terrier had simply not gone away when I blew the dismissal on the horn. He—I assumed the dog was male because of its awful persistence in the face of my making it clear I was not interested—had just trotted up the stairs behind us.

The man in the wheelchair had whisked away in a moment—I found it quite disturbing especially since I had no idea how he did it now I knew he wasn't going off into shadow like an ordinary person.

I am not a person whom people hug; it was especially disconcerting that these two women believed themselves to have some sort of relationship with me because of being avatars of my sister-lovers. It was especially disconcerting because they clearly thought of the relationship as familial in a more modern sense and not an erotic relationship at all.

I had given up explaining this to people some centuries earlier, because they think their arrangements are the only ones possible.

Suddenly the small apartment was even more crowded as well as cluttered.

"Oh look, it's the Huntress."

"She did show up."

"Just like the golden woman said."

"And look, she's got a doggie."

"I'm not going near it."

"Oh, but it's cute."

Aspara, or possible Eithne, bent down and started massaging the beast behind its left ear.

"I don't know how you can touch it. One made its mess all over my tree."

"Lots have, I'm sure. Don't be prissy about it."

182

Caroline broke from the hug and a second later so did Emma, which was something of a relief. Yet there was a part of me that didn't want it to be over—it had been a long time. Yes, I realized, somehow these were Sof and Lillit reborn however unlike them they seemed—they smelled the same even though they were pallid skinned and far too tall.

And, for the first time I could remember in this century, or possibly this millennium, I wept. Because I wept, I also blushed.

The worst of it was that it was in front of the dryads, but they did not say anything. Each of them reached out a hand and touched my shoulder and then they retreated into the miniature trees that sat on one of the many small tables.

I have never given them any great reason to be kind to me, and even now I did not know how to thank them.

Tom returned at this point, coughing to indicate that he had arrived. He managed to give the impression of not paying attention to any of this—he went off into a mood of abstraction, counting ammunition in his head or something.

He'd mentioned being a clairvoyant and had clearly been watching at a distance, which made his pretense of tact both redundant and irritating.

There was an awkward silence. Caroline reached into a box made of card and handed me several thicknesses of tissue paper, and, when I looked blankly at her, took it back and dabbed at my eyes with it until I got its purpose.

Emma walked into the small area with pots and pans, and filled a cylinder with water and then pressed a button on it so that a small light turned red. Soon it was humming and a little later steam came out of a hole in its top.

She put out four teacups and put sachets in them and then hot water from the cylinder.

"I don't think it's right to use godlike power to make cups of tea when I still have an electric kettle."

I approved of this woman, whether or not she was a part of Sof.

183

For a god, she seemed comparatively simple in her tastes and not especially obsessed with her own prestige. It also impressed me that she had a lover who was back from the dead—very few manage that trick and to do so from the Hell of Lucifer rather than from Hades—well, I didn't know anyone who had managed that before.

No wonder she had become a god.

I sipped the peppermint tea she had made while she and Caroline sat in front of the big glass screen and fiddled around with—oh, I got it—it was like a typewriter only flat and the letters appeared on the screen and not on papers. Mostly when I had seen those screens they had not been lit up and I had taken them for another entertainment device.

"So," Emma said after a while, "who's going to talk to the environmentalists and who's going to talk to the philosophers?"

I had very little idea of what an environmentalist might be, but I certainly did not want to talk to any philosophers.

I said so.

"I haven't liked a philosopher since Philo and even he was a follower of bloody Plato." Then I thought a little and said, "Does Marx count? I sat and watched him get drunk once. He was reasonably pleasant. For a philosopher."

Emma shook her head. "I don't think the philosophers are going to talk to me—I'm supposed to be a bad influence. You see, the way I've got away with being involved in the wonderful world of gods and demons is to pretend I do vaguely mystical things. Which are all a load of hooey, and they're quite right about that, but because what I actually do sometimes works, and all sorts of influential people kind of know that, philosophers—well, the sort of philosophers who write for the newspapers anyway, they see me as the principal source of a load of hooey. So if I go to see them, it will be all confrontation and no information."

She was clearly right, or at least was convinced and convincing. I pulled a sulky face to show that I was making a concession and hoped for one in return—since she was in so many ways Sof, it made sense to me that I could use the techniques that had served me well all those centuries ago, when we were little girls.

And I was right. She caught the way I was looking at her and nodded wearily. "You get to pick who goes with you, though."

It didn't need even a moment's thought. "I'll take your lover. She's clever and if she is Lillit, she's even more clever than I think. I can't imagine we need more than one fighter with the philosophers. Whereas if the other lot doing something with the fungus, your friend here's capacity to beat a rapid retreat is going to be needed."

I didn't know why I was so worried about the fungus—after all, setting fire to it had just been a mercy. It would have withered and died in any case. But the world had changed and—"Tell me." I might as well ask. "You know how it's possible to stop people getting smallpox, either by giving them it, or giving them cowpox…And how they give fields of wheat medicine from the sky…Is there some way of changing something that would otherwise just die of all the diseases there are, so it's stronger?"

They looked at me as if I were a little bit stupid, but I have become used to that down the centuries. It is always wiser to ask and be considered foolish than not ask, look wise for not asking and be death's fool at the end.

"Of course." Tom seemed to understand these things most confidently.

"When I met it last time, the fungus got sick and died. That might not be the case now."

"Oh, like Wells' Martians."

I was aware Herbert had written some books, but I had not read any of them. "Just so."

Since I had already made myself look a little stupid in their eyes, there was another thing I thought I ought to ask,

"Explain to me what an environmentalist is, exactly."

*\*\**

Actually, Emma did not think that was an especially silly question at all, the more she thought about it.

She had thought she knew—salt of the earth they were trying to save, and all that. Possibly slightly irritating personally, and inclined to the sort of vegetarianism that is all about explaining to people like her why she shouldn't eat that bacon sandwich. Good on the weather getting too hot and too wet and on crops that weren't real wheat any more…Maybe now she was a goddess, she ought to pay more attention to these things. But, gang warfare with philosophical terrorists, and the cultivation of some sort of fungus that clearly scared the Huntress. That wasn't what she gave the Friends of the Earth shop her used paperbacks for.

She had kissed Caroline goodbye and given Mara an awkward hug, and now she had to set her mind to business.

"So, Tom. Where are we going? Obnoxious man with a beard and shorts and a sports bike—smells of mushrooms—where was he going if not to the place that blew up?"

Tom thought for a moment then asked, "Can I use your landline? I may as well get Polly's people to look it up—they probably have all the data. If I were up to no good, somewhere around here, I would do what bank robbers and terrorists have always done. A lockup under a railway arch—lots of those round here and they mostly take cash and don't ask any questions. Just because these people are apparently some sort of high-minded plotter doesn't mean they're going to change a winning formula."

If he was talking to Polly, he probably didn't want to be overheard—not even by her and certainly not by the dryad house guests. She remembered the cone of silence from an old television show, and made it so.

Then she let herself relax for a moment—that seemed like the most sensible way to kill time.

Tom talked into the phone for a couple of minutes, waited and listened. Then he did that slightly disconcerting going blank around the eyes while he used his other sort of sight. Or Sight rather.

"Got it. Emma, take my hand. You probably won't be sick this time."

186

"I don't think I get travel-sick anymore. What with being a goddess."

"Suppose not."

It must be hard for him—he'd known her when she was just a fledgling celebrity fake magus—but then, she'd got used to his being a notorious international assassin, so he could just suck it up.

Emma took his hand, and this time it was simply a matter of stepping into another room. A rather scruffy reception area, as it happened, with a lot of posters on the wall of dead whales and dying sea lions and devastated forests with butterflies dancing in the foreground to provide a note of optimism. There was also a big sign that said Planetary Voice, so at least she had a name for these people.

A young woman with pink hair and some moderately becoming piercings was sitting at a desk that wasn't a spare door on a couple of trestles, but looked as if it would quite like to have been. It worked as a barrier, though, because this was not an open-plan office—the door behind her was solid looking wood and clearly led into another area entirely.

She had her eyes shut as if dozing, but opened them, slightly startled, when Emma coughed significantly.

"Where did you come from?" she stammered. "How did you –?"

Emma narrowed her eyes in what she meant to be a sinister manner. "You've come to Our attention." Imperiousness was the way to go.

The young woman looked awfully embarrassed. "I'm sorry; they made me a good offer. I won't do it again."

This wasn't how this discussion was meant to go; Emma hadn't expected to secure a confession this quickly just by giving a withering stare.

Tom, clearly more on top of this situation than Emma felt, broke in smoothly. "We're not from the secretarial agency. We're not checking up on you personally."

It had never occurred to Emma until this moment that temps worked for agencies and then took actual jobs behind the agency's back; it wasn't a sin anyone had confessed to her—which probably meant that it wasn't a sin anyone had ever been sent to Hell for, which was reassuring.

The pink-haired young woman breathed a sigh of relief. "That's all right then…They'd have threatened to sue me, that's what they said they do, and I'd probably have got the sack from here. They're awfully secretive here and when they hired me behind the agency's back, they made a lot of spy jokes, sort of 'We never heard of you' and 'we'd have to kill you'…Which was a bit uncomfortable, because they don't make many jokes, here."

She was looking at Tom in that sort of 'shame he's in a wheelchair but he's quite fit otherwise' sort of way that Emma had noticed him attracting before. And he was playing up to it.

"I used to temp, before I got a better job." He smiled at the receptionist in a 'things we share' way.

Yeah, Emma thought, before he became a teleporting mutant ninja assassin…But actually, it occurred to her, he probably isn't even making it up; after all, he has to have been doing something before elves started trying to throw him under trains.

"It's always weird being the outsider," he went on. "Like they can't be bothered to tell you what they're doing because you probably won't be there next week."

The pink-haired woman made clucks of agreement and so Tom went on. "You feel so stupid when they make private jokes that you're left out of because you started off as a temp and they're all clever people who show off."

This was all clearly working beautifully. Emma found herself being glad that this young woman was probably straight because she didn't think she would have been nearly as good at exchanging vague sexual charisma for information.

"I know, right?" the pink-haired woman said. "Take this lot—they don't make jokes, like I said, except they're always going on about this and that, weird stuff, and it's obviously meant to be funny, but I don't get the joke."

"What sort of thing?" Emma thought she should be the one to ask because otherwise this woman and Tom would just sit being gooey-eyed and never actually getting round to the interesting stuff. "I thought these people were just the Friends of the Earth or something."

The woman looked scornful. "They tell all these jokes about bubonic plague and Ebola and stuff. Like they were good things. Like they wanted people to die. They don't like people very much."

Emma looked at Tom and Tom looked at Emma.

"Makes a sort of sense," Emma said, thinking about the man who went out for bagels. After all, why bother being nice to shop-keepers and restaurant owners if... "If you kill everyone, well, you save the planet all right, don't you? You save it from, well, us."

The pink-haired woman looked alarmed and disgusted. She really must remember not to do the whole thinking aloud in front of civilians.

"Just who are you people?" the woman asked.

"We're the authorities." Tom was clearly trying to keep her from panicking and it equally clearly did not work, because the pink-haired woman picked up her bag from under the desk, stood up, collected her coat from a set of hangers on a rack by the door, and paused for a moment as if daring Emma and Tom to stop her.

In a defiant voice, she said, "Well I'm sure you've got it in hand. They know where to send my money."

Tom shrugged. "We'd hoped you could be of more help. But thank you anyway."

Emma walked over and shook her by the hand authoritatively. The young woman froze a second and then relaxed as Emma beamed reassuring thoughts at her. "You've been of great service."

Emma also summoned a quantity of small gold coins and magiced them into the woman's bag. She was pretty certain that they wouldn't turn into dead leaves later. After all, she'd just talked her into walking out of her job, and her suspicions might be wrong.

She'd rather be wrong.

Tom wheeled himself round to the other side of the desk. "That's convenient. The whole point of receptionists is to stop uninvited guests going past their desks into areas they are not supposed to see. But there isn't a receptionist here, is there? She'd left before we arrived. So we had better try to attract their attention."

Emma followed him to the other side of the desk and said, "Hello, is anyone there?" in the quietest voice she could manage, and then again only slightly louder.

Then she tried the door. It was locked and so she knocked on it twice.

Tom had been inspecting the appointments diary on the desk and shut it again, firmly. "Too much to hope there would be anything there."

He saw what Emma was doing and reached into his pocket.

Emma tried the handle again and thought hard at the lock until it responded to her will by disintegrating into its component parts, which flew gently and politely out of their setting into her outstretched hand. She placed them gently onto the desk. "We might need to put it back neatly later. I think I can make it reassemble itself if I ask it nicely."

Tom shook his head. "Only the other week you were having to be rescued and throwing up all over Polly's office. What happened to you? Well, I know. But it's amazing."

"It wasn't the other week for me. It was thousands of years ago, though I've wiped most of the details."

"Oh, OK. That's a thing?"

She pulled the door open and walked in; the room on the other side was empty, but then the man in cycle shorts came in from the door at the other end. Beyond it, there was a room full of vats and centrifuges and that sort of thing. He looked a little perturbed. As someone that obviously guilty might.

"You were in the bagel shop, having some sort of weird conversation about your role-playing game or your psychosis or something. Why are you here? Where's the receptionist?"

"She decided she didn't like working here. What with the plotting genocide bit."

Emma had always liked the way Tom cut to the chase. The man in cycle shorts looked even more perturbed. "What are you talking about? We're just a small NGO devoted to saving the planet."

Emma smiled. This bit was hers. "Actually, I've saved the planet at least once. I'm not convinced that you're up to the job. Your last office blew up—friends of mine were in the building next door. They're all right, but not because you took any precautions to ensure they were all right. I appreciate you were dealing with someone trying to kill you—but you seem to have been rather more keen on retaliating than looking after collateral damage."

Tom finally flashed his warrant card. "So, a friendly word. If you will get involved in private wars, keep them private, OK sunshine?"

And then he just had to do the Colombo bit.

"There's just one other thing, sir…"

He had the pregnant pause down pat. Emma supposed that he got to do it a lot, just before he shot people in the face.

"We'd like to talk to you about your shorts smelling of the primordial malevolent intelligent fungus you're trying to bioengineer. And what's that about?—I thought you disapproved of genetic modification."

The man in the cycle shorts laughed scornfully. "We are bringing back the lost brain of Gaia. And you people are in the way…"

From the room behind them there entered two young women with machine pistols. They had cycle shorts too, but rather more becoming ones.

*** 

"So, what passes for philosophy these days?" I asked, not really wanting to know. "And why would it lead scholars to try and plant explosives?"

I had never thought of Lillit as having an especially expressive face or as someone who constantly used her face, her hands and her posture for theatre. Somehow, in spite of that, Caroline was most like her when she was showing off—perhaps it wasn't her who had changed with the years, but me.

When I was young, what did I notice about my sister-lovers, except that I loved them and could occasionally manipulate them and had never thought of what it would be to be without them. And then perhaps to find them again…

This version of her was a clown, a clever clown who used clowning and masquerade as the visible manifestation of thought processes, the way her lover used sarcasm.

I felt like an intruder when they were together, even though they had made me welcome.

Sof and I had had our rhythms and our perpetual conversation. I found myself realizing what it must have been for intimate outsiders we had welcomed in, back in the old days. For Josh and for the Impostor—I blushed at what I might have done, unknowing, and in that moment I finally forgave Judas, in a way I had not when Emma had spoken of him fondly and said that he had cast his masquerade and service to Jehovah aside.

She hadn't explained to me how that had come about—there was something she wasn't telling me, that neither of them were telling me.

I had a feeling that they had a good reason for this, a confidence that they were respecting. Could it be that Josh had finally shown his hand in the game I suspected he had been playing in secret across the centuries?

It would be nice to see him again.

Caroline had been playing around at the keyboard and staring at the screen. Didn't it hurt her eyes when it flickered back and forth like that?

It seemed to take up all her attention for the next ten minutes. I was so bored that I stroked the dog behind the ears. It looked up at me with moist little eyes and the most abject fondness. It reminded me of why I have never much cared for dogs. Once you let something worship you, it could get to be a habit.

Eventually Caroline turned to me with the toothy smile of someone who has come to a realization.

"Not philosophers—I mean, he was, and quite a few of them are, but...There's scientists and a couple of abstract painters and a couple of politicians. They call themselves the Human League, which is the name of a band I used to quite like, when I was alive. Apparently, they get together and worry about stuff, things that might kill us all."

This sounded useful.

She caught my expression. "Not the sort of thing we deal with. Big rocks falling from the skies. Tiny machines that turn everything into soup. Artificial intelligence—things like this computer but that can actually think. I think they know about your fungus friend...I looked for our backless stiff and he's all over their letter-head—if he turned to blowing things up, perhaps they all have."

"So, people doing science they disapprove of?"

"And people who get in the way of things they like—I mean, the space programme never entirely stopped, even when the Soviet Union disappeared. So maybe that's not about going to Mars at all, just to watching for big rocks and –"

I'd never realized we had to worry about big rocks; Jefferson hadn't believed in them and I had assumed he knew what he was talking about.

We should certainly go and talk to these people. Maybe we could persuade them that the Rituals were just the sort of threat they were interested in...

I said so, but Caroline shook her head. "That really isn't going to work. Atheists and rationalists the lot of them. The moment we talk about Jehovah and what an utter dick he is, they'd stop listening. And magic—that would be worse."

I remembered Tom Paine. I could not imagine that a modern group would be as polite or considerate.

"I think we should go and offer our condolences." Caroline pulled a solemn face. "Gesture of respect at their loss of a much-loved colleague. We could take flowers. I went to one of his seminars once—really frustrating because I wanted to tell him how wrong he was and no-one could hear any of the really brilliant things I said. Normally Emma would come, and gain an entirely unfounded reputation for brilliance, but she was researching a possessed kestrel at the time."

That was a story I wanted to hear sometime—these two seem to have spent years tidying up small messy situations and learning their trade.

I'd had to deal with major situations pretty much from the start.

Caroline caught me looking unimpressed. "It was easy—we had this boss and she used to send us out on missions. Mostly they were things we could handle easily—sometimes they weren't but we coped anyway. Emma's always been amazingly good with people, even before she got to be a goddess."

"So this boss of yours?"

Caroline looked at once embarrassed and resolute. "You'll meet her in due course...In her own good time..."

It was clear that she was dying to tell me some piece of gossip that she equally clearly really was not going to explain to me. It was all very annoying, but I imagined they had their reasons—still, I could hazard a guess.

"So how is Hekkat—Morgan as she calls herself these days?"

"Very well, last time we bumped into her." Caroline laughed. "But no, she isn't our boss—guess again. She is, though, still utterly in love with you, in case you didn't know. She has this picture gallery."

This was further into my business than I wanted this version of Lillit prying, which I supposed indicated that I really shouldn't press them further about their mysterious boss.

"We'd better stop dawdling here," I said brusquely.

Caroline nodded agreement. "Their offices then."

She read off an address in Camden and I took her there, as quickly as possible, through shadow. The dog followed, at my heels. Apparently it could cross shadow under its own powers.

I'd assumed we would have to trick or bluster our way in, but a number of people were going through the front door of a rather elegant building and we simply followed. In the second hall-way a harassed woman with a clip-board was trying to get people to give her their names but most of them flashed a card out of their wallets at her and kept going, while a number ignored her altogether.

Caroline had two cards, and showed them, and smiled at the woman rather than ignoring her.

The woman looked down at the terrier. "I'm afraid you can't bring your companion animal in here. Not unless you were actually blind."

The dog faded out of mortal sight, though it was still there, being annoying. It yapped, arrogantly; I could have sworn it smirked at me. The woman with the clip-board looked around in confusion.

It was a surprisingly talented canine, I supposed, but this changed nothing.

Caroline looked at me with the trembling lip of someone who is finding the world too funny to talk about it.

Once we were through the doors of a large meeting hall with a lot of very old and expensive wood panelling, and glowering our way into good seats, I indicated how impressed I was at her forethought.

"I'd like to take credit for that, but actually resurrection in hell-flesh has apparently given me some skill at picking pockets—or maybe it's something the boss, or my other self, implanted in me… Or perhaps it's just a skill that goes with a poor moral character."

After a while, a harassed looking elderly gentleman arrived on a podium. "Lord Smith will give a short statement on behalf of the Human League about today's tragic events. He will take a few questions afterwards for ten minutes."

Another, rather more dignified man took his place. He sipped from a glass of water and then pulled a sheet of paper out of his jacket pocket.

"The Human League is shocked and appalled by the allegations made against our dear late colleague Professor Braithwaite. It is inconceivable to us—who have worked with him for many years to secure the safety of the human race—that he would have planned or executed an extreme act of terrorist violence. We are sure that there is a misunderstanding, or that he was coerced. We ask you to respect our grief for a fallen colleague and not question his integrity further."

Caroline whispered, "So, no opening attack on the other group. Look at his eyes; he's not a very good liar and he knew something might happen. He totally knows."

I looked round the room. Several people were already raising their hands, and a lot of them had the sarcastic inquisitorial look of officials and spies—even if they were pretending to be journalists. No one I recognized from Polly's offices.

There was also a young woman with pink hair and a couple of facial piercings—I'd seen her sneak in between the speakers. She raised her hand rather diffidently. Lord Smith smiled at her—a little lasciviously I thought—and nodded in her general direction.

If he had thought her a softer touch than the harder-faced men who surrounded her, he was mistaken.

"So, you and Braithwaite have both written about what you call Dark Greens, environmentalists that regard the human race as surplus to the planet's requirements. Do you think Planetary Voice is that sort of organization and do you think it poses a convincing threat to human existence?" Her voice had a crisp harshness that overlay something gentler and more rolling.

He chuckled. "Planetary Voice is a small, powerless group. A couple of its spokespersons sometimes use unfortunate rhetoric. No, I don't think they pose a credible threat to anyone's life or limb. The late Professor Braithwaite once suggested that the rhetoric they use might legitimate altogether more dangerous individuals."

"So he wanted to punish them to scare worse people?"

She really was not going to let this go.

Lord Smith went red in the face. "That's a monstrous suggestion. No more questions."

And suddenly the young woman with a clipboard started shooing people out of the meeting room. The pink-haired young woman was quietly smirking.

I glanced at Caroline and we pushed our way through the departing crowd to where the pink-haired woman was standing out in the street, obviously waiting for us, which was a cause for mild concern.

"Do you set out to make important people your enemies quite a lot?" Caroline smiled at the young woman. "Do you find it a useful way of finding things out?"

The young woman flashed a smile back. "People tell you an awful lot when they are telling you to shut up. Not usually with words."

She looked at Caroline quite intently as if she were trying to remember a face she had seen somewhere, and then she looked at me equally fiercely. As if by concentrating, she could see through the glamour I was wearing so as not to make my presence too obvious.

She bent over and patted the dog; it was still invisible to most of the people around us. Clearly she was either mad or psychic, or possibly both.

Then she looked back at Caroline and smiled to herself as if she had solved a problem. "I think we should go for coffee. My treat."

She really was a remarkable young woman.

"I have a lot of money, so it should definitely be my treat. Oddly enough, it was given to me by Emma Jones. What a coincidence that I should meet you two here. If one were a Fortean, or believed in conspiracies or the supernatural, one might even not think it a coincidence."

"What's a Fortean?" It seemed to be my day for asking questions, but then education is an ongoing process even after seven thousand years.

The pink-haired woman giggled.

"I meet someone who is probably one of the most powerful supernatural entities in the world and she doesn't know what a Fortean is. Bliss."

I had already noticed—it was one of the things which was gradually persuading me that Caroline was, as she claimed, in some sense my sister-lover Lillit—that Caroline liked putting people very slightly at a disadvantage. It was amusing to watch her very much not enjoying someone playing her at her own game.

She raised an eyebrow slightly. "Clearly you have the better of us." Her voice was shaved ice. "And you are?"

The pink-haired woman was, for some reason, anxious to enlighten us, and spoke in tones she clearly meant to be significant. "I am Dawn Blake."

I hadn't expected this to mean anything to me and it didn't. It meant nothing to Caroline either. But was clearly meant to.

Dawn narrowed her eyes. "My mother named me after my aunt."

This still didn't register with Caroline. "Sorry, doesn't ring a bell."

A couple of pink dots appeared on Dawn's cheeks, even brighter than her hair. "But you were at her funeral. Mind you, you were a ghost at the time. Mum pointed you out where you and that Emma Jones sat at the back." By now she was practically hissing.

I could see that Caroline had suddenly registered what was going on.

"Oh, Dawn Blake. Your aunt was Aurora Blake because Aurora is Latin for Dawn. We really do need that coffee."

I remembered a London where coffee had been a new thing, and you had to travel into the City to find it. And a London where you could find it rather more easily, and it was weak and tepid. I had been in London in the late 1950s where it came out of big hissing machines that no-one cleaned properly so that it was only slightly improved from Victoria's time.

Now, it seemed, there were coffee shops on every street corner and half-way down the street as well—from where we stood I could see four of them, two of them called Starbucks.

We walked into the nearest one; it smelled of sugar and cake, but also somewhat of moderately good coffee.

The dog stayed faded. At least it was a little less annoying if people couldn't see me with it.

The other two found themselves a table and sat down at it, glowering at each other. I went and, after looking at the menu, got three large Americanos, the least obnoxious thing they place served, hoping that left alone they would get things sorted out before I returned.

I don't carry money but for some reason people never ask me for any.

When I got back with the tray, they were still glowering.

"So, who do you think we are? And what's this stuff about her aunt?"

Dawn sniffed scornfully. "Well, you seem to be the Huntress, which is interesting because if you're real, then probably a lot of other things are."

"I might just be dressed as the Huntress."

"Nah, lot of power behind that glamour—took me ages to get past it. You're the real thing. She—well, there's the saw her when she was a ghost thing, but that's not why I recognized her so much because she was wearing a veil in the crem. There was that whole business with the internet—I wrote it up but it was just too weird for anyone to run the piece. Using the internet to break a powerful forget spell— don't think anyone's done that before." She laughed. "Getting a whole bunch of people to look for photos. So they wondered who the cutie in the background actually was. That's smart magic your friend Emma did for you; props even if she did kill my aunt."

Caroline winced. "That's really not what happened. We would have saved her if we had had a chance to. But the sort of thing she was trying to do never ends well—she was mostly gone before we got there, and eating people and getting eaten…"

It clearly was not a good memory.

Dawn did not look convinced, so I thought I had better add my weight to the conversation. "These things happen, with magic. So, you had some talent to begin with—goes in the family—and you wanted to find out. About this thing of ours. And maybe take a bit of vengeance?"

"I know my limits. Just a bit of the Sight, enough to help me find stuff out. With my aunt dead from meddling, it would hardly be bright for me to start playing around with actual magic would it? Kind of like having a drunk in the family and staying dry just in case." She shrugged a bit. "I always assumed that you and Emma Jones had been a bit hasty and that's why Aurora ended up dead. But if you say not...?"

She was looking at me rather than at Caroline, but I probably have a more trustworthy face. People fear me, if they are wise, but I can smile. So I did.

"So, Planetary Voice and the Human League?" Caroline asked. "They don't seem terribly your sort of thing."

"They're totally my sort of thing. Big rich organizations with a smiley face in public but some sort of dark secret doctrine. Lots to write about there. But I got interested in them for something else—they're part of my big magic drug story."

We looked at her, waiting for more; she was very good at the pregnant pause.

"There's this guy, Aurora used to date him. He may have been the father of her kid. Back in the day he was part of the whole Hoxton thing but none of the big dealers liked his work and his friends moved onwards and upwards. He wasn't very good, so no loss, but I'm biased because he done her wrong which may have been why...? Looking at her journals, well, he doesn't come out of that well. He was her dealer too; got her into stuff."

She had acquired from somewhere that habit of dying falls in her sentences that sound like a question but actually the question is always 'do you know about this important stuff or am I going to have to take time and tell you about it because I'd really rather not...?'

"So periodically I watch him. Thing about Sight is, you don't have to trail people?"

"We know." Caroline sounded a little testy. "Tom told us."

"He's that guy hangs out with Emma Jones?"

Caroline smiled a 'you may think you know stuff' smile.

I knew it well, but not on her.

"Top assassin."

"Cool," Dawn said in what attempted to be a bored voice. "So anyway, this guy's started selling this stuff again that he sold to Aurora years ago. I guess there was a duff few harvests or something—so anyway it's this black powder. Amazing expensive and I don't try stuff I don't know anything about? But he's been delivering it to both offices like it was milk for their tea."

I sat back in my chair—this was worse than I had imagined.

"Black powder, you say."

I hate to plan, but I really should have followed that up.

The dog gave an admonitory woof.

The man who had read the statement at the press conference—Lord Smith—came to our table and sat down.

"Miss Blake, and—I'm sorry, I don't know your names though I noticed you at the press conference... Anyway, I'd been looking for you to talk off the record, and I couldn't help hearing you mention some black powder. So clearly you are already ahead on the really interesting bit of the story... The thing we really don't want sullying Braithwaite's memory. But someone ought to know our side of it, just in case."

\*\*\*

Emma eyed the two young women appreciatively. If one is going to be menaced, it's nice for once to be menaced by someone cute. Then she remembered that she was a married woman, and a goddess, and she really should not be having objectifying thoughts like that.

It seemed that her subconscious had reacted to young women with guns by stopping time a little—maybe part of being divine is having a subconscious that does magic faster than you can think. How convenient. Or maybe it was some left over bit of her armour.

She walked over to the two young women—one had honey blonde hair elaborately moussed into peaks while the other had a black fringe that would have dropped into her eyes if she hadn't been wearing a sort of satin bandana—and removed the magazines from their guns, and, while she was at it, the bolo knife that the blonde wore strapped to her leg. Emma imagined that being able to attach easily reached weapons to your thighs was one of the plus points about shorts that well-cut.

While she was checking them for other weapons that might inconvenience Tom if he hung around and did not teleport out of there instantly the moment she turned time back on, she noticed that the woman with black hair had recently had a nosebleed. There were traces of something black crystallized in the fine dark brown residue just above her upper lip.

It was a kindness to wipe it off—also, a sample might be useful later—so Emma gently cleaned it off with a paper handkerchief she moistened with a small quantity of her divine spittle. Then she put the paper handkerchief in her pocket in one of the small plastic packets she kept about her for such purposes.

She walked over to where she had been standing before and tried to remember what her expression had been. Oh, yes, turned round slightly to face the oncoming menace but with her feet just so. No point in giving too much away when she started time again; apart from anything else it would be useful to know whether she was about to be threatened, taken hostage or shot out of hand as a possible enemy of the planet.

In the event, the two young women raised their guns as if to fire a warning salvo over Emma's head.

"Can we kill them?" shouted the blonde.

"Can we totally kill them?" shrieked the one with dark hair.

The effect was more or less ruined by the fact that both guns entirely failed to go off and their shouts were punctuated by the dull click of utter failure. Tom disappeared, and reappeared behind the two women—his hands now on his own weapons—but when he realized that Emma had already taken steps, he put his guns back wherever there was a place for them in his elegant suit and high-tech wheel-chair. His hands really were amazingly fast.

Just to make the point, he teleported back where he had been.

"As we were saying," Emma continued, "what do you think you are all doing?"

The man in cycle shorts sneered, then flicked his fingers. After he had done this a couple of times, a small flame appeared, which went out a second or so later.

"So you two know some magic. So do we."

Then he tried again, with less success. Emma began to feel embarrassed for him.

"Actually, I'm the only magic worker. As Tom here will tell you,— at great length if you let him—though a person of formerly elvish heritage, what he has are mutant super-powers. Just so we have things straight." She made her own small flame and danced it about on her left index finger. She didn't have to click it any more. "You really need to practice that more—it's not enough to make the click loud, you have to sort of reach into the sound and pull fire out of it. Then after a bit, you just pull the fire and don't need to click first."

She decided that she had better say something nice as well even at the risk of sounding patronizing. "Your bicycle spell is quite good though."

She stared fixedly at his left nostril.

"Generally, taking pills and powders isn't very good for one's magic. Concentration, that's the ticket."

The man in cycling shorts looked outraged. "He told me it was special. That it was an enhancer. It's improved our magic no end."

The two young women nodded in agreement.

Emma realized that she didn't know enough about this sort of thing. Maybe there were drugs you could take that would enhance your magical abilities and maybe she was just being smug about not needing them because she was a goddess. She decided to temporize. "That's as may be, but those of us who are really really good at magic regard that sort of thing as cheating if it works and remarkably silly if it doesn't. Also, given that it is already giving you all nosebleeds"—the blonde was pulling faces as she tried to make some spell she'd bought work and suddenly her left nostril turned into a small red mess—"it can't be good for you."

"Just say No," Tom cut in. "Apart from anything else, that powder does nothing for your judgement. In case you don't know, Emma here is one of the gods of the Underworld formerly known as Hell and it really is not a good idea to annoy her—she'll probably judge you. Quite soon, if you go on doing silly things like threatening me with guns."

"He does assassinations," Emma explained. "Threatening him with firearms is a bit of a faux pas."

The blonde sneered. "None of that matters. You'll all be dead soon and the Earth will be free of your kind."

Emma found this at once intriguing and baffling. "Which particular kind would that be? Goddesses, lesbians, redheads?"

"Humans."

"But surely –?"

The dark-haired one looked at her pityingly. "Well, obviously we're more highly evolved than you. We have a planetary consciousness. We are the new species that will live in harmony with the Earth once you are all gone."

Tom laughed sardonically.

"And you know this how?"

"Well, obviously –" the man in the cycle shorts began.

Clearly sensing an explanation coming on, Tom cut him off. "Did you know about it before you started using the black powder?"

The man in the cycle shorts looked blank as if he were trying to remember something.

"We've always known it." The blonde was getting angry again.

The dark-haired one looked slightly confused. "I haven't. You explained it to me only last week after you'd been to that meeting and came back with the powder."

"Oh." The blonde was still angry, but now a bit confused herself. "That's right, but it felt like something I'd always known. So I probably had, really, because evolved."

"Anyway," said the man with cycle shorts, "we have powerful friends and you do not. So shut up and go away and wait for the end." He looked as if he were going to start crying.

"These friends?" Emma thought she had better try and get some actual information. "I have quite a lot of powerful friends. There are those who would say I am their powerful friend, actually."

"I certainly would," Tom admitted with a cheesy smile.

"These friends of yours?" Emma went on. "Presumably one of them is a primordial fungus."

The man in the cycle shorts looked disconcerted.

"Well, yes, we do have a primordial fungus, next door, since you seem to know about it. But you could hardly call it a friend. It's a fungus. They don't do conversation."

A voice came into Emma's brain, whispering and insinuating. "You don't think I'd talk to these idiots. They are hopelessly confused; their brains are addled."

Then it added, "I think you know the Huntress? Oh, I see you do. Tell her that she probably did the right thing setting fire to me. But I did tell her I would be back."

Emma gave a psychic yell that left everyone in the room, including Tom, shaking their heads as if a very loud bell was ringing.

"Don't do that," her mind shouted. "I have a lot of people's secrets in here and people have to respect my privacy."

She formed a room in her memory palace with a large glass bottle in it, and a few ferns for decoration—if the fungus was primordial, it would probably appreciate old species of plant—and a chair next to it for handy conversation.

"You can talk to me in here. But I don't trust you so for the moment you stay in the bottle."

It intrigued her that a fungus could do that whole thing when someone who has taken a liberty because they are an utter chancer sort of shrugs and smiles. It had no face, it had no shoulders, it was just a pile of grey goo in a bottle, yet somehow it was surprisingly socialized. Also, remarkably relaxed about having its mind stuffed into an imaginary bottle in someone's memory palace.

"I was here before," the fungus explained in Emma's mind. "Jack grew me in chopped heart and rainwater and then Herbert grew some more of me in blood from his finger. A very bad man and quite a good one, so I think I had the measure of you people. And then the Huntress and the Hunter, and their dogs. They were harder to read."

It added, "But these people are utter idiots. Jack was a murderous lunatic, but at least he was interesting."

Emma knew without being told who Jack and Herbert and the Hunter were.

Meanwhile, outside her mind, she was watching Tom take his wheelchair over to the table where she had set the magazines from the machine pistols and put them somewhere about his person that she could not make out. He waved one of his own guns around in a desultory fashion and the other three backed against a wall.

Emma put the conversation she'd been having with the fungus on hold for a moment.

"The fungus says you people are idiots. I agree. Didn't you know it was intelligent? You were going to use it to wipe out the human race, and you think it's the brain of Gaia and you didn't bother to find out about it."

The man in the cycle shorts took exception to this. "Intelligence is over-rated. It's what is driving the planet to destruction—it's made humans a menace. Doctor Berinson says so."

"Doctor Berinson? Now that is interesting."

She turned to Tom. "Gosh, I think it's m'tutor back. For some reason he likes names with those letters."

Tom was having far too many moments of entire amusement today; he chortled then said "Oh it's probably a way of mocking our puny brains or something. Villain stuff."

The fungus couldn't really rap on the inside of the glass, but it made a sort of admonitory squelchy sound. "Didn't like him at all.

He was there when I woke up, with them. They have no minds worth reading and he was just a big blob of smelly emptiness when I tried to look. I'm not sure whether he saw me or not."

Emma turned back to the three people Tom had backed against the wall. "I'm not going to ask you about Berinson, because he would probably kill you and I don't want you to die. Even though you are murderous idiots."

The man in cycle shorts looked at her and there was someone else behind his eyes.

"But of course I'll kill them, Emma Jones. And all of their friends. Because they are no more use to me, now you've noticed them. You can choose to regard their deaths as your fault. As I always told them, intelligence is over-rated and dangerous. I can see that the fungus is not going to do what I wanted—sometimes things just don't work out. Still not a total waste of my time. It amuses me that their deaths will upset you, and the Huntress. Because you cannot save them all. Or indeed anyone."

*\*\**

I never got used to this modern habit of saying one thing in public and another in private, off the record, except that it never actually is, is it?

I blame Cato the Elder. He went on and on about how Carthage must be destroyed, and of course as you know it was. But all the time in the build-up to actually getting Scipio Africanus to do his dirty work he was smooth as the new silk from the East, pretending to be reasonable and saying, "We have to say that to put the wind up the filthy child-killers but actually we'll just force trade concessions on them."

Actually that's not a good example, because the version of history where all that was part of the background got mislaid in the Vatican somewhere. I remember looking for it the last time I was there and couldn't find it.

The Emperor Claudius had a nice turn of phrase at times, and asked me very politely why I hadn't done anything about the big statues of Baal that babies got thrown into. He was slightly disappointed when I told him it never happened, but then he reflected on what history would probably do to him and looked even sadder.

He put the truth down as I had told him, though. I wish I could say I had something to do with the man Graves but I was asleep at the time.

This man Smith reminded me of him a little, a scholar with sad eyes out of his depth.

"Actually," he explained. "I know for a certain fact that Braithwaite was as guilty as Hell, but I'd rather not admit it. The believers would have a field day—famous atheist turns terrorist. And the story is even sadder. It was the drugs, apparently. He got out of his mind on this black powder he had been told would be good for his asthma…"

That's what had happened to Crowley after he put me to sleep. Some opium called heroin, for his asthma. A bit sad, really, if it were anyone else.

Lord Smith cleared his throat, as if there were something distasteful he wanted to dislodge. "We never set up the Human League to do anything like that. And since I've been through his papers, it's all very awkward. He had a private benefactor, you see, and he used the money for, well, stuff I can't justify. I mean, we talked about it. Of course we did, but only late at night after a couple of whiskeys…"

"So he was killing people."

He had no idea who I was, but I have a certain authority to my voice. He stopped excusing himself and just nodded.

Dawn smirked as if it was her birthday and she was just unwrapping gifts long-expected. "So the Japanese AI project that blew up?"

He nodded.

She thought a little harder. "The American senator who thought the earth was flat and NASA a fraud?"

He nodded again.

Caroline did not want to be left out. "And eventually his benefactor stopped, well, benefacting, and he couldn't afford professionals any more and he thought he'd try his hand…"

If he nodded much more vigorously, his head was going to fall off.

Dawn's smile grew even more sinister. As if she had a personal stake in this, and, I realized before her next question, she had guessed that she had.

"He was buying the black powder from a man, and I happen to know that the same man was selling it to the people at Planetary Voice, Presumably he weighed one customer against a whole set of them."

I thought I had better explain. "We think they're cultivating a dangerous fungus. Presumably that's his scheme as well as theirs."

Caroline butted in. "What's his name?"

Dawn shrugged. "Back when he was dating Aurora, he told her his name was Brannen."

"And Braithwaite's benefactor, what was his name?"

Smith looked baffled, but said, "Some Italian motor-cycle manufacturer called Barono."

"Browning was the name of Emma's tutor, the one who got me killed. So, at the same time, using a different face and name, he was selling drugs to Aurora, teaching her magic and fathering her child that died and came back as a giant polystyrene giant that ate her and would have eaten the world. He was Berin, in Berthe von Renssler's opera, and some myths. He has this obsession with the letters B and R and N—Berthe found out when she was looking at the clay tablets her father had excavated. That's why he had her killed."

Caroline was becoming very excited indeed. I could sort of follow her and found myself sharing her excitement. Dawn was clearly excited on general principles.

"Miss Blake," Lord Smith said in a regretful huff. " I don't know who your friends are, but I thought you were a serious journalist, not a conspiracy theorist. This is all madness."

I stared at him, until he quailed.

"You silly pompous little man. You've just described a conspiracy, with your own mouth. You're part of a conspiracy yourself, even if you are too mealy-mouthed to accept that you didn't notice scientists and politicians you'd been denouncing to anyone who'd listen getting killed. You've been the dupe of a conspiracy—colleagues doing things behind your back. There are conspiracies in the world, get used to it. There's also a lot of chatter about conspiracies that don't in fact exist; there's probably a conspiracy to make imaginary conspiracies up so as to devalue the real ones. The entire economic system you live under is a conspiracy—Adam Smith told me that once, and smiled as if it were funny."

I waved him away. I get very tired of men who think that because I look young, and am a woman, that I am a fool. There was a fool at the table—or at least someone who had been much fooled and not known about it, and then lied—and it was not any of the young women.

The dog, which had been quiet for some minutes, sensed my mood and growled at him. Smith stumbled off, all the more hurriedly because he could not see the dog that was nipping at his heels until I called it back.

Dawn Blake looked after him as if saying goodbye to the world she had lived in up to now, a world which had a little bit of magic in it, a little bit of insanity and murder, but only so much as she could cope with. She pulled the face of someone about to drink something bitter, but good for you, or perhaps merely intoxicating.

"I think we're done here," I said. I'd finished my coffee and the dog was pacing round my legs as if it needed to leave.

"I'm not worried." Caroline clearly was. "I mean, I know Emma can handle herself but she and Tom seem to have drawn the short straw this time. All we've had to do is sit in a dull meeting, talk to an eminent and obtuse dull man, and meet someone charming." She smiled at Dawn.

"Just so you know," Dawn stammered, slightly flustered, "I'm straight. I don't know why almost every nice woman I meet in the Hidden Sector isn't."

Caroline laughed. "Emma and I—well, we're an old married couple practically except that we only got to have sex for the first time last night. The whole me being dead thing. Oh, and she had that fling with Elodie back around the time your aunt died and I think there may have been a bit of gallivanting and flirting going on back when she was in Hell, but nothing she's felt she had to confess or anything."

Dawn looked ever more intrigued. "So, clearly, there's a lot more going on in the world than I ever quite believed. I think you'd better tell me. I am now officially dying of curiosity."

Caroline reached out and took her hand a moment. "Don't say that. This is a world in which dying of curiosity is a thing."

She had just finished speaking when someone outside the door screamed and there were five shots.

They don't ring out; they are not hammer blows; they are shots, and for several centuries I have lived in a world where I hear them.

I got up from the table and ran to the door, which had been blocked open by the body of the now deceased Lord Smith.

Another elderly man, who wore a smart suit as if it were a uniform, a suit cut to hide a holstered gun from most people, but not from me, was squatting close to the body, checking for a pulse. He was one of those men whose white hair and lined face nonetheless glow with vigour and resolve. who always know precisely what they are doing.

He shook his head, and for a moment his face showed a sorrow that was not merely cursory and formal, and then looked up at me, and at Caroline, who had joined me. Dawn was with her, looking as if she wanted to be sick and was just managing not to be.

There were two large men standing near him, looking, in a brutal way, as if they were not in fact there, or rather, daring people to notice that they were.

Caroline recognized him. "Chief Inspector Sharpe—or is it something higher these days…"

211

He looked carefully at her. "We've not met," he pointed out. "I mean, I assume you've been in the same room from time to time, Caroline, but you were a ghost at the time, so… Of course, I knew your face from the photographs in Emma's file and Tom has talked of you often. I heard from him that you were back, and there was CCTV footage from the Brick Lane bombing."

"Goody, that saves explanations. This is my friend Dawn and of course you know the Huntress."

But the terrier was yipping at me, so I reached down, pulled the horn from its wallet and blew. The pack appeared outside the cafe, under and around the tables and under the feet of the customers and various pedestrians.

The terrier yipped again and they were off and I followed them, feeling a little redundant.

After a few moments, I could see what we were chasing: a motorcycle with two riders, one of whom fired several shots which did that thing that bullets do—they just fall to the ground a few feet from me.

The first couple of times people shot flintlocks at me they actually did bounce off me, to the detriment of the people standing near me, but I trained my magic to think of them as very fast arrows and it got the message.

I don't like people shooting at me, though, because there is always the risk that they might miss and hit someone they could hurt, so I took one of the small knives from my hair as I ran and threw it, carefully, so that it pierced and smashed the wrist of his gun-hand. He dropped the gun and fell off the bike—I ran forward and put my foot on his neck, ungently.

The motorcyclist had abandoned him but only got a few yards more before the Pyrenean mountain hound bounced at him and knocked him and his bike to the ground. The Doberman got him by the scruff of his neck and held him firmly.

The man Caroline called Sharpe came and joined us. Two of his companions held guns to the heads of the assassin and his driver.

He looked at me with a slightly amused face. "Normally, I'd ask you to come and give a full statement, but being as you're an ancient supernatural being—even your dogs are ancient supernatural beings—I don't much reckon our chances of getting CPS to regard you as a usable witness. So hop it and I'll say you were a random passer-by with dogs and I failed to trace you."

That did, on the whole, seem like the most sensible idea.

I took my foot off the man's neck; unfortunately this made it possible for him to speak. "Deathless whore," he screeched between coughing fits. "You will be punished for interfering in godly works."

I'll own to the deathless part but I take exception to slurs on my chaste fidelity, so I kicked him a bit until Sharpe put a restraining hand on my elbow.

"You know, Miss, regulations against police brutality do sort of imply that we're not allowed to let helpful members of the public beat them up either."

There are disadvantages to civilization, I have always thought, but I desisted.

Sharpe started the usual formalities.

"We don't need any goddamn Mirandizing," the assassin shouted. "You needn't think Burnedover ever leaves its men behind. We have our orders and God's. We shot the atheist son of a bitch and you coppers should be thanking us for saving you the work."

Caroline wandered over for a look—the visor of his motorcycle helmet had cracked and chose that moment to disintegrate.

"Oh look," she twinkled annoyingly, "he looks just like a younger version of Reverend Green, and so does the other one. Emma said that the Burnedover people in Iraq all did, too."

Dawn had a bored expression. "Everyone knows that. They all look the same. I wrote a story about it but everywhere spiked it, so it must be true. I used to think it was inbreeding somewhere in the Appalachians, but the accent is sort of Californian. Maybe it's cloning."

"Or just boring old magic," Caroline said. "Pretty much everything unpleasant turns out to be magic these day."

"Maybe it's magic cloning," Dawn came back at her. "That could be a thing."

"If there's one thing I hates worse than dykes," the motorcyclist said, "it's dykes flirting in front of me."

"I'm straight," Dawn blushed.

"I'm not," Caroline said.

"Sodomites," the assassin muttered. "That's why the Lord Jesus destroyed your empire."

"Well, actually," Caroline started, and then shut up with a guilty expression.

Sharpe made little shooing motions with his hands. "I'm trying to conduct a serious arrest, not some kind of feminist comedy hour. So, if you don't want to spend hours making a statement, I suggest you piss off. Now."

I took the horn again and blew the dismissal, and then I looked down at the terrier which had stayed, looking anticipatory and devoted, when the others had gone away.

"Emma," I said, and then took the hands of the other two and followed it into shadow. The man who sold it to me had said it was a good tracker and he had so far been understating.

\*\*\*

Quite suddenly the man in cycle shorts leaned across to the woman with dark hair, opened his mouth and very messily bit into the big vein in her neck.

He wasn't a vampire so his teeth weren't good at it. His eyes were glaring, but only because there was some sort of fire building in his head, as in hers. The blonde looked at her friends, confused—there was something building behind her eyes as well, but so far it was just a scream...

Emma hated that, even as they died in front of her, and there was nothing she could do to save them, she was calculating that with all his gloomy power, he could only manage to kill two of them at a time.

"I can put you in her head," whispered the fungus, "If you want to fight him there…"

Inside the room in her memory palace, Emma took a small hammer of trust and shattered the bottle, reached into the squelchy mess of the fungus' presence and followed where it pointed.

She'd never wanted to be a telepath, too much chance of finding out what other people actually thought of you and actually the inside of the blonde's head was a mess that she'd never have wanted to explore except in an emergency. Too many pictures of fat people and dead animals and burning jungles and a sense of the blonde as the one who would punish the fat people and put out the fire and save the small furry animals and—Emma seized on that image of putting out fires and reached back into her own head for an evening of torrential rain once in Mumbai. And that soothing bit from the Faure requiem and a cello note infinitely sustained and the taste of meringue with cream and—

Then he came battering in like a firestorm, and the bits of black powder that lay around the surface of the blonde's brain and mind like dust on furniture started to ignite and she looked at each spark and killed it dead. Emma took his firestorm and blew it, like a candle.

"Not this one. Too late for the others. But not this one. I hurt you once and I had no power then. GO AWAY."

Browning, Berinson, Berin, whatever his name was—oh god he was vast and strong but she was strong too and he was not expecting her. And the fungus was there too, like a warm squelchy blanket that lay over the flames damping them down.

It felt as if he could have beaten her, probably, but he was no longer quite sure, was not prepared to take the chance. And Emma blew on that doubt and watered it and it grew like a hedge of thorns that kept him out of the blonde's mind. He thrust at the fungus, hoping to cut Emma off from her link, but by now, Emma knew that somehow she had the trick of it; more power that she really did not want...

But her distaste with it was a pin beside the blonde, who was crying over the corpses of her friends and Emma was flooding along some landscape that lay between minds like a great cooling wave. And she stopped where she was, because maybe Berin was retreating strategically.

She caught at a fragment he left trailing, but it was only "the sleepers will awake and the ring of flesh will burst and all will be undone."

Obsession, much.

Though there was something like a crack in him and she hoped that perhaps it was fear.

She stopped where she was and shook a figurative fist at him in her mind and in the fungus' mind and god it was old so old and the blonde's mind. And he tried to kill three people and only managed two, which was hardly a victory but was something. It proved he could be beaten.

Also, if the fungus had ever had any delusions that it could take back all it had lost—and yes, there they were, locked away in its memory like toys it had outgrown—now it just wanted to live and find a space for itself.

"I just don't want to die again," it whimpered. "I fought the long campaign when they came onto the land and I lost and then I woke, over and over, and each time I woke I withered and died. And that was bad enough, but then I burned. Every cell of me burned...I slept in the fire for so long, but I could not feel it. I do not want to wake again knowing burning. Or worse, rotting. The Huntress gave me to flame but she saved me from the rot."

And then, "I used to dream of ends of the human world. I am not sure that they were my dreams for all that I could put them into people's heads. I just want to live..."

Emma stroked the great squelchy mass in her mind, but it was the blonde who needed her more right now.

"What was that?" Charmaine moaned. Emma had not thought anyone was called Charmaine but you can't be inside someone's head without knowing who they are, even if they normally go by Greengirl, and wouldn't you? "How are my friends dead?"

"There's stuff in the world you don't know." And Emma was not going to tell her anything she didn't know already. "Leave it at that. It wasn't your fault you are alive and it wasn't theirs that they are dead. Someone very wicked killed them, and I managed to save you, for the moment."

This really wasn't the time to point out that trying to cultivate something you could use to wipe out most of the human race was liable to have consequences. Emma was the Judge of the Damned and so she wasn't going to start having opinions about the living—especially when the balance of their mind and so on. So she continued to sit and stroke the poor bloody woman's forehead.

"He talked about killing the rest of your group. I think now would be a good idea for you to pull yourself together and get in touch with them. I don't know how to go about saving them like I saved you, but it would be a good idea for them to get rid of the black powder. That may not be how he gets inside you to burn you or makes you start gnawing on throats, but that's how I would bet."

She walked Charmaine to a desk with a computer on it. "Do an e-mail. Do it now. Tom, you'll inform the authorities?"

"I already did. While you were busy, doing whatever it was you just did. It was very loud, in my mind…There's a number I text—and they'll be here in a bit. For the bodies."

Wherever we go, Emma thought, we leave bodies behind and someone has to clean them up.

***

As we made our way through London's shadows, the terrier cocked its leg and pissed on the shadow of the Bank of England.

"Sound instincts, that dog," said Caroline.

Dawn looked around her, intrigued. "So—this is kind of like magical hyperspace that you can use to get places fast."

217

"It's so much more than that." I let Caroline do the talking on this one. Explaining things is a safe way of flirting when trying not to. "It goes off in all directions and there are a lot of weird places that aren't there in the Mundane. And gods and monsters."

"Apart from anything else,"—then again, I thought I'd join in— "it's where a lot of things go when we fill the world too much for them to be comfortable in it—dragons and hippogriffs and things."

"Unicorns?"

I gave an involuntary shudder. "I really hope not. Horrible creature."

"Apparently Emma fought one in Hell," Caroline said.

I hadn't known that, and was impressed.

"She had help. Judas. The enemy was trying to scare your old friend Crowley into silence."

I had no reason to like Crowley, but the idea of even the enemy managing to shut him up for more than five minutes made me laugh. The unicorn would be a good start, I supposed. "Not much chance of his being able to hold it off, I'd think."

Dawn said, her tone very mildly sarcastic, "So, when you get to be major adepts and powers, you spend your whole time on gossip about each other?"

"Pretty much," Caroline replied.

"So who's this enemy?"

"That's one of the things none of us know. One of the reasons we gossip," I explained. "I've only known for certain that he—pretty certain it's he—exists for about five hundred years. He's very good at working through cats-paws. His schemes are like onions, only they do far worse than make people cry."

"So basically it was he that killed my aunt. Seems a bit trivial for some sort of ultimate master-mind."

Caroline looked at her consolingly. "I'd give you a hug if we didn't have to hang on to the Huntress. Who knows how he thinks? It may have been that spell she ended up doing trying to bring your cousin back—if we hadn't been there it could have done a lot worse

218

than kill her and a few critics. Or it might have been a scheme to put Emma in danger, again. You just can't tell what's part of an endgame or what's just a small building block. Also, he likes messing people up. His idea of fun while he waits for the world to end."

I added, "We hope he's too clever by half. We're worried that he is even more clever and that every time we defeat him or his emissaries, we're doing exactly what he wants."

I reflected, not for the first time, that my never planning anything was probably not just my personal inclination and ethical choice—it was probably sound thinking.

We left shadow and walked down a backstreet to the address Tom had found.

Caroline panicked for a second when she saw an unmarked van and a couple of nondescript men with body bags, but then Emma came out with Tom, who was signing papers on a clip-board. Then it was Dawn that rushed forward—Emma stepped forward and took her by the arm.

"A couple of your former colleagues are dead. The blonde one, Charmaine, is badly traumatised, but –"

She was obviously surprised to see Dawn back.

Caroline stepped in to explain. "Actually, she was there undercover—she's a journalist who does conspiracy stuff. She's also Aurora Blake's niece, Dawn, so she's practically one of us already."

Dawn averted her eyes from the body bags. "So if Greengirl's OK, it's Rhodri and Giselle…They're the ones who were in the building when I left?" Then, still not looking at the body bags, she asked, "How did they die?"

Emma looked at her carefully as if unsure that she really wanted or needed to know, then said, "Berin got inside Rhodri's head and made him try to tear her throat out. Then he set fire to their brains. They were using some sort of drug—a black powder—to help them learn magic, and it turned out to be deadly. In several ways."

"Bastard bastard," Dawn sobbed. I was glad to see that she was not entirely the cold-hearted efficient person she pretended to be—

it is important to have a heart. "Rhodri was a dick, but he was going to marry Gis. She'd said yes when Greengirl broke up with her…"

Then she dashed into the building, and came out again a few minutes later with a blonde woman who was presumably this Charmaine or Greengirl. She was also carrying a small glass jar with something familiar inside it.

Emma explained herself, looking slightly guilty. "Someone had to get an e-mail out to the others in the group to warn them to ditch the black powder and take care of themselves. I had to get her to do it."

Dawn looked daggers at her and said coldly, "I get it, I do. Judgement calls, burden of command…" But she did not sound or look convinced. Clearly she had not forgiven Emma for the death of her aunt.

The clean-up squad turned out to have a nurse as well as people with body-bags.

"We'll look after her," the nurse said. She produced something that looked a little like a small gun. "Out of the way miss, I need to give her a sedative."

Greengirl was weeping as if she would never stop, great racking sobs. "What have we done? We ended up just wanting to kill everyone and it was us who got killed. All we wanted was to save the trees, to live lightly in nature and do no harm. We loved each other and they're dead…"

Tom took Dawn very gently by the arm.

"She'll get good care. They deal with bystanders all the time."

I knew that Dawn was going to need to do something practical— it's always the best way to deal with grief over people you didn't actually like very much.

"So, this dealer of your aunt's? What do you know? Not to make you feel under pressure or anything, but you're the best lead we've ever had on the enemy for years." I was fairly sure he'd be long gone, but I blew the horn of Cernunnos and suddenly we were surrounded by the rest of my hounds. The terrier barked excitedly.

Emma brought the glass jar over to me.

"By the way, Huntress, if we're looking for the enemy, we may as well take someone who might manage to read his mind. Say hello to an old friend."

The fungus coughed inside my mind.

It was a cough at once meaningful and conciliatory.

\*\*\*

Emma reflected that they could hardly leave the fungus to fend for itself, or to work out some scheme whereby it could stop being a humble suppliant and become a devouring menace again. She had been in its mind and thought she could probably trust it—but there was no point in putting temptation back in its way. Also, well, even if they were going after Berin, the fungus was probably safer with them than sitting in a jar while the agencies of the state cleaned up round it. They might not be as trusting of it as she was prepared to be.

Times like this, she thought, a girl needs her handbag. Just because she hadn't seen it for millennia of subjective time…So she whistled.

It came, looking sulky. The little hand inside it reached out and stroked her and then recoiled a little—that would be the goddess thing.

She put the glass jar into the bag very carefully. "Fungus, meet bag and hand. Behave yourself in there."

The fungus thought at her. "Gosh, these two have really interesting minds…"

"Don't tell me," Emma interrupted it very quickly. "I respect their privacy."

The pink-haired woman—Dawn—thought she had better brief Emma and Tom. "Aurora's old boyfriend used to sell her the black powder; that's how she learned magic. And he's turned up again, looking pretty much as he did then, selling it here and to Braithwaite and maybe some of his friends…"

Mara cut in. "I came across it before the War, the one you people call the First World War. I didn't know it could blow up in people's heads—Berin's always been capable of burning minds from the inside. I saw him do it once in Heaven."

Since everyone was sharing, Emma said, "Looks like he can only manage to burn a couple of brains at a time. That's handy to know, and handy that he knows we know…" She turned to Dawn. "Do we actually have an address? Is it a fashionable one?"

"Just off Hoxton Square. One of those new blocks they've built to cash in on Britart." Then she thought a second and added, "There's this thing that happens when I watch him with Sight—sometimes his face changes and it looks wrong."

"What do you mean, wrong?" Emma and Caroline and Mara all turned on her, agog and eager.

"Wrong," was all Dawn could say. She struggled to say more, but clearly language just wasn't up to how wrong, and why wrong and in what way wrong, "But surely that's not as important as the fact I know where he lives."

Mara bounced up and down with excitement. "After all these years…" She crouched down and petted the dogs as if she had forgotten ever hating them. The small terrier licked her face and she let him. "We can track him and tear him; tear him and track him –"

There came a meaningful cough from Tom. "Actually, I'm supposed to discourage all of you from going in and settling him, if he's there." He sounded almost but not quite apologetic. "It's a heavily built up area and yes, you did a stellar job of keeping everyone alive earlier, but you can pretty much guarantee there will be a bomb or something worse. It was all we could do to hush up what happened in the college chapel at the funeral, and I won't even talk about what you briefly unleashed in Iraq. And you, Huntress, rumour is it that you are far worse."

Then he added, confidingly, "Atlantis? Really. I'd say, look you two, you're not superheroes, you know, but that probably wouldn't be true."

Emma saw Mara about to ask a question, and put her finger to her lips in the universal sign of I'll explain to you later.

He pointed at the black van, which was poised to drive away, taking Charmaine and her two dead colleagues with it. "None of us want to see any more of that today, thank you very much. I'm sure that, if he is all he's cracked up to be, he can kill a small robot with his mind. One advantage of small robots is that they're built to last even when they meet a big bomb socially; another is that they're more replaceable than people. And I should be able to spot most possible traps without even going there—clairvoyant, you see."

There was a pub opposite, and some benches outside, and so they went over and sat down. Tom looked up imperiously and some minion who had been hanging around unobtrusively on the corner of the street brought them drinks.

Dawn offered to help. "I have the Sight too; it's why I get scoops. Two eyes are better than one."

Tom looked at her appreciatively. "Beautiful and smart and gifted. You know how to pick them, Caro..."

"I'm not..."

"She isn't..."

Emma laughed. It was nice to see Caro so flustered and, yes, she probably was interested in the child, and good luck to her with that.

Both clairvoyants went inside themselves for a few minutes.

"Well," Caro eventually said. "We can guarantee that he is out?"

Tom looked uncertain. And so did Dawn.

"Robot, definitely."

"Couple of bodies. Quite old ones. I didn't know you could do that to a person."

Tom looked at her patronizingly. "They call it the Blood Eagle."

Mara reached over and patted her on the shoulder. "If you need to be sick, we've all been there. I envy you being able to be shocked."

Dawn shook her head like a dog after swimming, as if she could force the image out of her head. "I've always meant to ask—just how bad was it with my aunt?"

Caroline pulled a face. "We've both been to Hell when Lucifer was still in charge...Pretty bad."

There was a sudden noise from around the corner of an engine racing. A motorcycle came into the street, drew to a halt at the curb just by Tom's chair and a courier in a black opaque helmet handed Tom a large envelope from which he took a laptop, with a small joystick plugged into it.

One of the things I would never get used to was a world in which minions made themselves so interchangeable. Doubtless this courier had a life behind the black visor but we weren't allowed any sense of it.

Tom took the laptop, balanced on two struts that came automatically from the arms of his chair and seized the joystick. The screen came on.

"If you don't mind, ladies, I'll do the honours on this. It's handy to see what the robot can see and be looking at it with Sight at the same time. Harder to do illusions that will fool both, our practitioners tell me…" He looked at his phone. "Ah good, they've delivered the little darling to the right floor, and got everyone out of the building. This is why you should sometimes let the professionals do our work. We get warrants…"

Emma started to feel a little miffed with her friend. Just because he was getting boypain about having to work with people way above his pay grade in terms of power was no reason to pull rank quite so obsessionally.

"How are you actually going to get the robot into the flat?" Dawn asked.

"Hand of glory attached to the top and lit before it was sent out of the lift." His tone was matter-of-fact.

"Hand of glory." Mara looked askance. "That's not the sort of magic I especially approve of."

Tom looked at the ground like a little boy caught pilfering, clearly embarrassed to be criticized by one of his heroes.

"Old kit we're trying to use up. Newton made hundreds of the bloody things and put them under a preservation spell. Polly doesn't feel she should waste them but uses them sparingly—she's not even cleared the Monmouth rebellion backlog…"

224

Dawn had already looked round the flat with Sight, and so Emma and Mara watched over Tom's shoulder as he manoeuvred the robot around a very dull company flat with occasional patches of blood on the carpet and the glass in the entirely mediocre collection of framed posters smashed as if with a small hammer.

There were the bodies of course. Neatly laid out on plastic sheeting in the master bedroom. They'd obviously been dead for some months and somehow dried out rather than rotted; it was as if something had pulled water from the flesh at the same time that they'd torn them open and done the thing with the lungs. There was no blood or other fluids around them; they were as neat and slick as if they had been licked clean, and they probably had.

Though Emma knew Mara had been seeing horrible sights for millennia, it was reassuring that she could still look disgusted and vaguely ill.

Mara explained. "It's how you make the powder, I think. You do something appalling and the power you normally get from the Rituals—well, you make a powder from it instead of just using it normally. And with luck the people you give it to will do what they are told and produce more of it—Paris would have been much worse if you hadn't stopped it, when you were Berthe."

"So," Tom looked thoughtful. "It's sort of like a Ponzi scheme for producing atrocities. Except that he has pulled the plug on it for some reason."

He continued to manoeuver the robot around the flat, but in a desultory way as if he really didn't expect to find anything.

Mara looked hard at the fungus.

"I think he realized that I wasn't going to be interested in helping," the fungus thought at them from its small jar on one of the tables. "They brought in some livestock and left them where I could have eaten them. But I had decided that this time I would make a real effort to have good intentions and act on them. It's not as if I get hungry or anything. I mean, I can eat animals, eventually. I canker their skins and they die and rot and then the rot kills me

225

too…It really wasn't very satisfactory. Before, for millions of years, I was the only living thing on the land, except for the little things that blow around in the air. At least these days I am not bored."

Mara continued to look suspicious at what was, potentially, the most dangerous being present.

"Well, for a start," the fungus went on, broadcasting to all of them, apparently in the interests of transparency, "I can't imagine that even magic drugs that work for humans would have any effect on me. And I certainly wouldn't want to try, even now they've, what's their phrase, souped up my immune system. For another, I'd rather not be used—I got a taste of that from your friend Jack and it was not the sort of thing that sits well with me."

"Jack?" Dawn pricked up her ears.

"The Ripper." Mara sounded bored.

"Was he?" Dawn had her notebook out.

"No one you'd have heard of." Mara's tone was final. "I killed him in 1912."

The fungus went on as if they hadn't spoken.

"I used to rule a third of this shabby little planet—well, rule in the sense of being the only thing that inhabited it, practically, except for other funguses, that weren't intelligent and didn't count… Then suddenly there were other things growing that were green and creatures crawling around, and eating me, and the air was changing. So I sank my spores deep into the crust of the world and let myself die, and waited for eruptions, because my one friend was time.

"It took me scores of rebirths and deaths before I realized that the animals around me were actually thinking thoughts that I could pick up and eventually understand—I wasn't used to the idea of other minds…And you are alien to me, mostly, apart from the fear of death and the desire to feed. I had to teach myself to think thoughts that you could possibly comprehend."

"You think human very well." Emma was not sure whether or not she was coming across as patronizing.

The fungus gave a squelchy chortle. "It's because my mind

actually works. None of you is in control of yours—half of what you think is just you burbling to yourselves about what you're thinking or planning what you are going to think in ten seconds' time. My mind isn't like that—it's more like that spark that lives in your head. Though that's not really alive, so it doesn't have to do maintenance on itself all the time the way you and I do."

Emma started to form the obvious question, but then Tom let out an excited yelp and they all crowded round the screen of the laptop.

He'd finally thought to have the robot look up at the ceilings of the rooms it had been rolling through.

Once you saw them, you realized that this dull little flat was the Sistine of pain and butchery. Perhaps the crude scenes of hunters and hunted were memories or perhaps they were wishes; they were anger and they were brutality and they were, in their way, beautiful in their malign energy.

Emma turned to Mara.

"He's a lot older than you."

"The Lord of Salt once told me, and the Bird as well if I had been listening, that he was there before the Ice."

"This has been one of his private places." Caroline's tone was full of awe and distaste. "This is how he worships and what he worships."

Emma remembered what she had written when she was Berthe, what Berthe had read, more or less, in her father's Sumerian tablets.

*I speak of the blood of men killed on altars, of the blood of mothers torn from ruined breasts, of the smashed skulls of the newborn, of the blood that drips from the torn flesh of those who long for death and to whom it is denied, the flayed, the blinded, and those who stagger or crawl with one leg or with none.*

And then

*The blood, the shedding of blood, the creation of true godhead in death and screams and the breaking of bone.*

She shuddered. "He really is not a nice man." Because understatement was really the only way she could cope.

Tom looked up from the screen. "You're saying that this guy isn't just some dealer or some killer, but is, well, sort of the Devil."

Emma thought of Lucifer, also not a nice man, but comprehensible in his venality and petty spite. "Rather more than that." She looked round at her companions. "This would all seem a bit petty if we didn't think about it—he sells the black powder and maybe creates enough trouble to make some more and do more mischief elsewhere. But you've got two groups—one all about propagandizing for saving the planet and another for saving humanity—and he managed to set them at odds to the point where they are killing each other. And no one is ever going to trust either group as well—the Planetary Voice people, if any of them are left, are going to be seen as cult killers, and the Human League—well, I'm sure they will go on but there'll be a whiff of sulphur about them."

Caroline butted in. "Three groups, actually. Poor old Lord Smith of the Human League got killed just after we talked to him—and it was your old friends from Burnedover. A couple of them. Mara caught them and your boss Sharpe arrested them."

Emma looked at Tom.

"Your world and Polly's, it's all about perception these days. This bloody war—well, that's making money for someone—probably my unfriends in Burnedover—and a lot of people see that. But people believe this crap for about 45 minutes. It gives them an excuse to go along with what seems easiest. That's why Berin can always find someone to join him in killing…"

"That's why I don't think I like you humans all that much," the fungus added. "You're better than being on my own. But not much."

"We kind of suck," Emma said. She thought for a second. "I might be able to help you with that. There are nicer people around."

"Your bag and its hand are quite pleasant in a strange way."

"You're a primordial fungus," Emma snapped back. "How can they be stranger than that?"

"You told me not to tell you."

"Fair enough," Emma answered. Then she added, "I don't think any of us here like most people all that much. If you had to like people to want to save them, well, you wouldn't be up to the job..."

Worryingly, all the others nodded, even Dawn, who might not have caught the pervasive cynicism yet. But had had an early start, Emma supposed.

Tom sighed and closed the laptop. "Nothing much else there. Might as well let Forensics in. Whoever Chummy is, he's long gone."

***

What most people that know about me at all, never seem to appreciate about me, is this.

Most of the time, I don't catch the bad guys, I don't get to protect the weak against the strong. I am just there, and I catch some of them and I save some of them, and the most important thing I do is simply be there, for seven thousand years.

Though for a few moments just then I had thought I might finally get closure on Berin, whose shadow's shadow I had been chasing for centuries before I even knew he existed.

I found myself being jealous of Emma, within hours of meeting her and Caroline. She was living at an end of history where things were happening all the time, where it was possible for them to feel all of the time that everything they did was important.

She didn't seem to have to wait for trouble—it was always there around the corner.

We'd both lost people at the start of things, but she got hers back immediately though partially; where I had had to wait for Sof for a while, but, for centuries, got her back completely.

Jealous wasn't the word; fascinated was closer.

Mostly, she both was Sof, whom I love, and was not her at all; she was a Sof who had been forced to become something like me, but had never known me, or loved me. It wasn't an improvement, but it wasn't exactly a loss either.

I found myself wondering what she, and Caroline, thought of

me—they were civilized and kind in a way I had never had to be, but also ruthless.

They had taken me into their hearts, nonetheless, and seemed capable of doing that to a lot of people. From what I could see, they had even done it to Hekkat—mostly by not taking her as seriously as she takes herself. Did they know what she had been capable of, was still capable of? Almost certainly, they were not naïve—and perhaps they were right. She had at least tried to change, even when I had last seen her.

Again, I had respected the fungus, but I had not thought of liking it.

Tom—I understood their attitude to him, more or less. He was a valued colleague and if there was a bat squeak of sexual attraction on his side, they did him the favour of ignoring it. Or rather, acting as if they did not know. A remarkable man anyway, or elf, even if he was a cold-blooded killer by profession.

Some would say the same of me.

Then there was Dawn—whom they had met and within minutes recruited to their cause as if they had known her for years. She had had some sort of grudge towards them, over her aunt, and they had charmed her out of it almost at once, simply by honesty. They had used no magic. I would have known.

I sat with them, thinking thus, in their small, and now very crowded room. They saw me thinking, passed me cups of tea, and let me be.

They had their rituals for the aftermath of adventures and investigations—rituals mostly concerned with the eating of food they had delivered and the consumption of small amounts of alcohol and vast quantities of tea. I had more often than not been on my own at the end of such things and had never felt the need to have such rituals, though, looking back, when I had been with Sof, she had taken care to provide me with them without describing them as such.

Another way in which Emma was like her, of course.

After a while, I noticed that I was, unthinking, constantly ruffling the top of the terrier's head as it sat quietly between my ankles. I fed it a torn off bit of kebab and some spiced bread, which it gulped delightedly.

I was still the Huntress, but somehow I was no longer alone.

***

There was a light drizzle in the air, but, standing among the trees, they could hardly feel it.

"We've asked the trees," Eithne said.

"And they'll hold up their leaves as much as they can," said Aspara.

"To give you a bit of shelter."

"While you dig."

"Thanks."

Emma was conscious of being in the dryads' debt, though actually she was doing no more than taking up a version of an offer they made to her long ago. They were, as she had said before, nicer than human beings even if she did find them a little bit irritating.

Caroline and Mara—whom she knew found them rather more so—stood silent and bowed their heads in respect. There had been a lot of that in the previous week—Greengirl's email had not reached everyone connected with Planetary Voice in time and Berin had been murderously busy. The financial institutions through which he had sent funds to Braithwaite and a couple of other members of the Human League had closed down, more or less overnight; some of their officials had disappeared, but not all.

Some of them were even alive, after a fashion.

To no one's especial surprise, Sharpe hadn't been able to hang on to the Burnedover people, the assassin and his driver. He'd only just got them back to New Scotland Yard when a car drew up alongside and showed him a warrant for their transfer. When Tom had asked him who had signed the warrant, Sloane just said that that was above Tom's clearance, and went white with suppressed rage.

Emma had attended every funeral she could make it to, and so had her lover and their guest.

231

"We cannot save them all," the Huntress acknowledged. "Perhaps I would feel better about that if I had, down the years, done more open grieving for that fact."

Even though she could hardly stand for constant weeping, Greengirl had been there to mourn every one of them, and Dawn had held her hand.

As she did now.

"Now you're sure about this?" she asked.

"Gis and I always wanted to live somewhere like this, not doing any harm. And that's what I want to do, and bring her ashes with me..."

"If you change your mind," Aspara said.

"Not that you will," said Eithne.

"You can change back."

"If you ask your tree nicely."

"We picked a friendly one."

Greengirl smiled a sad little smile.

"Where would I go? What would I do? This is as good a place as any to wait."

No one asked her because they all knew that she meant, for the end of the world, even if they were themselves determined to fight against that end no matter what it cost them.

Eithne and Aspara took her hands and she breathed in deeply. After a few minutes, the shade of her skin changed and she was Greengirl indeed. With a look of joy on her sad face, she stepped into a sycamore and was gone.

Its leaves and the leaves of the other trees around it sighed, but not in sorrow or because of the breeze.

"And now for you," Emma thought and spoke at the same time.

She took a small trowel and passed it round, Mara first, and then Caroline, and then Dawn and the dryads. Each of them dug—the small depression became a hole a couple of inches deep—and then Emma poured out the jar of fungus into it, and smoothed over the soil.

She blanked it out while it said goodbye to the bag and the hand. Privacy.

"Are we sure this is safe?" Mara was still sceptical.

"I think we can trust them both—they will be company for each other, and they will also watch each other. And we have two powerful clairvoyants to keep track of them as well. I am compassionate, but I am not stupid; also, goddess. They would have to be quite stupid to risk offending me. Or you."

"I am not a goddess," Mara protested, but, Emma thought, more for the form of the thing.

"Not in the old sense of the word—I get not identifying as a goddess, because most divinities we meet seem to be the most awful people who give themselves terrible airs. Sobekh's quite nice, though."

"Almost all of the Egyptians have nice manners and know how to behave themselves," Mara admitted. "You'll like Isis…"

"You two are working goddesses," Caroline suggested. "Call yourselves what you will—treat it like a job and you won't get above yourselves. Speaking of which, now I am back from the dead, I should get a job. Dawn, maybe you need a researcher?"

Emma knew that this was less Caroline chasing the next cute girl than Caroline reminding her that Emma had work to do and that Hell was her new commute. Still, better that than the Underground in rush hour.

"Mara," she said, "I have to ask. Now you've worked with us, do you accept that we are telling the truth about whose incarnations we are?"

Mara looked at her searchingly.

"Hmmph," she snorted. "I knew my sisters—Sof in particular— for millennia before you were born, Emma Jones. And yes, you are she, or a version—which means I know most of your tells and in particular when you have a juicy secret…"

We really are her sisters, Emma thought. Which means that there are five of us, and one the Quintessence.

Maybe all this is some colossal scheme of the Enemy—or maybe, just maybe, he is going to learn, at long last, that he just pissed off the wrong girls.

# Down and Sideways

## London 2003

I had been here before. I had never been here before.

I settled into a sort of family life for the first time since I was young. Emma and Caroline were not Sof and Lillit, or rather, they were, but the song they sang was in a different key. We were friends and they were lovers—they retired to bed and I sat up all night alone except for the dog at my feet and the dryads sometimes whispering to me from their pots. I sometimes left and roamed the streets or wandered off into the shadows of this London of steel and glass, yet still also of brick and stone, or further afield, and yet I could not bear to be from their side for more than a few hours.

As soon as it was clear that I had moved in, Emma's bird fluttered up to the ceiling with a suspicious glint in its eye.

"You despise me and my kind, I can tell from the way you glare at me," it chirped in a hurt voice. "If you didn't, you'd let my brothers at least come and visit, so you could get used to them. They're awfully bored with their current owner. He doesn't take their advice any more. We appreciate that you might not want to talk to Ghost."

It made that sound like some sort of bad thing which, I acknowledged, it probably was. He hadn't made that many dud moves in the millennia they'd been his trusted counsellors and I am loth to assume any god gets that bulletproof on natural talent.

I shrugged. "You were Lucifer's bird for a long time and I don't care for him, because he hates me, so I regarded you as part of a bundle with him. But you are Emma's bird now, so I'm sure we'll get along just fine."

It fluttered down to look into my eyes to see if I was lying, and if even a child of the Bird could tell that these days I'd worry I was getting old.

The terrier woke up and batted playfully at the red bird's tail feathers.

It pecked at the paw and the terrier gave a warning snarl.

"And then there's that brute," the bird said. "With that here, I don't feel at all safe. I think I should go back to Hell. Where Asareth appreciates me, and I am not stuck in one room with a smelly dog and two idiot dryads."

Aspara and Eithne did not say anything, but their bonsai trees drooped slightly to convey their hurt feelings.

The bird preened maliciously and conceitedly.

"I am Emma's bird, but only when she remembers that she is the Queen of the Area formerly known as Hell. I am not Emma's bird in the flat above the bagel shop."

Given how many smoked salmon and cream-cheese bagels I had seen it eat in the last few days, this seemed an ungrateful remark, and possibly a short-sighted one. I have noticed that goblins can hear pointed remarks through several walls and floors.

It fluffed its feathers and was gone.

I made a point of apologizing to Emma as if the bird's behaviour were in fact my fault.

"Silly feather-brain," Caroline said consolingly. "I don't have thousands of years of history with it and its siblings and I already can't stand it."

Emma looked a little disapproving, but only for a moment, then she and Caroline looked at each other, smiled and gave me a consoling hug. "You've done nothing wrong, dearest Mara," she whispered in my ear. "That bird was always going to go off in a huff sooner or later. It's not really a Brick Lane sort of bird."

They had asked me into their lives. I sometimes thought that they were waiting to ask me into their bed and I did not know what I thought about that, except that it had not happened and I did not need to know what I thought until they asked. I had never thought before that I would ever again be in that sweet ache of anticipation and dilemma.

We think we know our hearts, but we do not.

Sof was, I realized, lost to me for the moment—the message that she had sent through her other self was unequivocal. There had been too much pain in our last partings for things to be easy for her—perhaps that would change but there was nothing I could do to bring that about, nothing that would serve except time and her own will.

And Lillit. Lillit had become something so strange that I had not known her in the Quintessence. She had not engineered Sof's centuries of agony but she had not shortened them by a day. Sof might be able to forgive her for that—she was sometimes frighteningly rational in such matters—but I was not sure that I ever could.

Also, I suspected that she had been close to me at times down the years and I had not known her. Malinche had seemed other than a stranger; I had guessed for a second that she was my sister come back to me and perhaps she had been, but not the sister I thought. I had felt sisterly affection and lust towards Georgiana but I was certain she for one had only been what she had seemed. There had been the Trung sisters for a moment during their war—but no, that was just their wit and ferocity.

But what I now knew about Lillit made everything in my past uncertain, except that in her way she loved me, that all her deceits were intended for my good.

And Caroline—I could believe that she was Lillit in a sense because of that wit, and there was steel there but well-hidden.

I thanked fate for giving me these two new sisters and missed my original sisters as I had for most of the last years—even when Sof was reborn and in my arms.

I am, as you will have noticed, good at making the best of things. I have had to be.

I sat and watched quietly.

My terrier batted at Emma's handbag with a paw and the bag snuggled up against him. The little hand came out and stroked him just behind the ears.

Days passed, and weeks and months. I learned to use the Internet so that I could see if there was somewhere else I needed to be, but all the blood that was being shed was of an ordinary and predictable kind. A couple of times I followed leads and revisited my homeland, and the place where Hassan's homeland had been, and the battlefields of Menelek's time, but there was nothing. I was usually back in Brick Lane for supper.

Emma too was neglecting her duties—she sent her bird back and forth to Hell and Asareth sent back reassuring messages.

One afternoon, I got back from Madagascar and found Tom sitting in his chair in the flat, with Emma and Caroline and Dawn, who seemed to be calling round increasingly often and who always grilled me mercilessly for information, something I always find attractive in a person.

"Oh good." Tom was hardly effusive in his greetings. "You hardly know poor old Sharpe but I suppose you may as well come along. Not your fault of course."

"Come along?"

"Farewell drinks thing. The Powers that Be weren't pleased about those two killers you arrested for him—not happy at all. Questioned

238

his judgement. Truth to tell, he's not well anyway; had been talking of moving on."

He was drinking some of Emma's coffee—personally I tried to avoid it because it was thin stuff by my standards.

"They kept him out of the loop on so many things; they starved him of budget and nonetheless he saved things by sheer intelligence so many times. Once he's gone, they'll tear the Spook Squad down, you see if they don't."

"That's awful." Emma seemed seriously concerned but I had already gathered she had known Sharpe as long as she had known Tom. "Where does that leave you?"

Tom pulled that sardonic smug face which was one of the things I liked least about him, myself.

"It's all set up. I shall take a secondment to work with Miss Wild and after a while no one will remember that it was not supposed to be permanent. Sharpe was obliged to send me off to kill people his own bosses designated and, over the last months, that has sat less and less well with me. It's not killing I mind; it's stupidity. Polly needs me more for the Sight than for my other skills."

This made me like him a little more. I have lived in enough allegedly civilized societies to know how to do at least the more important sorts of small talk.

"So what sort of event is this going to be?" I have no great taste for social occasions.

"We show up," Caroline explained. "We avoid awkward explanations to people who don't know who we are. We drink as little as is polite and listen to Sharpe's speech—which might be fun if he is really upset with some of the people there and decides to tell them exactly what he thinks of them. And as early as possible, we drag the poor old man off to the proper party which will be a bunch of us eating Vietnamese food and him telling stories about the Spook Squad which will be quite entertaining and which you and Dawn will never have heard before."

It all sounded, if not delightful, at least acceptable.

"And if he gets a little tipsy, and starts crying over his dead girlfriend Ruby, well, we will hold his hand."

"Oh," Dawn explained, "That Sharpe. Aunt Ruby—well, she wasn't a real aunt, but you know how it is—was always very mysterious about her copper boyfriend..."

Actually it was all a lot more boring than I had expected.

Apart from anything else, the room smelled of excessive amounts of sprayed on furniture polish. No matter how chromed steel and glass government offices were in this time, they always had a room somewhere in them that pretended to be part of a Georgian manor house, with oak panelling and undistinguished portraits of long-retired dignitaries and two or three unpleasantly beige abstracts that look vaguely embarrassed at having wandered in from another century. The wine was sour and white; the beer flat; and the potato crisps stale.

I didn't know anyone and neither did Dawn, but we couldn't have any of our usual conversations because some of Sharpe's senior colleagues knew nothing about what Dawn kept referring to as the Hidden Sector—which is one of the more sensible things I've heard it called—and because the same older men assumed that we were both together and available, neither of which was an impression we had tried to give.

So we sat in a corner, by one of the bigger windows, sipped our drinks and played with my currently invisible dog, which bounded around the room chasing a ball that only he and we could see.

Sharpe looked very much older than the one time I had met him a few months earlier. I wanted to wander over to see if I could sniff magic or poison on him but decided it would be tactless and could be deferred until later in the evening. He was sat in a comfortable arm-chair near the wall of the room. Tom sat next to him—clearly not only his talented subordinate but his friend—and fetched him drinks, most of them not alcoholic.

Some policemen I took to be Sharpe's superiors clustered around him and looked down at him in a way that meant he was already gone and irrelevant. Their skins were ruddy and their voices were loud.

Tom was suddenly at my side "You're sticking around a lot." His voice was bitter and whimsical. "I'd have expected you to be haring off in all directions looking for malefactors."

"I keep going off and looking for them, but there are none to be found. This probably means there is some superior predator picking them all off and accumulating their power."

"You'd know all about that, I suppose," with a hint of disapproval. Then he added, "I see myself as the girls' more violent younger brother. You will be careful with them?"

"You know the situation."

He nodded. "I think I get it—pretty bizarre. I suppose that since they're not related to you in this life it doesn't count as incest..."

I thought about lecturing him about his provincial morals, then I thought of explaining to him the difference between blood sisters and heart sisters and clan sisters and the way that people could be all three of those things, or only one. I was not ashamed and I owed him no such explanation—nor you.

"They have not asked me to their bed nor will I ask them. I wait for a summons to shadow, and until I receive it I shall wait. And make myself useful, as usual."

"Before you ask," Dawn cut in, "me neither. Conveniently."

I do not, as a matter of course, drink wine, nor was the wine on offer of a quality that inclined me to change my custom, but when Tom raised a solemn glass in response to my words, Dawn and I raised our glasses of water in acknowledgement.

"Wot are you three being so serious about?" Polly Wild had quietly joined us. She was dressed less informally than usual—her outfit was sharply tailored in that precise way that is at once timeless and of the moment and indicates that a particular effort is being made. I do not notice such things—not as a code I can read the details of—but I have watched men and women enough down the centuries that I can spot the attitude that goes with a particular

241

quality of cloth, a particular attention to detail around collars or ruffs or the hang of a robe.

She was also wearing white gloves, something I had never seen her do in all the time I had known her.

Tom caught my eye as I assessed Polly and, guided by my cue, he did the same.

Dawn pulled a face which I recognized as that of a journalist into whose lap a story has dropped.

"Polly." Tom's voice was suddenly very serious. "What have you been doing?"

She shrugged. Then she looked pointedly at Dawn. "This is off the record, unattributable and all that."

Dawn pouted, then did the recently universal gesture I had never understood until people showed me a zip fastener in 1962.

Polly nodded, satisfied. "Not what I've been doing, mostly." Her voice was more amused than sorrowful but there was a bittersweet finality to it. Also, she was making less effort to be the grand servant of the state, and more the beggar queen I had first known "What's been done to me, more like. Dismissed from the service of the Queen, dismissed without a character like a serving girl what has made free with the spoons. Budgetary cuts, he said. Funds needed for more precise intelligence on the ground, he says. Serious questions about my length of service—files that make little sense, he says. As if he would know sense from the lies he commissions from every Tom, Dick and Aziz as will tell him what he wants to hear." She took a hefty sip of what was in her glass, some transparent liquid that clearly was not water. "Mother's ruin, 'Untress. Best thing Dutch William brought in with him. And no bloody Jesuit's root with it, filthy habit."

We waited in silence for what she had to tell us.

"So I told him what I think of the Yanks' damn stupid war and the damn stupid lies that went with it. And I told him what I thought of him and his jobbery and his bullying that he calls discipline. He says, I want the keys to your buildings and your files.

And I says, that building and those files ain't the property of your government and nor am I—we serve the realm and not the fucking state and that's how it's always been, check the fucking charter of my service what was drafted by John Bloody Thurloe himself back in Noll Cromwell's day and refined by Sir Isaac, miserable precise bastard that he was. Any service any of us do to the state is free gratis and polite, but we answer to the Lord. And he looks all pious for a second and I says, not Nameless, you crypto-papist—the Lord who guards this realm of Britain, as will have words with you one of these days. So he presses a button on his desk and a couple of flunkies come in and he says, Miss Wild will be leaving now. Which I does."

Tom looked serious. "Shouldn't you be making sure they don't simply seize your office and the files?"

Polly laughed. "I'd like to see them even manage to find the place. I has an arrangement with the Lord and that whole building is now hidden from view save by invitation. It belongs to the Land hitself, not to the bloody Prime Minister who currently thinks he stands for it."

She drank the glass straight down.

I turned at the sound of oak splintering—suddenly there was a hole in the panelling and the wall behind it. Another crash and the hole was big enough for a man carrying an enormous axe, like a butcher's cleaver with a long handle and better balance, to step through.

I could not be sure that he was the assassin I had allowed Sharpe to arrest and then let go, but he had the same face.

"Here's Johnnie," he shouted for some reason.

Various of the people in the room screamed or ran out through the doors; Sharpe struggled to get to his feet but sank back into his chair. He clearly was not at all well.

The assassin glanced over at me as he stepped into the room. "I'll get to you in a second, Huntress," he shouted, "but I have my orders and priorities."

I did not like the colour of the edge of the axe's blade—it was the same rippling non-colour as That Which Devours.

I ran towards him, but before I got there he had reached out and tapped his blade delicately against Sharpe's neck. His head fell into his lap—I have seen few men die so suddenly. There was no blood; it was as if both halves of his neck had been seared.

"Recognize it, Huntress," he shouted. "We've made a few improvements to That Which Devours. It was always a nuisance as a liquid. Splashed. But you know that, you've a scar on your cheek to remind you. Emma Jones next, because she killed the Reverend Green for being a man of God."

Emma did not seem at all fazed by this—I waited a second, trying to work out how I could duck under the swing of his axe without, I realized, possibly getting killed or maimed.

I suspected, in any case, that he was not aware that Emma was now unequivocally divine

She glowed like banked embers and her voice grew very loud, but he ignored this.

"Reverend Green was a torturer, a murderer and a fool. I killed him in self-defence and because he had killed my friend. You deserve the same."

Suddenly she had a gun in her hand—it hadn't been up her sleeve. It was as if she had pulled it from nowhere—actually she probably had. She pointed it at him, and suddenly the top half of him just wasn't there any more.

His bowels and bladder let go because there was no brain to stop them. Half of the axe's handle was gone too. Emma swept her pistol down and blasted the axe-head out of existence before it could reach the floor. "Better not have that around," she said in an irritatingly sensible voice.

I was impressed; she'd probably saved my life as well as her own. A blade like that could either have killed me, or condemned me to Sof's fate.

Tom reached out and closed the eyes on Sharpe's severed head, and then he wept.

I looked around the room—as did Emma. "They usually go in pairs," I said.

Most people had left the room—they were mostly police and the like so did their running away in an efficient and orderly fashion. Those that were left looked stunned.

"He was the head of the Spook Squad," Tom shouted angrily. "What do you think we do all day?"

Through the window I saw a red light flash from the building opposite us. Even as the glass of the window smashed, I had my hand out and caught one, two, and three bullets, but the fourth I failed to catch and it caught Polly in the arm as Tom flashed across the room and pulled her down against the wheel of his chair. Then he flashed away.

I looked at the window opposite from which the shot had come, and saw two sudden flashes in the darkness of the room.

Tom flashed back. "Sorted," he said. "Oh, and thanks, Emma. I owe you one. Poor old sod, he taught me everything I know. I knew he'd go soon, but I thought he'd have a little more time."

Then he reflected a little.

"Worrying that Burnedover people now think they have utter impunity."

"They do." Polly started to push herself up from the ground and sank back with a moan. Dawn helped her to her feet. "Bugger," Polly said. "This suit cost me a small fortune."

There was a neat hole through her arm and no blood.

"Is there something you've not told me?" I asked.

She winced, not just in pain, and pulled a resigned face.

"It's the bloody elixir, ain't it?"

This was not going to be good news.

She took off one of the gloves, and there, down the palm of her left hand, was a thin seam of silver.

"It happened a couple of months ago, didn't it? I got a paper cut and it didn't heal and then it did, and it was wrong. I've had it assayed—just a scratching of it that grew back in hours. Pure as anything it is—I could have the bloody Lion Passant stamped there if I wanted. There's a patch of gold foil somewhere I won't talk about where my skin sometimes chafes, and I stubbed my toe the other week and it's grown in porcelain. Nothing to worry about, for the moment, but clearly something like this arm—well, I don't imagine I can take too many of those. I remember what happened to my daughter and granddaughter—well, at worst, I've had a good run and the Lord will find hisself a shiny new servant when I'm gone. I was thinking, Tom—he could do worse, and the elf thing, well, that might give you some years…"

"Who has done this?" I shouted, and cast the three bullets on the floor so that they clattered like the dice thrown by desperate men and spirits of doom.

She had only had a couple of centuries, but Polly was as dear to me as if she were one of my sisters. I do not lose my temper, in general, but I will not have my friends hurt.

"You know how it goes, 'Untress. Who will rid me of this turbulent bitch, someone says when he's in his cups or in a mood. And then it's all someat as can be denied."

"I won't have it." My voice drowned out all the other conversations in that room. "Tom, I would borrow you for a few hours…"

"Don't do anything foolish, 'Untress. I'll just retreat to my offices and see if we can find a cure. Don't worry about me. That goes for you too, Tom. But you're neither of you listening to me, are you?"

We were not—I could see from his cold stare that he had made a decision, and that decision was the same as my own.

She waved Emma and Caroline over to remonstrate with me. Tom and I looked at each other and then I blew my new sisters a kiss and was gone from that place, to Tom's office, which was empty because of Sharpe's party. Tom joined me there, with the usual lack of noise save for the gentle chafe of rubber wheels on expensive carpet and we planned.

246

He rolled his chair over to a thin, tall cabinet in the corner and took out a crystal decanter full of some liquid or other, which he put on a small elaborately carved table next to a leather armchair—to which he directed me. I noticed that, on the other side of the table, the carpet had depressions in it which matched the wheels of his chair when he brought back two glasses.

"Poor old bugger."

He poured himself a glass of whisky, and then another which he emptied onto the carpet. "One for the road for poor old Sharpe, and for his lovely Ruby, who died too young. And one for you, if you want it." He filled the second glass again, and passed it to me, before swilling his own glass down, and then refilling it.

It was not artificial courage but something that looked like part of his personal ritual of preparation for killing or death. I knew without being told that it was a ritual which had always before included the dead man, his commander.

I do not, in general, drink—I am immune to the effects of all poisons, including alcohol. However, when he offered me a glass of something that tasted like smoke for all that it was clear, I took it. As part of his personal ritual.

Tom knew where the Burnedover offices were, and their out-stations, but they were deserted. They looked as if they had been decommissioned. I looked for computers—the many workstations were covered in tiny crumbs of metal and plastic and glass.

"Well, clearly we need to go up the food chain a little." And Tom smiled a smile that his targets presumably saw just before he killed them, and off we went.

The room was dark when we woke him. His wife was there, snoring gently, and did not rouse when I took him by the shoulder and shook him gently. To be certain, I cast a light glamour on her. I knew enough about her to feel she had nothing useful to add to the conversation.

"Don't put the light on," I told him. "You don't need to see my face, or that of my companion."

247

He blustered at me—most of what came out of his mouth was platitudes about the rule of law and how had we got past and who was paying us.

"It's very simple. Someone attempted the life of a friend of mine this evening, and killed the commander and friend of my companion here, and I and my friend are visiting some of the people most likely to have asked that they be killed and suggesting to them that this would not be a good idea, for them personally, or for the offices they hold. Or who signed off on the killing when it was requested. Just a word to the wise, or in your case, just a word."

Tom added, "We know she had harsh words with you early in the evening. You'd be ill-advised to dispense totally with her services, you know. The world is not entirely as you think it is, and this is why we are in your bedroom in the middle of the night and left no trace entering and will leave no trace leaving. Nor in the bedrooms of the heads of Five, Six, Special Branch and a couple of secret agencies that report to you directly and which even the Home Secretary does not know about. Yet. And you dismissed Sharpe, who had served the State better than you ever will, and you let him be slaughtered like an animal in an abattoir."

"We'll keep it short and to the point. Polly stays safe. No more assassins."

"We're holding you collectively responsible. You can police each other. All for one and one for all—your lives are in one another's hands. Are we making ourselves clear?"

He tried to bluster at us some more, but he was a coward who had suddenly felt the knife at his throat. Not literally, at this point. "But what if someone else kills Miss Wild?"

"You'd better all be very careful and watch each other and protect her. Because the thing about killing all of you if anything happens to her, is that you're all guilty of so very many bad things that the ones that are innocent of her death will deserve to be killed for something."

"In your case, the War, mostly. In their cases—well, there are a number of things that you at least know about. If you are doing your job."

I wasn't quite sure what Tom was on about but I was fairly sure I did not want to know. I stick to my main concerns, mostly.

I thought I had better at least mention those.

"You've not been doing the Rituals?"

The fear in his eyes was that of ignorance.

"Good. You don't even know what I am on about, and that's a good thing. And if anyone offers you or your wife some black powder, just say no."

To reinforce my point, the terrier appeared out of shadow and pissed against the side of the bed and then rolled on the carpet as he had earlier rolled in something unpleasant.

The room stank, but we had no reason to be there any longer. In, do what you need to do, leave in good order. That's what I did these days, and if I had been inclined to give the people we'd been speaking to some good advice, those would have been my very words.

Polly was quite vexed with us when we turned up in her offices and explained what we had done, Tom and I.

"It shows a good heart. And I'm not saying that giving that pop-eyed sanctimonious liar a hard time don't gladden my heart. As for the others, well, one day the stupid awful things they've been up to—of which, young Tom, you may think you know, but believe me it ain't the half of it…Well, me and the Lord have discussed whether we ought just to kill them all and let God sort it out, but the charter says we can't, because Old Nol didn't trust even Bloody John with the high justice, and Dutch William had this thing about separation. But you really shouldn't have. I know you kept the lights off, but they will know it was you, so you really ought to leave town for a while."

She considered for a second. "I'll apologize, over-zealous subordinates, grieving for Sharpe—rub it in that he knows how it is because that's always his excuse. It'll blow over. As for you,

Huntress, it's nice you care, but how bloody old are you? Acting like a stroppy kid? Disadvantage of eternal youth I 'spose. You asked him about the Rituals and the powder—yes of course I know about the powder, Tom tells me that sort of thing and you should have mentioned it back a century ago but other things on our mind a couple of years later. You need to be about your travels and the girls need to go judge damned souls some more. Makes me uneasy having a new-minted goddess swanning round the East End like she was just ordinary proper people…"

Back at the flat a moment later, Emma tutted at us a little like a responsible elder sister, which was spoiled by Caroline giggling. After a bit Emma admitted that, if we had asked her first, she'd probably have wanted to go along. She didn't even know Polly all that well; Sharpe, though, well—he'd always been good to her.

"I liked what I saw of her," Caroline agreed. "Obviously we haven't ever had anything you could call a conversation, given that I was a ghost at the time. Saw a lot of Sharpe down the years, and he was a lovely man, for a cop. And that bloody man you just went and scared, well, he's an arse, I always said so."

"I'm worried about this transmutation thing." Tom looked at me anxiously. "Does this always happen eventually?"

I looked at him equally seriously. "Most people the Elixir kills pretty much straight away. If it's going to. The one other person I knew well, it made her young again and then it kept her alive. Let's just say, no one should have to live like she had to, and I didn't know…This is why my actual sister Sof, that Emma is a sort of rewritten copy of, isn't here and doesn't want to talk to me; it was that bad. This thing of Polly's, it's not anything I've seen before. She'll just have to be really careful. I wouldn't want to go through that again."

The girls—who knew the whole story—in Emma's case, had actually experienced it all—nodded.

"I think," Emma said, "that at this point you really need to talk to Sof whatever she thinks. She actually understands these things and knows how to go about putting them right."

I looked doubtful.

"Look," Emma went on, "I know she'll accept that this is really really important. By now, because she doesn't like to be without it, she will have made the Stone—which is probably what Polly needs. And if you don't go and see her, the only other person who might be any use at all is someone you want to see even less. Apart from them—and I don't know Morgan could help, it's just that the Work is something she might have got into at some point just because Sof did—and there's Lillit of course but she's really not in the phone book. It's bad enough not knowing where people are, but in her case it's when. Oh, and there's…"

She bit her tongue and glanced significantly at Caroline. This was more of the important thing they weren't telling me, and of which, at this point, I had had quite enough. Sof had only had one pupil in alchemy that I knew of. And their whereabouts had been a mystery for almost two thousand years.

Tom clearly was not in on the secret.

"What about your other friend?" He was so full of bright ideas and wanting to do something about Polly that he didn't notice Caroline and Emma looking daggers at him. "Her from the House of Art? Josette? She's some sort of shapeshifter or something? As well as amazing hot."

Emma sighed, then explained. "Caro sort of has her on telepathic speed-dial. Speaking of which, how come she got you to turn up on Eurostar, you and Sobekh?"

"Don't know about the croc. I just had a voice in my head that said you were in danger and where I needed to be. Very precisely, because teleportation onto a moving train is not something you do lightly. Told me what to say, as well. She seemed nice. In the pub afterwards, Sobekh came over all mysterious about her…"

Emma and Caroline looked significantly at each other some more.

There was a knock at the door.

Emma was suddenly flustered. "Mara, dear, this may come as a bit of a shock."

I once watched a lockmaker at his work. As the key turns, cylinders move and fall into place like a syllogism.

Caroline opened the door and a woman walked in, tall and imperious. Her face was not, at first, familiar but I would have recognized those eyelashes anywhere.

I was so glad to see her.

"Huntress." Her voice was like steel tempered to be as soft and pliant as silk yet hard as will.

I wanted to speak, but I did not know her name.

Caroline saw my predicament. "Josette," she supplied.

Which I was sure was just the most recent of many aliases, but would do. Oh yes, it would do.

"Josette." Sorrow and joy mingled in my throat so that the word came out almost as a sigh, almost like a whisper.

As I gazed at her, I realized that I had been a fool not to guess, back when she was young. Some things are the case and were always the case but we were too stupid to see them. It was thin consolation that her father and her brother and my sister had been as stupid as me.

I fell to my knees because sometimes that is the right thing to do when you have wronged someone so deeply.

"I am so sorry. So very sorry."

Josette laughed. "Huntress, you need not be. Without you, I would be dead. I put myself in the way of death—yes, so that I could not be used, but also to avoid thinking. Thinking about who I actually was. You killed me for my own good, to save me worse pain—and unknowing you gave me my life back, and made me make new choices."

"I knew you were somewhere. I thought you must be so angry with me."

"And I feared your disgust."

I reached up and held her hand. It was still the hand I knew, strong and tender and used to hard work. "I am not your stupid bigoted father. I am your friend. And the lover of your love. How could I ever think ill of you?" I thought back to the hills of my childhood and youth, and friends I had had back then. "It takes civilization to be cruel about such things. Or people who have forgotten everything about civilization save its hatreds and its vilenesses."

Josette reached down and helped me up from the floor. "I've wanted to talk to you, Huntress, so many times. But I feared, and I wanted to stay under the radar because of my work. I could not risk my father or my brother knowing where I was or what I was doing— and I could not trust you, you're still too fond of him. And then Sof... And what happened."

Caroline narrowed her eyes. "What work? I am a little upset, dear, that you come in and out of my mind without a by your leave and yet there's plenty neither Emma nor I know."

"Speak for yourself, love."

Caroline turned to look at Emma.

"I sort of worked it out when I was judging the damned. I would have shared but we've been a bit rushed and then we had company and... So anyway, we knew she was doing all sorts of conspiratorial sex anarchist stuff down the ages, and—work it out for yourself. What would that mean? What would be most important?"

Emma looked at me, and Caroline, and Tom as if we were her idiot pupils.

"Which I would find out about, inevitably, and have the sense to pick my moment to talk about, while we are cloaked by whatever magic it is that has kept Jehovah from noticing her all these years...Surprised Judas never got it, but the poor dear swamps himself with work so as not to have to think too hard. And Lucifer..."

I still wasn't getting it. Oddly, Tom started to look as if he had an inkling.

"She's been keeping all sorts of people from being bored in Heaven or tortured in Hell, haven't you? Obviously I got to a lot of gay men and sex workers and, well, general malcontents, but there were surprisingly few of them, less than I'd have expected. The House of Art is only a bit of it, isn't it? You've been building a third force for centuries. Where do you keep them all? Shadow?"

Josette smiled. It was a bittersweet smile.

"As Mara here always says, and you know too, I could not save them all. But—well, so much was being done in my name that I was not going to let stand. So I did what I could. And trained them up to save others, those that wanted to. And the rest—I left them to get on with it."

"With what?" I asked.

"With the Just City. Philo taught us well. And I had Judas' failures to observe and learn from—and the biggest of all was—let them do it. Don't try to do it yourself. I learned so much from you, Huntress."

I could not think of a single thing I had ever taught her.

"Letting it go. Not trying to plan."

Emma looked guilty, then defensive.

"Well, aren't you the special anarchist duo?" she said. "Sorry, I sold out to the system because it was the only right thing to do at the time."

"That's different," Josette reassured her. "You and Asareth inherited Hell. And a lot of badly traumatized people who'd been tortured and a lot of the people—demons and humans—who'd been doing the torturing It's Lucifer and Jehovah's mess, and you're clearing it up. I got to have a clean slate and handed it over the moment I could—as you will, won't you? You because you're righteous, and Asareth…"

"Because she'd rather be called the Queen of Hell than do much of the actual work." I cut in. They all gave me the same sharp look, and I shrugged, "I don't have to work with her and can insult her freely."

Caroline giggled. "I don't insult her, but I do get to trump her outfits. And sleep with my beloved which she so wants to."

She was suddenly in a vast red cloak and a massive head-dress that was like antlers made of cloth with individual chandeliers hanging from each tine. She draped herself around Emma, who looked at once embarrassed and pleased.

"Of course," Caroline added. "If she asks nicely, we'll consider it." Then she looked at Emma, who nodded.

"In case either of you two were wondering... Sorry Tom."

He shrugged. "Used to it by now. How long have I known you two bitches?" And smiled to take the sting off.

Caroline put an arm across his shoulder and kissed the top of his head. "I've known you so long, sweetie, and it's only these last few weeks I've been able to touch you."

Emma put her hand on his other shoulder, then looked at me. "You two really ought to get going, if London is too hot to hold you. And I really ought to get back to Hell. Caro?"

"Coming with you, dearest. Not leaving you alone with Asareth. I'm sure I'll find something useful to do."

Caroline pulled out her phone. "One thing we should do. Known associate and all that." She dialed.

"Dawn, sweetie," she cooed. "Friends of ours have done something a little daft and it might be a good idea for us to get out of town. You too, perhaps, since you're now part of Team Emma. Yes. Of course you are. Practically family. So anyway, road trip—no, you don't need to pack much– it's warm where we're going and we haven't set up the Internet there. We'll come and get you in five minutes." She smiled in satisfaction.

Emma glanced at Josette. "You, Boss?"

"I think we graduated out of that relationship quite a long time ago." Josette said. "But no, there are things I need to do in shadow and Mara and I have catching up to do. If you and Tom don't mind me tagging along."

"More the merrier, I'm sure." Tom turned on what I had already registered what was his quite considerable charm and charisma. Elf psychopath assassin—it amused me to see Josette taking him so utterly for granted, but then, I remembered, Josette had been observing him for years through Caroline's eyes. And had plenty of time to form an opinion...

Of course, Tom just knew she was Emma and Caroline's mysterious employer, and they'd only met one time before. As to Josette's past, well, that was a conversation that would doubtless be had along the way. Along with so much else.

Emma stroked one of the small shrubs on a nearby table.

"We'll be back soon, dear. Look after the place."

Neither Eithne nor Aspara appeared, but the shrub suddenly grew blossom that filled the room with scent. Emma picked up her handbag, took Caroline's hand, and they blew kisses and were gone.

There was only one problem I could now see—Tom's powers of instant travel were something quite different to walking even through the quickest back paths of shadow. I wasn't even sure whether he had ever learned to travel there...

Like most trained professional killers I've met, Tom was good at using a single glance to assess the next move or the next turn in the conversation.

"Anywhere I can see, I can go, remember. And just because I don't spend much time gazing into the far reaches of shadow doesn't mean I can't go there; I just mostly haven't. Sharpe and Polly were keeping me busy. And they haven't needed my skills in shadow very often. But there are Powers that need a favour from time to time."

I hazarded a guess as to which powers that might be—I could imagine that various deities who had retreated to shadow and had to eke out their existence on a few scraps of worship might prefer to use a Mundane killer rather than squander what thunderbolts they had left. I could think of one such, who had placed himself well strategically—as he always used to in the old days—where roads met and where gallowstrees stood.

We could do worse than ask him—most travellers came to his door and if Sof and Alexander had not yet arrived there, we could do worse than ask others if they had met them along the way. Though he and Alexander were unlikely to have had dealings, they would, inevitably, approve of each other, and he would welcome Sof, having a fondness for gold.

Josette looked at me and at Tom. I did not think she could have read my mind without my noticing, nor would I have expected her to trespass, knowing my distaste.

Nonetheless she echoed my thought, and, from his expression, Tom's.

"Valhalla." Her voice was sharp as a trumpet, thrilling as fire.

# The Glittering Roofs

## Shadow 2004

Neither of the other two had actually been there, it turned out, though Tom had seen it from afar after using his sight to track his client.

"Of course I knew who he was, old tough guy with one eye and interesting scars, hiring me to kill very old Germans in Latin America. He wasn't Mossad, and he was obviously some Power that the Lord was mates with. Pretty obvious. Apparently they'd started praying to him and he took exception to that. Reckoned it tarnished his personal brand or something."

"I've never been all that comfortable around that crowd," Josette said. "They're really not my kind of people—I met one of them in a tavern once, in Burgundy, and we dated for a bit. She was a bit serious, Battle Ready, but fun when she drank. But she had Daddy issues and then she killed herself over that idiot boy."

That was going to be interesting. As far as I knew Battle Ready was still healthy and well. It was a good cover story though.

"I tried to get to her, but I wasn't in time. And I saw the whole place go up—a spark from her pyre, they said."

"I liked the old place," I told them, "but I remember and always preferred the old old place, and the current version is basically the old old place with modern conveniences. That's the thing about the Wanderer; he's fairly pragmatic for a god. Which is why he is still around—I had a little word with him about the Blood Eagle, early in our acquaintance and he did his best to stamp the practice out. As we just saw the other week, it's more Berin's sort of thing. I checked, of course, but if it went on, and he got the benefit of it much of the time—well, I'm not going to kill a moderately socially useful god just because he can't make a bunch of Vikings do what he says. He tried killing a bunch of them, but Vikings don't take a hint. They went on doing it in his name even when they thought he had died."

For someone who knew all about coming back from the dead, Josette was remarkably surprised that other people could fake what she did for real. Really surprised—she was not, these days, the sort of person who normally lets themselves be seen taken aback.

She explained herself. "I saw the fire and didn't believe anything could survive that. When I heard he'd set up shop again, I have to confess I was sceptical. There are a lot of impostors around, they tell me."

She caught my eye, and we giggled. Which was a little unfair to Tom, who wasn't in on the joke.

"So," he said ruefully, "all those hours I put in at the opera house were useless from an intelligence point of view. I sort of guessed that when he turned out to be around to hire me."

I explained, "After Constantine, the Wanderer guessed the jig was up and started making his plans. The whole place going up in flames, the whole 'we died and it was the end of time' thing—that was just him and his family covering their exit. They actually fooled Jehovah and there haven't been many who managed that—by the

259

time he realized that Odin had just rebuilt off in shadow, they were sufficiently well established, sufficiently far away, that it just wasn't going to be worth his while."

Obviously Tom had no personal investment in the whole business, but was interested nonetheless. "But presumably his worshippers all died out or converted. Don't gods get pretty messed up when that happens, unless they start doing the sort of thing that brings them to your attention…"

I shook my head. "He'd set things up so that they could get by in the lean years with few worshippers. You think it's a coincidence that both they and the Olympians had access to golden apples—the Wanderer stole them, years after the strong guy did; they're apples, they grow back. Only the Wanderer stole the whole orchard, and shipped it in carts, off into shadow. And the trickster took the snake off somewhere and had his way with it. Their kid is just as terrifying as they say."

I shuddered. There are few things that make me shudder, but the Earthsnake—well, it's not as big as in the stories, but when it wants to be…

"Lots of less prudent pantheons only survive on his charity," I went on, "in years when there's a good harvest and the cider is a vintage. When gods go weak and senile and forget who they are, well, you saw the aftermath of one of those in Iraq. No one wants that, so he's doing a public service—another reason for Jehovah to leave him alone."

Tom looked amused. "The Power I met, he did seem like the sort of guy who would call one of his daughters Battle Ready."

"No, you're right, he is not a nice guy. I mean—he invented the Blood Eagle in the first place. But as gods go…" I thought a second and then clarified. "I always prefer gods who actually work for a living, who got worshippers by being useful—he was always that sort of god. Before he got worshippers, and started getting them to kill for him, he wandered the trails and kept them passable, like all of us back then; he killed monsters and wicked men. A few times we fought alongside each other, back in the early days. Like your father, he got ideas into his head, but even then it was as much about trade and diplomacy and controlling a vast confederation of peoples who didn't like each other very much, rather than picking a side and trying to make it win."

"So how does a god make a living in retirement?" Tom very sensibly asked. I'd noticed his reacting when I mentioned Josette's father—maybe I could leave it and he'd work it all out for himself.

"The same pretty much—bit of trade, a lot of gossiping that you'd call intelligence work. And mercenaries when war comes to shadow. He's still got his dead warriors and they've been practising for centuries, every day. He doesn't need them for defence—he has the warrior daughters, Battle Ready's sisters for that."

So, the three of us arrived, followed a second or so later by my dog, and we came to the river.

This was the third Valhalla Odin had built in a bend, and cut a channel to split the fast flow—it wasn't the showy fortress he once had, but it was defensible enough for a glorified trading post. It's a refuge and a dwelling and a place of work. What it is not, is a threat—or rather, only a threat that if you meddle with it, you will come to regret it. The Trickster is still blood kin to some of the most dangerous of Beasts and other beings, far far off in shadow—and there are alliances that such creatures take seriously.

Was it you who had the idea of finding a part of shadow that was never especially cold? Where there were cedars and aspens as well as pine trees? A clever move in ways that have little to do with comfort and as much to do with misdirection?

Even when Jehovah started to realize that his rival lived still, he looked for years in the wrong sort of place; he complained about it to me once and I somehow omitted to suggest to him that he was assuming high cold mountains or thick oak forests where the aurochs push their way through thickets in the snow or glaciers that shimmer in the magnetic lights of darkness.

Yes, I know you spent millennia in the cold because I rejected you. Was it really just that or did you actually think it through? Are you deceiving me on this? Your reputation would imply a longer, more complex game than that.

Otherwise, Odin stuck to what had always worked. With or without your advice.

There is a horn; you blow a blast; and Heimdall, or one of his many sons, lowers the bridge and inspects you. There are pickets in the hills—no one is going to bring in hidden troops and rush that bridge. And there are eyes watching from the skies. You two, obviously, but also all those daughters and those horses, Sleipnir's get.

I blew on the horn, as is polite and the bridge came down, as expected.

Heimdall was waiting at the other hand, surrounded by a score of his sons and as many dead warriors. I knew, without looking, that some of the Valkyries would have quietly landed and closed in on us from behind.

"Huntress." His voice was strong and deep as a hammer blow. The horn is his, though he never sounds it, because if he did, the hills would shake.

As his greetings went, it was non-committal, even hostile. I had put him down on his back with a spear at his throat on more than one of my previous visits. Still, I noticed that, however else his pantheon was getting on, he at least was as he had always been.

He looked at my companions. "I know of the Boneless One, the Quiet Bringer of Death. Killer of more men than Ivar in days of old." Then he knelt and patted the terrier's head. "And you too, latest but not least of Cernunnos' hounds and now the companion of the Huntress."

It is, of course his business to know these things, but news clearly travels fast.

Lastly he turned to Josette, sweeping an elaborate bow. "And I have heard rumours of you, Enchantress, Warrior, who was and was not always as you now are—Battle Ready speaks of you."

Obviously there were parts of Josette's story even the watchman of the Aesir did not know—he has never thought tact a virtue. She had clearly been really quite remarkably good at covering her tracks down the years.

Josette, though, did not bother to hide her surprise.

"She lives? I had been told..." She looked at me sharply, then smiled without losing that sharp attitude. "In the circumstances, Huntress, I can hardly complain about being kept in the dark."

"It was not my secret. I am sure she has her reasons for not contacting you."

A voice came from behind us.

"That I did."

Josette did not turn, but her smile grew tender and lascivious.

"And what would those have been, fairest of killers, shieldmaiden of the Wanderer?"

"We met in the wrong time, in the wrong place. I am sworn, as you say, shieldmaiden to my Father, who had needs of me. And there was a whiff of the enemy about you that I dared not trust."

"Fathers, always fathers." Josette's voice was bitter. "At least yours loves you."

Tom laughed. "I'm sure I don't know the details of either of your stories in full, but I bet I win. Get over it." Then he looked up at me, quizzically.

I looked at him sardonically. "We never thought it necessary to have a relationship to mere donors of seed... Uncles though—well I could say a thing or two there."

Later peoples have their prejudices, I know, but it is not always the case that things improve. Let older men regard you as the thing that gives meaning to their lives and deaths, as their purpose, and pretty soon they think of you as a possession that can be stolen from them. Who were never theirs to begin with.

And we had problems enough with mothers, which is part of the story of why my sisters and I kept that wayside house. I have never said that my people were perfect.

Josette had turned, and there, closer to her than most people could have got without her permission, stood her light of love, Battle Ready, or, as the moderns call her, Brunnhilde, her face hard and determined and her great broadsword drawn and shining with its own interior light, the light of the flames that had for so long deceived all of us.

"You would lie with me again?" Her voice was at once seductive and harsh, like the purr of a great cat or the first delicate flakes of a blizzard that might yet freeze you.

"Well met." Josette's voice was wary and yet yearning. "And yes, we had such sport all those years ago. Sport I would play again, if you wished."

Brunnhilde raised her sword to face-height and bent her arm back for a thrust.

"Then defeat me." She added, fairly unnecessarily, "For I have wronged you and would make amends. And I will not take easy forgiveness."

Josette shrugged.

"As you will. But I have no desire to fight you."

Her draw was almost too fast to see and she parried the thrust that followed with an ease that against any lesser opponent would have looked too easy to be fair. Their swords scraped along each other.

Tom looked at me, pulled a face and tapped his watch.

Both women turned and looked at him, Josette amused and Brunnhilde with the air of someone who is not best pleased ever to be interrupted, least of all by a man she did not know.

"Culturally fascinating though this is, and I am always up for watching beautiful women fight each other, we are on the clock here. I have a sick friend who needs an alchemist and who knows how far we are going to have to travel to find one."

"But my honour!" Brunnhilde protested, shocked.

"Her honour." Josette clearly felt she had to back her ex up if only out of sexual tact.

Tom pulled a patient face. "You know your own minds, of course. But I have little tolerance for charming old folk ways, since my father's taste for them cost me the use of my legs and a brother I might have come not to dislike."

I found myself compelled to agree with him. "After all, Brunnhilde, what you're guilty about is no fault of yours. You slept with some hero and then pretended to kill yourself over him as part of your father's really very effective escape plan. I have a sister who swans back and forth in time pursuing some complicated agenda of her own which, among other things, involved the horrible death of my other sister at my hands. Yet I am sure that, when and if we all meet again, we are just going to have to get over it. I am sure she had her reasons. You two are old enough by now that you should take the long view of these matters. Have sex sometime, and get over it."

I had no watch to tap and so I copied Tom's gesture without one; it was an expressive gesture which I rather liked.

"And speaking of my sisters, the other one, Sof, newly returned to the flesh, is travelling in shadow in the company of the manslayer, the destroyer of empires, Alexander of Macedon. We need to find them—have they been this way?

Heimdall shook his head. "I have not had that pleasure, though any sister of yours, Huntress...And I am glad to hear that Alexander has risen. I heard rumours that he was fighting wars in the Hell of Lucifer and thought he deserved a better fate." He stepped aside. "But you should ask my lord. Sometimes he knows things that even I do not, for Thought and Memory are constantly at his side."

And then Heimdall added, almost as if an afterthought, though clearly not, "Welcome as you are, I trust you do not come empty-handed. We do not, in these dark days, offer counsel for free or guest-right without trade-right."

This was, of course, mere sophistry—no one ever got a favour from your master without something passing favour for favour or

265

trade for trade, and few have ever got the better of him in such dealings. They say he was born a sharp dealer and tricked even the trickster in the cradle they shared out of a fair share of wet-nurse's milk.

Loki is a wise and wily god, but it is Odin who has always played with a stacked deck, even before there were cards.

And Heimdall is the strong arm who collects debts for him.

Josette kissed Brunnhilde long and hard.

"I bring him the happiness and peace of mind of his most beloved daughter and shieldmaiden, for she has long been unhappy and now she is forgiven and once again loved."

And Brunnhilde laughed in delight for that her lover had found a way of making use of their love and thus sealed it after the manner of the Aesir, who are all about bargains of wit.

I was glad of this, for one day I would woo my sister Sof again and it was good to see a potential rival happy in love with someone who was not her. Much as I have always loved Josette after a fashion, more so now that I understood what I had always known without knowing.

Tom looked up at Heimdall.

"You will know that, as part of a trade of favours between my master the Lord of Cliffs and Shores and your master the One-Eyed Wanderer, I have slain those followers of the Crooked Cross who use his name for their abominations."

Heimdall nodded and Tom continued.

"Knowing that one day—though that day might never come—I might need to do business with your master as I do now, I have slain several more of those followers of the Crooked Cross that I have come across in my travels. On account, as it were."

Heimdall nodded again. "That will be satisfactory. Their deaths are always welcome. Huntress?"

I thought for a moment, because I had little time to spare and nothing I cared to trade with Odin, but then the terrier reached up with a paw and patted the bag in which I had placed Cernunnos' gift. I had to confess to myself that having this beast's company forced on me was going to be considerably more tolerable if it made itself useful and showed initiative, and it had not occurred to me as relevant that I was now mistress of Cernunnos' pack.

I took the small horn and blew, and we were surrounded by dogs, of various sizes, all barking or howling until the terrier growled them to order. He patted the floor in front of him three times and they formed in three ranks—the mastiffs, great Dane and wolfhounds to the back and the smallest dogs in the front. He barked three times and the other terriers, and the smaller dogs from breeds that chivvy creatures out of holes formed into a flying wedge.

He looked up at me and fixed my eyes with his left one, and winked.

I smiled and turned to Heimdall.

"My companions would appreciate being directed to your granaries and store-houses. They have come far and would feed on the rats of Valhalla."

Heimdall blustered. "We have no problem with rats. Our granaries are famously secure from such and the produce we sell across shadow is free from scat and bite-marks and –"

"Don't be silly, uncle." Brunnhilde's voice was full of long-suffering hardly held in patience with official cant. "Of course we have a problem. Not an especially bad one, but we waste a fair amount of what we would otherwise sell, and waste the time of many serving women sifting through. And of late it has grown worse—Huntress, you make this offer timely."

Valhalla was, when you got close to it, and realized that its glittering roof was mere fool's gold laid out in vast hammered sheets and that every outwards facing window was shuttered with iron blinds that could be pulled down to make the place almost impenetrable, at once a vast fortress and a large farm-house surrounded by a system of ditches which could be flooded or fired if needs be, and its cellarage was not the least strongly fortified part of it.

Then I looked again, and the fool's gold was gone and replaced, foolishly, with real. I knew that Valhalla prospered, but this was almost absurd.

She led us from the bridge to a path and then another bridge over the ditches and through a great iron door that currently stood ajar and into a series of courtyards where warriors, stiff as chess pieces in their great suits of mail and plate and leather, drilled unceasingly in files and firing positions, spinning like dervishes while clashing swords together, or firing arrows that flew like ranked wasps to unerringly hit targets. Had I had the time, I would have wanted to take exercise there for even after thousands of years there are lessons I might take from such swordplay, and the discipline would be restful to my soul. Though I had remembered their practice as a little more like individual combats co-ordinated by an over-seeing mind; drill had obviously had an effect on them.

In another courtyard, Brunnhilde's many sisters—more than I remembered or Wagner ever named—were at their practice, on the ground and in the air. They at least still looked and sounded as an unruly mob as they had ever been.

In one of the inner courtyard, in its far corner, was the start of a ramp, broad enough that three wagons might pass each other on it that led down tier upon tier deeper than I had thought even the foundations of Valhalla would be.

She caught my glance. "We trade, of course we trade, and we make much profit in that trade. But first and foremost we store and we preserve. When the Lord Jehovah brings his siege train here, as one day he will, he will have a long wait before he can starve us out."

I shook my head. "It will be a long time before he comes for you, even if he knew where you are. The heavenly host is not what it was—the campaign against the Hell of Lucifer cost the existence of many angels, so many that Jehovah has put many of the saints of war back into the flesh to fight his battles for him. And many of them are better strategists than the archangels he used to rely on, but they are also more reasonable, less likely to pursue war without question for the sake of his glory alone."

"The All-Father is aware of this, and is not prepared to let it lull him into a false sense of security. Did you actually see this happen? Jehovah is a long-practiced liar."

Given Odin's own many deceits, this was a bit of a nerve.

Josette patted her on the arm. "It is as Mara says. I was there and fought my way to the City of Dis through the chaos of the aftermath alongside Emma Jones, my former servant and pupil, who is now co-queen there. And no friend of Jehovah, who tried to betray her to her death."

Brunnhilde nodded and then smiled and kissed her old and, it seemed, renewed, lover.

Once the dog pack saw where they were going, the ranks of dogs raced down the ramp, baying as they went and my terrier in the fore, leading with encouraging yips and yelps.

I found myself smiling—I looked back at the endlessly drilling warriors and thought of him in Cernunnos' hall, doing the same with the other dogs of the hunt. I hunt alone—or rather I always had—but suddenly it seemed I had a small army at my back with set tasks and a habit of obedience.

I followed them with Josette and Brunnhilde at my side; I had my small lance in one hand—it had killed gods in its time, and one of the friends at my side, but it was not fussy; it had also killed small game for my meals and vermin when I needed a clean place to sleep.

The ramp led us down into a circular staging area with rooms off it in every direction and long rows of pallets and shelves or bars with hooks; at this level, Valhalla was floored with stone flags that shone with their own interior light and lit the whole cellarage, save those rooms where things needed to be stored in darkness. I knew how far from here in shadow was the quarry where such stone was mined and was impressed at so much of it—Odin must be trading very successfully in apples and warriors.

The terrier stood passant in the centre of the hall at the bottom of the ramp, his right paw raised to direct the smaller dogs of his troop a few at a time in each of the obvious directions. At a glance from him, the larger hounds and mastiffs started an almost deafening baying. Had I been a rat or a mouse, I would have found it like the trumpet of doom.

And doom was upon them—the small dogs dived under the pallets and shelves and reemerged triumphantly in seconds with tails dangling from their mouths or small furry creatures held by the neck between their teeth. There came a scurrying and a skittering from the further reaches and suddenly the larger dogs ceased their baying, because terrified rats and mice were flooding from the rooms into the hall, and the hounds were busy with killing, tossing each dead rat into the centre of the hall where their lord, my terrier, laid them out in piles as if counting each dog's kills so that he could rank them later.

Some of the other dogs looked at the pile of corpses hungrily; there was some drooling, but my terrier stood over them and growled gently. Then he looked at me and pointed to the whiskers of the large rat nearest to the top of the pile.

I looked and the whiskers were beaded with black powder, that black powder.

Here, stored in Valhalla?

Then from one of the darker rooms came yelping at a higher note—not of fear, for these were brave dogs, but of concern and enquiry, and then a hissing and then a smell of lightly singed dog fur, and the snarl of a dog which had lost its temper and the death scream of something small and vengeful that was not a rat, but, when one of the small dogs—I did not recognize its breed—came and dropped its prey by my terrier, had a rat's tail and ears, but the scales and flared nostrils and venomous teeth of a tiny dragon, that had rat somewhere in its ancestry.

Or, perhaps, it was a rat that had eaten the black powder, and fallen asleep and dreamed of dragonhood.

The terrier yipped the recall and then, shoving it gently and carefully with its paw, pushed the dragonrat until it lay at Brunnhilde's feet. His eyes looked reproachful.

"I did not know of any such creatures, lord dog," she said courteously. "I thought we had left all our foes behind us in High Germany when the last Valhalla burned and we tricked so many of them into its flames. They were forewarned of our supposed deaths and thought to snatch our gold as we burned—but it was not there and swords and flames were. Many died that day and most of them were the sons and daughters of flame given back to the flame."

I had not known that Odin had more enemies than the one, Josette's father, but it was of course plausible that he was a foe of dragons. I had heard the legends of the creature that gnawed at the root of the world-tree, and guessed that the world-tree was little more than metaphor. Odin's world centred on one thing apart from worship, and it was not a tree, though it grows and its branches and roots are everywhere in the world.

Jehovah was his rival, his successful rival, in the pursuit of worship and worshippers; Odin had enemies as deadly who like him pursued gold wherever it was to be found. So like him to plan a strategy that deceived his more dangerous enemy while tricking other enemies to their death and to his profit.

Because I was, of an instant, sure that the hoards of any dragons that died that day had not stayed in the caves where they lay stacked. I looked closely at the flagstones—they shone with their own light but also with the light of what lay beneath them, down another staircase that I had not yet seen yet knew was there, in a deeper, better hidden cellarage.

"He robbed dead dragons, whom he had tricked to their deaths, and brought their hoards here and buried them. Does he not fear their curse? And the black powder? How came that here to be eaten by rats?"

Brunnhilde had the grace to look confused at this last and so I considered her, at least, probably innocent.

"Have his birds not warned your father of consequences?"

271

Because while I may have rejected you from the egg, I have never disrespected the pair of you. You gave Odin good counsel that he profited by when he followed it, and saved him over and over when he was rash and greedy.

But, as it was to prove, not this time. I had been mistaken, the roofs of Valhalla were not after all fool's gold, they were the gold of a fool, or rather of a wise man who had turned to folly in old age.

One of the reasons, the many reasons, why I allow myself so little in this life is that it is always best to move lightly through the world. Those who tread heavily bring consequences down on themselves so often. Gold—well that has more weight even than one might think, especially in shadow.

But my dogs were not here to fight even half-breed tiny dragons; that had not been my promise. I would not squander the lives of my pack even if they were not overmatched—one small dragonrat might be taken down, but what if there were a squadron of the things, and they were larger than this pathetic piece of dead flesh?

And if this was a creature half-rat and half-dragon, there had been a rat and a dragon there to breed it. Such couplings are less unlikely than one might suppose, I have found. Rats are to be found where there is grain, and dragons where there is gold—Odin really did need to take greater care of his cellars. And his ill-gotten gains.

I looked at my friends and I sounded the recall.

There was a goodly enough pile of dead rats in any case to pay for any information Odin might have for me—or rather for the privilege of asking him a question that he might well be unable to answer.

He expected payment in advance for most things; he was the lord of sharp practice as well as of gallows and crossroads. And, if he was trading in the black powder, to whom had he sold it, from whom had he bought it, was he making it or merely trading in it, and was he making use of his own supply? I did not see the profit for him in any of this, but was sure that if it were there to be found, he had found that profit.

I turned back to his daughter, who was snuggling against her lover; she had turned from warrior to minx quite remarkably quickly and this pleased me—it meant that she was her own person as well as her father's shieldmaiden. This might be crucially important to the future happiness of my friend.

In any case, I wanted to be gone from this place. There was no particular reason for my uneasiness, save that there were things I had not known and which no one had either thought to mention to me, nor to particularly hide from me. Odin slaughtering dragons and other dragons now lurking deep in his cellars—this made little sense that I could see. How could he be so cavalier about the vengeance of beings who are all about fury and covetousness?

"I would like to talk to your father," I said to Brunnhilde. "I have questions, and not only the one I came here seeking answers to."

At the far end of the hall in which we stood was a spiral staircase which led back to the upper floors of Valhalla.

I looked at Tom and he looked back at me.

"I can manage the ramp, but if someone could show me to wherever it is you are seeking audience?"

Like me, he had realized that his capacity to teleport and to see in advance where he was going was a tactical advantage we should not remind people of. Heimdall might know it, probably did, but more likely his knowledge of Tom's professional activities was not detailed enough for it to be in the forefront of his mind.

Most of the dogs disappeared back wherever it was that they went, though one of the larger wolf-hounds stayed alongside the terrier.

Brunnhilde looked at me for permission, and then pummelled them both behind the ears. "Bare is the back without brother beside it," she smiled.

I was not sure that the relationship between these two dogs was precisely brotherly, but it was certainly solicitous. The wolf-hound had taken some bite or scratch and as we walked to the staircase the terrier licked at it until it ceased to bleed.

"A remarkable dog, that," Josette remarked. "I could hardly heal faster than that."

The stair was not steep—it was rather too easy to climb as if there were some charm upon it to speed our feet—and it ended by bringing us to a grand corridor that led out into the open air in one direction and in another to a room so vast that it seemed too large even to be the hall of this mighty building, a hall that served as a banqueting area for tables were laid out at on both long sides, so many tables in so many ranks that even without anything further they would have been a boast of immense power.

Beyond them and the carpeted path that led between them was a platform on which sat the Aesir, still as statues and Odin highest of all, and you two perched on the high back of his throne. After a few minutes Tom joined us from the courtyard.

"Remarkable how still those warriors stand when no one is watching them. Such discipline…"

I could tell from the set of his jaw that the lightness of his tone was an illusion. He said "remarkable", but his meaning was "disturbing," if not "terrifying".

As we waited to be shown in—Odin, like many potentates, does like the petty power of keeping even me waiting before being presented to him, something which I have tolerated down the years because I do not waste my power on protesting such matters.

Then Heimdall was gone from Tom's side and back out towards the bridge and the gate.

When he returned, he was not alone. Next to him there walked a woman in a smartly turned out long skirt and tight-waisted jacket with a jaunty boater pinned to her thick dark curly hair and a deeply serious expression.

She walked over and pecked my companion on the cheek. "Josette. Not surprised to see you here, I s'pose. Didn't know as you'd have heard." Her voice was that thick cockney of a previous century, that you hardly hear nowadays.

"Mary Jane," Josette scanned her outfit appraisingly and approvingly. "I like the hat." There was a note of surprise in that last word.

"Normally I hates hats," Mary Jane replied, "but they said that, since I was being a fucking Hambassador to a foreign power, I had to dress up sharp and ladylike."

Josette looked a little apprehensive. "You do know who it is you're going to be seeing?"

"What, old One-Eye? Not completely uncultured, me. I had a nice old gentleman take me to the opera once, back in London, what it amused to dress up a sixpenny shag like I was a lady. Went on a bit, but there were a couple of nice tunes…Funny thing, he had eyelashes just like yours, Miss."

Josette looked slightly appalled, as well she might.

Then Mary Ann looked at me.

"Here, you're the bloody Huntress ain't you? Her what did for Fucking Jack in the end? Respect for that, I s'pose, though you might have got round to it sooner… Still, if'n you had I might never have made it to the Just City, so swings and roundabouts, eh? 'Ope you made the fucker scream under the knife, just for me."

I felt I had to be honest.

"At the end, he was tired and wanted to let go. All I did was not stop him and not catch him." She looked a bit disappointed, so I added, "It was off a very high building though."

Mary Ann smiled—clearly she was a woman used to making the best of disappointments.

"So." She turned around to inspect our company, and noticed Tom for the first time. She gave a slow admiring whistle. "Who's the pretty boy? Shame about the chair."

He nodded his head in respect. "They call me Thomas. I kill people for a living."

She sniggered discreetly. "Oh well, if you're a professional…I had enough of amateurs back when I was in London…But 'ow? Smile them to death do you?"

She gasped a little when he was suddenly six feet further away and then right next to her with the left barrel of a shotgun pressed gently against her right nostril.

"Don't worry, Miss Kelly." Tom put the gun away somewhere in his chair. "It's not loaded…"

Heimdall coughed discreetly.

"Lord Odin will see you all now."

He hadn't received any signals that I could see, and I wasn't aware that the Aesir went in for mind-reading, so my suspicion that there was a set time for visitors to be made to wait.

Mary Ann went storming in ahead of us. Josette caught up with her and put a hand on her arm, but the Cockney hissed back at her. "When you lets us run our own affairs, and said you wouldn't interfere, well, that meant something didn't it? I know he's a fucking god and I don't fucking care—I can handle it, what's the worst he can do, carve me to bits and pull out my innards? Guess what, been there."

She's a tigress, that one. And the right person for the job because she was utterly fearless, which is the only way to go with the likes of the All-Father…

She started shouting long before she got to the foot of Odin's throne.

"So what's all this fuckery about, then? Don't try to fucking deny it, you old fucker. Who else 'as dead-eyed humourless buggers with helmets over their eyes wandering around bleeding shadow carving holes in people's sodding backs and pulling their lungs and lights out through their fucking shoulders? We fucking trades with you, you old cunt; we sells you our milk and our fucking honey and you don't pay us enough to put up with this shit."

She paused for breath, but only for a second.

"I mean, we resurrect and all because Miss here fixed our new bodies that way, but it's not fucking nice. Is it? Not fucking neighbourly. If you're going to pull that shit, pull it on someone a bit further away that doesn't have to see the miserable faces of them as pulled you apart every time we deliver the fucking milk."

I was saddened that Odin had returned to old ways because it meant I was going to have to take measures and Mary Ann at least was a civilian, and I thought Tom and my dogs overmatched in what might ensue. Josette could handle herself I was sure, but there were an awful lot of the Aesir and the dead warriors and Brunnhilde and her sisters and… I really had thought Josette and Brunnhilde were going to get a happy ending.

Worse, it meant that he was in the black powder trade up to his neck—repeated torture of the vulnerable and self-renewing was exactly the sort of thing I had seen be part of its manufacture.

Then you spoke, the pair of you in chorus.

"Say that it is not so, Master Odin, say not that you have ceased to heed our counsel."

There was silence in the hall of Valhalla and I noticed that the eyes of the Aesir were dead and pale and stone, each of them save the one who sat in golden shackles at his brother's feet. All those eyes dead and the eyes of the sister shieldmaidens that stood in tiers behind them and the warriors who filed in and took their places at the many many tables.

Odin stood, and he was taller and younger than I remembered him and his one eye glinted with grim pleasure.

"I need you not, birds, to whom I have listened too many years by a half and more. What need of Thought or Memory, when I have Will that never fails? Advise my brother here, whose tricks have led him to folly, or the Huntress who stands before me for the last time. For I will have no more of you."

You cawed scornfully.

"You are done with us? Old fool, for all you the appearance of youth and wisdom. We are done with you."

You fluttered up to the ceiling and away from the hall through an open skylight.

Odin turned and looked down at Mary Ann. "Has not your former mistress, who is still your mistress for all she claims otherwise, for she has made you in her whore's image just as she made herself from what she was before—has she not told you that I respect courage, but not insolence? You will die today, little whore herald, die once and for all and be gone. Fear not—you will not be alone when it is over." His voice was as resonant as an actor's in the role of his life, as rich and sweet as honey and as sounding as virgin bronze.

Mary Ann looked up at him with a sublime expression of not being impressed in the slightest. She spoke no words, but the gob of saliva she hawked at his feet was eloquence enough.

We had advanced into the hall some way and I had placed hands on my lance and my sword Needful, but I had not drawn yet. There would be time for this once Odin had ceased speaking and I sensed that that would be a while yet.

From behind us there came hoofbeats loud as hammers on iron and a sorrowful whinnying like the wing befor rain, and the delicate scent of well-groomed manes and tails and suddenly the horse herd of Valhalla was around us and behind us, never quite trampling or rearing but pushing up against us firm as a lover for a moment just to make us aware that they were serious beasts. It was a little like gentle bullying and a lot like an oath of transferred fealty.

Gram went to her mistress Brunnhilde, who produced an apple core from somewhere and fed it to her. I felt a long tongue tickle me behind the ear.

"Lords leave learning for goldlust and folly.

Servants seek saner. Not a betrayal;

Mistress we make you in midst of madness.

Long have we lingered here—light is this moment.

Darkness dims to death, delight follows after."

I reached up and stroked Sleipnir behind the ears.

I looked up at Odin and narrowed my eyes a little—I find this perturbs most of the mighty because normally I do not do it. It is a reliable sign that I am displeased and that violence may ensue.

"Lord Odin, I had come seeking your counsel, but this is obviously not a good time. Nonetheless, let us be clear. My companions here, human and otherwise, are under my protection, as is the ambassador of the Just City, Miss Mary Ann Kelly. Though in her case the usual rules of the sacredness of all envoys should in any case apply."

There was a flutter of wings and I felt your weight on my shoulders for the first time.

"Does this apply to us as well?" you both cawed.

I saw the madness and rage in Odin's eye and knew that things were about to come to a head, and that, yes, given those I was protecting, I needed all the advice I could get whether it came from the children of the Bird or not.

Millennia before, I had rejected your counsel and had probably been right to do so. Circumstances, though, alter cases.

"Yes." I raised my voice because it was a time for solemn proclamation. "I accept the gift that was made to me as Atlantis sank, finally. It is time—I would hear the counsel of Thought and Memory, freely renounced by their former master Lord Odin—and I take them into my service and my protection, along with the horses of Valhalla and the dogs of Cernunnos. And the terrier who was one of those dogs but who had given his heart and loyalty to me beforetimes."

I thought a little more deeply and looked once again at the dead eyes of the Aesir and the dead soldiers and the ranks of the Valkyries.

I have seen such eyes before and have not liked what came next after.

"If you will take my protection until such time as Lord Odin desists from abusing the fealty of his people, I swear to protect you, Brunnhilde, the daughter whose heart he chose to break, and Heimdall the watchman. And you too"—I looked with misgivings at the one in gold shackles, but kinslaying is a powerfully wrong magic and kinslaying was in the air—"Lord Loki, if you swear that no harm will come through your means to any of my companions and servants and other wards."

His voice was sly and insinuating and ironic, and yet...

"I swear the loyalty of me and my children—those of my children not already sworn to her—to Mara the Huntress, and renounce fealty to mad Lord Odin who has betrayed me and plans worse. Do likewise Heimdall and Brunnhilde, if you wish to live."

I wondered what he meant—he spoke in the plural and the only child of his who was sworn to me was the horse Sleipnir—and the deposed goddess Hel, exiled from her realm when Lucifer annexed it, and the Earth Serpent, were not servants or allies I would have chosen for myself.

I had always hunted alone, and suddenly I was almost overwhelmed.

Heimdall spoke to his brother Odin.

"What is it that you plan that is so terrible? What have you done to the rest of us?"

"Father, what have you done to my sisters? Why do you look at me with eyes so fell who have always been the most loyal?"

She was never going to swear to me until it was too late, and I saw Josette's sorrowful eyes and realization that she again could not protect her.

Then both Heimdall and Brunnhilde collapsed.

Tom put two silver handled guns back in their holsters in his chair.

Josette and I both looked at him, shocked.

"They were going to go on dithering. And you seem to like them, so I thought I would do the sensible thing. You can thank me later."

Heimdall snored—it was definitely a snore because I know better than most what a death-rattle sounds like.

Tom chuckled. "They're perfectly all right, just asleep and so immune to any unpleasant suggestions he might be about to put into the minds of the rest of that lot."

"How do you know any human sleeping drug will keep a god and a demi-goddess quiet?" Josette wondered aloud what I had been thinking.

Tom looked a little shifty momentarily, then confessed. "It's a version of what Crowley used on you, Huntress." When I did not instantly lose my temper, he went on. "Well. With everything that's been going on in his part of the world, your old friend Hassan decided he could not be bothered fighting the Taliban or the Ayatollahs or anyone else, so he and his little magical commune hopped it. And they're all very comfortable in a safe mansion somewhere in Surrey."

"Why did you and Polly not tell me this?" Sometimes I ask the stupid question.

"Need to know, Huntress, need to know. And not telling you was one of his most important conditions when he turned up one morning at the office…"

Heimdall snored even louder.

It is true that sometimes respect for people's free will is over-rated. Josette—I could never get over how strong she was—lifted the paralyzed god and her lover the Valkyrie in a hand apiece and slung her across the back of Gram and him across some other random horse who was standing nearby.

"Take them from this place," she said to the horses in tones at once forceful and ingratiating.

This turned out to be one of those occasions when the taciturn Gram felt like speaking.

"We shall, but because she is my mistress whom I would protect, not for that you order me, whoever you are."

The two horses galloped out of the halls of Valhalla, their hoofbeats echoing in a silence that grew more ominous the longer it persisted.

I turned to Sleipnir.

"Most noble horse, who carried my friend with us to Alamut and Shamballa, and whom I promise to ride when this is done and give you sugar and apples, take these your companions, the horses of Valhalla, and go to safety, some little way away in the fields, where you may graze. And from which, if things turn out not to my advantage, you can at least try to flee…"

Sleipnir nuzzled my shoulder.

"Fare we forth, for fair weather or foul,

Loyal at the last, to you losing the struggle,

to you victorious, valiant, we come."

And gave a high commanding whinny and solemnly led the horses of Valhalla from the hall.

All this time, Lord Odin had been waiting in mounting fury for us to start paying him some attention…I saw no reason to give him what he wanted. If he was about to do something unutterably vile, well, a pause to reflect might be good for him.

He knew I was here, and what I was capable of.

Evildoers, though—they always think that they are going to be the one, the one who beats the odds, the one who kills me before I can kill them. There have been those who escaped me for a while, like the Ripper, even those who escaped me long enough to die in their bed like Crowley… And there was of course the Enemy, he who was for a while the Lord of Smoke and Mirrors, the one Emma believed was called Berin and had been Browning.

For a god whose professed worldview was all about Fate and Bleakness and the End of Things, Odin was a bit of an optimistic chancer. Yes, I reflected, he might well think he was going to be the One, and perhaps he was.

I have always known that someone someday would beat me, but with so many allies around me, I suspected that this was not that day.

"Lord Odin." I used my most resonant voice and filled it with the sorrow of those who deal with old acquaintances turned to evil folly. He was a lord of rhetoric and lies and would regard the absence of an attempt to persuade as disrespect. "I entreat you to reconsider whatever it is that you are about."

The look he fixed on me was full of hatred.

"Threaten away, Huntress. I have your measure now. You were never my friend and now you seduce my servants and daughter and brother away from me. As you always meant to at such a time as this."

Perturbed, I replied, "I had no such plan. I came into shadow to ask whether you knew the whereabouts of Alexander, Lord of the Wild Damned, and my resurrected sister Sof who travels with him. I have need of something she carries to cure a sick friend. And that is all."

He laughed cynically. "Jehovah is at his weakest and you just happen to pay a social visit when I am preparing for my vengeance against him. And have an army already on hand in shadow, led by your sister and your hireling thug. You claim innocence. I think not—your plots with him are well-known. I have been told of late what you did in Mexico..."

A little light dawned. The Lord of Smoke and Mirrors?

I must have mused aloud, for Loki laughed. "As a trickster god, I felt myself outmatched by that one. He finally persuaded my brother to throw me in chains for real. I suppose I should be glad you dispensed with the woman, the serpent and the bowl..."

"That, Lord of Flames," I said consolingly, "is that it is your nature that you are a trickster and little more. He is everything more. He is a death god, Lord Odin, far more than you have ever been; he is a god, I fear, of the death of all things, whose tricks are to pass unseen while he prepares his gambits. He brooks no rival, so if he has made you promises I would not trust to them."

"He has given me more than promises, you foolish girl."

Odin reached into a small leather pouch that hung from the great leather strap, boar hair still fresh and untanned on it, that bound together his fur robe and took a snort of something.

"The black powder?"

Odin sneered. "You know of it? You surprise me, Huntress. It has given me such wisdom and such insight. If you had taken it, you would not be foolish enough to come to me at the time of my ascension."

"Your ascension?" He spoke as if he were not already a god. Before he could clarify, though, I went on. "You know where the powder comes from? Of course you do. He didn't give it to you—he just gave you the recipe. Which is why you have been sending raiders to the Just City of my companions. You have become vicious as well as foolish, Lord Odin."

Because there was no point in not being polite.

"Enough chatter, Huntress. I have things to do which do not—for the moment—involve you. It is time."

He turned to his kinsmen, his children, his wife, his servants—an entire pantheon of gods and demigods.

"You have served me well; now serve me one last time. As I become. I need to challenge Lord Jehovah. I thought, once I attained godhood, that the Rituals had nothing further to give me, but the Lord of Smoke and Mirrors has told me otherwise. I say to you now—kill and die the final death and let the black powder you have taken consume you utterly so that all you were is mine. This, at last, really is the Twilight of Gods."

# Honey Still for Tea

## 2004

Meanwhile in the place that was no longer Hell...

Given that she'd only recently learned how to walk in shadow at all, Emma was conscious of being a bit smug about it. She'd got herself back, more or less, in a two minute slide-show of flickering backgrounds. She'd also brought Caro and Dawn with her, not only without a hair out of place, but without either of them stumbling.

It was as if she'd brought them through on a little cushion of air that she let down gently on a smooth bit of lawn—actually, she reflected, that was pretty much precisely what she had done. Being a goddess had its compensations to go with all the responsibilities and one of them was just being suddenly hugely more competent at things.

She would need to watch that—she'd seen too many smugly competent villains in her time and knew where self-satisfaction gets you in the end. Still, for the moment, nice not to drop your beloved and this new young woman they both seemed vaguely to be crushing on.

Dawn was looking round at the gardens with a slightly dazed expression on her face. In the weeks Emma and Caroline had been away, Aserath had added a lot of topiary, some water features including one that was like the Bernini in the Piazza Navona in Rome, only with a lot more sex going on, most of it involving images of Asareth, and a rockery that went on almost to the horizon, or rather what looked like a horizon but wasn't. Even as a goddess, Emma's maths did not extend to the more complicated applications of non-Euclidean geometry to the topology of Hell...Dante tried but really you couldn't begin to get it right with mediaeval maths.

"So this is Hell?" Dawn was trying ever so hard to sound unimpressed. "Not very hellish."

"Oh, you should have seen it before we fixed it up." Emma was worried she was sounding a bit too labouredly cool. "It used to be pretty unpleasant under the previous managements, but we changed the mission statement. Also, my colleague, whom you will meet in a moment, is mostly a fertility goddess so she has a head start when it comes to relandscaping."

Caroline reached up and picked a purple grape the size of a small mango, and started to nibble.

"She's improved these quite a lot," she said, with her mouth full and juice trickling over her lips in a way that made them even more kissable than usual. So Emma kissed her, and then stepped back politely.

Dawn blushed a little.

"Really, you might as well." Caroline picked another of the huge grapes. "It's only a kiss."

Dawn walked over and pecked her on the cheek. By this point, though, Caroline had got grape juice everywhere so Dawn's lips ended up sticky anyway.

There's a lesson in that, Emma thought. But it's almost never just a kiss.

There was a clatter of china and silver-ware from behind the next hedge and the three of them walked through a small tunnel of greenery into a shaded bit of lawn over-shadowed by vast, almost translucent flowers, satiny white and pink cones veined with scarlet that somehow seemed to float on the air as if they were made of silk or clouds.

Three older women were sitting very decorously around a spindly mahogany table on chairs that at first sight were equally spindly but on a second glance had a solidity to them that matched the women's air of authority.

They looked around and Aserath waved her hand, stretching the table somewhat and producing three more chairs. She was wearing a nifty little outfit that was obviously a piece of design Emma should be able to recognize.

"Chanel," Caroline whispered inside her head.

Morgan, who was wearing something extravagant and spiky in purple leather, gave a little wave.

"Hi Asareth," Emma said to her co-ruler. "Hi Morgan—Asareth said you might look in."

She looked closely at the slightly older, and therefore almost certainly much younger, third woman. They'd not met before, but her face was vivid in Sof's memories. Also, the blue and white robes were a bit of a give-away.

Given what Jehovah had said a while back, and Judas' long-standing habit of being only a spirit and an appearance, and in spite of Catholic doctrine, Emma was quite surprised to see her in the flesh. She guessed that it was a matter of when in Rome, or possibly Jehovah had gone on relaxing the rules—after all, if he was putting his troops back into the flesh, he could hardly deny the mother of his children.

Now, Emma thought, this was a moment when a certain amount of tact is called for, because she really did not know what this woman thought or knew about the current status of her children.

"Hail, Queen of Heaven," seemed the only appropriate thing to say.

"The Ocean Star?"—some deeply Catholic part of Dawn clearly took over unbidden and incredulously.

Mary laughed—her laugh was intoxicatingly light and breezy.

"Hail, Co-Queen of former Hell. And friends."

Then there was an awkward silence, broken by Asareth saying, "It's all right, she knew. Apparently she's always known."

Emma and Caroline breathed a joint sigh of relief, as they and Dawn took the three new chairs.

"Best bit of gossip in two thousand years," Morgan said irritably. "And I'm the last to know. I mean, the last. I don't know who you are," she looked at Dawn, "some girlfriend of those two I imagine— and nice to see you back in flesh Caroline. But I bet you knew before I did."

Dawn looked apologetic. "Actually, I've no idea what you're all talking about. I sort of gather who you all are. I'm new to all of this."

"Oh, how sweet," Morgan grinned. "Fresh meat. So who are you again?"

Dawn was clearly struggling for the right self-description, so Caroline stepped in. "We met her on a case. She's the niece of this mad artist and sorcerer we stopped and failed to save a few years back. We felt responsible. Also, she's delightful."

Morgan tutted at them and Asareth smirked.

"She's smart and resourceful and really good at lying to people," Emma added. "Just like me when I was getting my start. Now I have responsibilities here, someone will have to pick up the slack back in the Mundane world and she seems like a good prospect. I'll ask Josette to help train her, and Mara…"

Dawn looked slightly flattered and slightly apprehensive. "You never told me that. I've been looking you up and asking around. I could never –"

"Her shoes aren't that big." Caroline looked at Dawn's feet assessingly. "The world always needs heroes and somehow they always emerge. What do you think you were doing when we met you? Finding stuff out so you could fix it. That's pretty much the job description; the magic comes along later. In her case she had me, of course, when I was still a ghost, but she would have coped. Probably."

Caroline turned back to Dawn, with what almost passed muster as a big sister taking care of a younger one on introduction to high society. There was a concentration in her smiling eyes that Emma recognized; should she care, she wondered for a second, and then shrugged in the realization that she didn't need to, was not entitled to.

Caroline caught her glance, smiled almost apologetically, and patted Dawn's arm.

"These other two... Well, this lush creature is Asareth, Emma's co-ruler of what we will go on calling Hell until we decide on a better name for it. She's a fertility goddess, and a part-time dragon. The other one is the enchantress Morgan who used to be the goddess Hekkat—or the enchantress Hekkat who is now the goddess Morgan. Don't fall in love with her—she breaks hearts more or less routinely. If you're male, she probably rips them out as well. And how is Gustavo these days?"

"Perfectly well, and still composing." Morgan smiled nostalgically. "I must have gone soft. I remember back when I was just an angry young woman who made some bad decisions. Killed a lot of monsters though, me and my girls, before the Bird got them."

Dawn looked slightly baffled.

"It's something to do with Atlantis," Caroline explained. "There was some huge adventure involving Morgan here, and Mara, whom you've met, and Jehovah and Lucifer when they were boys, and they all ended up not speaking to each other. And it's all to do with some Bird which had children, one of whom now belongs to Emma and should be turning up around now."

Tsassiporah fluttered down through the flowers and perched on Emma's shoulder, retracting their claws, mostly.

"Miss me?" they chirruped. "Who's this?" Then they sniffed. "I see Hekkat is here. We don't like her. She killed our sib the Morrigan."

"She took my eye." Oh, that's what happened, Emma thought. "If it ever grows back, I'll think about it."

"Think about what?" chirped Tsassiporah, suddenly very interested.

"Letting the Morrigan exist again," Hekkat said. "Sometimes I miss it. And I could bring it back any time. If I chose."

The red bird gave a sceptical sniff, then turned its attention back to Emma. "Anyway, mistress, your companion?"

"Our friend." Emma kept it terse because she really didn't want to explain Dawn all over again.

"Their trainee." Dawn kept it brief.

"Ooh," the bird whistled on a high note and fluttered over to Dawn's shoulder.

She hardly flinched at all—more evidence that she is the right stuff, Emma thought.

"We're going to have such fun, you and I. I can tell you so much about Emma's mistakes when she started out."

"You weren't there." Emma was slightly hurt.

"Vretil knows everything," the bird said. "I bring him Vick's Vaporub for the sniff, and Piriton for the allergies. You really should have thought to try those. He's ever so grateful, and that makes him indiscreet."

"Oh." Emma really hadn't thought of solving the Recording Angel's sniff by going to a high street chemist. Then she asked, "So where is he?"

Asereth explained wearily. "I sent him and Judas off to bake brownies together while the three of us had a girly chat. Jehovah's ears must have burned."

"Couldn't you just have summoned some brownies, like Morgan does? From the Ritz?" Caroline asked.

"The Ritz doesn't do brownies with that particular recipe. Stuff I make or grow doesn't last if it's too far away from me, unless it's cooked. One of those silly rules that goes with magic if it's who you are not what you do. Mary here wanted some to take back with her. You can't get decent dope in Heaven."

"You can't get anything much in Heaven," Mary said wearily. "My ex got weirdly stuffy at one point—it's all high culture and plotting and very little in the way of fun. I don't know what you think, but... But all of that's changing now he's letting some of us be in the flesh again, and brownies are currency."

And what does that currency pay for, Emma wondered. None of her business, she felt.

"He's totally up himself." Caroline was in a ranty mood. "I know he's master of the known universe and all that, but he's a patronizing old sod. He tried to kill Emma and even before that he was trying to micromanage our love life. He lets things get away from him far too much given all his pretensions. The whole recent mess here –"

Aserath smiled. "Well, if he and Star hadn't screwed up so very badly, we'd none of us be here and I'd still be having to pretend to be a cartoon demonic French maid. So let's count our blessings, such as they are, shall we?"

"It ought to be a lesson to us all," Emma put on her serious voice, "not to get lazy and complacent. Caro, Dawn. You two aren't particularly known in these parts; could you go for a little walk and pay attention to our subjects? I'm sure they've got grievances and we may as well find out what they are, but I've probably still got a backlog of judging to do, if Judas is spending his time 'cooking'." She did air quotes. "Aserath, sweetie, I don't suppose you've..."

Aserath stretched langourously. "As if. I do gardens and orchards and ornamental terraces. The formerly damned have got a nice place to live where they can eat themselves plump with minimal exertion and the rest of it really isn't my sort of thing."

Emma raised her voice just a little. "We had a major demon revolt a few weeks ago. That's what I mean about not getting complacent. We do have to do some work, you know."

Aserath pulled a bored face.

"Time I left you all to it," Morgan yawned slightly. "Complicated and morally dubious enchantments don't cast themselves. If I did that sort of thing any more. Which I don't. Obviously."

She looked rather pointedly at Mary.

"What's said in Hell, stays in Hell," Mary shrugged. "Jehovah never asks after any of you. I think he thinks I don't know. None of either of our businesses any more anyway."

Aserath looked sceptical. "Really?"

Mary laughed again. "I am a respectable married woman, remember. Part of why so many people worship me. I know you two old sluts"—the other two older goddesses laughed—"don't get him, but Joseph really is very sweet. He's a lot more like Judas than any of you seem to understand—he is his father after all. Worse things in Heaven than being a little bit dull, bless him."

She put on a more serious face.

"Like Jah, for example. You've kept yourself well clear, Hekkat dear, apart from that one time."

"Two actually," Morgan said. "There was an awkward grappling after Emma here saved the world."

Mary nodded, thoughtful. "Ah, that makes sense. He doesn't handle rejection well."

Emma and Caroline thought back.

"What rejection? He never asked," Emma realized as she spoke that she was not entirely sure about that.

"I told you so," Caroline giggled. "Told you he had a thing for you. Called it, totally called it."

"He doesn't ask." Mary's voice was just a little bitter. "Not usually. Sometimes he lunges, mostly he just assumes women will throw themselves at him. I was special, so he sent Gabriel to do his dirty work, creepy little sod that one is. For all the poems are good."

"You were lucky." Aserath was more bitter yet. "First I was this elder goddess from whom he wanted to learn his trade, then I was just an occasional visit expected to help him with miracles, then I was the spoils of war and then he just forgot my name."

"So basically," Caroline smirked, "he's an utter dick if he cares about you and worse if you're just a fuckbuddy. Narrow escape, Emma; no wonder he was so objectionable about you being a big old dyke."

"He was jealous of Sof and Mara, too. Part of the reason he forced Sof to marry Josette back when…"

Having memories in the abstract, Emma realized, is not the same thing as knowing what they actually meant at the time emotionally to the actual people actually involved.

"Oh crap, I've been a bit insensitive."

"Don't worry about it." Mary got up, walked over and patted Emma on the forehead. "She didn't know who you were until very recently and actually you're not, are you? You seem very sweet but you've met Sof, and you're different now, even if you were once the same person. Her and Mara, I regard as my daughters—you three…well, we will see."

Emma felt vaguely patronized, something she hadn't expected to feel now she was a goddess, but if she was going to be, well, her sort of ex-mother-in-law was entitled. It was like being smothered in pillows of fond regard and really not unpleasant at all.

Morgan laughed. "She does it to everyone, Emma, and somehow we all let her get away with it, even those of us who are way older. She and Isis had a face down about it, and Mary won. It's a number of worshippers thing, a number of images thing. Not sure she couldn't pull down on Jah himself if she set her mind to it."

Mary set her jaw, while still smiling benevolently, even with her eyes.

"That won't ever be needed."

"What happens when someone tells him about Josette?" asked Morgan.

"That, dear, will never happen, though it would be unfortunate for whoever let it slip. Luckily there isn't anyone apart from us six who know."

"I still have no idea what you're all talking about," Dawn stuck up her hand, "so you can keep that down to five."

Emma pulled a don't blame me it's sort of my fault face.

"Well you can add Mara, and Sof, and Alexander, and Judas. And Vretil. And probably Tom Matthews which probably means Polly

Wild, which probably means the Lord of Cliffs and Shores. And certainly Sobekh."

Mary narrowed her eyes.

"The ones on that list I don't trust are the ones I don't know. I don't much care for the Conqueror but he spent enough time in Josette's head that he's practically her other brother. I haven't talked much to the Lord since the late Tudors, but he knows how to keep his mouth shut. The other two?"

Mara looked at Caroline and Caroline looked back at her.

"We trust implicitly."

"Good," Mary said. Emma had heard many actual threats that were less scary.

"But here's the thing," Emma felt she had to make the point. "If I guessed, anyone could. Lucifer didn't guess, even when she healed him of what Simon Magus had done to him—but he almost did and he has the best motives for making trouble. Telling Jehovah, or selling the secret on to the Adversary, if Berin hasn't worked it out long ago. Or, I don't know, the Burnedover people or somebody I've not even come across yet."

Mary's eyes stopped smiling. "Well, if that were ever to happen, Jehovah would have to behave himself. He just got a lot of his angels killed and the heavenly host—well, he does take them rather for granted. And the Saved. But that will never happen."

"What won't happen?" Judas entered with a large plate on which many pieces of brownie were cooking. They smelled delicious.

"That's the great thing about being back in the flesh," he said, looking round at the women. "I like to cook, you see. No one ever remembers that." He put the plate down on a small table that Emma was certain had not been there a second earlier. "So, mother, what's not going to happen?"

"No-one is going to tell Jehovah about Josette, and if he gets upset about her, he is not going to do anything stupid."

Judas nodded assent. "Sounds sensible. He wouldn't take it well, but you can usually calm him down." There was a remarkable amount of certainty in his voice, but then, Emma reflected, he did know his stepmother awfully well.

"When I can, when I have to. That's because sometimes, probably too often, I let things go, really stupid things. So that when I really need to."

Emma felt reminded of her place in the great scheme of things—she was used to older gods being colossal show-offs, present company included, but Mary—well, it was a good thing she was on the right side. She was so very focussed on a few things, like the safety of her child, and those she regarded as her children. Emma hoped, that if she were very good, one day Mary would adopt her, because it would give her a tremendous sense of safety.

She fixed her lover and their friend with a serious glance. Caroline nodded, equally seriously, and after a second, so did Dawn. Yet more evidence that she was the right stuff.

"Judas,"—Emma thought she had better try to have a quiet word—"we should perhaps go and judge some souls. Where's Vretil? We could do with him too."

"He's off taking depositions. He knows what people did—usually—but there are always gaps, even he can't be looking at everyone all the time. And there's evil intentions and bad thoughts—he really has to ask what people thought they were doing at least sometimes. And there's a whole bunch of American immigrants who got caught up in something called the Johnson County War—there was a huge argument about land tenure, and then everyone started shooting. I really don't want to get involved—some of them were Magyars and I'd have to go into my memory palace and open all those dusty rooms about customary tithing and all of that, and I really really don't want to."

"Take him a brownie," said Mary. "He's an angel, so it won't affect him much. Might take the edge off a little. And make sure he is not going to say anything out of turn about your sister, next time he sees his. I trust him to keep his big mouth shut, but she's a gossip. We really don't want your 'father' getting wind of it prematurely, by which I mean ever."

Judas nodded, went over to the table and picked up a brownie. Then he licked his finger where he had burned it slightly.

"Don't get it all over your fingers," his mother reminded him. "And don't paw poor Vretil's food. Summon up some napkins for Jah's sake. Honestly…"

She turned to Emma. "Such a mess, that boy. Always was. Being out of the flesh for so long didn't help, of course. I really should have put my foot down on that one a lot sooner. I'm sure Jehovah saw it as putting himself out of temptation's way, there not being any flesh to get fleshy with."

Judas trotted off dutifully and Mary took Emma by the arm.

"Now send your little friends away to do their inquisitions and let's have a proper chat while the two girls there gorge themselves and probably do something stupid. I've heard great things about you as judge of the damned and I want to see you in action."

Emma's office was exactly as it had been when she had last seen it, except that someone had been in and tidied her desk and dusted. She sat down on the chaise longue, with her bag beside her, and gestured Mary to the most comfortable chair.

"If that's all right for you," she added deferentially.

Mary shook her head and gestured. Suddenly there was a perfectly turned and polished three-legged stool which she sat on, wrapping her blue and white robes around her knees. From somewhere, Mary produced a small case of needles, some thick thread and a pile of white robes that reached to the ceiling.

"Don't mind me," she explained, "I like to take charge of the Heavenly Host's robes—they never look after them properly. Seraphs especially, all those limbs and wings to get tangled in arm-holes. The personal touch—it's part of what makes Heaven a pleasant place to be in rather than a tiresome chore. You'll hardly know I'm here."

Emma rang the small bell on her desk—so convenient not to

have to reach over and actually touch it. Then she worried that Mary would disapprove of using power for something so trivial.

Mary looked up a moment, smiled and went on with her mending. "Really," she said softly, "don't mind me."

Emma realized that there was something she needed to do that she should have come back and done straight away, but she had been distracted.

The two idiot environmentalists probably had not gone to Heaven, in the circumstances. She hoped, she really hoped, they were here, because they might have been utterly annihilated otherwise.

She thought her way down the queue and, breathing a sigh of relief when she found them, got one of her clerks, who had appeared at the bell and were waiting attentively, but not slavishly, to fetch them.

They looked a little surprised to see her.

"Tom did tell you I might end up judging you, you know, but you were too off your faces to pay attention. I really am the co-ruler of what used to be Hell—which just goes to show that you should listen when people tell you important things. So, anyway, Rhodri and Giselle, what am I going to do with you?"

They looked shifty.

"Can it not involve demons playing tunes on a trumpet up my arse? I've always hated that painting," Rhodri said. "And can you let Giselle off? It was my fault."

"No, it was mine," Giselle insisted. "And where's Charmaine?"

"Charmaine didn't die. I managed to save her. She's gone off to be a dryad. She loved you lots. She is hanging out with the fungus."

They both looked relieved, but for her not themselves.

"We don't do punishment here any more," Emma explained, "except perhaps the queue. You tried to end the world, so rightly I ought to put you with the Dukes of Hell for a bit, bad people who did bad things. You two are idiots though, so here it is. You wanted a simple life close to nature, growing things—well, that's what we do here. Mostly. If you get bored, you can always come and work for me. Good clerical work always useful."

She thought them away into an orchard.

"Next," she called out.

The first two hundred cases were pretty straightforward release hearings—the usual peasants whipped to death for failing to touch their forelocks, or mothers who smothered their children to stop them starving or to save them from rape and other tortures. Yet again, Emma remembered that, for all the unfortunate side effects of her choices, she had done the right thing and there were a lot of people who were better off for her intervention.

And at least with Mary silently present in the room they were too awed and worshipful to be irritatingly grateful.

After a little, Mary looked up. "I'm impressed. A lot of divine personages would be at least a little annoyed if I came into their place of power and diverted attention from them, and soaked up almost all the worship in the room. You really are a very sweet child."

Then she went back to her stitching and Emma went back to listening to tales of rural woe and stamping release orders. This was an easier batch than most—she didn't have to take more than three confessions of carnal knowledge of domestic animals and she still nodded those through. There were a couple of nasty incestuous rapes in people's self explanations and she sent the victims on their way while remanding the fathers back to the blood vats to think about what they'd done and come back in a few months' time.

Mary looked up, smiled and nodded.

Emma was making a note in one of the incest files when the next person entered. She heard his limping foot and recognized him even before she looked up.

"Joseph," she purred. "I hadn't expected to see you appeal for a while yet."

For someone fresh from the blood vats of Phlegethon, he had managed to acquire a very natty black suit. Not Hugo Boss, Emma noticed—Versace? No something much newer and sharper.

Somehow the creepy little man kept far more abreast of fashion than she had ever had time for.

He shrugged cynically and she gestured him to the comfortable chair Mary had refused.

"The limp?" she asked.

"Every time they put me back in the flesh," he winced. "I'm just used to it. It comes back. This is a farce. Just send me back to Phlegethon and have done with it."

Emma shook her head.

"It doesn't work like that. It's a system that's totally fair. Every few hundred ordinary souls, I have to put up with the distasteful task of at least giving the Former Dukes of Former Hell a hearing. You get a chance to think very hard about what you've done and why you're still imprisoned."

"Feeble-minded bourgeois resentful nonsense," he spat. "A goddess like you ought to be above such things. I take the consequences of my actions and being imprisoned is one of those consequences. I regret nothing except defeat."

He clearly wasn't going to get away from the blood vats any time soon; he was treating Emma's office as if it were an arena with a public address system.

Emma found this very tiresome and was just about to terminate the interview—which was exactly the same as the previous twenty times—when she thought to ask.

"I see you considerably more often than most of the Dukes."

Goebbels looked at the carpet.

Then he looked up, malice in his eyes. "A lot of them don't want to break up their poker game just to come and be told they aren't eligible for release yet. And they are annoyed with me because the great rebellion failed, and Simon just doesn't exist any more to be blamed. So they make me come in their place."

Emma could not bring herself to be sorry for the nasty little man.

Then Mary—whom he had not previously noticed—waved her pile of mending out of sight, put away her needle case and stood up.

She had not changed her expression and yet somehow she was the most terrifying thing Emma had seen in a while. It was as if she was a ray of light seen among storm clouds—motes of holy dust flickered in the light around her.

Her voice was still light and mellow and yet now there were thunderheads clashing in it; as Emma watched, the hairs on Goebbels' head stood up and he quailed, then fell to his knees.

"Joseph, Joseph. Listen to your betters. Emma here has better things to do than listen to you show off. She is here to help you, as am I. To help you to be your better self."

He prepared himself for more bluster—Emma could see harsh words hovering on his lips as if they were written there, but Mary fixed him with a look of infinite compassion mixed with mild scorn.

"Joseph, Joseph. Named after my sainted husband, and what a disappointment you were to him. I remember him saying it once on his feast day—even the Georgian managed to find his way to repent."

Emma thought she had better mention…

"He works for me, these days. He's a very competent clerk— Vretil and I don't know what we'd do without him."

"You see Joseph, even a sinner so much more effective than you, repented and made something useful of himself. You could do that. And don't say you'd rather die, because you did and took poor wronged Magda and those poor children with you…And you weren't always a liar and an adulterer and a bearer of false witness and a murderer; you were not always angry with the world for not recognizing your genius or envious of better stronger men; you were not always a lecher who took young actresses and tried not to notice how much they despised you and hated you for what you made them do as the price of working at their art."

She paused, but not for breath, only to look more sorrowful because still.

"And you were a sweet boy when you used to pray. You'd ask me to persuade God to twist your foot back the other way, and to take the fever from your lungs; was that where you went wrong? Resentment that there was nothing to be done for your health? Except give you the patience to work through it? Everything you grew to be came from that patience, poor Joseph, and it was grace and not something that was in you. You studied and you learned to be charming where you could not be handsome, and you had so many virtues that we helped you gain. And then you turned them all into sins…"

She wiped something imaginary from her face. She was spell-binding, Emma thought.

"You spat in my face, Joseph. Over and over again. All I had done to help you endure, you turned to murder and lust. Joseph, Joseph. You were so sweet once. Why did you do that?"

And she fell silent.

By now Goebbels was on his knees, blowing his nose messily into a fine linen handkerchief he had acquired from somewhere in his natty suiting. And the more he wept, the younger he looked and the more his suit hung on him loosely. Quite suddenly he was a little boy of seven or so; Emma wanted to pat him on the head and give him an apple.

"Now run along." Mary's voice was indulgent and kind. "Find some other little children to play with. Your foot is all better now. Maybe you'll find your children that you killed or some of the Jewish and Gypsy children you helped send to their deaths—if you do, mind you say sorry. Now run along."

He wiped his eyes some more and blew his nose free of snot, and then a cheeky, endearing grin crept over his face as if he had forgotten his life and his crimes. He skipped from the room.

Mary sat up straight on her stool and looked at Emma.

"You're really pretty good at judging, young Emma. But don't think an old lady can't teach you a trick or two. Sometimes you just have to tear them down and build something better. He's the same person, but he really probably won't ever do anything bad again, so other people are safe round him."

Emma was not sure how she felt about this.

"Josette has all these ideals about letting people work it out for themselves but, well, you were there when Tomas sought self-annihilation. She really is too soft and it doesn't always work out for her, or for them. Be warned."

Mary packed up her needle case and whistled softly—the stack of white robes appeared and then floated up to and through the ceiling.

"Time I was gone. Give my love to the girls."

She followed the robes in a flurry of blue and white, and was gone.

After that, Emma felt any further judging would be an anti-climax. She got up and walked through to the ante-chamber. There were a only a few of the formerly damned hanging around, most of them looking bored except for one who had a stack of old New Yorkers in front of him and had clearly settled in for a long wait.

"Any of you done anything really bad? Don't lie because I'll probably know and if I don't Vretil will."

The man with the pile of magazines stuck up his hand.

"I doodled fornicating couples in the margin of the Bible I was illuminating."

Emma waved this off as a peccadillo.

"It's really interesting. I didn't know you could do drawings and then make up your own texts for them." He clutched the pile of magazines to him. "Can I take these with me?"

Emma gestured to him to wait a couple of minutes.

"Any of you commit any rapes or murders I need to know about. You over there, what were you damned for?"

The woman looked slightly shame-faced. "Tried to sell myself for bread, I did, didn't I? Only first day on the street, the beadle caught me and stuck me in this room where I had to go on pumping or drowned. So eventually I got tired and I drowned and they said it was suicide. But I was just so tired."

"You can go," Emma walked over and kissed the woman on the

cheek. "You experienced Hell while you were alive. I am so sorry that you got Hell afterwards again."

She looked around the room.

A couple of the men were looking just a little too smug for her taste.

She beckoned one of them over and whispered in his ear.

"What do you know about your friend over there? Anything I ought to know?"

He whispered back, "He was a judge in a witch trial once, I think. And he lent money at extortionate rates and had defaulters whipped. Disgraceful I call it."

Then she wandered to the other, looking sad and hurt and angry.

"I gather you've been a bad boy and not told me about it. Anything you want to say?"

He shrugged. "I'm in trouble whatever I do, aren't I?"

"Don't think of it as trouble. Think of it as a longer period of personal reflection and improvement before you get to move on."

Emma's smile showed a misleading number of teeth—the important thing was not to let them think you were being soft or letting them get away with a thing. Even so she was, and was.

He looked at her suspiciously. "This is how I make my position worse. No one likes a sneak, do they?"

Emma allowed as how this was correct.

"So if I tell you what he did, that shows I haven't grown as a person, which means longer sitting around thinking about that witch and the forty-two per cent compound interest."

"Pretty much. It all adds up to how long you spend in the queue, mostly."

He smiled at her. "Saying nothing, then."

"Good boy," she nodded, "your new place in the queue is ninety-nine thousand, seven hundred and sixty-two..."

She waved a hand and he was gone. Then she turned back to the informer.

"Something in the two hundred thousands I think..."

303

"Do I get time off for full confession? And if I stop off on the way to my place to apologize to him?"

Emma showed even more teeth.

"That depends. The apology is a nice touch. We like good manners."

"OK." He took a deep breath. "I was with Cortes, when we burned the flower barges and when their gods died. I did some very bad things that day. We'd seen what they did in their temples and we got very drunk on the last of the wine and killed a whole bunch of their priests. Well, they'd killed a couple of us and we thought it would be funny to give them a taste. But I hadn't realized how bad it would smell—not just the bowels letting go, but when the skin came off and there was nothing but blood and bone—so I went for a walk to clear my head, and I fell asleep on the quay-side and some local kid bashed my head in with a bit of jade on a stick. And that's the worst day, but I did what soldiers did, you know…"

Emma had heard far worse. She made a mental note to find Cortes and give him her special attention.

The informer caught her expression.

"One good thing happened that day," he ventured. "Some half-naked Turkish girl was running around fighting things we couldn't see, but one of the priests we killed wept that she was destroying his gods… Anyway, she gave Cortes a right going-over like she was a drill-sergeant and he was some clod hopper who did not know one end of a sword from the other. Am I allowed to think that was funny? Because it was."

Emma guessed that she knew who the young woman had been, and smiled herself. And made another note about Cortes—anyone who had been thrashed by Mara got a bit more time off.

She thought for a second. "When you go and apologize to the other one, you can wait just behind him. The pair of you can discuss your sins—some people find that helps see why sins are what they were."

She waved him away.

By this point everyone else was standing near the exit waiting for her to send them back to the queue or off to the fields. And the monk was patiently waiting still. She waved away all the mostly blameless peasants and all the children and all the consumptive factory-workers and all the civilians who had died horribly in other people's wars and...that pretty much covered it. She really didn't see how anyone had ever thought any of them belonged in Hell— but then, she reflected, once you'd build and staffed it, you needed to fill it.

The good thing about learning how to be tough with sinners was that one day she was going to have far more serious words with Lucifer and his former friend than she had had thus far, now that she knew more. And Judas, well, he was her old comrade in arms now, but she'd at least mock him sardonically a few thousand more times. What did he think he'd been thinking?

She went to the monk, who was clutching the stack of New Yorkers as if they were the most precious possession he could have obtained.

She really thought she ought to make certain he understood. "You do realize that those drawings, with the words underneath... they're supposed to be funny."

He looked at her, intrigued and incredulous. "Really? I hadn't thought of that. It explains so much. So if I think about them really hard, I'll be able to understand the twentieth and twenty-first centuries. Because if that's what their jests are like –"

"Don't rely on that theory too hard." Emma was starting to be sorry she'd even mentioned it. "It's the New Yorker. The people who write for it think the cartoons are funny. The rest of us, well, not so much."

But he seemed like a bright lad.

"Want a job here?"

He nodded enthusiastically, and she showed him into one of the long halls full of filing cabinets. Stalin was knelt over a large drawer somewhere down in the Zzs.

"He'll show you…Don't let him bully you."

And then she thought herself back to Aserath's bower, where she found Aserath flustering around Morgan, who was busy throwing up her brownies. And some honey cakes which had all been eaten by the goddesses before Emma and the others had got there.

Emma wandered over and stroked the back of Morgan's neck in a solicitous way. It hadn't occurred to her that a goddess as old as Morgan could just suddenly get sick—her concern was at least partly selfish because she had just got used to the idea that she, personally, might never have to cope with minor physical annoyances again.

"What's brought this on?" she felt obliged to ask.

Morgan sat up but remained silent for a moment. Gradually she stopped sweating and her breathing returned to its normal rhythm; the blood came back into her face.

"Well, that was an unpleasant reminder of what it was like to be human." Her voice was slow and thoughtful. "For a moment, there, I thought I might be about to end. Just travel sickness, though. I thought I was over that millennia ago—not even when the Bird's minions netted us and took us to Atlantis—you'd think if I was going to get it again…"

"What happened?" Aserath was looking as worried as Emma imagined she herself did. "You got up to leave; you walked off into shadow; you were gone about ten minutes and then you came back spewing like a bacchante after her first riot."

Morgan's face was smeared, the corners of her dark eyes clogged, with a red dust. Aserath reached up with a white linen pocket handkerchief she had produced from somewhere, and wiped her friend's face clean. She sniffed the handkerchief and pulled a disgusted face. Then with a gesture, she burned the linen to ashes; its smoke smelled of distrust and despair.

"It's hard to say," Morgan began. "I set out and the further I got from here, the less I knew where I was going. Like most of us, I have my own route home, to my place of power, and somehow nothing along the way was where it was supposed to be, and I found myself in places I'd never been and couldn't remember. And there was this golden, reddish dust everywhere in the air and the further I got, the more it stuck in my throat and the more I got confused. So I set myself to get back here, and it wasn't easy, but gradually I managed to retrace my steps and... Something has gone wrong with shadow. I've never seen it before—not even when Crete died and there was pumice dust everywhere in the Mundane world and great stacks of it in shadow."

"I remember," Aserath shuddered. "My people choked on it and there was nothing I could do to save them except make them wrap cloth around their features, and even that. I nursed children and they looked up at me and they died, choking."

Emma had never seen two goddesses as worried as her companions. And not just for themselves. She really needed to get out of the bad mental habit of thinking of herself as caring more about her worshippers than other gods; there, she'd caught herself in another bad habit—she needed to stop thinking of ordinary people as worshippers.

"I've been around volcanoes," Morgan was thoughtful. "Nothing like this."

"I think it's a weapon—the enemy has this black powder, I was going to tell you, but it didn't come up straight away. Mara's seen it before—it's like essence of Ritual and people get high on it and the enemy can use it to burn out their brains and their minds. So that's not his only powder—bet it's what fuels the annihilation guns and bombs. And this time he's just royally screwed up contact with the Mundane—Mary isn't back so I imagine she got through to Heaven—but she went straight up so that's probably easy...For her anyway, but I pity the dust weapon that tries to get in her way."

The other two nodded. Shit, Emma thought quietly, they're agreeing with me. We really are in trouble.

Then Caroline, Dawn and Tsassipporah turned up.

Emma noticed with amusement that her lover and their new

friend were now wearing identical sharp black suits with tapered skirts, low cut waistcoats, men's white shirts, dark glasses and clipboards. To indicate that she had noticed, she changed to an identical outfit only with slightly higher heels.

Caroline smirked at her; she smirked back. After a pause, Dawn did a very slight double-take and smiled embarrassedly.

"We really have a problem," Caroline pulled a concerned face. That almost never happens, Emma said to herself, but then this stuff with the dust is really that much of a problem.

"Didn't know you could walk through shadow by yourself yet, sweetie. Shame you've started just as it all goes wrong."

Caroline walked over and hugged her. "What are you talking about? Of course I can't walk through shadow."

"Well, that's what I'm saying," Emma explained. "No-one can any more, looks like. Morgan tried and got sick and dizzy. Aserath and I haven't tried yet—I guess it was going to be the next thing one of us did…"

Tsasipporah chirped, "Oh I'll do it" and disappeared. Thirty seconds later, they came back, hacking like a cat with a furball.

"Oh, yuk." They spat a pebble from deep in their crop—it was coated in saliva flecked red and gold.

"That looks bad," Emma reached out a finger and then thought better of it. She plucked a pair of tongs from the air and a phial, and put the crop stone into it.

She looked around at her friends. "Since I have Sof's memories, I should probably set up a workshop and look at this properly."

"That's a good idea, but there's this thing we really need you to look at first." Caroline's voice was as urgent as her hand that tugged on Emma's arm.

Morgan looked impatient. "If she's got Sof's memories, she knows how to make the Stone, and if she can make the Stone, she can presumably give me my eye back."

Emma shook her head apologetically. "Unless someone else has been doing alchemy, I can't make the stone without I make the elixir, the adamant and the alkahest first, and I can only do the first of those in the Mundane, and for the second I need Mundane materials. So, we need to sort out the dust first and then I promise I'll do your eye. Or Sof will somehow get here, and then she can do it."

"I've been waiting two hundred years and change," Morgan said, her voice weary. "I didn't ask her to do it last time I saw her, because she was mad at the time and I didn't trust her. I've regretted that— teaches me to be unselfish."

Caroline and Dawn started to look really impatient.

"Look," they said in unison. "There's another crisis, and Emma needs to slow down time, and go to a couple of the nearer villages –"

"There are villages?" Aserath asked, clearly actually surprised. She really doesn't take this being queen of Hell thing seriously, Emma thought, except for the gardens, the orchards and the lying around looking decorative thing, does she? At least I wasn't here while they started doing villages.

"Look, just go already," Dawn said. "You two, other goddesses, go with her and we'll hang out here because I can't stop time and Caroline can sit and talk to me. Yes, just talk, dirty minds the lot of you."

"Oh," Aserath stretched. "I'm sure Emma can deal with it. I'd rather just sit and watch you two…talk."

"Me too."

Morgan was gleeful—clearly having to wait for her new eye, now she'd thought about getting one, was rankling and she wanted to spread the misery a little.

Then a thought caught her.

"In case I'm not here when you get back, Emma, I completely forgot to thank you for my new librarian. He's quite good at the job and just the sort of pompous poseur I love to torment when I am bored. Wickedest man indeed—honestly he wasn't even the wickedest man in Hastings. To my certain knowledge."

If Caroline was worried, Emma really didn't have time for any more chitchat. She was annoyed with Aserath for not taking care of whatever the problem was Caroline and Dawn had found, and she was annoyed with herself for thinking Aserath wouldn't act like a scatterbrain the moment Emma left her in charge.

The thing with the dust was bad and so she couldn't take any short cuts—but she could stop time and she could run.

So Emma ran.

# Twilight of a God

## Valhalla 2004

Odin took the great spear from the side of his throne and banged it three times on the floor.

I could not stop what happened next—I had companions to protect and I could not quite believe what I had just heard and was about to see. And I cannot, I could not, save them all.

So many died in the next few seconds—most at their own hands, though in a few cases at others'. Bragi the harpist drew the small knife with which he trimmed guts to string his harp and suddenly for a second his eyes cleared and he made to put the knife in his belt, but his wife Idunn, she who had the apples of youth in her care— she sat next to him and had already drawn the scissors with which she cut cloth for his robes across her own throat, reached over, spraying blood on him and ruining her past work, plunged those scissors into the great vein at the side of his neck.

Tyr of war and the skies and Njorthur of the seas and wealth strangled each other, equally matched and dead in two minutes.

Freya, Odin's own consort was one of the ones who seemed to wake a moment from her stupor—and her Odin slew with a great sweep of the spear in his hand, plunging it deep into her breast. And her last look at him was of concern, love and terror, but neither the concern nor the terror were for herself.

The warriors were disciplined to the last, as if they had been drilled in self-murder. On a foot-stamping count of three, they drew their swords on one, plunged them into their own chests on two and beheaded the man standing next to them on three. The Valkyries just dropped as if they had had their strings removed—they were most of them extensions of their Father's will and died when he told them to, as they had always killed when he told them to.

Josette looked on in sorrow, pitiless to herself in her compassion for those who were dying around us.

Then she spoke into the silence. "Fear not those who can kill the body alone, but rather fear those who can kill the body and the spirit."

And Josette wept.

"Oh," Tom had solved a problem in his head. "You're—you used to be –" and then he fell silent in the silence.

And as each body dropped, it crumbled slowly as it lay, body and clothes and weapons and spirit into small piles of that black powder which feeds madness and death and turns its victims into more of itself, and Odin took a great breath where he stood and the black powder rose up like mist from where there had been a holocaust of bodies and there was now nothing whatever left save us and him, and his brother, under my protection, cowered and weeping and angry at the foot of the throne.

Odin cupped his hands to receive the bounty of the dead and he looked at Loki at his feet.

"One last chance, my brother, to join me in greatness."

Loki spat, and his spittle was white fire that scoured the floor at his feet to whiteness.

"I will rather die, than join you in madness. Here's a jest—at the last it was Odin who turned traitor and Loki, they will say, who stayed true."

Suddenly he turned to fire and the fire ran across the floor leaving that whiteness where he went and suddenly he was at my side.

"Well met, Huntress," he laughed, and bowed and took my hand in his and raised it to his hot lips like a gentleman seducer in a romance. I noticed that the shackles were still at his wrist, not attached to the staple in the floor as they had been betimes, and that they were curiously carved, one like a great snake and one like a long thin tall woman with a face like a skull but a skull that compelled with its empty stare, a skull that was arousing in its beauty.

He caught my glance.

"Ah yes, two of my children whom I have placed under your protection along with myself."

He shook the shackles from his wrist and as they fell to the floor they rang once and spun once and then Hela that was once Queen of her own Hel was there, towering over me but thin as my wrist; fell yet lovely. And next to her stood a man almost as tall and quite as thin; I have seen serpents turned men with fewer scales but not many. His eyes were glimmering jewels and his bald head was tattooed with runes and his tongue flickered forked from his mouth, yet had one met him otherwise one would not have known him for the Earthserpent.

"Welcome to my side." Because they were now my allies, if not my dependents, and I might have need of them in moments.

Her voice was like mist over a cemetery that lies at the shoreline of life and death, like the beating of waves on desolate shores, like the making of love in the instant before extinction—Hel was lovely as the death she was and terrifying as an executioner's blade.

"Huntress, you have been kind unknowing to our brothers; how could we not share their devotion to you?"

Loki laughed and his face changed and there was bacon and tobacco in his suddenly sprouted white beard.

"If you really want to go after rats, and be absolutely sure, what you needs is a good rough little terrier. The which, as it happens, I have for sale at a very reasonable rate. Lovely little chap even if 'is ear is a bit chewed orff.'"

And my terrier was at my feet and up licking my hand and suddenly towering over me tall as his sister and his brother, and so was his wolfhound companion with whom I had hardly made friends yet whose tongue licked me with affection, though also a deadly beast's slaver.

Loki reverted to his usual face.

"They don't talk much, any of my three sons, and these two don't even try to look human. But they know you, Huntress, and I hear good report of you from them. My boys, Garm the Dog and Fenris the Wolf."

I don't plan; I certainly don't lay snares that only snap shut on a person's heart after a hundred and twenty years. But then I am not a god or a trickster and I could see by the smirk on Loki's face that he was a very happy god and a very happy trickster, and there was a childlike glee to him that I could not resent.

After all, with you two on my shoulders, I had to acknowledge that the Bird had worked a plan on me that had taken millennia.

It is also true that time and chance are a plan without a planner that is always coming to fruition and no one knows how or why until perhaps afterwards. Not even my sister Lillit, I suppose, who wished to avoid them and thus became their servant.

One or other of you—I had not yet learned to tell you apart and am still not entirely sure which is which—nibbled my left ear and the other scratched my right with a claw. The feeling was not unpleasant.

I reached up and rumpled Garm's half-chewed ear and then,

314

slightly experimentally, I stroked the top of Fenris' head—his fur was coarse and yet under my fingers grew sleek and soft.

I am the Huntress and the Dog and Wolf of the End of Days were now leaders of my pack; this was less reassuring than it might have been because it meant that the End of Days was probably approaching.

But something more pressing was going on and I watched to see it evolve.

Odin was ignoring us, for the time being, and taking snort after snort of the pile of the black powder held in his cupped hand. I did not think good would come of this, for him or for us, but there is a side of me that enjoys seeing a wicked fool reap the fruits of his acts, a grim satisfaction. I was sure that he at least would die this day but did not see why others, less powerful should.

"Tom –" I spoke in a whisper, "– I think this is all going to be a little out of your class. Perhaps you could take Miss Kelly out of here." I turned to her. "Trust me on this. Tom has ways of getting himself out of danger that you just saw—he can be worlds away with a thought."

She sat down, squirming gently and sensually, in his lap, and she and Tom smiled at each other.

"I don't know about you, Miss Kelly, but, given that I really can jump us out of here in seconds, I wouldn't miss what comes next for the world."

She kissed him on the lips.

"Me neither. I want to see that old fucker get what's fucking coming to him."

I looked at them concernedly, and suddenly he was gone from my side and appeared yards away, in the open doorway.

He called back, "I think this is what my and Emma's friend Saeed would call a safe distance."

"Fucking spoilsport, that Huntress."

"We will manage quite nicely to enjoy ourselves, Miss Kelly. After our fashion…"

315

Odin gave a great yawn as one who was about to sleep or one who was full up, and then he dusted the last crumbs of the Aesir from his hands. His smile was toothy and unpleasant.

"I think I shall Ascend first and kill you all second. That way you get to watch and be terrified and your fear will make your flesh more tender—I've always thought you a stringy old bitch Huntress, under the glamour of your eternal youth, but that is a question I shall answer to my satisfaction in a few moments. And the rest of you, well, I like to vary my diet and what a range you are, dog wolf snake bird horse—tasty, even raw."

I tried one last time, knowing it to be useless, but I am fair-minded to a fault.

"Whatever you think, Lord Odin, I have not conspired against you. I claim guest right for my companions and envoy right for Miss Kelly. Who is also my companion. You dare not break those rules."

"I dare anything. For I will eat you and then I will crush Jehovah and then I will take all of shadow, and the Mundane, and Heaven and Hell. I shall kill whom I choose and eat them too, and I will collect all the gold that there is."

"Many wicked men—who aspire to be gods—mis-think during the Rituals and become powerful and strange, but not as they would have wished. You are already a god, so you will not become a Flat Ogre. But beware, Lord Odin, beware of over-reaching."

But I was too late and he had begun to grow.

When I had been staying with Emma and Caroline, I had watched them do the washing up of all the china and cutlery they used for the large number of takeaway meals we ate in their flat. After a while Emma made me help, since I was eating at least some of the food. She showed me how to dry rubber gloves, turning them inside out so as to dry the inner part. Only the fingers remained tucked inside. "Bunch it tight at the end," she said. "And blow and the fingers will pop out."

I found that her suggestion worked, and also that there was something weirdly satisfying to the way that the fingers reappeared, and the knowledge that I would get to do it again when the inside had dried and I needed to turn them again.

Odin began to grow, massively, but he did not grow evenly and parts of him would pop out like the fingers of a glove. His clothes tore from him in rags and he stood there naked before us, with his massive penis engorged with blood but not in lust. Sometimes it, like the other parts of him, went purple as if it were choked and other times it went white as if it were a dying thing.

And he screamed in agony.

"Go on, you old fucker," shouted Mary Ann from the end of the hall. "Scream some more. I hope it fucking hurts. Because you owe me and my mates for what they tore out of us. Bloody foaming lungs laid across our backs like fucking wings."

It may have been her words, or some other justice, but as she spoke his neck crooked and crooked again as if he were hanging from the tree again only with ropes around his throat that broke his neck once and twice and then it looked as if he had always had joints in it. And then he twisted and turned and had his back to us, and the bones of his shoulders burst forth and then snaked back in, tearing the skin of his back to rags, rags that grew and then his shoulder blades burst forth and grew spike after spike as if they were great new ribs, or the branches of a tree or the spars that hold a sail in place and then the torn skin wrapped itself around and between those ribs and what was tearing out of him was great bat-like wings.

I began to see where this was going.

Next his hair fell from his head in great swatches as his skull stretched and flattened and grew to a point and then his beard peeled away as his jaw stretched to accommodate new teeth and all the time he screamed.

I do not know, given what he had done, and what was going to have to be done to him, how I could pity him, and yet I pitied him. Though not enough to intervene and stop this process before it was done. Sometimes things have to be watched in a spirit of enquiring justice so that you can tell the tale to others tempted to the same crimes.

317

His skin crackled into scales and his spine stretched and broke free, taking flesh with it that mended itself around the exposed vertebrae into a great lashing scaly tail, and his new talons clawed their way out of boots that strangled his new vast feet, and he fell to the ground and grovelled there because he could no longer stand upright.

The one part of him that had not grown—had shrunk rather—was his arms, which became little stubby things, almost vestiges with paws at the end that had once been his speaking eloquent hands but now waved ineffectually, not even able to claw or catch—and behind his eyes there was little except one flame of wit and will and intelligence going out and another of ferocity and cupidity and appetite being born.

Whatever and whoever this new vast dragon was, it was no longer in any meaningful sense Lord Odin, the king of the north, the uniter of tribes, the wise, the wicked, the treacherous, the ruthless, the wilful.

He could still mutter after a fashion and I heard in his mutter and his growl as it gradually muted to a mere burble like a pot that is simmering to a boil, the words "Gold" and "Meat" and "Pain."

I hope—there can be no forgiveness or mercy beyond this hope—that he only had a few moments in which he could know what had been done to him.

He would not have chosen to become a beast—he was tricked into it by his ally—who promises friendship and takes the price of his friendship in madness, death and worse. Odin had had intelligence, and male beauty of a kind, and they had been taken from him by his own act.

The adversary clearly loved to despise those foolish enough to think him their ally, and to punish them. When and if we ever found him, there could be no compassion, no mercy.

As for Odin, best kill him as soon as possible, if we could. A dragon this vast and strong—if it chose to ravage all of shadow, well, shadow is vast but it would get to it all in time and leave nothing but blood, ash and ruin of all the peoples and creatures that lived there. Dragons do eat, but not often, and a dragon forged as this one had been would sustain itself on the deaths that had made it for a long time.

Berin, or the Lord of Smoke and Mirrors—his plans were rarely so obvious and this, I feared meant that his stratagems were coming to a head. I had thought this increasingly often, recently. Taking off the board by seduction and treachery a powerful god and transforming him into a weapon of pure rage—that was a master stroke that I had to acknowledge I appreciated.

Yet it might be brought to nought if we could destroy the brute before it woke into its full strength from the torpor that transformations this entire tend to bring with them, and the torpor of dragons who have had to exert themselves a lot.

And then a wind arose, a wind that blew in all directions and blew towards the dragon. I say a wind, but it was more like the force that drags a magnet across a table to a hunk of iron. And there was a rumbling and the panels of the roof above our head came darting down like cards thrown on a cardtable by reckless gamblers, but with more direction, for they formed themselves around the new creature, not his hoard but his armour. A series of plates across his breast and around his loins and a vast codpiece for that great scaly erection; braces around those thighs and shins and small delicate yet strong talon-less gauntlets around those tiny arms and hands.

There came a chinking and a rumbling and a whispering from beneath our feet and up the staircase we had used earlier came coins flocking like locusts to skitter across those parts of his skin that remained unarmoured, ducking and weaving and forming themselves into a tough yet flexible network of mail.

My guess was that Odin had planned this before he knew what was to become of him and had cast the spells while he still had a mind to cast them with, but all I could think that this skin of gold over the naturally tough scales of dragon kind was going to make him inordinately hard to harm, let alone to kill.

"What shall we do, Huntress?" asked Loki, and if the Lord of Crooked Counsels was at a loss, well, I am not even noted for strokes of brilliant planning, quite the contrary...

"First things first –" because I had no plan but everything begins with a first step, "—if he takes to the air there will be no stopping him and he will burn us with impunity from above. So we must bind him and most especially bind those wings, and look, the gold is not yet about them, so we must cripple him there first, and if we cannot hamstring him, we should seize his ankles and those tiny paws and hold him close to the ground. And blind him, for he cannot burn what he cannot see—Serpent, cast mist and poison and acid saliva into them; and birds, peck at them. If he tries to breathe flame, Loki, fight fire with fire. Dogs, seize him by the scruff of his crooked neck and shake him like the rats you killed anon. Josette, you and I will take those wings for we are agile. And the webs of those wings are delicate and new and raw—Hela, cut them and slice them and ribbon them to ruin. For the dragon that was Odin is a beautiful evil thing and we must mar it as best we can, for it will do harm to much that is more beautiful and all that is good."

And I knew that this was no more than a first step because the marring and maiming was no more than a holding action—what I did not know was how well the dragon that was Odin could heal and how fast, and whether he would tire before we did. These were the beasts of Ragnarok and I am the Huntress and Josette, well, many think her the one whose return brings apocalypse and that must have some effect.

So we hacked and we struggled and we wrestled and we blinded and we burned, and it was filthy enough work and hard labour to hew not through dragon skin alone but through armour new-cast from the gold of Valhalla. Yet my sword Needful sang in her work and remained as perfect and unmarked as the spirit that lay within her, for all the wreckage that we made, slicing the wings from the dragon's back.

Needful whispered to me that she would know the name of the

blades that were partners with her in this destruction of the dragon's wings, and Josette's sword and Hela's whispered their names back as she whispered hers. "Needful," she whispered. And "White Death," whispered the sword of the Goddess Hela, and the sword of Josette whispered simply "Nails and Coins," for those were the materials from which it was made, those and the magic that came to those nails and those coins from the deaths of Josh that became Josette and of Judas her brother.

Yet I feared that it would not be enough. Odin bucked and Josette and I were almost thrown from his back; Hela, who was standing tall to reach his wingtips and break free the poison claws that tipped them, fell but tumbled and rose to her feet in seconds, only to be knocked from them by his lashing tail. She walked to where the spear lay that had taken Freya's life, and raised it, whispering to it.

"Spear of worst murder," she hissed, "guilty yet guiltless, avenge your victim."

She plunged the spear into the meat of the tail halfway along its length and pinned the lashing rope of bone muscle and gold to the stone flag as if it were a butterfly that someone had killed and collected.

"Stick there, kinslayer."

Yet this too would not be enough, I thought, as I hacked the last sinews from the base of the dragon's wings and threw the leathery sheet aside, just as Josette did the same. I noticed with concern that the bloody stumps where the wings had been healed over almost instantly, and the gold armour flowed over them.

All the time the dragon muttered in a voice that was and was not the voice Odin had had beforetimes. It was that fine-tuned instrument but played by some stupid pair of hands that knew not how the tune should go or the placement of the notes.

"Kill you," it said most. "Pain" and "Gold" and "Eat" and every so often "Mercy," as if there were any mercy we could offer save the killing stroke, if we were to think of a way of delivering that stroke.

Mary Ann had sauntered over from the doorway, as if she were taking the air in Haymarket or strolling in Miss Coutt's park in Hackney. I noticed that she had left her hat behind somewhere.

"Old bugger giving you some trouble, is he? I know a few fucking tricks as have served me well with stubborn old buggers who think they're fucking smart, I does."

She daintily lifted the hem of her skirt to step over the pool of dark purple blood that had dripped from the stumps of the dragon's wings before they healed.

"Give us a fucking hand up, would you, Huntress? Miss?"

We reached down and pulled her up—we had no idea what she could possibly be about but she was a young woman who clearly believed herself competent to deal with the situation though I did not see how. She walked the dragon's back as if it were a tightrope and then, as she reached them, patted the dog Garm, my terrier, and his brother the wolf, and clambered up the neck they were tearing and twisting, using them dextrously as something to hang on to for support. I was impressed that they let her—clearly they sensed something I did not.

"Nah, you old fucker, I fucking owed you this." She spoke with calm certainty, and I realized why she had taken her hat off, as she took the long sharp hatpin and plunged it, elbow deep, into the hollow of first one ear and then another, taking care to do it slow and wiggle it around through what she found there.

The dragon screamed and then, as she wiggled some more, ceased to struggle, ceased to lash its tail.

It was not though, dead, and I had already seen that it could heal, remarkably quickly.

"I've got this." Tom was suddenly near at hand, looking carefully up at the dragon and doing some sort of calculation in his head. "Huntress, could you be a good sport and pass me one of your larger knives. Don't usually carry the damn things myself because I prefer guns..."

I reached into the knot of hair at the back of my head and

322

produced a long thin blade, which I tossed down to him—he seized it from the air, spun it, poised it on the tip of a finger to check the balance and then ran his finger carefully along the blade to check for sharpness.

A thin line of blood on his finger—"That will do nicely," he said.

Then, suddenly, he was gone for several long seconds, and when he reappeared, he was covered in blood and had, pierced with the blade of the knife he held aloft, a huge lump of flesh that I realized was a heart.

"I thought you couldn't safely teleport inside solid objects." Josette sounded almost put out at not having understood.

"Bodies aren't solid inside," Tom explained patiently. "Bodies are squishy. I displace stuff all the time, otherwise I would be cut to pieces by air molecules...It had pretty much stopped beating, so I think we credit this one to Miss Kelly's score. Just went in to be absolutely sure. What's that thing you say, Huntress?"

"Dead is good, but dismembered is better," I said.

It took a while for it to be sure, even so. Dragons do not die easily; even heartless, eyeless, deafened and with parts of its brain pierced and scraped away, somehow it breathed, somehow it struggled, somehow it lashed its tail.

It took half an hour before we could be entirely sure. There was no more movement, no more sound. There was a stillness in Valhalla and Loki wept, and his children Garm and Fenris, Hela and the serpent, they all wept with him.

Three or four horses tentatively poked their heads around the door, and Sleipnir trotted up to join their siblings and share their grief.

"No poem for your uncle, child?' Loki mocked.

"Grief when greatness falls, gap in the world.

Fell into folly, fell to betrayal.

Once Odin ruled over us mighty in wisdom

Treason and torment, turned into night.

Let us be silent, nothing to speak of him."

323

And then gave a whinny and a sigh that was more like a keening.

The wolf and the dog and the goddess and the serpent and the god their parent joined in that wail.

Tom, who was still holding the heart, and covered in the blood, looked embarrassed—so very English of him.

Josette flung her arms around the trickster god.

"I lost my brother for two thousand years, but I always knew there would be forgiveness and that I would see him again. I cannot imagine knowing him gone forever, his spirit maimed and blasted like dust."

Loki continued to sob for a few moments more and then kissed her in an exploratory way.

She pulled back, though she smiled at him.

"Not a chance with that one, bucky." Mary Ann walked over, and stroked the dog, the wolf and the horse. "Plays for the other fucking team, don't she?"

Loki smirked some more.

"That could be arranged," he said slyly. "Some of my children I sired, and some I bore."

"My heart belongs elsewhere." Josette was firm.

"Not your heart I want."

Mary Ann clearly thought she had better intervene. "Anyway, wanted to say, sorry for your loss. Even though fucking good riddance from my point of view."

Loki turned back to his children. "I am done with this place for good. We should fare forward, children. I fancy throwing myself on Jehovah's mercy; I am sure he can find a use for a trickster and his family now Lucifer is done."

"Hell is under new management," I warned him. "I would not try conclusions with them."

"Whatever." He laughed that proud laugh, then looked slightly less smug as the dog and the wolf and the horse trotted over to my side, and all three nuzzled into me.

Hela thought for a little and joined her siblings—for someone so very thin, the nuzzling part was surprisingly pleasant and yielding and unbony. Only the serpent stood with their father.

"Ah," Loki smiled a bitter-sweet smile. "Sometimes I am so sharp I cut myself. And sometimes I believe other people's self-assessment, always a mistake when it's blatantly untrue. Hunt alone? As if that's ever been true."

"You could stay?" I felt I had to offer. "You've actually met the adversary."

"Not so much met," Loki acknowledged. "More eavesdropped from behind a tapestry. All I could see was this very impressive negative image, total darkness in the shape of a man."

"That's what I saw through Caroline's eyes," Josette shared. "What Emma saw. Except when he was being their tutor."

"You saw that?" Loki snickered. "When she hit him in the balls with his own staff? If I'd done that to my brother a few times when we were younger, maybe things would have turned out better. As it is…" He gestured at the vast corpse, and then peered more closely. "I don't like the look of that," he added, in a concerned tone.

Then he nodded to the Serpent and they were gone.

I followed where his gaze had been. The corpse was still there, still glittering with gold and with spilled blood, but it was as if there were a mist surrounding it. It did not flake away but just turned to a copy of itself in gold and red powder, gold and red powder which suddenly swept up into the skies of shadow in a vast funnel and was suddenly gone out of sight.

I could not help but notice that a small tendril of red and gold cloud disappeared on the very spot Loki had just left.

"That can't be good." I had already noticed that Tom had a taste for saying the obvious.

But for the moment our attention was distracted. First the rest of the horses ceased their dithering and entered the hall. Among them was Gram with a half-awake Brunnhilde just about managing to ride her, and Heimdall still asleep on his. From behind them there came a sharp blare of trumpets and the beating of feet and then, mounted on two great wingless birds with sharp and terrible beaks, Alexander and my sister Sof at the head of their troops entered the now almost empty halls of Valhalla.

It was almost as it had been when we arrived, except that where there had been dour warriors and the carriers of the slain in mail and helmets, now there were Persians and soldiers from the land of silk in their flowing robes and warriors from beyond the cataracts in leopard skins and ox-skins and a bunch of Redcoats with their regimental drummer and piper and…

"Fancy fucking bunch of troops," said Mary Jane Kelly. "Regular fucking Lord Mayor's fucking parade."

The normally taciturn Gram explained as tersely as she had it in her.

"I met these people on the road. They were coming here anyway and I told them you were here. Their two leaders are known to you."

She looked around the hall.

"I told them that your arrival here had precipitated some sort of crisis. Clearly it did and clearly it has been resolved. Frankly, I stopped liking the All-father some time ago; clearly my judgement was sound, but no one cares what a horse thinks."

Which was unfair, to me at least, since I have often found even mute horses a reliable source of information and creatures of sound instinctual judgement.

Brunnhilde looked at the emptiness of the hall and, without even asking what had happened, began to sob, great wracking sobs. Josette rushed over, lifted her from her horse and held her, wiping her tears with a big sheet of tissue paper she had produced from somewhere.

I, though, had my sister to look at, and speak to, knowing how little she wanted to be in my presence. My heart has broken so many times over her, and Lillit, that I will not say it broke again. As it was, it was long seconds before I could bring myself to speak.

"Sister," I said at last.

326

"Sister," she acknowledged unsmilingly.

There was an awkward pause.

Tom, still covered in blood and other fluids, wheeled himself forward, and cleared his throat.

"Lady Sof," he began. A degree of courtly gallantry is usually a professional attribute of assassins as it is of the disinherited princes of lost kingdoms, and he was both, I gathered.

She turned and looked at him enquiringly.

"Lady Sof," he continued. "It is at my request that the lady Mara, the Huntress, is here—I needed her to plead with you for a mutual friend who is in peril. I know some little of what has passed between you—no details—and I can assure you that she would not have sought you out without need. "

Sof indicated with a nod that she was prepared to listen.

"My superior and friend, Miss Polly Wild, took the elixir some three centuries ago, and it did not kill her but rather gave her life. Until now, when even minor injuries, let alone major ones, are causing spontaneous transmutations, which will either kill her or leave her in some state in which she would not wish to continue."

Sof winced, and I winced in sympathy. Perhaps I should have briefed Tom more thoroughly.

He caught that he had put his foot in it a little, but had no option but continue. "Might the Stone relieve this affliction? If you have some of it with you?"

She was suddenly all business. "Perhaps, if it has not progressed too far. In which case desperate remedies would be called for. We have not a moment to lose."

She held out her hand and suddenly the Stone was dancing there.

She turned to the Conqueror.

"I have enjoyed being your fellow-traveller, but…"

"Josette," she continued, "we will see each other again shortly, no doubt. And you and my sister can explain to me then what's become of the Aesir. I don't have time right now."

Then she walked over and brushed my scarred cheek with her lips.

"Sister, you were right to come fetch me. Other people's welfare comes ahead of our personal problems."

She turned to Tom, who took her by the hand.

"Lady Sof," he said, "since we are in a hurry, we will not use the roads of shadow. I have my own ways of travelling, which are rather quicker."

And they were gone.

That could have gone a lot worse, I thought. And once they've fixed Polly they'll be back in half an hour or so. Until then, well, Odin had probably left some files somewhere that I really needed to go through. If he was working with the Lord of Smoke and Mirrors, well, there was a being who always got his minions to do all sorts of dirty work without realizing how much they were doing for him…

It was a shame, I thought, that I had not insisted that Loki hang around and tell me everything he knew—but then, presumably one of the reasons he had gone was that he didn't want to have to answer my questions.

Only at that moment, he and the Earthserpent, still more or less looking human, stepped back into the space they had disappeared from a few minutes earlier, looking confused as anything and wiping their streaming eyes as if they had been in a sandstorm or had smoked something ill-advised.

By now Brunnhilde was fully awake. She looked up from where she was resting her head in the crook of Josette's arm.

"What did my Father do? Where is everyone?"

There was no way of softening the blow but her lover took on the job of delivering it.

"Dead, all of them save Loki. Dead and gone to dust, and then Odin transformed himself, and we killed the beast he had become, and then he went to dust…"

"Dust that is mischief of its own." Loki held out the handkerchief he had been wiping his eyes with. It was coated in the gold and red dust we had seen swirling away a few minutes earlier.

"I thought we should take a look at the World, before trying to make contact with Jehovah," he explained. "Always some information to worm out of people that might be currency. And these days they have these amazing machines—you can find out almost anything, did you know?"

The Earthserpent hissed, "Father, don't let them think you understand the Internet. That's my job."

The trickster god's other children all mocked him according to their kind—the Dog and the Wolf lolling their tongues and panting, and Sleipnir and her sister tittering genteelly. I had not noticed before how strong the family resemblance was—but then, sardonic mockery was a trait their father had passed to all of them.

"In any case," he continued without acknowledging his get's teasing, "either the World is not there any more or, more likely, we just got turned around endlessly. I found myself in the eternal reed banks of Isis and then up in the high ice where the mammoths rut –"

"– Where I joined him," the Earthserpent said, "After a difficult conversation with centaurs who have no love of the snake kin. But it was mere chance that we ended up in the same place so soon or that we found our way back here."

I have never been inclined to trust tricksters or snakes—on this occasion I guessed that they were telling something like the truth but I always verify.

I stepped away from Valhalla and at once found myself choking on dust that I had to spit out and blink away, and there I was on the shores of Oceanus, on a beach of pebbles every one a sapphire or an emerald, or the dust that gathers when the tide tosses them against each other. A great shell lay on the surface of the sea, like that which artists show Venus rising from, only it was closed all save a chink from which eyes peered at me.

I stuck out my hands in a placatory manner, but the shell opened just a little more and the creature within, whatever it was, started to bombard me with more of the blue and green stones.

I took a handful and then stepped away—again the dust—and

found myself deep in the earth in a cavern which I lit with my own light, that glistened off the stones in my hand.

Something clattered at me—in the shadows I saw a shape that half-emerged from the rock.

Kobolds are touchy about their territory and hold grudges, and so I stepped away again, turning myself about—and feeling my way through the dust and back to the beach and then to Valhalla.

"There seems to be a trick to it." I looked round at the others. "You can retrace your steps if you try, but I felt for the World and it is as if it is not there. And I had little control over where I went, just over coming back."

"We wondered, or at least I did," Josette said, "what the Adversary's secondary scheme was. And perhaps the devastation dragon Odin might have wrought was the secondary scheme—because here we all are, several of the Mighty, and we are unable to get back to the World, for the moment, which gives him all kinds of free hand."

"And what of that nice young man? How's he and your sis going to get back?" Mary Anne was disturbed enough that she forgot to swear.

"I think," I explained "that Tom travels by means that are not quite the same as most of us. Perhaps they are all right…"

But I could not be certain and, as the hours went by, I realized that my sister was perhaps lost to me yet again.

I sat in silence brooding. After a while Alexander, Josette, and Loki cane and stood around me.

"We've talked," Josette said. "We need a plan."

"I hate to plan," I replied.

"Yes," Alexander said impatiently. "You are the Huntress and you hunt alone. Sometimes we have to do things we don't want to do, and we have to change into these new people, with responsibilities. Apart from all of us, who are your friends, there's this whole menagerie which you seem suddenly to have acquired. You don't hunt alone, not any more."

"You never did," Loki added, "when it suited you not to."

"Look." Josette at least was my friend but she was as merciless as the others. "Personally I would prefer a committee, but these two, and most of the others, are stuck thinking in terms of leaders. And really even if we think of it as collective leadership—there's got to be someone that this lot will all listen to. And that's you, Mara. You're stuck with it."

You two fluttered around my head. Giggling.

Garm and Fenris and Sleipnir snuggled around me licking my face and hands with their vast tongues.

"I need to think," I said and went away from them. Somehow you followed.

I hated the knowledge that planning and leading were useless in any case because our Enemy would have planned many of his moves centuries in advance. Or at least had a knack greater than I possess of turning everything to his advantage.

Or, perhaps, I and those allied with me were just unlucky.

Sometimes, down the years, I had thought that much of what the Enemy seemed to be was my imagination excusing my incompetence. But perhaps this was not, after all, the case. Perhaps he was so fond of one prophecy as a way of teasing me that he knew large chunks more of what was to pass. It was clear that he had targeted Emma from the beginning.

I rejoined the others for a while.

"Alexander, I need you to tell me where the passes are in and out of Hell. I need to send word to Emma and Aserath, if I can."

Alexander called over his scouts who knew the passes well because they were where the Wild Damned had hidden from Lucifer for centuries, passes through the mountains that have surrounded Hell since it was Tartarus and Elysium and those fields of asphodel which Lucifer uprooted and I doubt Aserath will have replaced— she never liked those particular flowers.

I turned to my followers. "I will do what I can. But you will excuse me if I take a little time alone first."

I ran in the direction I had been told and soon found myself at

331

the foot of mountains. Mountains unlike those in the Mundane world which have never been blunted by time and rain and the movements of the earth, mountains as sharp and high as geometry.

Passes that had been fine when Alexander and Sof and their force had come through them mere hours before—and which were now as blocked with great rivers of ice as the air was choked with the red and golden dust. And the ice was threaded through with the dust.

I tried to pass through the solid ice or the solid rock but somehow the effects of the dust were the same as they were in the open air—I could not pass. I have passed through solid rock and solid ice in the Mundane world through shadow and in shadow through itself so often that it was a shock to me that I could not do it now, that I choked and was obstructed if I tried.

I tried and I went on trying and I wasted hours on the attempt. The dust was a physical thing, but it was also a magical miasma. It had been designed and was not merely an accidental by-product of Odin's metamorphosis and death. The Enemy had allowed for every circumstance.

I had travelled easily through shadow for seven thousand years. No barrier was closed to me; even a block of adamant was something through which I could pass as if it were mist. Losing that ability was like having a limb chopped off suddenly. It was a limitation and a blow to my pride, as if I had been struck in the sinews and forced to crawl in the sight of my enemies.

And the ice that had suddenly closed in from nowhere was high as the sky and more slippery than it had any right to be and I tried to climb it but my steel and my fingers could gain no purchase on it.

You both fluttered up to me, at once arrogant and tentative and terrified, as I stood frustrated.

"We did not know," you both cawed. "Our master deceived us more and more—he would send us on crucial missions and when we came back, we understood him less each time."

And watched me sideways as if waiting for the moment when it would be best to fly from my reach.

The worst of it was, I did not know then that I could trust a single word. You claimed that you had been waiting all these years for me to accept the logic of my situation, but you were children of the Bird, and your temporary master had proved almost as great a traitor.

I had to assume you lied—listen to what you said and then discount it as probably poison.

What I most wanted, most needed, to know you could not tell me. Odin had kept secrets from you too well, you said, and why should I believe you who had been his thought and his memory for millennia? And how could I believe you deceived by him, how could I believe that he had managed to keep secrets from you? It was easier to try to plunge through solid rock than to untangle this. And I could do neither.

It would have been so easy to reach out and twist both your necks like chickens for my dinner, but I held my hand. Out of prudence but also out of a sense of justice.

You might, after all, have been telling the truth, I thought. And of course you were.

There would be time to throttle you, if that was the right thing to do. I had other things on my mind, so many other things.

I had no one else there to voice my fears to and so I voiced them to you, and perhaps that choice to speak to you was the beginning of a degree of trust, even though there was no reason save the desperation that silence would have been to even begin to trust you.

"It could be worse," I said, haltingly, because my mind was flooding with images of the few ways in which it could be worse.

"Perhaps," you cawed tentatively and yet in unison.

"He could have arranged for Odin to turn, when slain, into something that would kill us all."

"This might," you, Thought, answered, "just slowly."

"If that is the case, there is nothing to be done," I spoke after thinking a little more. "But I think that he wishes us to suffer longer. To feel his power like a foot on our face, a pressure that could crush and does not yet."

"You are right, we think. Evil likes to toy. It is one of the marks by which you can tell the evil from the merely selfish and misguided."

I reflected that, after all, this is why and how I knew that Nameless, for all his pride and scheming, was not an enemy in the final analysis. He had done great wrongs, but he was not evil in his heart.

For all our estrangement, I wished I could speak to him at that moment. There were, though, others I missed more. Sof had gone to the Mundane world while it was still open to us—I had seen her for mere moments and then she was gone again. Doubtless, sooner or later, Emma would find a way to contact me. She was a woman on whom I could rely occasionally to outwit the Enemy, as I, it appeared, could not.

In the meantime, we would do what we could.

I could have run to Valhalla but I made one last attempt to scale the peaks.

Hell was so near, I knew, and yet we could not get to it; the World was near too and so was Heaven and they were beyond my reach.

I clung to the mountain and I wept.

In the sky, to what might be the east if anyone could ever have charted Hell or shadow, something glimmered that was not a star. I wondered whether Sof or Emma could see it too.

## Some Things About Roz Kaveney

She has been a professional writer since her twenties but is publishing her first novel *Rhapsody of Blood: Rituals* and her first collection of poetry, *Dialectic of the Flesh*, at the age of 63. Asked why, she says, "Well, I was quite busy."

Friends say it's hard to be out with Roz in Central London and not find yourself being randomly greeted by other people she knows. Some say this happens in New York, too, on the rare occasions when she goes there. This is because Roz's circle of acquaintance includes everyone from politicians to poets, art historians to dominatrixes, at least one serial killer to at least one Poet Laureate.

She helped negotiate changes to the law that helped trans people—Roz is a proud trans woman—change their legal status; she helped block a law that would have imposed stringent sexual censorship in UK bookstores.

She once rescued a flatmate from a Chicago mob hit.

She and Neil Gaiman once sold a two-book deal on the basis of a proposal they improvised in a meeting at which the publisher had turned their original idea down.

She discovered in the British Library an unknown verse play by a major Victorian poet; later, she told this story to a leading contemporary novelist, who based an award-winning novel on it.

She knows that British Intelligence has a file on her—she's seen the letter in which an Oxford don denounced her to them as a subversive. She does not know what the don meant...

She co-founded both Feminists against Censorship and The Midnight Rose Collective. Look them up.

She's contributed to reference books that vary from *The Cambridge Guide to Women Writing in English* to *The Encyclopaedia of Fantasy*.

She was deputy Chair of Liberty (The National Council for Civil Liberties), and active in the Oxford Union debating society, the Gay Liberation Front and Chain Reaction, a dyke SM disco she helped run in the 80s.

She's been on television talking about sex, alternate worlds and who should have won the Booker Prize in 1953 if it had existed then; she's been on radio talking about fan fiction and film music.

She was a contributor to the legendary Alan Moore anti-Clause 28 comic book AARGH! (Action Against Rampant Government Homophobia).

As a journalist, she's written about everything from the Alternative Miss World competition to the crimes of the Vatican.

Her acclaimed books on popular culture include *Reading The Vampire Slayer; From Alien To The Matrix; Teen Dreams;* and *Superheroes.*

"I was reared Catholic but got over it, was born male but got over it, stopped sleeping with boys about the time I stopped being one and am much happier than I was when I was younger."

She likes baroque opera, romantic string quartets, the music of Kurt Weill and Bruce Springsteen, the singing of Ella Fitzgerald, Ricki Lee Jones and Amanda Palmer.

She makes adequate chili, perfectly decent scrambled eggs, and a good cassoulet if she's got a couple of days.

She will write you a goodish sonnet in about five minutes if she's in the mood—sestinas usually take an hour.

When she grows up, she wants to be awesome.

For more about Roz, visit her Glamourous Rags website at:
glamourousrags.dymphna.net/index.html

www.ingramcontent.com/pod-product-compliance
Lightning Source LLC
Chambersburg PA
CBHW022205010726
47493CB00002B/418